NOTHING SPECIAL

A. E. Via

A.E. VIA

Nothing Special

2nd ed. Copyright © November 2014, A. E. Via

Cover Art by Jay Aheer of Simply Defined Art

Edited by Ally Editorial Services

Formatted by Fancy Pants Book Formatting

Trademark Acknowledgments

The author acknowledges the trademarked status and trademark owners of the following trademarks mentioned in this work of fiction:

21 Jump Street: Columbia Pictures, Metro-Goldwyn-Mayer (MGM), Relativity Media
44 Magnum: Aldila, Inc.
Air Jordans: Nike, Inc.
Ardesia Stone: Pavestone
Brokeback Mountain: River Road Entertainment & Focus Features
Cap'n Crunch: The Quaker Oats Company
Coke: THE COCA-COLA COMPANY
Converse: Converse, Inc.
Coors Light: Coors Brewing Company
Corona: Crown Imports LLC
Desert Eagle: Magnum Research, Inc.
Easy Bake Oven: Hasbro
Facebook: Facebook, Inc.
Atlanta Falcons: NFL Enterprises LLC.
Food Network: Television Food Network G.P.
Ford Explorer & F350: Ford Motor Company
Google: Google Inc.
Grand Theft Auto: Rockstar Games, Inc.
Guns & Ammo: InterMedia Outdoors
Harley-Davidson: H-D
Hennessey: HENNESSY
Hustler: Larry Flynt
Jacuzzi: Jacuzzi, Inc.
K-Y Jelly: Johnson & Johnson
Keurig: Keurig Green Mountain, Inc.
La-Z-Boy: La-Z-Boy, Inc
Levi's: LEVI STRAUSS & CO.
Lifetime: Lifetime Entertainment Services, LLC, a subsidiary of A+E Networks.
Micarta: Industrial Laminates / Norplex, Inc.
Muscle & Fitness: Weider Publications, LLC, a subsidiary of American Media, Inc.
NASCAR: National Association for Stock Car Auto Racing, Inc.
NyQuil: Procter & Gamble
Phenergan: Pfizer Inc.
Playstation: Sony Computer Entertainment America LLC
Ray-Bans: Luxottica group
SportsCenter: ESPN Internet Ventures
Washington Redskins: NFL Enterprises LLC.
Saving Private Ryan: DreamWorks Pictures, Paramount Pictures, Amblin Entertainment
Similac: Abbott Laboratories
Colt Slick: CeC Products, Inc.

Smith and Wesson: Smith & Wesson
Starbucks: Starbucks Corporation.
Superman: DC Comics, A Warner Bros. Entertainment Company
Timberland: Timberland LLC
TracFone: racFone Wireless, Inc., a subsidiary of America Móvil
Twilight: Summit Entertainment (presents)
Velcro: Velcro Industries B.V.
YouTube: Google Inc.

Acknowledgments

A Very Special Thank You to the LaSalle Sisters (Stephanie, Cheryl, and Iza) of Man2Mantastic.Blogspot.com for writing the synopsis and coming up with an awesome title for this great work. Your wordplay was absolutely phenomenal. Thank you so much for helping me meet a very tight deadline. It was a pleasure working with such talented ladies. Your thoughts and feedback really helped me to develop the hilarious intensity that is Cash and Leo. Cheryl, I can't wait to see the trailer!

Contents

How He is Something

"I expect my officers to be diligent, dedicated, focused, and work together as a unit. Most importantly, I expect my officers to not get themselves killed."

Detective Cashel Godfrey groaned and rolled his eyes at the captain's obvious statement of their goals. He was pretty sure that all the officers just graduating the academy didn't want to die anytime soon. Fifteen new recruits were squeezed into the meeting room eagerly anticipating who they'd be partnered with and how soon they'd be able to hit the streets. The ever-present hero complex shinning in their eyes.

Godfrey tried to inconspicuously survey the freshly shaven faces. He didn't recognize any of them. Most of the cliché rookies were sporting gelled hair, large, tattooed biceps, and backward Ray-Bans resting on their thick necks. He tried not to be obvious while looking into their eyes—seeing if he could make a connection with his future partner. He wasn't prepared for the light brown eyes that locked onto him, unblinking.

Godfrey quickly took in the man's lithe, strong physique. Although he was sitting, Godfrey knew he couldn't be any taller than five-foot-ten, five-eleven. His hair was dirty blond, free of product, and longer than he'd expect a rookie to wear it. His trendy five o'clock shadow was already present at eight a.m. Godfrey unconsciously fingered his own neatly trimmed goatee and saw the man quirk up one side of his mouth, his gaze still steady on him.

His arms were crossed over his chest and the short-sleeved, blue polyester uniform shirt allowed a peek at the skull and crossbones tattooed on his left biceps. Godfrey had to squint his eyes to see the simple lettering on the three-inch nametag just above his right pocket. DAY. When he brought his eyes back up, he could see Day's intelligent eyes were sizing him up just as hard.

Godfrey heard the captain clap his hands together once, breaking their stare-off.

"All right, officers, you'll spend most of today in admin getting your IDs and log-ins for the database, there'll also be a few uniforms to do tours of the station: interrogation rooms, holding tanks, records room, gym, locker rooms, blah, blah." He trailed off. The captain looked hard at everyone in the room. "When you're finished today, I want you all to go home, fuck your wives, and kiss your kids; because from tomorrow forward, I don't give a fuck about office hours… you're here until I say you can leave. I own your rookie asses until you prove otherwise. Got it? Any questions?" His voice boomed in the small room.

Godfrey watched Day raise two fingers.

"What is it, Officer Day?" The captain turned hard, dark eyes on the man, already sporting a sarcastic smirk.

"What if you don't have a wife to fuck, sir?" Day quipped, his mouth twitching at trying to hide his amusement.

"Then fuck your boyfriend, Day, I don't give a shit, just make sure you can still drag your ass back in here at zero-dark-thirty tomorrow, smart-mouth." The captain snatched his paperwork off the podium and left the room.

"Yes, sir," Day whispered after the captain slammed the door.

The men started to gather their stuff, getting ready to file out of the room. Godfrey lingered, watching Officer Day pull out his cell phone and use a thin stylus to manipulate the small screen.

"Well at least we've spotted the faggot early on, so we know who to protect our junk from in the locker room."

Laughter rang throughout the room.

Day's head eased up slowly and leveled what Godfrey assumed was his annoyed face at the wannabe *21 Jump Street* cop who'd stopped to see if he could push Day's buttons while securing his reputation as the homophobic, asshole cop.

Godfrey slowly eased around the table, approaching the cop from behind and Day immediately locked on to Godfrey's eyes over the asshole's shoulder.

Day looked at the man's nametag. "I think your pencil-dick is safe, Ronowski... you're not my type anyway. I have a strict no-bastards rule. Now move on."

"Oh, so you're a selective faggot. I thought you guys fucked any dick that's available." Asshole cop sneered.

"I wouldn't fuck you if your dick jizzed liquid gold." Day smirked while a few other officers laughed.

Ronowski took a couple steps closer to Day and things suddenly turned real serious, drawing several of the officers in the room in closer.

"Just make sure you stay the fuck away from me, ass-licker."

Godfrey was moving up the row when he saw Day pocket his cell, snort, and flick the side of his nose with his thumb, the telltale sign that he was getting ready to knock this asshole out.

"I said: move on," Day growled, his furious hazel eyes now the color of burning amber as he closed the distance between him and his bully. Godfrey was now directly behind the asshole, who was completely oblivious to his position sandwiched between fury and disgust. Godfrey was actually beyond disgusted. He couldn't believe there were still people with this hick-town mentality. He'd had to deal with prejudices and bigotry all his life, growing up in Clayhatchee, Alabama. Just when he thought he'd escaped it... it rears its ugly head again.

11

The asshole spun around and ran into Godfrey's large chest. The man rubbed his forehead as if he'd run into a brick wall. His eyes traveled the rest of the way up, until he reached Godfrey's green eyes, which he now knew glowed with intensity.

"Who are you, his boyfriend? You gonna make me leave him alone?" Ronowski sneered and made a move to get past him.

Godfrey reached out at lightning speed and gripped the man by the throat, leaving him zero time to react. His knees buckled and his eyes bulged as he scrambled to get a grip on Godfrey's large forearm. Godfrey dragged the man in close and snarled in his face.

"No, I'm not his boyfriend. But if you don't shut your fucking mouth, I will make you his bitch."

"That depends... does he swallow?" Day asked casually.

"What the fuck is going on in here!" Captain Murphy's loud voice made Godfrey release the small throat from his hand, but not before glaring hard at the asshole, daring him to say a word.

"Just getting to know each other, Cap," Day answered. "Officer Ronowski was just showing my partner the correct technique for choking the shit out of a suspect." Day grinned. "Isn't that right, Officer Ronowski?"

Day gave the still-coughing officer a hard smack on his back, while Godfrey gave him the look of death.

"Yeah. We're just fucking around, sir," Ronowski barely huffed out while rubbing his red throat.

"Well knock that shit off and get your asses down to admin, now!" The captain barked, then walked off, mumbling something about them slacking off already as he made his way back to his office.

Godfrey and Day looked at each other for a few moments before Godfrey quirked one eyebrow up at him. "Partner, huh?"

"Yep," Day said with confidence.

Godfrey shrugged. "Works for me."

The other officers moved out of their way as Godfrey made a hole for him and his new partner.

12

Four Years Later Yes. We are The Baddest

Four years later

"Atlanta PD! I said freeze! Don't you fucking make me chase you!" Day yelled as he pushed his legs to move faster. He shrugged out of his leather coat and easily hopped the car in the intersection while keeping his weapon trained on the man who was currently thirty feet in front of him.

"Stop!" he yelled again.

His suspect turned to see how close he was, and Day took the opportunity to leap, successfully knocking the large man to the ground, and rolling with him. Day immediately scrambled to get on top and kneed the man as hard as he could in his kidney, immensely satisfied by the loud wail that burst out of him. Day looked around first before dropping another knee onto the man's other kidney. "That's for making me run, asshole. I just had a bean burrito… you do not want to know what's going on in my fucking stomach right now." Day removed his handcuffs from his back pocket. He looked up and saw Godfrey smiling down at him from the driver's side of his truck.

"Are you gonna fuck him or arrest him, Day?" Godfrey smirked at him.

"Fuck you, God." Day grunted as he pulled his suspect up off the ground. "Why do I always have to chase the runners?" He huffed and threw their suspect none too gently into the police cruiser that'd also pulled up.

"My suspects are always too scared to run," Godfrey said with a shrug.

"I can't wait to get back to the station. I'm going to kick James's ass. There were twice as many guys in that drug house as he said there'd be."

Day took his leather coat from the uniformed officer who'd picked it up for him and jumped up into the big F350's passenger seat.

"Yeah, I definitely think we need a new snitch," Godfrey responded while pulling smoothly into traffic and then flooring it down the boulevard.

"So, good cop bad cop?" Godfrey smiled at Day.

"We're both bad cops, God." Day smiled back.

"This is true, but you're more convincing as good cop." God stroked his goatee. "Hey, uh, you know Cap is gonna chew our asses out for not calling for backup."

"Which is whose fault? I told you to call it in, God... but no... you gotta be Billy Bad-ass and kick the door in before we even got the plan down," Day argued. He tried to stretch his legs and hissed at the pain in his knees. "God, I swear you're chasing the next one, man, my knees are killing me."

"If you stopped dropping down on them in back alleys, they'd be fine when you're at work," God replied easily, taking the toothpick from his mouth and flicking it out the window.

"Oh, wow, aren't you just full of shits and giggles today." Day pulled one of his 9mm handguns from his holster and checked the safety before locking it back in place and putting his leather coat back on. He held on to the oh-shit bar as God made a hard right turn into the station's parking lot. They saw the squad cars pulling into the underground tunnel with their four new arrests and the evidence van backing in to unload the fifty pounds of marijuana they'd just secured from their raid.

Day dropped down to the pavement and winced again at his aching knees.

"There's no way those idiots could bring that kind of weight into the city on their own, God. We're getting closer to the kingpin... I can feel it."

"Well let someone else feel it, princess. Long as we get the drugs off the streets, I'm good," God replied, and aimed the key fob toward his truck, activating the alarm.

Godfrey—or as Day and most of the force liked to call him, God—fell in line with his partner and strolled through the precinct's bull pen like they hadn't a care in the world. But Day knew they'd fucked up. They should've had backup when going in to make that kind of arrest, but their snitch had lied to them about how many dealers worked out of that house. Although he and God were able to take four of them into custody, three others had gotten away... and there was a little gunfire in there too.

God's tight black T-shirt clung to his body while his gold detective's badge, which hung from a sterling-silver link chain around his neck, swayed methodically as he walked. His dark denim jeans fit snuggly but comfortably. His gun holsters held his Desert Eagle on one side and his 9mm handgun on the other. His thigh-length black leather coat barely concealed the large firearms or the six-inch serrated blade with the pearl-handle grip secured under his left arm.

Day was about five inches shorter than him, but they complimented each other perfectly. Day was quick, witty, smart, skilled, and very dangerous. He'd graduated at the top of his academy class and already had commendations for marksmanship. It'd only taken four years for him to make detective and after overseeing several of the city's most successful drug busts along with God, both were promoted to the Tactical Narcotics Team. God and Day were known on the street, they were respected, revered even. When drug kings saw them busting through their front door... they knew their reign was over.

Everyone also knew Day was gay and out, but ever since that first day in the conference room when God choked Ronowski without a second thought, no one bothered Day about it, because no one wanted to face the wrath of God.

"So we hear you two busted up that cartel over on 33rd street." Detective Seasel strolled up beside God as he sat at his desk with his boots propped up on the edge. Day was perched on the corner, looking down at his partner, silently communicating with him like always.

"That's right, sweetheart, another righteous bust for us," Day bragged. He looked around Seasel to her partner, whose electrifying blue eyes were shooting daggers at both of them. "You got a problem with that, Ronowski? You look like you're dying to get something off your chest."

"I don't have a goddamn word to say to you, Day. Come on, Vikki, let's get out of here, we have a planning session to get to. Unlike you fuckups, there are some of us who believe in working as a team to get the job done right."

"Tsk, tsk, tsk." Day shook his head sadly and sucked his teeth at the angry man. "Mad because we didn't invite you to come along, Ronowski?"

Ronowski gritted his teeth. "What-the-fuck-ever. This unit is about working as a team. Every time you jackasses go off half-cocked, someone has to come behind you and clean up your fucking mess." The detective fumed.

God just shook his head watching the angry exchange. There was no love lost between Day and Ronowski, obviously. Ronowski's partner, Vikki Seasel, was cool though. She was a pretty woman with an even hotter body. She had plump lips and long sandy-brown hair that she kept pulled into a tight ponytail at the base of her neck. Her warm brown eyes were beautiful and although she was tough as nails, she knew how to bat her eyes to throw a suspect off during an interrogation. Her hips were nicely proportionate to her small waistline, and Day didn't miss God's lustful stare whenever she approached.

"All right, let's go, Ro. I'll see you guys later." She gave God an extra-long stare before turning and following her partner through the bull pen.

Day waited until they were almost to the other side of the room before standing up.

"So, Ronowski, same time as last night... my place, right? I bought the extra large condoms this time, so we don't have that little problem again," Day yelled for all to hear.

Ronowski spun around, his face a bright shade of red and Day thought the man was going to burst a blood vessel in his neck.

"Fuck you, Day!" Ronowski yelled back at him, his fist clenched at his side.

"So you want to do me this time? That's cool; I'll let that tight ass of yours have a break tonight." Day feigned confusion before adding, "I guess we won't need those extra large condoms after all, huh?"

The room was buzzing and many of the officers had turned their attention on a livid Ronowski, laughing hysterically. Even God had a hard time concealing his smile.

Ronowski looked like he was about to charge back across the floor until God slowly stood.

"All right knock it off out there! Get back to fucking work," the captain bellowed out into the bullpen from his open door. He turned his sharp eyes on them and shook his head.

God looked at Day. "You just can't get enough can you?"

"That's the same thing Ronowski said last night." Day winked.

17

"You sonofabitch," Ronowski growled as he was dragged out of the bullpen by Vikki, while the other officers laughed at Day's last jibe.

"I said, knock it off!" Their captain looked around, daring anyone else to laugh. "Day, God. In my office, now."

They got the scolding of their life and a threat of demotion if they ever pulled a stunt like that again. Day gripped his coat in his hand and exited the captain's office fifteen minutes later.

"Thanks a lot, God, I really enjoyed that." Day shoved his partner's arm hard, barely moving him at all. "Just because the captain was best friends with my dad doesn't mean he's going to go easy on us."

"All right, sissy-queen, you don't have to be so dramatic," God teased.

Day didn't care about God calling him names because he knew the big man was crazy about him and would kill anyone who insulted him for real.

"I don't like getting my ass chewed out, man." Day plopped back down in his desk chair and let out a long sigh.

God leaned against the desk and stared at him. "I thought you did like getting your ass chewed. Umm, what do y'all call it?" God snapped his fingers. "Oh yeah… tossing salad."

"Fuck you." Day laughed.

"Not even on your best day, sweetheart." God winked, removed his large frame from Day's desk, and sat back in his own chair facing him.

Day picked up his favorite coffee mug and told God he'd be back.

"Yeah, yeah, I know. You're a damn addict, dude. What would you do if there was ever a shortage of coffee beans in the United States?" God shook his head at him.

"What do you think I'd do... I'd move to a country that didn't have a shortage, dumbass. I swear, God, as smart as you are, you sure do ask some stupid shit." Day dodged the paperclip God threw at him and started toward the station's kitchen.

Day made quick work of starting his three-hundred-dollar Keurig coffeemaker. It was the best one on the market and he had carousels holding a variety of flavors. The kitchen had other, industrial-size coffeemakers, but Day had to have a freshly brewed cup each time. God was right about Day being addicted to coffee. He drank ten to twelve cups per day. Although he griped about his inability to sleep, he refused to sacrifice his coffee, or switch to godforsaken decaf.

Day hummed while he took inventory of what was left and saw that someone had brought in Vanilla Biscotti flavored cups. *Yes, been meaning to get some of those.* Everyone knew the elaborate coffee machine was his. Other officers were welcome to use it, as long as they kept it clean and contributed to the stash.

"Well, hello there, handsome." A rich, deep voiced crawled up Day's spine. *Great... of all the precinct kitchens in the world... he had to walk into mine.*

Day turned around slowly, his steaming cup of coffee held right under his nose, letting the bold aroma calm him.

"Detective Johnson, it's such a pleasu—It's nice to—" Day stuttered sarcastically. "Well, let me just say hi."

"Ouch. You hurt my heart when you say things like that." The tall detective rubbed his hand over his ample chest like he really felt an ache. "You're way too beautiful to act like that."

Who said I'm acting?

Day watched Johnson crowd into his space, using his height to try to smother him, but all he was doing was overpowering the smell of coffee with the cologne he wore. Day refused to look up into the detective's eyes. The man was an arrogant prick and he didn't deserve Day's respect.

19

Just because the detective was out and proud too, he somehow thought that made them a great couple. But Detective Johnson was a spoiled rich kid. His father was the police commissioner and the man wasn't ashamed to throw big daddy's weight around, which Day and God hated. There was no way in hell Day would ever consider dating him, no matter how handsome the bastard was.

"Where you been hiding yourself, Day? I called that number you gave me, but it was an adult video shop. I really didn't like that. It was rude and childish, don't you think? If you didn't want me to have your number, all you had to do was say so."

I did shit-dick, but someone can't take no for an answer.

Day didn't bother voicing his response as he sipped his hot coffee, refusing to let this man ruin his Zen feeling. Detective Johnson was far from an ugly man, actually he was fucking stunning, but he was also pompous and not Day's type. The man really thought he could have whatever he wanted because he had a trust fund.

"You gave me that number and said you didn't mind me calling you." He propped one arm up on the cabinet next to Day's head. His cinnamon breath was wafting down on top of him... *and into my motherfucking cup of coffee.*

"I know I said you could call me, but there are two explanations for that. Now either I was lying... or I was wrong about the number of explanations." Day smirked and took another sip.

"That slick mouth of yours is going to get you in trouble." Detective Johnson turned his lip up at him. The man really couldn't take a damn hint.

He had Day up against the counter with only a hair of breathing room between them. Day could've easily gotten out of there, but he liked fucking with the smug detective. Detective Johnson was a ballistics expert who went from precinct to precinct assisting on cases where needed. Obviously Cap had called him in to assist with the guns that were recovered during their recent bust.

20

"Well, umm, I gotta get back to the grind. Wouldn't want you to tell Daddy I'm slacking off." Day gently set his cup of coffee on the counter, spun, and ducked under the detective's arm before the man could blink twice. Day grabbed his mug and made his way to the other side of the room.

"So me and you, dinner this weekend?" Detective Johnson said to Day's back.

Day snorted, while grabbing a muffin for God.

"So is that a no, Day?"

"That's a fuck no." Day opened the door and left the room. He could hear Detective Johnson's curses as he walked away.

Day made his way through the office and when he was a few feet away from their desk, he tossed God the blueberry muffin. God looked at him for a few seconds, using their soundless communication.

"You're welcome," Day said, dropping down in his chair. He took another long gulp before releasing a deep breath. He cracked his neck on both sides and leveled his hazel eyes on his partner. "So you ready to do the nasty, God?" he asked him with complete seriousness.

"As ready as I'm gonna be. Give it to me, baby," God replied with a frustrated huff.

Day began downloading the multitude of forms and printing them out to be completed. God groaned at all the papers printing on their small desktop printer. "Uhhh, fuckin' paperwork… shit! Hate it!" God all but yelled.

A.E. VIA

Now You See Me, Now You Don't

After two hours of paperwork, they were both exhausted and Day felt like he'd been rubbing his eyes with sandpaper.

Day heard God clearing his throat before he coughed again. "I'm going to stop by the convenience store on the corner and grab some cough drops," God said.

"Good, I want some coffee," Day groaned as he reclined in God's comfortable truck.

"Of course," God replied between coughs.

"You all right, dude? You have been coughing like that for over a week." Day kept his eyes closed while he spoke.

"I'm good. I think it's just allergies," God said with a shrug.

Day didn't think anything else about it. God was as stubborn as a mule, especially when it came to his health or, heaven forbid, going to see a doctor. He couldn't even recall the last time his partner had a checkup. Not even after his biceps got cut by a perp they arrested last year. Day had tried to convince him he needed stitches, but God insisted it was just a flesh wound—the jagged scar was still very visible.

God jerked into the parking space and slammed on the brakes right before his front bumper came into contact with the brick wall.

"Jesus, man. You trying to kill us?" Day huffed. "You don't always have to drive like you're auditioning for the Grand Prix."

"Stop bitching, Miss Daisy. If you don't like my driving, you can always ride that crotch rocket to work," God replied with an annoyed expression.

"Whatever. Let's just hurry up." Day made his way into the small store right behind God's massive figure. Before the overhead cowbell could stop ringing, Day asked the clerk, "You got a fresh pot back there?"

"Yes. Just started it five minutes ago," the clerk replied with a thick Asian accent.

"Good man." Day made his way to the back of the store. God turned down the cold medicine aisle.

Day hummed as he poured the steaming brew into the largest cup the store had and popped open about fifteen creamers. Day liked his coffee with a lot of cream and sugar, and he wasn't ashamed to open a ton of the mini-servings until his cup was just right.

Day was stirring the golden-brown liquid and was about to take a sample taste when he heard the store's cowbell ding. Five seconds later he heard a demand shouted by a male voice.

"Don't move, old man! Empty the drawer right now!"

Then something, or things, went crashing to the floor.

"Don't do anything stupid. I don't want to hurt you. Just give me the money!" the guy shouted.

Day couldn't see over the rows of shelves, but from the sound of it, the robber had to be in his late teens, early twenties. *Great.* Day took his cup and went by the coolers across the back of the store. He peeked down the aisle that God was in and saw him reading the label on some cough syrup as he popped a cough drop into his mouth.

Really, God?

Day eased up to his partner, careful not to make a sound. "Did you find what you needed?" he whispered to God.

"Yep." God turned to look at him.

"Don't you hear the place being robbed?"

"Yep."

24

"Are you going to stop it?"

"Yep."

"Now you see me, now you don't?" Day winked.

"Yep."

God put the cough syrup and drops in his coat pocket and strolled to the front of the store.

Day went back around to come up the aisle closest to the door. He heard the young man yell again.

"Open the safe! Hurry up. Don't try to stall me."

Ugh. Fucking amateur.

God turned at the end of the aisle and saw a small figure in front of the counter shakily pointing a .22 caliber handgun at the terrified clerk. The boy couldn't be over eighteen years old. He had a red-and-blue Braves ball cap pulled down low on his face, and his black hoodie was zipped up to his chin and pulled up over the cap. The jeans were faded and extremely tight, and God found himself wondering if the guy's balls were pissed off at him.

God took quiet steps toward the counter and was only a few feet from the boy before he whirled his gun around and pointed it at God.

The kid jerkily moved his head up and down, taking in God's appearance. His chiseled face, massive bulk, and sheer height had the boy's eyes widening to two times their size

"Hey! Don't move! Put your hands up!"

"No," God said, crossing his arms over his chest.

"W-what," the boy stammered.

The pain and uncertainty in the kid's eyes was familiar to him.

He gave God a pleading glare. "Look, man. Just get down okay. I don't want to kill you."

"Good, 'cause I don't want to die," God said with a stone face.

"I have the gun. Now put your damn hands up!" The young, pimply face was a mask of anger, but his shaking hands betrayed his fear.

"Hey, how much for the cup of coffee?" Day yelled in a voice that was way too loud. "Oh shit, my bad. I didn't see you over there with the gun."

The teen whirled around toward Day. "Yeah, so get your hands up," he snapped.

"Not you." Day pointed around the kid's shoulder. "Him."

When the kid spun back around he was staring down the barrel of God's very large Desert Eagle, looking like he was going to piss himself.

Now you see me, now you don't. Works every time.

"Mine's bigger than yours," God said casually.

"Literally," Day said around a smirk.

God rolled his eyes at his partner while focusing on the kid. "Slowly drop your weapon and kick it over, then put your hands behind your head."

"Okay, easy, man." The boy slowly eased his small handgun to the floor. "Please. Just don't shoot me."

"Not gonna shoot you, kid," he said while pulling the silver chain from inside his shirt and revealing his gold badge. He saw the kid push his gun toward God's feet and scramble to get all the way down, putting his cheek on the dirty floor. He hadn't asked him to lie down. This kid was obviously not a hardened criminal. He took his eyes off his suspect and saw that Day was reading a *Muscle & Fitness* magazine from the rack. God rolled his eyes again.

"Day, get over here and pay for our shit. I'll handle 'world's dumbest criminal—the high school edition.' Get your ass up and come with me, kid." God pulled the boy up by his collar and took the small handgun, tucking it into his waistband at the small of his back.

He walked them around to where he was parked and threw the boy against the side of his truck. He patted him down—none to gently—and yanked a worn Velcro wallet from his back pocket. *Fucking Velcro Twilight wallet… are you kiddin' me?* He spun the kid so that he was facing him, and pushed him hard against the truck's bed.

"Officer, please. I'm sor—"

"Detective," God barked, cutting him off. "What the hell are you doing, sticking up a mom-and-pop store? How fucking old are you?"

God yanked the ID out and scanned it. Curtis Lamont Jackson, he lived four blocks from here and was only seventeen.

"I-I'm seventeen, sir," the kid stammered. Sweat was pouring down his face and his arms shook while he kept them raised with his fingers linked behind his head.

"Put your fucking hands down for Christ's sake," God snarled, looking the kid up and down. "You're a goddamn baby, out here playing a big boy's game."

He stepped back from the trembling kid and saw that his light blue eyes were glistening with fear, or maybe it was sadness. He couldn't tell.

"I'm not a baby, sir."

"Pfft, please. I can smell the Similac on your breath from over here." God huffed.

Day came around the corner with a small brown bag, and leaned casually against the hood. "Dude, is that team Edward on his wallet?" Day doubled over with laughter.

"Shut up, Leo. Did you get a statement from the clerk?"

"Yep." Day held up the piece of paper.

"Sir, I'm really sorry. Please, I swear I wasn't going to shoot anyone," he whined.

"I know that. Your gun doesn't have any bullets in it," God said drily.

The boy looked at him in shock.

"I didn't know that until I picked it up… it's too light. But I still could've shot you before I knew that."

"Sir, my mom is sick. She's on a hemodialysis machine and she has to use it every night, sometimes twice during the day, or she'll get extremely sick. She has acute renal failure. They cut our power off last night." Curtis looked down at the pavement. "The machine runs on electricity."

God knew the boy wasn't lying. No one—especially his age—could come up with that kind of lie and look as heartbroken as he did.

"So robbing someone was your solution?" Day asked.

"I'm so sorry. I didn't know what else to do. My entire paycheck went to the rent, and I didn't qualify for another extension for the electric. I did try to think of other options… but there are none. I can't go to jail, please, my mom needs me. I'm all she's got." A single tear fell down his red cheek.

"Get in the truck," God ordered.

Curtis's gaze frantically darted between them. "Please, I'm begging you. I can't go to jail. My mom will die. I have a good job. If I don't show up tomorrow, I'll be fired." The tears were flowing down his face, and God's heart clenched. He knew what it was like for a young man to take on the responsibility of caring for his mom. It wasn't fair, but it was life.

"Get in." Day backed him up.

God practically tossed the boy in the back seat and went around to the driver's side. Day climbed in on his side and turned to look at him. They were looking at each other, communicating just as effectively as if both were talking. He knew what Day was thinking… he usually did. They turned and looked at the kid. He had his knees pulled up to his chest as he rocked back and forth.

"I swear, I'd never hurt anyone, even if I'd had bullets. I would never have shot him, and I would've paid it back. See?"

God watched the boy pull out a crumbled piece of paper from his back pocket that had IOU written in large bold letters.

Curtis wiped more tears. "I was only borrowing it. During the middle of the month, I usually have enough to pay back any loans I get because I get a bonus at work for best sales. Please don't make me lose that job. No one else will take a chance on giving a decent job to a teenager. I can work something out with you guys if you let me go."

God's and Day's heads both jerked up at hearing those words.

"I can do community service or some volunteer work at a shelter. I'll go back in and apologize to the clerk, and I'll do any type of work he needs done in the store. I'm pretty good with basic maintenance stuff."

Oh thank you, Lord. For a split second God thought the kid was offering *something* else.

Curtis's blue pleading eyes were zipping between them.

Day reached out his hand asking God for the kid's wallet and pulled his cell phone out of his coat pocket.

God knew what he was doing. Because he knew the sensitive man that was his partner.

Day dialed the three numbers for the information operator. "I need the number for the power company."

He's too fucking generous for words.

God drove Curtis home and pulled into the narrow driveway. It was a small house with tan siding and blue shutters. While there were no flowers or landscaping, the yard still looked neatly maintained. He could immediately tell the boy really took care of his home. He didn't bother to ask where the father was, because if he was around, he wouldn't have his son robbing stores to get their lights back on.

After Day called and gave the power company the boy's address and paid the bill—which was one hundred and five dollars—he told the power company to call him if it was ever scheduled for disconnection again.

Curtis thanked them so many times, God almost wanted to tell him to shut up.

"The power should be back on in an hour." Day pulled out his card and scribbled his cell phone number on the back. "Call me if you have any other problems."

Curtis just nodded in agreement. His tears had left streaks on his flushed cheeks.

Day grabbed the boy by his collar and damn near pulled him into the front seat. "No more crime. Got it?"

Curtis looked ashamed but he eagerly responded. "Yes, sir. Yes, sir. I swear. Oh, my gosh. Thank you so—"

"If you say thank you again, I'm going to pop you in your lip." Day cut the boy off.

"Oh, sorry." He blushed. "Man, I've never seen cops like you guys."

"And you never will," God rumbled in his deep voice, his harsh cough cutting off what he was going to say next.

"You know, Detective Godfrey, you should really get that cough checked out. It doesn't sound good at all. I do a lot of medical online searc—"

"Curtis, get out. Go inside and take care of your mom." God cut him off.

Day snorted. "It's useless, kid."

Curtis smiled and climbed down from the truck.

"Curtis."

"Yes, Detective Day?"

"Stay out of that little store. The owner thinks we arrested you and took you to jail. He doesn't need to know we didn't."

"Yes, sir."

God and Day watched the young man jog up his driveway and go inside before pulling away. Neither one of them commented on what Day had done. He knew his partner had a soft spot for kids... especially the ones he saw good in. Curtis was definitely a good kid; he'd just been dealt a bad hand. He knew that feeling.

30

God popped in another cough drop and drove the few miles to Day's home. He pulled into the paved driveway and put his truck in park.

"You wanna stay to watch the game tonight?" Day turned to ask God before sliding from the big truck. He looked at all the leaves that had blown around his lawn and figured he could probably convince the big guy to rake them up while he grilled them dinner.

"Nah, I gotta go by my mom's and get some work done while her and Gen are both working," He responded. He stretched his large frame out in the spacious cab. His leather coat was thrown in the back and his biceps flexed against the white-knuckle grip he had on his steering wheel. Day cocked his head to the side at the unconscious movement. *Something's not right.*

"Why do you go over when she's not there? Don't you want her—"

"Don't go there, Leo. Just let me handle my business. Maybe I'll have time to come by later. Alright?" God cut him off.

"Sure." Day looked unsure and lowered his eyes to the ground.

"Stop looking like that."

"Like what?" Day stared at him.

"Like I just tried to fuck you without lube. You know what look I'm talking about. I said I'll try, okay?" God's mouth quirked up on one side, making Day surrender as always.

"Fuck off."

Day watched as God easily maneuvered the big vehicle back out onto the street and took off like a bat out of hell.

It's been four years, partner… what the hell aren't you telling me? Day thought as he strolled into his home.

He immediately removed his holster and weapons. He readied one handgun and put it underneath one of the couch cushions and tucked the other in the back of his jeans. He went to his very clean kitchen and took out two T-bone steaks, just in case God did come back.

Meet the Family

God sat around the corner from the little two-bedroom single-family home, making sure no one was there. With help from an old flame, he was able to put the mortgage in an alias so that neither his mother nor his little brother knew that it was him that had moved them there. They thought it was their deceased father's friends from the force that helped them and made sure they were cared for. God not only ensured they had everything they needed, but that they also had just about everything they wanted.

With God paying his mother's mortgage and utilities, his salary didn't leave him much for himself. He didn't have extravagant needs anyway… all he had were his PlayStation 3, his sixty-five-inch smart television, and… his truck. His little one-bedroom apartment was a piece of shit in an even shittier neighborhood. But someone fucking with him was the least of God's concerns.

He pulled the throwaway cell phone from underneath his driver's seat and re-read the text.

Mr. Eudall, I know you said to text this number if we had any problems, so I am, because my mom and I tried to fix the kitchen sink and couldn't. The plumber we called wants $500 to do it and Mom don't got it right now, since she's saving for a computer for me. Can you help please?

God had mailed a letter to his mom when they were settled into their new home. He had to move them to Atlanta, Georgia where he could watch them better. He gave them the fake name Mr. Eudall and left this number for them to text if there was a problem. All they knew was things got fixed when they requested it—always when they weren't there. The bills got paid on time, and groceries were delivered every month. His mom had a little volunteer job at the retirement home since she was disabled. His father had seen to it that she'd never again be able to walk or stand for long periods of time. God shuddered at the memory of that accident… that's when he'd made a deal with the devil that cost him his home.

God desperately wished he could hear his mother's voice again, taste her cooking, feel her warmth from an embrace, or throw the pigskin with his kid brother. He was in high school now. He probably had questions about girls and shit that God would never be able to answer. He wouldn't be able to have a beer with him when he turned twenty-one.

Although they probably wouldn't recognize his voice if he answered the phone as Mr. Eudall, he didn't want to risk it. He explained in the letter that he—Mr. Eudall—lived in another state, but would always be available. God sighed inwardly, his chest constricting painfully with each thought. He wanted to tell his mom he was the one doing all those things. Heaven knew he missed them like crazy, but many years ago he'd had to protect them at all costs… and unfortunately it had cost him their love. There was no way they could ever know it was him… that he was Mr. Eudall, the made-up friend of their father.

When he got out of the military, he'd made the mistake of turning up at the tiny apartment in Clayhatchee where he'd once lived with his mom and brother, hoping that bygones were bygones. To say it didn't go well would be the understatement of the century. His mom had cursed and yelled for him to never come there again… that he was dead to her. His brother, only eleven at the time, threw things at him. He ran from there as fast as he could and never went back. That was six years ago. Now he could only love them from afar, and it made him sick to know that his love would never be returned.

God shook his head and pushed down those thoughts. Mr. Eudall had a job to do. After watching the place for twenty minutes, he was sure that his brother Genesis had stayed for football practice and his mom was doing her volunteer shift. God left his truck parked on the dark corner. He pulled his toolbox from the back and trotted the couple blocks to the house.

He went around back and got the key from under the third stone along the path to the door and let himself in. Stepping into the dark kitchen, his throat immediately formed a large lump in it that had him bracing a hand on the counter trying to catch his breath. It was the smell of what had been recently baked and still lingered deliciously in the air of the tidy room. He'd never be able to forget that smell for as long as he lived. His mother's made-from-scratch cinnamon-raisin bread that she used to make for him when he felt bad. God wondered if she did that for his brother, Genesis.

He turned his flashlight toward the stove and saw the small loaf wrapped in plastic wrap, a few pieces already eaten. He was sure Genesis could probably eat the whole loaf, since he was obviously taking after God in height and weight. He walked to the stove and picked the plate up and put it under his nose.

Oh man, what I'd do for one slice.

God carefully set the plate back down. He wouldn't dare do that. No handyman would come in and make himself at home with a plate of fresh-baked bread and a large glass of sweet tea.

He turned on the small light above the sink and placed his toolbox by his feet. He had a job to do and then he'd hightail it out of there before either of them got home. He'd gotten pretty good at knowing their schedules. He figured the sink repair would only take an hour, that was plenty of time to get packed up and out of there before they came home… which was always together. Genesis would pick his mom up on his way home from practice and they'd come in about seven thirty. He'd watched them follow that pattern every Thursday for many months.

35

It was rare he had to make an appearance in their home since he usually sent someone to make repairs. However, to have a plumber replace the drain and garbage disposal was more than he could afford right then. He'd just paid their mortgage, his rent, and his truck payment, but he'd be damned if he let his mom go another two weeks with a broken sink.

God pulled out his flashlight and wrench, and began to make quick work of the sink. He had to refer to a how-to YouTube video once, but he'd been able to get it done in the time he'd allotted. He closed up his large red toolbox, took his small hand towel out of his pocket, and began to shine up the sink. He bent down to pick up his toolbox when he heard the front door open and his brother's deep voice reach his ears.

"Fuck, fuck, fuck!" God whispered while anxiously looking at the back door, gauging whether he could run past the kitchen opening without being seen… highly doubtful. He looked at his watch. It was only five-thirty.

Why the hell are they home now?

"Mom, are you sure you're okay? You look exhausted."

"Just need a little rest, son. Thanks for picking me up early."

"No problem, go on up and rest. I'll bring you a cup of tea."

God was deathly still and probably pale as a ghost knowing he was about to come face-to-face with his brother. He wished it would be a nice reunion, but he wasn't a fool. He watched Genesis drop his book bag and football gear in the laundry room, turn around and jump five feet in the air at the sight of God's hulking frame leaning against their kitchen sink.

Upon realization of who he was, a hard scowl formed on his face and his fist immediately balled up at his side. "What the hell are you doing in my house?" he barked.

God looked into green eyes that were so much like his own. His mother had given those intense eyes to both of them. His brother was at least six-foot-two already at the young age of seventeen. The

36

black-and-white Muddleton High School muscle shirt he wore
showed off his solid chest and well-formed biceps. He immediately
found himself hoping he didn't have to ward off an attack by his
brother… because it wouldn't be pretty. God just stood there silently
staring at his brother, wanting to hug him so bad his arms burned.

"Did you break in here, asshole?"

God flinched at his brother's language.

"Honey, who are you yelling at?" His mother's voice reached
him before she rounded the corner and gasped at the sight of him.

She still had on her pink-and-white-paisley print volunteer
smock. Her hair had a few strands of gray that had detached from her
tight bun and curled haphazardly around her worried face. Christ, he
missed her so much. For a split second God forgot that he was
persona non grata and took two steps toward his small mom before
seeing Genesis jump protectively in front of her.

"Cashel," she said barely above a whisper. "Is that you?"

She doesn't sound angry… maybe she's not anymore.

"Yeah, Mom. It's me," he replied, his heavy bass drawl filled
with emotion and hope.

"She's not your damn mother," Genesis barked.

"What?" God gasped at the absurdity. "She'll always be my
mother."

He watched his mother ease from behind her youngest son and
limp toward him. God thought maybe she was going to embrace him
and scold him for staying away so long, then offer him a huge slice of
raisin bread. Maybe she'd hug him and tell him she understood why
he'd done what he had all those years ago, and it was okay, he could
come home now… she'd missed her big boy so much.

He hadn't even finished the fantasy before his mother drew her
hand back as far as she could and slapped him so hard across his face
that his hair came loose from the elastic band and fanned across his
now-stinging cheek.

Genesis was at her side in three large steps, pulling her protectively to him. God kept his head down and tucked his hair behind his ear, his eyes burning with unshed tears.

"How dare you come here? How did you find out where we were? You bastard!" she screamed. "You killed my husband. Get out! Get out now! Don't you ever come back here, or I'll call the police on you!" She hobbled away, but not before God saw the tears, the hurt, and the disgust all playing across her usually angelic face.

He watched her do her best to get away from him.

"I'm sorry, Mom," he whispered after her slowly retreating form.

"I *said* she's not your mother." Genesis shoved him hard, causing him to stumble over his toolbox, still on the floor at his feet. His large frame hit the floor with a heavy *thud*, making him wince at the pain now radiating from his shoulder. God saw the pride in his brother's face at feeling like he had the upper hand.

"If you ever break in here again, I'll kill you." His brother stood over him.

"Gen, can I please talk to you for just a minute?" God asked quietly while working his way to one knee.

"Fuck no. You killed my father because a gang leader told you to, and because of a technicality, you didn't serve one day in prison." Genesis's eyes were filled with a hatred he'd only seen in the hardest of criminals.

"You don't understand, Gen. If I could just talk to you." God tried to recover. He saw Genesis pull back his fist but didn't bother trying to dodge it. He let his brother hit him across the same stinging cheek his mom just had. His head hardly moved but he still rotated his jaw a little. "You got a pretty good punch, baby brother."

"You asshole," Genesis snarled. "Don't call me that. I'm no brother of yours. Now get out of my fucking house and don't ever come back if you value your life. Although maybe I'd be able to get off on a justifiable homicide defense too." His brother came closer, his voice an ice-cold snarl. "Do you live in Atlanta now?"

38

"No, I still live in Alabama," he lied.

"Good. I don't think I could stomach living in the same city with you."

Just when God couldn't feel any worse, his brother spit in his face and turned his back on him to open the back door. God used the hem of his shirt to wipe the salvia off his face while picking up his toolbox and heading for the back door.

When he got to the threshold he paused, thinking he'd give it one more attempt, but his brother shoved him hard in the back and slammed the door with enough force to shake the house's foundation.

God squeezed his eyes shut at the pain now radiating in his heart.

Jesus... was it worth it? Fuck yes, and if the piece of shit resurrected from hell, I'd send him back all over again.

What the Hell is Going On?

He wasn't sure how long he drove around trying to calm his racing heart before pulling into a bar that was about an hour from his apartment.

Fuck it, I'll sleep in my truck if I get too drunk, because I desperately need a drink.

God slid his 9mm under his seat. He put his detective's badge back around his neck, but tucked it inside his shirt. He put his handcuffs in his back pocket and tucked his knife into his boot. He locked up and took long strides across the parking lot and into the crowded dive.

The oblong bar stretched all the way to the back door. God noted its proximity right away, also any obstacles that might keep him from getting to it. He made a quick survey of the patrons before deciding to bypass the bar and slide into a booth that provided him with a full view of the place and the front door. Four or five couples gyrated on the small dance floor to the soft rock music coming from a jukebox. There were a few college-aged guys occupying one of the three pool tables on the far back wall.

He looked to his left and saw a plump waitress coming toward him. Her breasts were ample, and her tight black jeans showcased her very wide hips. God never understand why women with considerable midsections wore halter-tops. He was a believer that it was actually sexier to wear clothing appropriate, not only for your age, but also for your body type. It was apparent this waitress immensely enjoyed the southern cuisine served at the multitude of buffets Atlanta had to offer. Her cornbread sashay brought her to him, her wide mouth presenting him with a grin that was more than a little obvious.

"Hey there, tall, dark, and handsome. You by yourse—"

"Double shot of Hennessey straight up with a Corona back," he ordered, quickly cutting off her flirting. He took a deep breath and ran his hand through his unruly waves.

She balanced the tray on her round hip and put one hand on the table. "You sound like a man who knows what he wants, when he wants it," she purred. "Is there anything else I can get you, gorgeous?"

"Yeah, silence," he said on a sigh.

He figured cornbread got the message, because she sauntered off without another word. When she brought his drinks and a bowl of pretzels back, she plopped each one on the hard surface and left without asking if he wanted anything else, which suited him just fine.

God picked up the beer and took a long gulp before dropping it back to the table. He kept his head down, picking at the nicks that'd been made in the table's wooden surface. The pure hatred he'd seen in his brother's eyes was branded in his mind and his mother's shrill scream radiated in his ears. *"You killed my husband."* He threw back the shot and winced at the burn in his throat, but relished the feeling as it traveled into his system.

No. I didn't kill your husband… I killed an animal.

He put two fingers up in the air to signal cornbread. When she came back he didn't allow her to even ask the question.

"Yes, another… and keep 'em coming. When it looks like I'm about to pass out… bring two more."

Day ate the final bite of his steak and stuffed the last few homemade steak fries into his mouth. "You missed a helluva meal, buddy," Day said before grabbing his beer and leaning back on his couch, settling in for a satisfying evening of Thursday night baseball.

He was nodding on and off when he heard his cell phone vibrating on his coffee table. He picked it up and read the single line text.

You on your knees?

He snorted at the line. "Fucker," he said and typed a reply.

You're just pissed I don't get on them for you.

Day waited for what his partner would say next.

i'm pretty drunk right now, I might let you if you beg hard enough.

Day typed back immediately.

even if your dick was rolled in powdered sugar and your come tasted like raspberry jelly… I still wouldn't beg for it.

Day was waiting for the next reply but after five minutes, he figured his partner had given up. He turned up the volume on the post-game show to see who'd won since he'd fallen asleep and saw his phone light up and vibrate again.

figures… no one would want a useless fuck like me.

Day bolted upright on the couch and reread the text. "What the fuck?" he whispered while dialing God's number. He cursed when it went to voice mail.

"God, where the fuck are you? Call me right now," he barked into the phone.

He knew his partner. He didn't talk like that. If anything, the guy was annoyingly arrogant, constantly reminded Day how much he needed him, and how worthless Day would be without his guidance.

Day bounced his knee nervously. He wanted to know who and how the fuck someone had gotten into his partner's head. He called God back again… no answer, and figured it useless to leave another voice mail, so he texted.

wtf? where are you? answer me now.

Day waited fifteen minutes, but it felt like hours. *Fuck. Damn you, Cash. You better not be screwing up.* Day got up and started pacing back and forth in his spacious living room. He stopped and ran his hands through his blond hair thinking about where God could be… then an idea hit him like a ton of bricks. *Our tracking apps.*

He and God had been toying with each other's phones one night while at his house. Day was teasing him about all the bitches' numbers in his phone, some of them actually had stars by their names, and God joked with him about the text messages from some of the twinks Day dated. One guy actually sent Day a picture of his asshole spread open. God still made fun of him for that one. Day had to admit, that did embarrass the shit out of him, because that guy was a pure slut.

After the teasing, they began downloading apps and games into each other's phone. When they saw a track your lover app, they both thought it'd be funny to put it on their phones to see if it worked… and it did.

Day picked up his phone and opened the app, praying that his friend hadn't uninstalled it from his own phone by now. When it opened fully, he clicked on God's pic—an image of a lion—and sure enough, a red dot was blinking on a miniature map of the city and an address came up. Rugley's Bar, Piedmont Road off I-85.

"Yes!" He quickly rejoiced before frowning again at the location. *What the hell are you doing in Buckhead?*

Day figured he'd let God answer that question right after he punched the man in his throat for scaring him. Day called a cab all while taking his stairs two at a time to throw on some jeans and a T-shirt. He was waiting at the door with his badge in his back pocket, his 9mm tucked snugly behind his back and a two sets of handcuffs in the inside pocket of his leather coat, when the cab pulled up. He slid in the backseat and told the driver, "Buckhead." Day settled in for the nearly thirty-minute ride, all the while keeping his eye on the stable red dot. If God moved, he'd know.

44

You Can't Fool Me

God really didn't know what round he was on. All he knew was he was completely smashed and no longer thinking about his brother having spit in his face four hours ago. He'd put his phone in his back pocket after sending Day that stupid "woe is me" text. A momentary slip in judgment. He knew it would raise Day's hackles, but he'd have more time to explain later... after he'd sobered up. He'd moved from his booth to the far end of the bar after a saucy redhead in a low-lying blouse sent him a shot of Jack.

"You wanna get out of here, honey?" she moaned in his ear while nervously looking around and scanning the bar.

He turned his face toward her and took in the long, fake lashes hiding her timid brown eyes. The dark eyeliner was smudged in the corners as if she'd been crying... or maybe sweating. The long auburn hair was thick and not styled. The oily strands looked like she hadn't washed it in a couple days. Her breath smelled like whisky but her lips were full and he found himself wanting those lips someplace else.

"Yeah, why not," he slurred. God was a damn good instinctual cop and even though he was highly inebriated, he recognized this wench's hustle immediately, but he'd hoped he could get his cock sucked and get out of there before trouble started.

She led him into the dark seclusion of the back alley and maneuvered him up against the wall. He looked down into her eyes and saw the mischief dancing within those giant brown orbs.

"Suck me," he demanded. He wasn't gonna wait for her boys to show up.

She looked at him nervously.

"Don't act like it's your first time." He smirked. He watched her slide down his long muscled torso until she was squatting in front of him. She slowly undid his zipper and clumsily fumbled his semi-erect cock out of his jeans. "There you go, sexy-lips, get that big cock in there."

God rested his head against the bricks while his dick was engulfed in that hot, moist mouth. He fought not to close his eyes, knowing he had to keep a look out. She sucked him hard and fast. She wasn't great, but she wasn't terrible either.

"You let them use you like this?" he said in between moans. She paused and looked up, pinning him with a look that said, "Why would you say that?" But he just put a heavy palm on the back of her head and guided her back to her job. "If you don't mind them using you, then I'm not gonna feel bad about using you either."

She pulled off him with a slick pop and huffed an annoyed breath. "What the fuck are you talking about?"

He yanked her up by her forearm and glared at her. "You know what I'm talking about."

As if on cue, three guys came down the dark alley toward them. He turned his hard eyes back to her and shoved her away from him. "That's what I'm talking about. So how many guys have you set up tonight, huh?"

"Leave, Brenda. Now!" One of the guys approaching barked the order at her, making her jump and scurry to pick up her purse off the ground. She ran toward the other end of the alley without a backward look at him.

God groaned and slid his zipper up. "You guys could've let her finish."

"Give us your wallet." The guy who'd commanded his date to leave, spoke up.

"So you're the leader... the one I need to take out first," God answered.

"What?" the punk said with a confused look. His hair was pulled back and tucked under a black skullcap. There wasn't anything notable about his attire... any of them actually.

God quickly brought his steel-toed boot up hard into the man's midsection, easily causing him to crumble onto the concrete. While the other two were shocked at his move, he used that to his advantage and rounded on the second guy. He threw a right hook, catching the man's cheek, and heard a loud crack at the sound of his jaw shattering. God growled, swiftly spun around, and gripped the third around his neck, driving him back into the wall so hard his eyes crossed when his skull made contact with the unforgiving bricks.

God could no longer see the faces of the men, only a red and orange haze. He heard taunting voices in his mind spurring him on, calling him a "pussy," and saw old, hairy hands reaching out to grab him. His gripped tightened on the punk's neck and he cocked his right arm back, ready to do some serious damage.

"Let him go."

God shook his head at the familiar deep voice.

"I said, let him go now!"

He felt two strong hands land on his shoulders and heat seeped its way into him from behind.

"Put him down, God. Right now, before you kill him. Listen to my voice." Day was up on his tiptoes speaking into his ear. His breath was hot on his neck and it made his spine tingle. "Cashel, stop," Day whispered.

God put his right arm down and released the man from his grip. He didn't wait to see the man's body drop. He spun around, looked into his friend's eyes, and was relieved when he didn't see judgment, sorrow, or pity... all he saw was relief and then concern. Day grabbed him and held on to him tightly. His embrace was strong and confident... exactly what God needed to feel right then.

"Come on, we gotta get out of here." Day gripped the back of his arm and moved them quickly out of the alley and into a waiting taxi.

"Wait... my truck."

"It's taken care of." Day stopped him from getting out of the vehicle.

"What do you mean?"

"I mean you owe me two hundred dollars because that's what I just paid the bartender to follow us back to my place in your truck."

God spun around and saw his huge truck's headlights behind them.

"You have a stranger driving my truck... my fucking guns are in there, Leo."

"You should've thought about that earlier, Cash," Day growled right back.

"If you're going to lecture me, Leo... fucking save it." God slid down and let his aching head rest against the seat as the cab accelerated onto the highway.

"You know me better than that, Cash. I'm not going to lecture you. I'm going to kick your ass," Day said matter-of-factly and turned to look out the window. Neither one said anything else the rest of the ride.

Thank You Tracking App

Day climbed out of the taxi and told the driver to hold on while throwing a few more bills at the man. "Take that guy back to the bar."

The bartender turned into Day's driveway and parked God's truck at an awkward angle. He hopped down out of the cab full of energy.

"That's a cool truck, dude. Wish I could've opened her up on the freeway. How fast does she—"

"Just get away from it," God grumbled while walking over to inspect it as if the guy had done something to damage it internally.

"Hey, man, I just did you a favor and that's the thanks I get." The bartender turned offended eyes on Day.

"You don't need thanks, you just got two hundred bucks... now go," Day said while holding the cab's door open. The pissed-off man slid into the seat and turned back to say something to Day, but he quickly slammed the door and banged twice on the roof telling the driver to go.

When the cab was out of sight, Day turned and strolled up to his partner, who was now checking his truck for his weapons.

"Let's go inside, God," Day said around a yawn.

"I'm going home, I'm fine to drive now," he said quietly.

"The hell you are. You can sleep on my couch, man, it's almost four in the morning," Day said quickly.

"I'll be fine. Doubt I'll be sleeping anyway," God responded, already pulling himself up into the driver's seat.

Day jumped inside the truck door to prevent God from closing it. He heard him let out a frustrated breath.

"Cash, talk to me, man. What the fuck was that all about tonight? The text, the liquor, you trying to kill a man with your bare hands... that fucking rage?"

"Nothing, Leo. Go in the house. I was just blowing off some steam. I'm a man. It happens to all of us every now and then... right?"

God didn't look him in his eyes when he spoke, and Day knew something wasn't right.

"Try that bullshit on someone with a GED, okay. I saw your anger, I saw the pain, I saw the confusion, and I saw when that punk's face turned into an enemy's... so out with it. Is someone bothering you, Cash? I'm your partner, man, you should know by now you can trust me with this, just like you trust me to watch your six when we're out there on the streets."

Day was shoved back when God jumped out of the truck and barely made it to the side of the house before he wretched up all the high-octane comfort he'd had tonight.

Day walked over to his partner, placed a warm hand on his muscular back, and felt it tense and contract while he coughed and dry heaved after there was nothing left in there but his stomach lining. Day's hand was forcibly shrugged off.

"A little fucking privacy, Leo," God barked.

"All right." Day put his hand up and turned to walk back to his partner's truck to take the keys from the ignition and pocket them. He went in the house, leaving all the lights off except the hallway. He went in the kitchen and put on a pot of coffee and popped two pieces of bread in the toaster. He was adding two spoons of creamer to God's mug when he heard his front door slam.

"My keys, Day. Or are you going to hold me hostage?" God said from the entrance to his modest kitchen.

He stalked over and rinsed his mouth out repeatedly in the sink before taking the offered coffee mug and saucer of lightly browned toast. He raised those striking green eyes up at Day and said thank you without speaking.

Day figured he'd leave his partner alone to deal with his demons for now. Obviously the guy wasn't up for sharing time. He clamped his palm down on a broad shoulder.

"I'll see you in a few hours, buddy. I'll put some blankets and a pillow on the couch for you," he said, turning to leave.

"Hey, fairy. No jerking off to me down here practically naked on your couch either." God slipped in before Day got out of the room.

"If I do, I'll make sure to run down and shoot my load on your face." Day laughed and took the stairs two at a time.

Day had only been upstairs an hour and half. He had his jazz music turned down real low so not to disturb his overnight guest. In the four years that he'd been partnered with the big guy, he'd never stayed at Day's house. They'd had plenty of visits—usually four or five times a week—but despite Day's persistence, God always got up and left to go back to his shithole apartment... no matter how late it was.

Day was reading his magazine and mellowing out when he heard God scream a gut-wrenching cry. Day was on his feet in a second, racing down the stairs with his 9mm in hand. He took in the entire downstairs but didn't see anything out of place. God was asleep on his back. He only had his pants on, the button undone and zipper pulled down. His hands were clenched into tight fists and his face wore a frown so deep that he was barely recognizable.

Day put his gun down on the table and moved quickly to the couch. He was down on one knee, but had to jump back when God's upper body jolted up off the couch and he yelled again, his arms flailing wildly. "Get off me! I said stop! Enough! Enough!" he yelled repeatedly.

Day was amazed that someone could yell that loud and not wake himself up. God looked like he was in so much pain it was breaking Day's heart.

Day used his quick wit and sarcasm to keep everyone at arm's length and protect himself, but none of that applied to the man in front of him. He'd had a soft spot for Detective Cashel Godfrey from the very beginning.

Day saw that God wasn't waking up on his own. He had to put an end to his nightmare before the man hurt himself. Day put both hands on God's shoulder's to keep him from jerking back up when he yelled again, "Dad, he's hurting me!" His six-foot-four partner sounded like a frightened boy, and this time Day yanked his hands back as if he'd been burned.

Oh no. Please don't let that mean what it sounds like… Jesus.

God began thrashing as if he was fighting for his life.

Fuck, wake up.

"Cash! Cash!" Day had a firm grip on God's forearms as he shook him with force, hoping not to scare the shit out of him. "Cash, wake up!"

God jerked upright and tried to yank his arms out of Day's tight grip.

"It's me… it's Leo. Calm down Cash, you were dreaming." Day watched him look around frantically, still not one hundred percent awake. God pulled at his arms again and this time Day let him go. "It's me. You're at my house, Cash."

The man looked like a cornered deer. His green eyes were wild and unfocused as he tried to get a grip on where he was.

"Cash, look at me," Day said forcefully and that seemed to jar God back to the here and now.

"Leo," he whispered.

"Yeah, Cash, I'm right here." Day sat on the edge of the couch and reached his hand up to run it over Cash's sweat drenched forehead. He saw him close his eyes and take a shaky breath while still trying to control his labored breathing. When God opened his eyes again it was like he was just recognizing Day, and his eyes immediately filled with water. God reached out and grabbed him around his waist, pulling him tight to his chest.

Day let out a harsh breath but threw his arms around his friend's neck. God was shaking hard and he was soaked with sweat. Day's own eyes filled with tears as he hugged his partner hard. "Cash, please, baby. Tell me what's wrong. I can't help you if you don't tell me." When God choked on a sob, Day squeezed him tighter.

"He wouldn't stop them. I asked him to stop and he wouldn't stop them." God cried.

"Who? Your father?" Day pulled back and looked into moist green eyes.

A.E. VIA

A New Insight

Fuck! He'd said too much. Day just asked about his father. No one knew about that—and if God had anything to do with it, no one ever would. He pulled back from Day's embrace and he could see the tears and concern shinning in his partner's eyes.

God knew the caring man really did want to help him, but what's done is done. Unless Day had a time machine, there's no way he could help. God felt his cheeks heat when he'd realized Day had called him baby... probably because he liked it. No one had ever cared for him... at least not for almost fifteen years. That's a long time to be a lone wolf. He had to get out of there he couldn't breathe. He pried himself out of Day's hold.

"I gotta go, Day." God swung his legs over the side of the couch.

"W-wait! No, absolutely not! Where are you going?" Day admonished.

"Where else? Home," God said, while wiping his wet eyes.

"No, Cash. I don't think you should be home alone right now."

"Who am I? Macaulay Culkin?" God chuckled humorlessly.

"I'm not playing around, and don't fucking mock me, Cashel," Day ground out through gritted teeth.

"Day, please." God sighed heavily and dropped his head into his hands, silently praying Day would just let this go. *Fat fucking chance.*

"I'll see you at work in a few hours, all right?" He still had his boots on, so he threw his black T-shirt over his head and snatched his keys off the end table before Day could grab them.

God didn't bother buttoning his pants back up. He threw his leather coat on, ran his hands through his sweaty curls, and moved to the front door, only to have Day race past him and block him from leaving.

"You are not leaving until you talk to me, because later at work you'll try to act like nothing happened and throw yourself into a case," Day said. He had his back pressed firmly to the door and his arms stretched out to the sides.

God thought Day looked wonderful at that moment, and he'd be damned if that realization didn't make his head swim.

"I'm tired, Leo." God's voice was husky and strained as he stepped in very close to his partner. Their chests were almost touching and he saw Day crane his head up to look into his eyes. What he saw reflected back at him through those caring hazel browns was stubbornness and concern.

Day had come for him tonight, had rescued him, had worried about him, taken care of him, but what he saw in Day's eyes didn't have a damn thing to do with being buddies. He needed to leave and process all these new feelings.

"Leonidis, I'm walking out this damn door, and I promise to talk about this with you later." God inched even closer, letting their chests touch. If Day had puckered his lips he could've kissed him on his chin, that's how close their faces were. He saw Day's eyes lower at their close proximity and his hot, heavy breaths were ghosting over God's neck.

"Well later is now. Because I'm not fucking moving." Day dared him.

God began to slowly bend his knees and slide down Day's torso, bringing his eyes level with his partner's.

"What are you doing?" Day whispered.

God brought his arms up and slid them under Day's, securing them behind his back as if he was positioning them for another hug.

"Cash." Day breathed his name into his cheek while bringing his arms up around his neck.

God squeezed his eyes shut and enjoyed the contact for a few seconds before lifting Day completely off his feet, up into a bear hug and turning him around so that he was no longer blocking the door. He slowly set his friend back down and did something that shocked the hell out of both of them... he kissed Day gently on the forehead before turning to leave.

It's Time for A Change

Day was sitting at his desk, trying not to get angry at the fact that it was almost noon and God wasn't at work yet. Day had called him at least ten times and hadn't gotten an answer.

"So where's your bodyguard, Day?"

Day mentally rolled his eyes and swiveled his chair around to face his most incessant headache. "I don't know, Ronowski, but I know where *I* am… I'm about ten seconds off your fucking ass. I'm warning you, now is not the time." Day glared.

"I bet you'd love to get up in my ass. Tell me, Day. Do you scream like a girl when a man is shoving his hard cock in your ass?" Ronowski said just loud enough for him to hear. He had both hands on the surface of his desk, sneering down at him disgustedly.

Day narrowed his eyes and shook his head. "You made a special point to stop what you were doing and come all the way from the other side of the station just to ask what sounds I make when I get fucked. Jesus, Ronowski… get a life. Better yet, come out of the closet and then get a fucking life."

Day saw Ronowski gearing up again but completely lost interest when he saw God stroll into the office in his typical tight black T-shirt and dark blue Levi's. He had on his leather coat and black boots. His long waves were tamed by an elastic band and his two-day-old scruff looked delicious. Day thought about how the coarse beard had felt against his face just nine short hours ago. Day leaned

59

back and blatantly tracked God as he moved through the maze of desks, stopping here and there to speak with other officers. God's sexy green eyes were fixed on him as well as he sat in his chair across from him. After several seconds, God broke the contact and blinked quizzically in Ronowski's direction. Day absently looked up at the wickedly handsome, homophobic officer and saw he was still standing there staring at him.

Day jumped up out of his chair. "Jesus, fuck, Ronowski! Why don't you just take a goddamn picture of me so you can jerk off to it later?"

Ronowski gasped and his porn star lips twisted into an angry snarl. "Fuck no! I hate you."

"Then get the fuck away from me! Why the hell are you standing over me?" Day fumed.

"No one gives a shit about you or where you put your dick," Ronowski fired back.

Day threw his hands in the air and exaggeratedly flopped back down in his chair. "You've got to be kidding me. Ronowski, I swear, you are the fucking stupidest smart person I know. How the hell can you have a master's degree in psychology and be so completely fucked-up in the head?"

Day looked over at God and saw him leaning back in his chair with his hands steepled together, smirking at him.

Vikki chose that moment to come over.

"Detective Seasel, can you call down to the records department, your partner needs to have a look at the de-nile file," Day said turning his glare back to Ronowski.

"Fuck you, Day."

"You wish, you closet case. But people in hell wish they had ice water… lesson here is you can't always get what you want," Day retorted.

"Come on, Ro, we have a call to follow up on," Vikki said while tugging Ronowski's arm off Day's desk.

"Call me a fucking closet case when your bodyguard's not around, ass-muncher," Ronowski spat.

"To thine own self, Ronowski," Day answered drily.

He watched the red-faced officer continue to shoot daggers at him. He rolled his eyes dramatically and turned his attention to Vikki, who was leaning on God's desk, not paying attention to his and Ronowski's feud. He watched her through squinted eyes.

"Good afternoon, Detective Godfrey. I like your hair when you pull it back like that... it looks sexy." She smiled and ran her thin fingers through God's chestnut waves.

Day didn't give God a chance to respond. "Didn't you say you had a follow-up to respond to, Vikki?" Day's harsh tone startled her out of her lust.

She frowned at him in confusion before turning and walking off with Ronowski.

God looked back at him. "You want to come cock your leg up and piss around my fucking desk too, Leo?"

Day didn't hesitate. "Maybe."

God watched him for several moments, those intense green eyes leveled on him. It made him think about how he'd look on his knees in front of Day, staring up at him.

"Come on, we have work to do." God unlocked his drawer and pulled out a few files.

"Of course... just like I said would happen. You stroll in here late as hell... we can't talk... all we can do is work," Day huffed.

"Stop whining, little girl. I'm gonna talk to you later." God tossed the file at him and they got to work.

Four hours later they had all their files spread out in the conference room while the ADA and two profiling detectives gave them feedback on their new theory. Someone was bringing large shipments of marijuana and cocaine into the city, and they were most likely using the water and the unmonitored ports. They'd concluded that it had to be someone with power and connections; all they needed was a break to crack this one.

God was standing in front of the dry erase board with his legs apart and his muscled arms folded across his chest. His eyes were focused on the notes and diagrams they'd drawn over the last few hours. Day couldn't put together any of the case's connections today, because he was having the hardest time concentrating. He kept picturing the open, emotional man that had clung to him on his couch this morning. During those few hours, something had changed between them.

After God had sent him that text, saying no one wanted him, Day had realized that *he* wanted the man. The bad-ass, tough-as-nails, cocky sonofabitch that had stuck up for him four years ago for no reason, Day wanted *that* man... and he wanted him bad. What was fucking up Day's head was the way God had held him and kissed him this morning. He knew God was straight—or so he assumed—although it appeared that he limited his conquests to one-night stands and quick hookups.

During the entire time that he'd known God, the man hadn't mentioned a love interest or brought anyone to meet Day. Day found himself wondering if God had ever taken anyone to meet the mother that he always jumped through hoops for.

Day's thoughts were interrupted when Detective Johnson strolled into the conference room and announced proudly, "Detective Day, you are going to love me, handsome."

"Oh yeah, you finally got me that date with Channing Tatum?" Day quipped.

Day heard God huff with annoyance, not bothering to turn around and face them.

"Whatever... even better," Johnson replied. He slammed a clear evidence bag down on the table, the contents making a loud clank against the wood surface. Johnson pointed at it. "That right there my friend, is the weapon that killed fourteen-year-old, street level drug runner, Enrique Lopez. Ballistic reports are a sure match. The number of rounds found at the scene is even consistent with what's missing from the clip."

Day waved his hand in a get-to-the-point gesture. "I'm not feeling the love yet, Johnson."

Johnson strolled over to Day, in what he obviously thought was a sexy strut, looked down at him with those dark brown eyes, and Day had to stifle an urge to let his gaze travel lower.

"Damn, you smell good," Johnson said out of the blue. His look full of lust, he completely forgot the evidence and everyone else in the room.

God spun around and barked, "Whose fucking gun is that, dipshit?"

Johnson jumped at God's hard voice. "It's Lamar Jenkins... the guy you busted last week, who's still refusing to roll over on his kingpin. The search team found this gun under his bed, along with several others. I think a bargaining chip of twenty-five to life will have him reconsidering his vow of silence."

Day looked at God with surprise and saw his devious smirk. They were talking again with their eyes, their look saying, *"Finally, this is just the break we needed."* God nodded his head once and Day moved from his perch on the corner of the table and headed to the door, both knew exactly where they were going... over to lockup.

"Hey, hold on, Leo." Johnson grabbed the evidence bag and jogged over to the door, pausing in front of Day. He leaned against the doorjamb and propped his arm up on the wall beside Day's head. Day hated when men used their height to stand over him... it grated on his nerves... *all men except for God.* Day refused to look up at him.

"You busy this Friday? My dad got me box tickets to the Braves game," Johnson boasted.

"Good for daddy, Johnson, but I'm not a baseball fan," Day lied and sidestepped to head out the door, but was again blocked by the tall man.

Day heard God let out a small growl from behind him in the room but chose to ignore it.

"That's cool, Leo." Johnson was damn near standing on top of him as he spoke, but he'd be damned if he was going to back up.

"So just talking would be nice... would you like to come to my place tonight for a glass of wine?"

"Not even if Jesus was pouring it," Day responded quickly. He heard God let out a loud laugh and the sound of it made the corner of his mouth turn up. God rarely laughed—hell, the man rarely smiled—but somehow, Day could make him do both.

"What the fuck are you laughing at, Godfrey?" Johnson moved away from Day.

"You, daddy's boy." God's smile disappeared as fast as it came, and he was back to typical, intimidating God.

"Fuck you. I know Day is just showing off for you." Johnson turned back to look at Day. "I'll be sure to catch you when you're alone."

"I'll be sure to have my rape whistle," Day retorted.

Johnson turned a frustrated look at God. "I'm not finished with you yet, either." With that hanging in the air, Johnson walked out the room.

"Duly noted," God said with an uninterested shrug.

Day slammed the door behind Johnson, leaving just him and his partner in the room alone. Day killed the lights.

"Setting the mood, Leo?" God grinned at him.

"I want to talk to you now."

"You can't always get what you want, Leonidis," God rebutted.

"I want you," Day said, with no hesitation.

The room was deathly silent. After a few long seconds God responded simply, "No you don't."

"I do. Isn't it obvious?" Day moved a little closer.

"You don't know what the fuck you want. I've watched you for four years, jumping from bed to bed and fucking your way through

64

half of Atlanta. I have one emotional night and all of a sudden you want me... fuck you," God said gruffly.

Day's body heated at the sound. He moved closer to where God was standing on the opposite side of the table.

"Oh, I'm sorry. I didn't realize I was supposed to be saving myself for marriage, and even more, I didn't realize you were a goddamn virgin. How many women have I seen you fuck in that pussy-magnet truck of yours, huh?" Day lowered his voice as he stood directly in front of God. "Just tell me you didn't feel what I did last night." He closed the small gap, not minding God's height at all, and looked up into electric-green eyes. "Tell me you don't want me too, and I'll back the fuck off."

God looked down at him and Day could see the uncertainty all over that ruggedly handsome face.

"Shit's complicated, Leo." God's breath ghosted across his forehead.

"Make me understand, Cashel," Day whispered, and slowly brought his hands up to rest on God's waist.

"What makes you think I'm gay or bi?" God asked avoiding Day's request.

"Really? Maybe it's this that makes me think that." Day boldly palmed and squeezed God's rock-hard erection.

"Fuck," he hissed.

God grabbed Day's shoulders and quickly moved him until his back slammed hard into the wall.

"Fuck yeah. That's it," Day groaned. He held on tight while God hoisted him up against the wall and attacked his mouth. It wasn't pretty or gentle. His partner kissed him with a fury that he hadn't felt in years. It was erotic, carnal, wicked, and Day loved every second. His feet dangled as God's bulk pushed hard against him, keeping him immobile and under his control.

"This what you want, you sexy fucker?" God snarled in his ear, then leaned in and bit the juncture of his neck and shoulder.

"Ugh, yes! I want you, goddammit," Day hissed into the darkness.

"Prove it." God released him and Day dropped back to the ground. He immediately felt the loss of God's heat and had to resist the urge to claw at the man.

Day palmed his own hard erection.

"Seriously. This isn't fucking proof enough?" he said while seductively squeezing his cock and licking his lips, now full and plump from their kiss.

"I don't give a damn about your wood. You get a hard-on when you drink coffee, Leo." God grabbed his coat and headed to the door. "If you want it, you'll have to earn it."

Day stalked over to him. "Did you make all those other bitches you fucked earn it?" Day fumed. Not liking that God was playing a come-and-get-it game with him.

God spun around fast and gripped Day around his throat, pulling him into his rock-hard chest. Day hit that solid wall of muscles with a thud and the air rushed out of his lungs. Day put both his hands on God's huge forearms that flexed against his touch. God bent his head and a few strands of his hair came loose from the elastic band and brushed against the side of Day's face.

God looked and smelled so fucking delicious, like masculinity and aftershave. Day knew the grip on his neck was not to hurt him, it was to show him who was in charge. God's sheer strength and power had Day feeling like he could come right there in the small conference room.

"Oh, so you want to be my bitch?" God's mouth was at the base of his ear. He roughly ground his pelvis into Day's stomach while the other hand got a firm grip in his hair at the back of his head. "Why didn't you just say so? You want me to have you face down and ass up in my truck? Then we can go do that right fucking now."

God loosened his grip on Day's hair and let the large hand around his throat turn into a gentle caress. He smoothed down Day's

66

hair and leaned in and took a deep sniff before nuzzling the side of his face. Day couldn't have stopped his whimper if he'd tried. God dragged two fingers down his throat and gently stroked his collarbone. His breathing was now even and calm, surprisingly relaxing Day as well.

God kissed Day's temple before speaking in a seductive whisper against the side of his face. "Or do you want me to put on one of your jazz records, lay your sexy body down on your bed, and slowly lick you from head to toe?" God ran a thumb over Day's parted lips. "I would kiss these soft lips for hours before I let you wrap them around my cock."

God let loose the sexiest fucking growl he'd ever heard while he oh so slowly massaged Day's leaking cock, trapped uncomfortably in his jeans.

"Then I'd lie on top of you and bury my dick so deep inside you that you'd feel me for days," he taunted sexily.

Day felt God's breath stutter and knew he was enjoying the visual just as much as Day was.

"I'd fuck you slow and deep, Leo, until you came screaming my name." God released his dick. "So tell me... which do you want?"

Day had to figure out how to speak again before he was finally able to reply. "Yes, Cashel. I want you in my bed."

"Then prove it." God laid a lingering, gentle kiss on his forehead before stepping back from him and leaving the conference room.

Good Cop, Very Angry and Scary Cop

God was glad Day wasn't on his heels when he walked out the door. The way he'd described wanting to fuck his partner had his dick ready to detonate and him practically running to the locker room—which he was hoping would be empty.

He burst through the heavy door and quickly stepped past the assigned lockers, his head scanning the aisles. He pushed through the glass doors and shouldered his way into the last stall. He slammed the metal door shut and leaned his back against it. With his head tilted back, his eyes shut tight; he unbuttoned his jeans with shaking hands, lowered his zipper, and forcefully dug into his briefs, yanking his dick out into the cool air. He tried not to groan but failed miserably.

He spit in his palm and got a punishing grip on his cock and rapidly pumped his fist up and down his steel rod. He thought this had to be the hardest he'd ever been. No woman or man had ever excited him to the point of having to jerk himself immediately. The smell of Day was still on his body and the scent of the man's soft hair lingered in his nose.

"Fuck, Leo," God moaned as quietly as he could manage.

His body jerked violently when he felt his orgasm barreling to the surface. He dug his other hand into his underwear to free his balls, and that was all he'd needed. He fingered then pulled at his tight sac.

"Ohhh, fuuuck."

With a tight hold on his blushing cockhead, he squeezed it repeatedly, letting his seed spill into the toilet. God slammed his eyes shut and bit his bottom lip to muffle the moans threatening to break free. He braced his legs apart trying not to fall, his knees buckling at the intensity of his thoughts of Day underneath him taking his load deep inside him.

"Ugh, damn."

More come shot from his slit, knocking him back against the stall.

Holy shit.

He let his head fall back and hit the stall door again, trying to catch his breath. If he felt like this just from thinking of him and Day together, God couldn't imagine how it'd be if he ever got to fuck the gorgeous man.

God had thought of him and his partner together plenty of times, but decided never to act on it. More than a few times he'd caught Day looking at him with want in his pretty eyes. He didn't consider himself gay, straight, bi… who gave a fuck? God would do whatever and whomever he wanted. Period. It was just that simple to him, because his life was complicated enough without him worrying about a damn label for his sexual preference.

God flushed the toilet and made sure there was nothing on the seat, then left the bathroom. He washed his hands and splashed some water on face. After pulling back his hair, he went in search of his partner who he figured was waiting at his truck.

God pulled on his leather coat as he stepped outside and noticed Day leaning casually against the passenger door. He wanted to wipe that condescending smirk off his face.

"What are you grinning at?" God frowned while unlocking his truck.

Day boldly swept his eyes down to God's groin and licked his still red lips. "You missed a spot," he said, and jumped up into the cab.

God walked around the back of the truck's long bed and looked down at his jeans, and he'd be damned if there wasn't a small, not quite dry spot there. *Dammit.* He got up in the truck and started the powerful engine.

"Damn shame to have wasted that in a toilet. I could've thought of a couple good places for it to go instead," Day said nonchalantly, scrolling through his cell-phone messages as if they talked about fucking each other every day.

"Shut up," he said and peeled out of the parking lot toward the jail.

Day was inwardly pumping his fist at the knowledge that the always cool God had to jerk his dick after all the dirty talk he'd tortured Day with in that conference room. Day was imagining God fucking his hand in some bathroom stall, groaning and moaning his name when he came, and just like that Day's dick was hard again. Unfortunately he didn't have the luxury of getting some much-needed relief. Day gazed out the window and palmed his aching cock.

"You all right over there?" God's deep country drawl ricocheted around the large cab before smacking right into Day's balls.

"No. Why? You offering to help?" Day looked into God's eyes.

"Nope," God responded easily and plucked the small toothpick from his mouth and tossed it out the window.

"Come on, we need to shake this dude down." God swung into an official use parking space. "He's going to give us a fucking name today, or he's going away for way more years than he thought." God stepped out of the truck and came around to stand beside him.

"Is the ADA already here?" Day said while checking his weapons.

"He didn't need to come. The offer is the name of the kingpin for twenty years, possibility of parole in fifteen. That's a hell of a lot better than life." God was talking to him, but his eyes were scanning up and down his body. Day was going to have fun proving to the big man that he wanted him, and he'd have him too.

"Good cop bad cop." God smirked.

"Cool. This should be short but sweet… like me." Day winked

"Let's go, flirt. Stay focused if you can. And I don't mean on my cock." God admonished.

"I make no promises." Day yanked open the heavy door and they quickly made their way to the metal detectors, pulling out their badges.

While they waited for their inmate and his lawyer to come into the small interrogation room, Day and God stared openly at each other as if they were seeing each other for the first time.

"What are you thinking?" Day asked.

God leaned against the wall in the corner with his arms crossed over his broad chest, already in his position as bad cop. His job was to stay lurking in the corner with a hard scowl on his face to intimidate their suspect.

"Nothing in particular." God shrugged.

"Not thinking about me?" Day asked, his voice husky.

God looked up at him. His eyes held a seriousness that made Day lose his smirk.

"Of course I'm thinking about you, Leo," he whispered.

Day had to hurry to catch his breath and get his bearings when he heard the clanking of the heavy metal locks as their suspect stepped into the small room with his lawyer and a guard. His hands were handcuffed behind his back, the guard checked with them before he undid the cuffs and pushed the man down into the small metal chair.

Day pushed all thoughts of sexing his partner to the back of his mind and went into his role as good-want-to-help-you-I'm-your-friend sensitive cop. In a soft, professional tone Day spoke, "How ya doing buddy… ya holding up in here?"

72

"It's fucked up in here, Day. What the hell you think? You said you were going to get me in minimum-security."

Day looked at the man with what he hoped was his best I-understand face. Lamar's long dreadlocks were pulled back in a ponytail. His faded jeans and prison-issue shirt looked like they'd missed the last couple laundry rounds. He smelled like he was avoiding shower time as well. Day had no doubt that most of the cliques and gangs in the maximum ward didn't take too kindly to child killers. Word traveled fast, especially on the inside. There were men in there that were serial killers, rapist, robbers, you name it… but as soon as someone came in who'd harmed a child, even the most hardened criminal took offense. Had something to do with children being unable to defend themselves… inmates that were child abusers, molesters, or whatever would always have it worst in prison.

"I'm working on it, Lamar," Day said soothingly.

"You don't deserve a fucking thing. You don't cooperate, we're not cooperating." God barked from the corner of the room. He wore a menacing glare and stood to his full 6'4" height with his feet shoulder width apart, like a military drill sergeant.

Lamar snapped up out of his chair. "No one was talking to you, God. Everyone knows you don't give a fuck. I should've run from your big ass when I had the chance ya heartless bastard," Lamar yelled back at a stone-faced God, who never flinched at Lamar's rage.

"I would've loved for you to have run, Lamar, then I would've had a reason to put a bullet in your thigh. I find it baffling that you're the one that shot a kid in the back but I'm the heartless one." God snarled at him.

"Detective Godfrey, enough." Day frowned at him, like he was really upset with God. He turned his focus back to their suspect. "Look, Lamar, I'm still working on your placement, but let's talk about right now. I'm sure your lawyer has already counseled you about the handgun found in your home. We have your prints and a

73

ballistics report that confirms that gun was the one used to kill fourteen-year-old errand boy Enrique Lopez."

"Yeah. I know I can't beat that charge," Lamar said, casting his eyes downward.

"You can't beat it fuck-face because you're guilty," God huffed.

Lamar jumped up but his lawyer pulled him down before he could yell again.

"Look, detectives, we want to make a deal. My client is willing to give over the locations of the other guys that got away, in exchange for ten years with the possibility of parole in eight."

Day had to be careful not to break character, because he desperately wanted to slap that dumbass lawyer across his face for even suggesting something so ludicrous. Lamar had enough weed in his house to supply an entire reggae concert, in addition to three illegal automatic weapons, and if that wasn't enough to warrant twenty years, one of those guns was used to kill a kid. Day didn't have to say anything, because God would.

God rushed forward and slammed his large hands on the metal table so hard that Lamar and his lawyer practically fell backward out of their chairs.

"Eight years for drug possession, intent to distribute, guns, and murder one! Fucking kill yourself!" God roared, glaring at the lawyer. "If you're going to waste our damn time, then we're leaving. Let's go, Day." God stood up and stalked toward the door.

"Hold on, Detective Godfrey, give them a chance." Day put both his hands up as if to calm everyone. This was all part of their act. He looked back at Lamar. "Come on, Lamar. You gotta do better than that, buddy. Give me something good and I'll see what I can do for you. You and I both know that you're holding on to that kingpin's ID. You were the biggest dealer on the street; you carried the most weight. Tell us who he is, and I swear I'll do everything I can with the DA to get you a good deal."

Day watched Lamar drop his chin to his chest and knew he was thinking it over, so Day decided to go in for the kill.

"Come on, Lamar. Do you want to walk out of here when you can still have some kind of a life? Or do you want to leave when you're old and gray and your dick doesn't work anymore? Just give us a name and where we can find him."

"I want your word, Detective, that the DA is going to do a deal if he gives you a name," the lawyer added.

"We want the name, a location, and how the drugs are getting in here. Or else you don't get shit," God growled.

"Detective Godfrey, that's an awful lot of intel. What assurances are you going to give my client? Especially since his safety will be in jeopardy," the lawyer responded.

Day watched God size up the pudgy lawyer. His hands were fat and his hot-dog sized fingers were clasped together as he stared up at God with light blue, beady eyes. God snarled back at him and Day knew he had to jump in now.

"We're willing to offer twenty with parole in fifteen. That's a damn good deal for murder one and possession, Lamar," Day said in a low, sensitive tone.

"Twenty years, Day… come on, man!" Lamar yelled. "I can't see myself even doing a dime in this place, man."

"Well it's good you can't see yourself doing ten, because you're doing twenty, asshole." God laughed.

"Fuck. You. God!" Lamar stuck up his middle finger.

"Lamar, look at me, man." Day interrupted. He looked into Lamar's worried eyes; his lip trembled as the reality hit that he was indeed going to lose the next two decades of his life. Day played his sympathy card. "This is a good deal. I want you to be able to go back home and be with your mom and kid brother one day. If you keep your nose clean while inside, you can pull your fifteen and be out. You got a newborn son, man, he can still get to know you when you get out, he won't even be in high school yet."

A tear ran down Lamar's face when Day mentioned his son. "You could be looking at life if you take your chances with a jury. You killed a kid, dude. Even though he was a small time runner, the parents thought he would eventually turn his life around… and they want justice. I begged the DA for this deal, but we need the kingpin's name." Day watched Lamar take a deep breath.

"His name is Joe Hansen, they call him Sandman." Lamar looked up. "He's dangerous and he's got an army that's not afraid to kill for him. Not too many people can get close to him. He's got several houses, but his main one is on the coast."

Day watched God move closer and stare into Lamar's eyes. "Address."

Lamar huffed. "2021 Palisades Drive."

"Tell us about the shipments," God said in a harsh voice.

"We want this deal in writing," the lawyer started.

"Shut the fuck up," God barked. He looked back at Lamar. "Tell us about the shipments. Who's bringing it in where and when?"

Day wrote down everything Lamar told them. Finally they were going to nail this bastard. Day knew there was a kingpin… there always was. Lamar told them shipment times, ports, other big weight runners, and even the men that worked the docks that were on the take. They also got the next shipment date, which was a month from now… and it was a big one. It was going to require a huge multi-agency task force to pull off this seizure.

"Thanks, Lamar, you did the right thing," Day said as he got up.

"Hey, Day, hold up, man. When am I going to get moved to the minimum security?"

"Go fuck yourself," God said disgustedly; his handsome face a mask of hate.

Day turned around very slowly. They had their information, so good cop was off duty. He braced both hands on the table and lowered himself, firing a heated stare into the inmate's worried eyes, and spoke in a fierce snarl.

"You shot a scared kid three times in the back when he tried to run away. You took his body and put it in a goddamn Dumpster like he was motherfucking trash. You sold coke to high school kids right before they walked into class. You put guns into the hands of kids so they could kill for you." Day was in Lamar's face now. "I hope you spend the next twenty years with your back against the fucking wall, asshole." Day turned and left through the large metal door with God on his six.

When they were out of the jail and back in God's truck, they looked at each other for a long time. Neither one saying a word. Again, communicating without speaking. He stared into God's brilliant green eyes. Took in the man's strong features—his Roman nose and cupid's-bow lips framed by just the right amount of stubble.

It looked as if God was focused solely on Day's mouth. They knew shit was about to get real serious. They had the information and were going after the kingpin and his army. There was no doubt that he was a dangerous man, and one of them could end up getting killed.

"Have dinner with me tonight?" Day asked, his voice full of emotion.

"Yes," God answered immediately.

A.E. VIA

Aren't You Coming In?

God was waiting in the Starbucks parking lot for Day to get another coffee fix, and decided to check Mr. Eudall's phone. He'd only checked it once since he'd had the run-in with his family. He had a message thanking him for the sink. Gen had been so angry, God doubted that he'd put it together that God had had a toolbox when he'd thrown him out.

He pulled the small TracFone from under the seat and saw that he had a missed text. He looked to see that Day was still in line before opening the message.

Mr. Eudall, Thanks again for repairing the sink and im sorry to have to call you right back, but last night the hot water heater exploded and theres no hot water. If you cant help we understand. We'll make do.

God pounded on the steering wheel before taking a deep breath. *Fuck me.* "Dammit, that's gonna cost over a thousand bucks," he groaned. Even if he bought the heater himself, there was no way he'd risk going there again to install it. God didn't use credit cards, so he couldn't charge it. He was broke; but he refused to have bad credit too. God felt a terrible headache coming on. He had no clue how he was going to fix this one. He couldn't very well let his mom and brother go without hot water. How would they bathe, cook, or clean? God rubbed the back of his neck, he could feel the knots… they were huge. He cleared his throat a few times, it felt scratchy, and it ached now. He reached in the console and popped in another throat lozenge. He'd been sucking lozenges and downing cough syrup for weeks and nothing had worked on the terrible cough he'd developed. He hoped he wasn't coming down with anything serious, because there was no way he was going to the doctor.

He tucked the phone back under his seat, and when he rose his head was spinning. Day walked across the parking lot with the largest cup of coffee they had and a small brown bag.

"I got you a coffee cake," Day said, climbing back up into the truck. He tossed the bag into God's lap and took a long drink of his coffee, moaning like a slut at the flavor.

"Thanks," God mumbled.

He hadn't realized he'd closed his eyes until he felt Day's hand on his shoulder. "You okay, God? You look a little green around the edges, babe."

He looked into Day's concerned eyes and cleared his throat again. "I'm good." God had to blink a couple times before his vision focused enough to drive. His thoughts were all over the place, he was stressed the fuck out, and he knew that Day could see it. He pulled into Day's driveway but left the engine running.

"Aren't you coming in?" Day paused with his hand on the handle, looking at him quizzically.

"I'm a little beat. I think I'm just gonna go on home. We have a lot to do tomorrow." God waved his hand in the air. "You know… planning the raid."

"You can rest in my house too," Day said back softly.

"I know, but I just need some time alone, I don't think I'll be much company anyway," God said back. He rubbed his neck again and saw Day's hurt expression at the rejection.

"Hey, come here. Stop looking like that." God held out his arm, and watched Day hesitate before leaning over to him. God kissed him lightly on the forehead, rubbing his back tenderly. He tilted his head so his cheek was resting on Day's soft hair. "I'll call you later. I just got some things to handle."

"All right," Day whispered and climbed out of the cab. He walked quickly across his lawn without looking back.

Dammit. God was sure that Leo was thinking that he'd changed his mind about spending some more personal time with him, but that was the complete opposite. He did want to see how Day was going to prove himself, but he had to handle his business first… and he really did feel like shit. God blew out another weary breath which turned into a coughing fit. He put his hand on his chest at the tight pain there, and tried to breathe through it slowly. *What the fuck?* God rubbed the back of his neck again and moaned at the tension. *It would've been nice to let Day work these knots out for me.*

God backed out of the driveway, his head pounding like someone was hammering him in the head. He made a beeline for the drug store and picked up a couple bottles of NyQuil and drove twenty miles per hour the rest of the way home.

Where's God?

Day was working on a model kit of a nineteen thirty-four Ford Street Rod, listening to music. He picked up one of the micro-parts with the tweezers, applied an ultra-thin strip of glue, and carefully placed it on the car's frame. He tried not to think about God not calling him. They'd had a date. God had agreed to dinner... then all of sudden, he just changed his mind. Day couldn't pretend it didn't hurt. He was dead set on proving that he wanted God.

How about a little Blind-Eye Willie's saxophone? That was Day's favorite when he was upset. Day cautiously picked up the vinyl album and placed it on the player. He paced back and forth wondering if he should call God. He flopped down on his bed and looked at his alarm clock. *Four in the morning... great. I've got to sleep.*

Day tossed and turned on his bed. He was restless. He couldn't get God's lustful eyes out his mind. Yes, something major had definitely changed between them. Day had always thought God was strikingly gorgeous. In an I'm a-bad boy-and-don't-give-a-fuck kind of way. But seeing God break down in front of him, all needing and wanting, made Day yearn to fulfill those wants and take care of all his needs.

Day dragged his hand down his chest. His legs moved back and forth on the silk sheets as he imagined grabbing God's goatee and pulling his mouth down to meet his. Day wrapped his hand around his hard cock and arched his back off the bed at the first brush of contact. *Cashel.* Day grunted and jerked when another large bead of precome formed on his head. He used it to make his grip slide easier up and down his throbbing shaft.

"Fuck, God. I need you so bad," Day whispered, his orgasm building quickly at the sound of God's name on his lips. He wanted God on top of him. His weight crushing him into the mattress while he pounded his ass.

"Uuugh… fuuuck," Day groaned.

His head was thrown back, his throat pulsing, wishing it was being ravaged by God's mouth as his orgasm barreled through him. His body spasmed and he moaned deep in his throat when he dragged his tight fist up, slowly milking the last of his come out.

Day hadn't come that hard in a long time. He shot so hard that he had come on his neck and some on his pillow. *Fuck. God, you're going to be the death of me.* After Day got cleaned up, he had no problem falling asleep.

Day was fixing his coffee in the precinct's kitchen and of course, his mind kept wandering to God. It was almost ten and he hadn't seen him yet. Usually, God picked him up for work at eight so Day didn't have to ride his bike. God would automatically drive to Starbucks and then they'd talk shit the rest of the way to work.

By eight forty-five God still hadn't showed. After several unanswered calls, Day got on his bike and rode to the station, figuring God was still handling whatever shit he had to do. Day handled their normal morning duties. He knew his partner would be there for the ten-o'clock strategy meeting they had scheduled with several of the department heads, including SWAT, to plan how they were going after the kingpin.

Day looked at his watch and saw that he had five minutes until to the meeting. He finished his cup, fixed another for the meeting, and headed for the door. He stopped, turned back, and picked up a blueberry muffin before heading to the main conference room. *Yeah, I got it bad.*

When Day walked in, several of the officers began clapping and patting him on the back for getting the kingpin's information. He made jokes with a few of the officers and noticed that God was still MIA.

"Day. Where's God?" Vikki asked, looking around.

Day took his seat. "He'll be here," he said in a clipped tone.

She didn't need to worry about where the fuck God was.

"Maybe he got sick of you trying to fuck him." Ronowski shrugged nonchalantly.

Day glared at him and leaned across the table. His teeth were clenched so hard they ached. "You don't know how on edge I am, Ronowski. So if you have even an ounce of self-preservation, you'll shut your fucking mouth and not say another word to me for the rest of the day."

Day saw Vikki whisper something to Ronowski. The man sat back hard in his chair and didn't say anything else. Day wasn't sure, but he thought he saw a flash of sorrow cross Ronowski's handsome face. He quickly thought better of it.

The captain walked in with the SWAT team squad leader and the police commissioner.

Where the fuck are you, God?

The captain began the meeting. After all the introductions were made, and duties were assigned, the captain turned to him.

"Where's Godfrey?" The captain scanned the room again, his sharp eyes falling back on Day.

"He's following up on a tip, sir," Day lied.

"Okay. That must have been a damn important tip if it warranted missing a mandatory strategy meeting."

"It was, sir." Day kept his eyes locked on the captain, shutting out the other forty sets of eyes in the large room. After a couple seconds the captain resumed to talking to the group, and Day let out a breath he hadn't realized he was holding.

"All right people, you have your assignments. We'll meet back here at 0900 next Tuesday for an update and briefing. Dismissed." Day tried to leave before the captain snagged him. No luck.

"What type of tip, Day?" The captain looked at him with a cut the bullshit look.

"I'm going to find out, sir." Day didn't wait for a response. He hightailed it out of there and made his way back to the bullpen. He stopped by his desk to grab his leather coat and helmet, moving fast, trying to avoid any more questions. But there were a lot of officers who needed his and God's input on this case. It was priority one and he and God were the go-tos for information.

Day went out the back door and walked around to the parking lot. He saw Ronowski and Vikki getting into their squad car, choosing to ignore Ronowski flipping him off.

Closeted bastard. I can't wait for the day you beg to suck my cock, and then I'm gonna ram it down your throat.

Day kicked up his stand and raced the engine a couple times before taking off to find his partner.

Falling and Can't Get Up

Day pulled his bike onto the sidewalk leading to God's apartment. He refused to leave his Harley on the street. The complex didn't have front door parking and sometimes you had to walk a good ways from where you parked. Day took one look at the long row of cars that had broken taillights, cracked windows, and flattened tires and knew he wasn't leaving his bike out there. Day checked his holster and released the snaps that secured his weapons.

This was a shitty neighborhood with even shittier residents, but God had an arrangement with the dealers in the area. He didn't bust them and they didn't fuck with him, his apartment, or his truck. Besides, they were all low-level dealer guppies in a big damn pond, and God and Day only went after the big fish. For the life of him, Day couldn't figure out why God lived in this part of town. A detective's pay grade didn't allow them lifestyles of the rich and famous, but they could afford decent housing.

Day dropped his kickstand down, parking his bike right under God's kitchen window. He saw five thug-looking men standing a few feet away next door.

"You guys seen God?" Day asked them.

A man with tattoos completely covering his naked chest spoke up first. "Nah, man, he ain't been out yet. Some little kids knocked on his door about an hour ago wanting to clean his truck, but he didn't answer," he paused looking Day up and down. "You can go on in, it ain't locked."

Day quirked one eyebrow at the man. "And how would you know that?"

The guy blew out a large billow of smoke from the joint he was smoking before answering, "Because it's never locked. Besides, ain't no one going up in there."

Day snorted. "Oh yeah, why not?"

The thug wore a deadly expression and looked Day in his eyes. "Because he's God."

The respect that God demanded and obviously received from these men had Day's cock getting hard. His man was a badass and a force to be reckoned with. God lived in the slums of Atlanta, smack dab in the middle of the urban jungle... and the man didn't even have to lock his front door.

"We know you're his partner. Go on in." The man nodded his head toward the door. "Don't worry about your bike, ain't no one gonna fuck with it."

"Thanks, man." Day nodded once and went inside God's small one-bedroom apartment.

God wasn't a slob; the tiny place was tidy. His kitchen was to his immediate right. Day closed the door and went right to the mini-coffeemaker, and started a fresh pot. There were no dishes in the sink, only a bowl and spoon in the drying rack on the counter. It didn't smell like God had cooked anything this morning either. Everything was neat and in its place.

God's sixty-five-inch television took up over half of his living room. Since he didn't have a table for eating in the small dining area, God had combined the two spaces to allow room for his futon recliner. The small area rug in front of the TV had a moderately sized gaming chair on it, no doubt where God sat when he played PlayStation 3.

Jeez, how can he play those mindless games?

Day listened to see if he could hear God snoring, or any movement, since the bedroom door was closed. *Oh fuck. What if he has a chick in there?*

Day's chest jolted at that thought. "Hell no," he whispered, shaking his head at the ridiculous thought.

Day made his cup of coffee and took it with him as he walked down the short, narrow hallway. Day tapped lightly on God's bedroom door and waited impatiently for him to answer.

"Hey, slacker. You slept through a very important meeting this morning, and I covered for you by the way, since I'm such a good partner. You owe me, buddy." Day waited. He put his ear close to the door, but didn't hear anything. He got ready to turn the knob when he heard a low groan come from behind the closed bathroom door.

Day hurried into the bathroom, not bothering to knock and dropped his coffee mug to the floor at the sight of God's huge body sprawled out on the linoleum floor. His face was half-covered with his hair and what Day could see was so pale, he almost appeared transparent.

"Jesus Christ, Cash, what the hell?" Day stepped over God's long body and brushed the hair back from his face. He yanked his hand back as if he'd been burned... which he had.

"Fuck, Cashel. You're on fire, man."

God had to have a one hundred and five degree fever. He jumped up and pulled a small hand towel from the rack and ran some cold water on it while he pulled his cell from his pocket. He squatted down and began wiping the large beads of sweat from God's forehead with the cool towel.

"Cash, can you hear me? Open your eyes!" Day yelled.

He took God's usually handsome face in his hands and lightly slapped his left cheek.

"Leo," God whispered softly. Day saw him crack his eyes open just slightly. He was barely moving, but his face was scrunched up, and he was obviously in pain.

"Cash, come on, let's get you up." Day tried to hook his arm under God's massive frame, but God wasn't budging. "Help me out, babe."

"Can't." God let loose an agonizing moan and his body began to convulse in a coughing fit. Day pulled back as God's body hacked and dry heaved. It sounded like his body desperately wanted to throw something up, but there was nothing there.

"I'm calling an ambulance. You gotta get to the hospital. You have a really high fever, Cash." Day pulled out his cell and saw that God was shaking his head back and forth.

"What? Are you saying no?" Day squatted back down.

"No, you can't," God groaned. "I don't have insurance. It'll cost me thousands for an emergency visit and I—"

Day's hand stopped wiping his partner's forehead, and his eyes snapped to God's.

"What the fuck do you mean you don't have insurance? You're a goddamn police officer. It's mandatory. You must be mistaken," Day argued.

God coughed and hacked for a while, but when he saw Day pull out his cell phone again, he made a hard effort to try to grab it, but ended up yelling out in pain.

"Day, please don't. I can't afford that. Besides, no ambulance will come out here anyway. You must've forgotten where you're at." God panted shallowly.

"God, you're sick. You need help. Look, we'll get the insurance thing settled or I'll pay the bill my damn self." Day looked into God's watery eyes.

"I said no. Even if you did manage to get—" God's body spasmed and hacked some more, cutting his own words off. His eyes were squeezed shut, and Day didn't know what to do to help. "Even if you get a paramedic out here, I'll refuse to go."

Day knew God was serious, but it was obvious the man was very sick, and not like common cold sick, either. Day ran his hands through his hair in frustration as he watched God's body go very still. His eyes were barely open, staring at him. Day got all the way down on his knees and got very close to God's ear.

"God, you're sick. I can't lift you and your temperature is probably high enough to cause brain damage."

"Just leave me here. I'll be fine as soon as it passes," God moaned.

Day stood back up, wet the towel again, and went back to wiping God's forehead. *Fuck. He's too damn hot. Shit, shit, shit.* Day had to think of something fast. It was probably true. There's no way an ambulance would risk coming in to this neighborhood. He had to at least get God to his bed. From the smell of things, God had probably made it in here to puke but couldn't get out.

"Okay. Come on. You need to at least get in the bed." Day hooked both his arms under Gods armpits and used every bit of his strength to try to lift him, but he was dead weight. Day heard the big man moan and hiss, his body obviously in pain, but he wasn't helping Day out by supporting any of his own weight.

"Fuck!" Day yelled. He eventually stopped straining and slowly lowered God's upper body back to the cold bathroom floor.

Day stood and stepped into the narrow hallway, wincing at the pull in his back. Day watched God's eyes narrow before fully closing. God's chest rose and fell and to Day's relief his partner was breathing evenly.

What the hell am I supposed to do? I can't move him by myself. Day's eyes widened. *Oh. His neighbors. Those were some big motherfuckers.*

Day made determined strides through the hallway but jerked to a stop when he got to the front door. He thought about what the pot-smoking thug had said to him before he came in. *"No one's going to go in there... because he's God."*

"But if God is weak and unable to protect himself they won't be afraid anymore," Day whispered to himself.

Fuck. I can't show those punks how weak God is right now.

Day repeatedly ran his hands through his hair. *What now, what now.* He looked at his cell phone again and was thinking about trying to put some of God's symptoms into the Google search engine to see what it said when he got an even better idea. *Yes, why the hell didn't I think of that before?*

Day punched in the numbers he knew by heart, all while keeping an eye on God.

"Good afternoon, Waldon, Schmidt, and Day, how may I help you?" the bubbly receptionist said in greeting.

"Yes, I need to speak with Dr. Day immediately please, this is a life or death emergency," Day said back to her.

"Sir, you need to hang up and call 911," she said back quickly.

"No I don't. Please go get Dr. Day right now. He'll take the call trust me. Tell him his brother is on the phone."

"Hold one moment."

Day waited impatiently while an annoying woman crooned in his ear about rolling in the deep. After almost an entire damn song, the line was connected.

"Leonidis, what's going on, have you been hurt?" His brother's easy voice soaked into his soul and he felt better already.

"No, Jax, I'm fine... but my partner isn't." Day took a deep breath and told his brother everything that God had told him about the insurance, the lack of a medical response team in this neighborhood, and all of God's outward symptoms.

"It sounds like pneumonia, Leo. Try to keep him cool. If he's as hot as you say, you need to try to get that temperature down. Get some ice trays and dump them into a towel and rub him down with it, mainly his chest and neck. Are you sure you can't get him into the tub, because an ice bath would be more effective."

"Fuck no. He's almost three hundred pounds, man. I'm quick, not strong." Day huffed.

"Okay, okay. I'll be there in a half hour. I'll bring my two assistants, they're pretty big guys. We should be able to move him," Jax assured him and Day finally was able to breathe a sigh of relief.

"Leo. I'm concerned about his temperature. Are you sure you can't get an ambulance out there?" Jax asked again.

"No. I already said that." Day huffed. "Besides, he said he'd refuse it anyway and I told you why, so just make sure you don't mention that. I'll chew his ass out about the insurance when I'm sure he's not fucking dying."

"All right, be there soon, bro."

"Oh, shit. Hold on. Are y'all going to come with doctor's coats and bags of medical supplies?" Day stopped pacing.

"A white coat is not necessary, but I will have to bring supplies, Leo. Why?"

"No, you can't. If these hooligans out here see three doctors coming into God's apartment with medical supplies they'll know he's sick," Day said.

"I can't very well treat him without supplies, Leonidis. You're being unreasonable," his brother said, exasperated. "His neighbors should just mind their own business… or better yet ask how they can help."

Day barked a humorless laugh at his brother's ignorance. "This isn't fuckin' Mayberry, Jax. It's the jungle. Look, just tell your assistant to grab a few suitcases from over at the consignment shop next door to your office and then pack all your supplies in there. I'll take care of the rest." Day hung up.

Day swiped an empty coffee mug out of the kitchen cabinet, and hurried toward the front door. He took a calming breath before opening it. He strolled easily over to his bike and began digging through the side bags. He pulled out a *Guns & Ammo* magazine and stepped back up on God's porch when he heard the lead thug ask, "What's up with God? Playing hooky from the streets today?"

Day turned toward them as if he hadn't a care in the world. But his heart was racing a mile a minute, knowing that God was in there on the floor burning up brain cells, and he should be in there trying to cool him off. Day had to handle this first. He took a fake sip of his nonexistent coffee before answering with a shrug.

"I forgot he had relatives coming to town. He told me, but I don't remember irrelevant shit like that."

"Oh cool," the guy said and took another hit of his joint.

Day turned to go inside before backing up a step. "Yo, man, God told me to ask if y'all can make sure no one fucks with them when they get here. God's on the phone handling business right now."

"Tell God we got him."

"Cool." Day shrugged and strolled back into the apartment. He raced to the small linen closet that was right next to the kitchen and got a clean towel out. In the freezer he only saw two ice trays, but thank goodness they were full. He quickly dumped all the ice in the towel and ran back into the bathroom.

His chest hurt when he saw God panting heavily on the floor. He was drenched with sweat and his body was shaking violently with tremors. His eyes were closed tight as his body tried to fight the sickness coursing through him.

"Oh no." Day dropped to his knees, not caring about the ache in them and made work of lifting God's shirt up so he could get to his chest. "Hang on, babe, help is coming."

He saw God open his eyes slightly, a look of obvious worry on his face. "I didn't call 911, my brother's coming. Try to relax." Day began to rub the ice-filled towel all over God's massive chest. God groaned, shook, heaved, and coughed over and over as Day tried his best to keep working on cooling God down.

Day was beyond frustrated. God's temperature wasn't coming down. He was still hot as an oven set on broil. Day's eyes watered when God grabbed his hand and clenched his teeth when a coughing fit took control of his large body.

"It's gonna be okay. My brother will be here any minute."

God looked into Day's eyes again. Their usual intense green was now red-rimmed and as dull as dying grass. But Day could still communicate with his partner, and he knew what God was thinking.

"I told your neighbors that you had relatives coming and to look out for them. They think you're in here handling business." Day held God's hand tight while wiping at his brow with the cold rag held in the other. Day bent and kissed God's forehead, just like he'd done to him before, letting him know how much he cared for him.

Day heard a light tap at the front door, before it opened and his brother's voice reached his ears.

"So where's the beer and the girls," his brother yelled.

Perfect. The Day men were always quick on their feet, smart as whips. He knew Jax would catch on.

Day got to his feet and ran into the front room. He ran into his big brother's arms. "Thank you for coming so fast. He's back here." Day took the small rolling suitcase from his brother and said a quick hello and thanks to his brother's MAs before showing them back to the small bathroom.

"Damn, he is big," one of the assistants said letting out a short whistle.

"I told you. Come on, fellas. I need to get him into a bed and get the IVs hooked up. I can already tell he's severely dehydrated. So first things first," Jax said to his assistants.

It was ridiculously hard fitting four men into God's tiny bathroom to try to lift him, but somehow they'd done it. God hollered more than once as they gripped and pulled on him however they could to get him into his bedroom without dropping him. By the time they'd gotten him in the king-size bed that took up ninety percent of the space, everyone was breathing hard.

His brother was panting, but he immediately went about opening the luggage and laying out supplies. His assistants made quick work of removing God's sweaty T-shirt and sweatpants.

Day sat on the side of God's bed and rubbed his cheeks and forehead gently with a cool rag.

"I'm right here, baby. You're gonna be all right," Day whispered, and saw his brother's head shoot up at hearing his endearment for his long-time partner, but Day kept his eyes on God's face. He groaned some more and would probably be writhing if he had the energy to move his limbs.

"Cash, can you hear me?" Jax spoke in his stern doctor's voice. "Cashel, I need to know if you are allergic to any medications."

It appeared God tried to answer, but as soon as he opened his mouth he coughed violently and was unable to mumble anything intelligible, slowly shaking his head no.

"That will have to do," Jax said, digging out what he needed.

Day sat quietly, watching his brother and his assistants work quickly and efficiently. God was hooked up to an IV, and several vials of blood were being drawn while Day's brother used his stethoscope to listen to God's lungs.

"Get those to the lab and order the results stat," Jax said to the assistant who looked to be in his mid-thirties. He was average height and build, but he had beautiful blue eyes, and appeared kind.

"I sure will," he said and left the room. Day heard him close the front door behind him.

Day carefully watched God's face. He was calm right now, but his eyes were slightly open and fixed on him. Day gave him a small wink and he swore that a flash of love appeared in God's eyes.

His brother started injecting syringes into God's IV port. Day looked at the multiple medicine vials. "What are all those, Jax?"

Jax picked up each bottle as he named the medications. "This is an antibiotic to fight any infection; this one's intravenous Lidocaine to help suppress the coughing, Phenergan for nausea and vomiting, morphine for pain, and ibuprofen to reduce his fever. Jax injected each syringe, put his stethoscope back on and checked God's chest again.

He pulled back and blew a breath, "It's going to take a while, and I won't know the diagnosis until I get the lab results, but I'm fairly positive he has pneumonia brought on by bronchitis." Jax reached in his bag and readied another IV bag of fluid. "God's obviously had the bronchitis for a while for it to have brought on this nasty case of pneumonia. It's unlikely in this day of modern medicine, but people used to die of pneumonia if left untreated."

"Wouldn't I be sick too, or people in the office?" Day argued.

"Not really. If an adult does start to cough or get a sore throat, they most likely go to their doctor and get medicine or an antibiotic, and the symptoms go away. I will give you a couple of doses of antibiotics just in case, since you two are obviously," his brother paused and looked at him, "close."

"Thanks, Jax," Day said, ignoring his brother's insinuation. "So he's going to be fine?"

"Yes. I'll show you how to push the antibiotic every four hours and to give the nausea and cough suppressants every six. I'm going to give him a stronger dosage and see if it can help him recover faster. I'll be back after my morning rounds to check on him. In the meantime, just watch him for any significant changes and if there are any, call and I'll be right over."

Day came around the large bed and hugged his brother. "Thanks, man. I don't know what I would've done without you… as usual." Day grinned sheepishly.

"You would've figured something out. You always do." Jax patted him once on his shoulder.

Day watched him pull a bag and a long tube from out of the second suitcase, and hand the materials to the other assistant, currently struggling to position God fully on his back.

"What are you going to do now?" Day scrunched his brow at the supplies.

"He's going to insert a catheter. Since God is being pumped full of fluids, he'll have to urinate frequently. He'll be drowsy from the pain meds, and too weak to get up and go to the bathroom. Since you obviously can't carry him, I don't see any other way," Jax told him.

"Aren't those uncomfortable though? I don't want him in any more pain, Jaxson. I can get a pot or something for him to use while he's in bed." Day tried to reason an alternative.

At Day's suggestion, God turned his head toward him and looked into his eyes. The appreciation and care that showed on God's ruggedly handsome face stole Day's breath away.

"He'll be out of it most of the night, Leo. This is best. Joseph is a great nurse; Cashel won't even feel it being inserted. If he's constantly trying to stay awake to hold it in all night, that's more uncomfortable than the catheter." Jax snapped off his rubber gloves and tossed them in the small wastebasket by the bed.

"Don't worry, I won't hurt him. And not trying to brag, but I know my way around a penis." The cute man's feminine lisp told Day that the man was telling the truth.

"Okay," Day said, shocked at finally hearing the young man speak. He watched the nurse slather K-Y Jelly on the long, thin tube and insert it into God's limp penis. Day monitored his actions closely, all while keeping an eye on God's face for the first sign of discomfort.

"All done." The nurse hooked the bag onto the bed frame. "If you'll get me a large bowl, his body wash, and a towel, I'll clean him up real good and get him comfortable."

Day just stared at him with narrow eyes. *Keep fucking dreaming, tall and cute.*

"Day, get the stuff and knock it off. Joseph's here as an employee, and he's one hundred percent professional. Now let him do his job." His brother pushed at his shoulder.

Day gave the nurse the supplies and closed him in the room with his partner, while he walked his brother to the living room and got him a glass of water. Day listened to all his instructions as God's caregiver for the next several days and asked the necessary questions.

"I know it seems like a lot, but you are more than capable and a damn good partner. Oh yeah, didn't God say a while back that he had a mom and a brother that lived in the area? Why don't you give them a call so they can come and help take care of him?" Jax asked him.

"I'd rather do it myself," Day said without hesitation.

Day tried to ignore his brother's questioning glance while he sipped his coffee.

"Are you in love with him, Leonidis?"

"Yes." Again there wasn't a moment's hesitation, and even Day had to admit that he was shocked as shit at the confession.

"You never mentioned that Cash was gay," Jax said.

"I know."

"Leo, what are you doing? Falling for a straight man, and your partner at that?" His brother tried to make eye contact with him.

Day finally looked into his brother's eyes, soft hazel ones that matched his own, and told him. "He loves me back. Straight, gay, bi, goddamn tranny… whatever he is. That man loves me too. He just hasn't said it yet," Day took another sip, "but he will."

Day was relieved his brother let that subject go. He walked him and Joseph to their car, again playing the role for the neighbors, and came back in to take care of his partner… his man.

99

Might-As-Well Get Comfortable

The nurse did a great job with God. He smelled great; his teeth were brushed, hair combed, and even his sheets were changed. *Wow.* Day stared at a peacefully sleeping God. Jax said the pain medicine, along with the nausea medicine, would keep him mostly asleep for the rest of the afternoon and night. He still had sweat beads on his brow, but he didn't look to be in pain, and Day was grateful.

Since it was almost four in the afternoon, Day sat on God's small black and white futon in his living room and took out his cell to call his captain. After Day lied, saying that God had pneumonia and was in the ER all morning, he told him God could only be released if someone was going to be with him. He knew his captain wouldn't require any documentation, but Day knew his brother could whip something up if he needed him to.

"Yes, sir. I'm going to be available on my cell phone for any questions." Day paused and listened. "I would say a few days tops, sir." He promised to check in several times a day and hung up.

Day sat on the couch for a few more minutes, his leg shaking nervously. *I just admitted that I love God. What was I thinking? What if he doesn't love me back... or can't? Fuck. That would be the end of our partnership.*

Day went into the kitchen and looked in the refrigerator. There wasn't much to choose from and he settled on a turkey sandwich and a couple of apples.

Day finished his lunch and went back into the bedroom to watch God sleep. Every now and then he'd pick up the cool rag and dab his clammy skin. He was still hot, but not alarmingly so.

After a couple hours Day began taking his holster off, but paused mid action. *God's guns.* God kept two of his guns in his truck at all times. Day figured if God was going to be in the bed for several days, he'd better bring his weapons in.

He opened the front door and saw the same guys sitting on the porch next door. *Damn... nothing better to do. Must be nice to sit on your ass and smoke pot all day.* Day didn't want to have a conversation, so he jogged over to God's truck and used the key fob to deactivate the alarm. He reached in the glove box and removed a 9mm, then went around to the driver's side and felt under the seat. He pulled out a .22 caliber handgun and a cheap cell phone. He tucked the guns in his waistband and put the phone in his pocket.

Day gave a slight nod to the neighbors and headed back inside. After putting the guns in the closet, Day put the cell phone on the kitchen counter and stared at it for several minutes. It wasn't God's main phone, it was a throwaway. Day was a naturally inquisitive man, and every instinct he had told him that God didn't want him to know about this phone... which made it hard to resist... so he didn't. Day would rather know now than later if his anticipated lover was doing something that could hurt him. He pushed the small power button and went directly to the contacts. There was only one. *"Mom, Gen."*

It was God's mom and his brother. *Oh, okay.* Day didn't know why but he thought he'd find a bunch of tramps' phone numbers listed there. Day kind of laughed to himself and tossed the phone in one of the kitchen drawers. He turned off the lights and went into the bedroom to take care of the man he loved.

Playing Doctor

Day had showered and put on a pair of God's huge sweatpants that he'd had to tie as tight as he could so they'd stay up, and a black tank top he found in the dresser in the corner. There was a small television on top of it and Day turned it on to the food station, setting the volume just high enough so he could hear it and not disturb God.

Day quietly did his evening duties for his patient. He changed the IVs, emptied the catheter bag, inserted the pre-filled syringes of antibiotic and pain medicines into the port, and put some cool water and clean rags by the bed. Day climbed onto the other side, careful not to jostle God and propped some pillows behind him. He took a small sip of the coffee he'd sat on the tiny end table before turning on the bedside lamp.

Day flipped through his magazine until he found the article on the modern submachine handgun. He was engrossed in the article when he felt God shifting on the bed, perhaps trying to get more comfortable. Day absently rubbed God's shoulder while he groaned and rocked back and forth. He put his mouth close to the side of his face.

"Sshh, it's okay, Cash," Day whispered quietly.

That seemed to settle his partner, but a few seconds later God's large thigh shot out to the side, darn near knocking Day off the bed, and released a loud cry.

"Cash, calm down."

God cried out again. Obviously he was dreaming. *Fuck, another nightmare.* When he started thrashing more wildly, Day had to jump out of the bed. He ran around to the other side and quickly moved the IV tower out of reach so God didn't knock it over.

"No, Dad, stop!" God yelled, his eye squeezed shut, and sweat pouring down his face.

"Cash, wake up!" Day yelled. His heart was beating wildly and his hands shook as he got a firm hold on God's wide shoulders.

Day shook him more forcefully but that only seemed to make it worse. He climbed on top of his partner and tried to press his full weight on him. If God ripped the IV or catheter out, Day wouldn't know what to do. He held God's arms down to his side and yelled again. "Cashel, Cash, stop it!"

God's eyes opened but Day knew he wasn't awake yet. Day rose up and straddled his stomach, still pinning his arms to his sides. He leaned over and dipped the cool rag in the water and leaned back in to wipe God's wet face. "It's all right. It's just a dream, Cash, wake up." Day watched God's eyes come back into focus. Day began to lift up some, so his full weight wasn't pressing on him anymore, when he felt one of God's arms come around his back, preventing him from moving.

"Stay," God moaned.

"I'm too heavy. I'm just gonna slide over." Day eased off and settled in close to his side. God took in a shaky breath and coughed hard for several seconds. Day wiped his damp brow some more, his cheeks, his neck, and then his lips all with light tender strokes.

"It's okay. I'm not going anywhere." Day placed a soft kiss to God's temple and saw his partner's muscled chest fall with his exhale.

God turned his head to stare into Day's eyes. He could see the gratitude emanating from those beautiful green irises.

"Leo," God said in a half-breath, half-wheeze.

"Try not to talk. My brother said he'd be back in the morning, he said it won't take long for the worst of the symptoms to go away. You'll be weak for a while, but I'll be right here to help you. I'm going to get up now so I can give you some more cough and pain medicine. Jax said I could give them as needed."

Day watched how God stared at him wide-eyed. Day stared back. "I know. You're welcome." Day softly wiped the cool rag across God's forehead one more time before kissing him there too.

He moved to the other side of the bed and got out, moving around to God's side so he could inject the medicine. He pushed in the two syringes and realized that he only had two more for pain. *Shit. I hope he doesn't need more before Jax comes back.* God stayed with his back to him, and Day took the opportunity to raise God's shirt and wipe the cool rag over his back. Day couldn't help his body's reaction to the strong, muscular back. Day gasped at the huge lion tattooed across the upper left side of his back. The mouth was open wide in mid-roar; the full, bushy mane was so detailed, it looked like it swayed when the muscles moved. The paws were big and the claws were extended as if the beautiful beast was prepared to attack. A lion described his partner perfectly—fierce, protective, a king. Day had only caught glimpses of the exquisite work before because God didn't undress in front of him or anyone often, probably not wanting too many people to see the scars that accompanied the art on his body.

Day oh so gently traced his fingers around the lion's mouth and shivered when a slight moan came from God's lips.

"So beautiful," Day whispered.

He finished wiping God's back and was climbing back in bed when he heard the light snores. Sure that the medicine had pulled him back into a hopefully peaceful slumber, Day watched him sleep for most of the night, only stirring slightly when he tried to get more comfortable. Day had finally dozed of himself about three in the morning.

He was startled awake at seven by his phone ringing on the nightstand. He hurried to pick it up before it woke his still snoring partner. Day saw it was work, pressed the accept button and put the phone to his chest as hurried out of the bedroom, closing the door behind him.

"Yeah, this is Day," he said still sounding groggy with sleep.

He listened to Vikki tell him why she was calling. He gave her the location of the files regarding their kingpin case. "They're in my desk, the bottom locked drawer and the key is taped underneath my keyboard."

He was about to hang up when she asked how God was doing.

"He's fine," he replied shortly. When Vikki asked to come over and relieve him, he almost told her to fuck off. However, since that would be mean he simply said, "I got it, he'll be up and at 'em by tomorrow," and disconnected the line.

You won't get your claws in him Vixen Vikki.

Day made a pot of coffee and drank it black to try to wake himself up. After one full cup he poured himself another and began looking through God's cabinets, knowing that his patient would eventually require food. After a quick inventory, Day realized a trip to the grocery store was in order, and laundry would need to be done too. *Who's gonna stay here? Oh, of course.* Day dug in the drawer for the mobile phone he'd found in God's truck and typed a message to Gem, adding the address just in case. *I'm sure he won't mind sitting here a few minutes while I run some errands.*

Day took the one can of soup God had in the cabinet, poured it into a bowl, and popped it in the microwave. He fixed a small mug of hot tea. *I got to remember to get some lemon and honey from the store.* He opened a bottle of water and poured it into a clean glass.

Making his way back to the bedroom, he saw that God's eyes were slightly open. His forehead had tiny beads of sweat and the collar of his pajama shirt was wet from perspiration. "Hey you," Day spoke quietly.

"Hey," God croaked, his voice sounded like he'd smoked for fifty years.

Day set the bowl and drinks down so he could wipe the sweat from God's face and neck. "You're not as pale as yesterday," Day said while tenderly wiping his forehead. God turned his head toward him and sighed. If Day had to interpret it, it'd probably be an I'm-tired-of-feeling-like–shit-and-being-taken-care-of sigh.

"Won't be much longer, babe. Jax said you'll start to regain your strength in only a couple days. I brought you some soup. Do you want to try to eat it… or just the broth? I know you're starving by now."

"I'm not hungry," God said around a hard cough.

"Just try to eat a little for me, okay."

Day watched God twist in the bed to face him. He groaned and cursed, obviously not accustomed to being watched over or forced to eat.

"Okay," he finally conceded.

Day set the bowl on the bed beside God and watched him struggle to sit up so he could get the spoon to his mouth without spilling. Turned out he failed miserably. As soon as he brought the spoon mid-way to his mouth, he began to cough and spilled the few noodles and broth on his chest.

"Uhh, dammit," he muttered.

Day reached for the spoon, but God yanked his hand away from Day's touch.

"Cashel, come on, don't be like that. I'm here to help you. You're not the only man to ever get sick and need someone. Let me be that someone," Day spoke quietly.

Sad green eyes stared back at him for a couple seconds. He could've sworn that he was apologizing to him, and Day didn't need him to say it out loud. God handed him the spoon. Day took the washrag and was wiping the soup from God's chest when God put his hand over his. Day looked into those gorgeous eyes and felt

107

something click between them. Had he proven himself to God? Did he realize that Day didn't just want him for a fuck? He hoped so, because he realized that his partner was also his best friend, and the only man that he'd really cared about or loved since his college sweetheart.

Day leaned in and put his lips to God's ear. "When you get better, I'm going to show you just how much you mean to me." Day heard God moan sensually. He smiled against the side of his face and laid a delicate, chaste kiss on the corner of his mouth. "Now I want you to eat."

Day propped a couple pillows behind God and fed him almost half the bowl. By the time he finished helping him drink the lukewarm tea; he heard a knock at the door. He kissed God on his forehead before getting up to answer the door.

"Hey, baby brother, how's the patient?" Jax said coming in through the door with a book bag hung on one shoulder trailed by the same nurse who had cleaned God up the day before.

"Okay. He's still weak, though. He woke three times through the night. The coughing is not as hard and is less frequent. He ate half a bowl of soup and some tea this morning," Day said, making his way down the narrow hallway and into God's bedroom.

"That's good. I'll probably stop the fluids since he's drinking water now. I got the test back and it was bronchitis, which can cause flu or pneumonia-like symptoms if left untreated. It really is a good thing you got to him when you did. I brought some more antibiotics, anti-nausea stuff, and stronger cough medicine. You only need to give the pain medicine if he asks for it," his brother said to him since God had fallen back asleep.

He had on his stethoscope listening to God's chest. "Sounds a little clearer. By tomorrow morning I'll be able to take out the catheter and the IV, he can take pills after that."

"Great, thanks, Jax. When do you think he can go back to work? I'm sure he's going to ask that," Day said.

108

"Well he's not contagious anymore after twenty-four hours of antibiotics. By the way, did you take yours?"

Day huffed. "Yes. I took it last night and this morning."

"You probably took it with coffee." Jax laughed.

"That's irrelevant, as long as I took them. Now back to my question. When can he go to work?"

Jax raised God's eyelids and shinned a mini flashlight in them before answering. "You just play it by ear. If he feels well enough to go, he can go. It's Wednesday. I'd say let him rest for the rest of the week and then Monday he can go back in."

"Cool. I already called his brother… well actually sent a text because he's probably in school, and asked him to come keep an eye on him for me tomorrow while I go to the store and check on my house." Day sat on the side of bed, watching God sleep.

The nurse began gathering his stuff to clean God up again, so he and Jax went into the living room.

"It's good you called his brother so you can get a break, Leo." Jax sipped the bottle of water he'd given him.

"I don't need a break, but I do need to get some food in here and get the sheets washed since your nurse is putting the last clean set on now. I haven't met his mom or brother yet, because God said that they have kind of a strained relationship. He never went into specifics and I didn't press the issue. But I'm sure it's not that strained that his brother wouldn't help him if he's really sick. This will be a good way for his brother to show him that he loves him," Day said while flipping channels on God's massive television.

"Well hopefully you didn't do anything that God wouldn't want you to do," Jax said, always the voice of reason.

"Nah. Cash is always doing things for them. The relationship probably isn't as bad as he thinks. Sometimes it takes something like this to mend an argument."

"And you have no clue why their relationship is strained?"

"No, Jax. Like I said, God didn't really give any details."

"Okay, don't get antsy. I just want you to be careful." Day let his brother drape his thin arm over his shoulder and pull him into a hug.

Day wiggled out of the hold. "I'm good, bro. Thanks for doing this, and believe me; I'm going to kick his ass about not having insurance. This really makes no sense. He lives like a peasant and never spends any money. All he has is his truck, which is financed. Unless he's saving to buy a yacht or his own small island, I can't fathom why he'd cut off his insurance or how the hell the department would allow it." Day thought for a second. "Unless he told them he had private insurance."

Day finished talking just as the nurse came out.

"He's all clean. He wasn't as nice today as he was yesterday," the nurse grumbled.

Day smiled wide. "Was he all growly and snarling?"

"Yes." The nursed sucked his teeth and rolled his eyes.

"Yes! That means he's getting better already." Day pumped his fist in the air.

"You guys have issues." Jax shook his head. "Okay, you know the drill. Call me if you need me. He's on a bland diet right now until the nausea is completely gone. Give him the meds on time and let him get as much rest as he can."

"Got it." Day walked his brother to the door.

He went into the kitchen for another cup of coffee. After scanning God's freezer, he took out some chicken and a few cans of vegetables to make homemade soup until he could get to the store.

Hate This Helpless Shit

God was staring at the television but not really watching it. He was in complete agony. Not because he was sick, but because he was so weak he couldn't even get up to piss or feed himself. He had a tube stuck in his cock, which was extremely uncomfortable, especially after Day had given him a semi with the promise he'd made. God tried not to think about Day's lips caressing the side of his face or the way he smelled.

Day had come for him. He'd only missed one meeting at work and his partner… his friend, had come for him. God had barely made it to the bathroom to puke after he lay in bed for hours trying to muster the strength to get up. When he fell to the floor after retching everything out of his stomach, including what felt like the lining, he couldn't get off the floor. He'd never been so happy and so mortified at the same time to see Leonidis Day.

He was now lying there in bed feeling slightly better and slowly regaining his strength. He could hear Day in his kitchen and could smell something absolutely wonderful permeating the air. He tried to call out for Day but ended up coughing instead. "Fuck," he groaned.

Day came barreling around the corner. "Cash, are you all right?"

The bed dipped and God looked over at his partner. Day was in one of his APD T-shirts and a pair of his sweats—they were four sizes too big—but he looked damn delicious in them. Day began wiping his face with a cool rag, and it felt wonderful. His touch was tender and caring. Day winked at him and God had to take a deep breath to try to hold down his impending hard-on.

"Were you trying to call me, babe?"

God brought his hand up to rest on Day's solid thigh. Day picked his hand up and lightly kissed each knuckle. "Do you want another glass of tea?"

God shook his head back and forth. Damn he hated his partner having to take care of him hand and foot.

"Stop it. If it was me, you'd be doing the same thing," Day told him sternly.

God sometimes forgot that they could almost read each other's thoughts. He wasn't surprised Day could see in his face that he didn't like appearing weak in front of him.

Day moved the cool cloth down lower to wipe his neck off. "I'm fixing you some soup, and I don't want any problems about eating it either." Day leaned in and put his forehead to his. "I know what you're thinking, but: *You. Are. Mine.* I will take care of you until you are one hundred percent better."

God felt the pad of Day's thumb brush over his lips and he vaguely realized that he was holding his breath.

"Leo," God whispered.

"Shh. Don't talk, you need to rest. I'm going to give you some more medicine and when you wake up, I'm going to feed you again. If you snarl at me even once, I'm going to molest you while you sleep."

God quirked his lip up. It'd been so long since someone had cared for him like this. Day had his back on the streets; he never doubted that. But this was a different kind of care. This was the kind of care that led to relationships and eventually love.

God tried to get comfortable. He watched Day push two syringes into his IV port as if he had a medical degree. His heart almost exploded when Day bent down and kissed his forehead while tucking the covers under his chin. True to form, before Day walked out the door he threw God a sexy kiss over his shoulder.

Sexy bastard. You're mine too.

A.E. VIA

The Feud

Day was letting his soup simmer while God continued to nap. It was almost four and Day had to admit that he was getting a little stir-crazy or cabin fever, whatever the hell it was called. After leaving the station at the end of a day he'd either go home and work in his yard, build model cars, cook, always something. Day didn't like to just sit around and do nothing. After exercising, he'd showered and put on some more of God's clothes. He peeked in the bedroom and saw that God had shifted to his side, but still slept soundly.

He fixed another pot of coffee and went into the living room. After checking in at work he decided to see what was so special about the video games that God loved so much.

Hmm. Grand Theft Auto, *that sounds interesting.*

Day had been playing for over an hour when he heard God begin to cough.

"Hey, sleeping beauty." He sat on the side of the bed. He used the back of his hand to feel God's forehead. No fever at all and hardly any sweat. *Very good.*

"You've been asleep for almost five hours. I'm sure you're hungry by now. I kept the soup warm. Sit tight while I fix you some." Day waited for God to nod his head before getting up.

Day got God's food and some more warm tea. He was just getting ready to take the food back to the room when he heard the little boost phone buzz with an incoming message. He put the bowl down and pulled up the message. The text was simple.

I'll be there tomorrow at three.

Day smiled. He was finally going to meet some of God's family. He already began making a mental list of what he was going to ask the little brother.

He wanted to know if his partner was a brat growing up, did he have pimples, did he ever get caught sneaking out of the house, was he grounded a lot.

I want to know it all. Day took God his dinner.

God had slept a lot better last night. Now he was propped up against the headboard waiting on Jax to come take out the IV and catheter.

"You look a lot better, babe. How are you feeling?" Day asked, his body stretched across the foot of the bed. He had his head resting in his palm on his bent elbow. He watched God bring both hands up and wipe his face.

"I'm better. I want out of this bed, Leo," God huffed.

"Uh. Nope. As soon as my brother gets here we'll see," Day said, trying hard to stifle a laugh at God's irritation.

"I'm going to hurt you bad Leo, if you don't let me out of this—" God couldn't finish because his bitching caused a coughing fit.

Day jumped up and grabbed the washcloth. He rubbed God's chest in soft circles as the coughing slowly subsided.

"Fuck." God coughed. "Okay, maybe I'm not ready."

Day looked at his man and shook his head. "Lie down and get some rest before Jax gets here."

After Jax's exam, he regretfully informed God that he was not cleared to go back to work. While he may not be contagious anymore, he would still be impaired as long as he was on the pain medication. Jax only stayed about twenty minutes. He gave God a couple prescription bottles of medicine and told him to call if he was needed.

Day walked his brother to the front door and told him he owed him tickets to the next Braves game. After Day fixed another cup of coffee for himself, he prepared a large bowl of homemade soup for God and went back to the bedroom. God was sleeping so peacefully that Day hated to wake him. He set the bowl on the nightstand and sat gently beside his partner. The nurse had cleaned him up again and he looked more like God. His skin was back to its normal color. His facial hair had grown out some, but it looked sexy. He stroked the side of God's cheek with the back of his hand.

"Babe, wake up. I got your breakfast," he said softly.

God slowly opened his eyes. "I'm tired, Leo."

"I know. But eat just a little for me, okay. Then you can go back to sleep." Day was already propping him up on the pillows so he could eat.

"What's going on with the case?" God asked around a mouthful of noodles.

"Still doing surveillance on the locations, nothing major. Don't worry; there'll be plenty of asses to kick when you get back." Day smirked. His smile quickly faded when God grabbed his chest during a hard cough. "Here, drink some tea."

Day helped his friend sip the warm liquid.

"I think I can hold my own cup and spoon now, Leo," God said with a slight smile.

Day blushed and handed over the cup. He watched him take a few careful sips.

"I need to get up and walk around."

Day was already shaking his head no, but God ignored him and slowly began to swing his legs around to the side of the bed.

Stubborn man.

Day helped God sit up on the edge of the bed. God swayed a little in his arms. "Cash, is this really necessary? You just took some medicine. What if you fall?"

"Then catch me." God winked.

"That's not funny," Day chided.

"Not trying to be. But I need to build up my strength and I have to pee."

"Oh, okay. You should've just said that. You made it sound like you wanted to go on a field trip or something." Day let God drape his large arm around his neck. While he was still very heavy, God was supporting a lot of his own weight.

"My head feels like it's going to explode," God groaned.

"You can take a pain pill after you use the bathroom," Day said. He helped him into the small bathroom and moved to untie God's pajama pants until he stopped him.

"I can manage from here." God looked more amused than anything.

"Oh. Well I can hold it for you if you want." Day inched closer to God and gazed up at him with his sexiest leer.

"Get out, you nympho." God braced one hand on the sink while using the other to nudge Day out the door.

Day laughed and stood guard outside the door just in case he heard a thud. After several minutes he asked while trying not to laugh, "You need something to read?"

"Shut up, Leo," God huffed.

After several more minutes Day heard the toilet flush and the sink running. When God opened the bathroom door he looked exhausted. Day didn't joke anymore. He simply slid his arm around his friend's waist and helped him back to bed. It took several minutes but God was finally lying comfortably. He turned off the television and hit the lights on his way out.

After playing some more *Grand Theft Auto*, Day heard a hard knock at the door.

What the fuck?

Day pulled his 9mm from under the futon cushion he was sitting on and moved quickly to look out the peephole. Intense green eyes were focused on the door. Day was able to see the person's entire face and realized he was looking at a younger version of his partner. Day tucked the gun in his waistband and pulled his T-shirt over it.

He opened the door and smiled wide at his partner's baby brother.

"Hey, man. You must be Genesis. Come on in." Day stepped to the side, and waited for Genesis to enter.

His wide shoulders were set and tense. Day didn't know if the big kid was nervous or what.

"I wish I could say that Cash has told me a lot about you but he hasn't. I'm Leo, Cash's partner." Day held his hand out for the young man to shake. Day watched, as Genesis looked him up and down with a hard scowl while completely ignoring his outstretched hand. Day slowly pulled his hand back. "I can see the family resemblance," he said dryly.

"Who are you?" the kid asked again. He even sounded like God. That slow country drawl encased in a deep baritone voice.

"I'm Leonidis Day. Everyone calls me Leo. Has God really never mentioned me." Day said as a statement rather than a question. He couldn't believe that God never told his family about him. Day's whole family knew who his partner was, who he trusted with his life while out on the streets. God had been to so many of his family's barbeques, birthday parties, and even weddings. Hell, God was a pallbearer with Day at his father's funeral for Pete's sake.

Genesis was still standing there with a dumbfounded look, and Day began to wonder if the boy was slow.

"I work with your big brother. I'm a detective too." Day pointed his finger at his chest.

Day jerked his head back when he saw Genesis grinding his teeth together.

"Hey, look, dude, I know you and your brother have had your differences, I mean what brothers haven't. My big brother still rides my ass and I'm over thirty years old. Sometimes I have to tell my brother, 'Look, I'm a man now. I got hair on my chest and my balls. So stop treating me like the snot-nosed kid that used to follow you around.'" Day laughed and slapped Genesis on his back trying desperately to lighten the mood.

"Leo. That's your name?"

Day nodded, his brow furrowed with confusion.

"I don't know what Cashel told you, but he's no goddamn brother of mine." Genesis fumed. "Does he live here? Your text said he was sick. Is he dying? Because if he's not, I'm going to fucking kill him. He said he didn't live here in Atlanta. Is he stalking my mother?"

Day stood there with his mouth hanging open. This kid was outraged, and Day just realized that his feud with God's went way beyond the normal brotherly squabbles.

"Genesis, please lower your voice. Cash is sleeping and he's still very sick. Look, I called you because I needed to run some errands and I thought you could come over and keep an eye on him, but obviously that was not a good idea, so you can leave and—"

"Oh, hell no. I'm not going any damn where." Genesis glared at him.

Day's hackles rose and he was afraid he was going to have to remove Genesis by force. Before Day could react, Genesis ran past him down the narrow hallway. He burst into the bedroom and stopped short. Day stood in the doorway watching Genesis as he watched God.

"Please don't bother him," Day said in a stern whisper. "Whatever is going on between you two can continue after he's better."

"Fuck that," Genesis barked. "You asshole! You said you didn't live in Atlanta!"

Day grabbed Genesis by the arm but he forcefully yanked it from Day's grip. After Genesis's loud rant, Day saw that God was now fully awake and glaring at his brother. Or was it aimed at Day?

"Gen, what are you doing here?" God croaked. He tried to sit up but ended up coughing.

"What am I doing here? Really? What the hell are you doing here? You said you didn't live here. Are you stalking my mother?" Genesis yelled loud enough for the whole neighborhood to hear.

God continued to try to rise; he slowly swung his legs over the side.

"Cash, stay in bed," Day yelled over Genesis. "You." He pointed at God's brother. "Get out."

"You called me, asshole," Genesis yelled back at Day. "I thought you were Mr. Eudall, but you said your name was Day. So I want to know why you are helping this murderer."

Day saw God's eyes snap up to him. The look he saw in God's eyes was pure anger and Day couldn't stop the chill that flowed over him.

"You called him," God growled. He slowly stood to his feet. "Did you snoop around in my truck and get that phone and call my family... my mother? You had no fucking right, Leonidis."

Day didn't have time to respond before Genesis yelled.

"We are not your family!" Genesis charged forward, head first, as if he was a defensive lineman aiming for the other team's star quarterback. Day yelled out right before all of Genesis's two-hundred-plus pounds barreled into God's midsection, hurling them both over the bed and off the other side onto the hard floor.

God ended up on the bottom. Day leapt over the bed and grabbed at Genesis, but not before the bastard landed a hard left jab to God's midsection. The wail that escaped God's mouth was heart wrenching. It had to have hurt like hell.

Day was having the hardest time pulling Gen off his friend. The bastard was solid muscle just like his big brother. His entire weight was pinning God and God didn't have the strength to push him off. God yelled out again when Genesis elbowed him in the ribs. Day actually thought of pulling his weapon, but quickly dismissed that thought. He put Genesis in a chokehold that had him gagging and gasping for air.

"Let him go, Leo!" God yelled from the bottom.

Day couldn't believe God was yelling at him. This kid was trying to kill him, so why was he being told to let go? Genesis threw an elbow back and Leo just barely dodged the sharp bone hitting him in his cheek.

"Get off him!" Leo yelled.

But Genesis was a raging bull and he wasn't budging. Day could see God's face, not only was he in agonizing pain, but he was hurting emotionally. Day could see now that God wasn't even trying to fight back. In the midst of all of their yelling and fighting, Day heard the front door to God's apartment burst open and loud steps making their way to the bedroom.

Day quickly moved off Genesis's back and pulled his weapon from his waistband, thinking maybe Genesis came with backup. Seconds later God's thug neighbors appeared in the door to the bedroom. Day lowered his gun and let the big guys pull Genesis off God. While being dragged off, Genesis's large boot caught God in his thigh right next to his groin, the strike bringing tears to God's eyes.

The thugs pushed Genesis up against the wall. Two men had his arms while the other held him from behind with a meaty forearm around his throat. Everyone was so busy snarling and cursing at Genesis that no one saw God work his way to his feet until the room echoed with the sound of God's Desert Eagle chambering the first bullet. The loud click made everyone pause and shut the hell up.

"Release him and get the hell out!" God had the gun aimed steady but he wavered slightly on his feet.

Everyone was so shocked at the feral look in God's eyes that no one budged.

"I said get your goddamn hands off my brother, now!" God's deep voice was like thunder, his glare hard like steel.

The thugs released Genesis.

"Now get the fuck out." God spat the words out like venom. His neighbors didn't question what was happening. However, the look they gave God said, "all bets are off," and Day knew God had picked up on it.

Day heard the front door slam shut hard enough to rattle the thin windows. Day was breathing so hard that he had to flop down on the bed.

Day saw Genesis inch toward God again.

"Don't you even fucking think about it," Day snapped.

"You're not worth the fight, murderer. You get the fuck out of Atlanta and I mean it. We don't want you anywhere near us, and my mother doesn't want to see you." Genesis's face was hard and angry. His words were striking harder blows than his fist ever could. Day could see it in God's face, he could read the hurt in those beautiful green eyes, and it was breaking Day's heart.

"If you come near my mother"—Gen stepped even closer until he was right in God's face, looking him in his eyes—"*my mother*, not yours, murderer. If you come near me or her, I'll get a restraining order against you." Genesis turned to walk out the door. He paused at the doorframe and turned back to look at God. "You're dead to us, just stay away. We don't want to ever see you again. We'll never forgive you, so stop trying." On that note, he turned and left the apartment.

Day had fucked up big time. This was his fault, all because he couldn't keep his nosy ass out of other peoples private business. Day rushed to God's side.

"I'll help you ba—" Day didn't know how, but God had found enough strength after that beating to push him so hard that he flew into the dresser, knocking it and all the items on top of it to the floor, including the television. Day rolled a few feet, the dresser just missing falling on top of him.

"Cash, what the fuck!" Day cursed.

He rolled to his side and winced at the sharp pain in his ribs from coming into contact with the dresser.

"I was trying to help you get into bed."

"Get the fuck out, Leo." God's face was an unyielding mask. For the first time in their four years together, Day couldn't read what the hell was going through God's mind.

Day stood slowly. "God, I only called him because I needed to go—"

"It doesn't matter why you did it! You had no right! You have no clue what you just did!" God yelled. "Now get out!"

"Cashel, please. Just hear me out," Day pleaded. His eyes begged God to see the sincerity in them. He really didn't mean for any of this to happen. "Cashel, I swear. I didn't know any of this was happening between you and your family. You should've told me. Why was he calling you a murderer?"

No matter what, Day couldn't turn off his detective side.

Day watched God squeeze his eyes shut. He went down on one knee and clutched his chest when the hard coughing started again. God's eyes were full of water and pain. Day timidly eased over to God's side but God cut his eyes at him, daring him to come any closer.

Day had to fight the moisture in his own eyes. "I just want to help you into bed."

"Day, if you don't get the fuck out of my house, I'm going to show you why he called me a murderer," God said through clenched teeth.

Day couldn't stop the gasp that escaped his lips, or the pain that radiated through his chest, as if his rib cage had been torn open and his heart ripped out. Day kept his eyes on God as he knelt to pick up the dresser, then the television. God watched him as well. Day didn't say anything as the rogue tear fell down his face without his permission. Day went around to the opposite side of the bed and pulled a pen and piece of scrap paper from the drawer, still watching God carefully. He really didn't like the look on his best friend's face. He'd seen the look before, but he'd never had it leveled at him. Day scribbled a couple of phone numbers on the paper.

"This is Jax's office and cell number. Please call him if you're hurt." Day turned and walked out the door.

A.E. VIA

Chapter SEVENTEEN

I Want Him Back

Oh no. What have I done? God thought as he sat on the end of his bed. He'd fought his brother, challenged his neighbors, and thrown his best friend out of his place, all in a matter of minutes.

God felt Day had no right to go through his things, especially his cell phone, which was buried underneath his seat. He'd clearly been snooping around. God couldn't be with someone that didn't trust him. Now he had to clear out of there… immediately.

God slowly made his way to the front of his apartment. He peeked out the blinds in his mini-kitchen and saw that not only were his neighbors outside, but also about ten more guys. *Fuck.* He knew he'd ticked his neighbors off and they were no longer BFFs. God had to get his shit and get the hell out of there, before the shit hit the fan.

He went to his bedroom and called in a couple favors, then made fast work of putting on some jeans and a T-shirt. After dressing he loaded his gun holster, making sure the safeties were off before he went about packing up his stuff.

God had all his important belongings packed in forty minutes. He turned off all the lights and pulled his belongings to the door. While God waited for his backup, he popped a couple of the pain pills that Jax had left for him. He had to admit to himself that he was in excruciating pain from his brother's hits, but he'd be damned if he showed it. After the pain eased to a dull throb, God disconnected all his electronics.

127

He was discreetly looking out the blinds again when he saw the dark neighborhood was now lit up with red and blue swirling lights. He'd told his buddies to really put on a show and they most definitely were. Four police cruisers and a SWAT van came barreling across the field, stopping with a screeching halt right in front of God's door. His neighbors looked around at the police jumping out of the squad cars as if about to do a drug raid, and all the wannabe thugs began to scatter like cockroaches, not sure what the fuck was happening. God couldn't help but chuckle despite his aching heart. Because ordinarily Day would be included in this emergency evacuation plan.

God opened the door and stuck his hand out at the crazy SWAT leader.

"Someone call for backup?" the short man said with his mouth set in a wide grin.

"Good to see you, Joker. Thanks for coming, man." God stepped to the side while Grey's rookies hustled inside to get God's stuff in the SWAT van.

"Hey, we weren't doing shit anyway. Besides, that was fun." Grey laughed while shaking God's hand. "I told you I owed you one. You saved my ass in that bust over in Doverton Hills. If it weren't for you, G, I wouldn't be here."

"It's all good," God replied with a shrug. He was glad that Officer Grey—who everyone called Joker because the man loved to play practical jokes—didn't press the issue of why God needed to be moved right away.

"Move it ya pansies. If you break anything, it's coming out of your already little-ass paychecks!" He laughed loud enough to make God cringe.

"Those your rookies this year?" God asked but already knew the answer.

"Yep. Fresh out of boot camp last week."

God looked at the tender faces on bodies that were so heavily muscled they looked artificial. He shook his head.

128

"Is it me, or are these guys getting younger and younger. Some of these guys don't even look twenty-one."

Grey stood with his feet shoulder width apart and arms crossed over his chest. He had on a dark blue Atlanta PD SWAT Team T-shirt that hugged his firm pecs, and brown cargo pants. His boots looked military-style, the way he had them laced up over his pants.

"I know, dude. Guys are signing up right out of high school now. That's why it takes a little extra to whip these guys into good soldiers. Today I had them running laps for three hours before the sun came up." Grey grinned slyly.

God shook his head. "You do realize this is the police department, not the Marines."

"These rookies will learn the meaning of hard work and perseverance if it kills me, God." The man looked at the men struggling to haul God's big screen television. "If there's even a scratch on that TV, I'm taking it out of your ass first and then your paycheck!" he bellowed.

One of the men approached them, and he looked like he could've spit nails at God before he turned dark eyes on his SWAT leader. No doubt he was pissed for having to do a job that didn't have a damn thing to do with being on SWAT.

"Sir, with all due respect, what does moving your buddy have to do with training? We are all pretty tired from today's workout, sir."

God noticed some of the other men pause to see what their fierce leader was going to say. Grey stepped up until he was nose to nose with the man before he barked in his face.

"You should be happy to assist this man in any way you can! This man saved my life, so he's not my goddamn buddy; he's my friend and comrade! So you show some fucking respect, fish, because you may need God to save your sorry ass one day."

The chastised man nodded once to God and turned to walk away.

"And as far as you feeling tired and overworked, I'll just put that on my list of shit I don't give a fuck about!" Grey yelled.

God tried hard to stop his laugh but just ended up going into a coughing fit.

"Your captain told me you were out sick, dude. What do you have, PMS?"

God wrinkled his brow at him. "What the fuck?"

"You got Penis Muscle Strain, man." Grey cracked up laughing at his middle school level joke.

"Do you ever get tired of laughing, Joker?" God asked.

"Nope, never. It takes way more muscles to frown than to smile. I'm just conserving energy."

God checked his place one final time. They'd gotten his bed, televisions, video games, dressers, and clothes. He left everything else. God knew he had to take everything all at once. Those thugs would break in the moment he left. If he would've stayed the night, they still would've come in to test him, since he'd already shown them he wasn't one hundred percent. God wasn't coughing as much, but his body hurt like hell now after taking Genesis's beating.

God tried not to think about Genesis and he really tried not to think about Day right then. He didn't want the rookies to see his hurt.

"God!"

God jerked his head back around. "Yeah. You call me?"

"Yeah, like three times. Dude, you really need to get some rest. You look like shit. Go ahead to wherever you're gonna lay your head, and I'll get this stuff into my garage for now."

"Thanks, Joker. I really appreciate it." God gave him a one-armed hug.

"You sure you don't want to bunk at my place? I'm sure Shelia wouldn't mind. I got a spare bedroom." Grey turned serious eyes on him to show he wasn't kidding.

"No, I'm just going to check into a hotel."

"You sure? Tomorrow's sloppy-joe night." He smiled.

God smirked. "I'm sure, besides I don't want to bring any germs into your house."

"All right, man. It's an open invitation though," Grey said. He got in the all black cruiser and rode off with his team.

God climbed in his truck and left the jungle.

Chapter EIGHTEEN

I Want Him Back Too

Day used the garage opener to lift the door and coasted his Harley Sportster into the small space next to his SUV. He peeled his tired leg from over the seat and dragged his heavy body through the side entrance of his home. Day had ridden around for three hours after God had thrown him out like he was yesterday's trash. It'd hurt him in a way that he never fathomed. He'd been caring for God's every need for two days, pretty much saved his life… and one mistake made, and God wanted nothing to do with him anymore.

Being partnered for four years, they'd had their share of disagreements, but nothing like this, and God had damn sure never put his hands on him in anger. Day didn't want to, but his body wasn't obeying his commands. He went straight to his room to plug in his cell phone that had died during his long ride. He had to see if God had called him. Day shucked his leather jacket and draped it over the La-Z-Boy in his bedroom. He plopped down on the edge of the bed and waited impatiently for the phone to boot up.

E-mail. He might have e-mailed me.

Day put the phone on the nightstand and made quick steps to his laptop and turned that on too. Day had one hand in his mouth, chewing relentlessly on a nail, while his left boot tapped an erratic rhythm on the hardwood floor. He logged into his e-mail account and saw that he had fifty-two e-mails… but not one from God. *Dammit!*

Day picked up his cell phone at the sound of the message notification beeping. He couldn't believe he was actually nervous. He scrolled through his missed voice mails and then his texts… nothing.

"Son of a bitch!" he yelled, throwing his phone across the room.

Day dropped to his knees and cried out at the pain that action caused. He maneuvered until his back was against the bed and dropped his head into his hands. Day went over and over in his head what the hell happened today. How it started, why God got so angry. How could God hide this from him? But most of all, why had Genesis called God a murderer?

He stayed that way, trying to rationalize things in his head until his cell phone rang. *Damn, I thought I broke it.* Day jumped up and scrambled to get the phone from behind his dresser before it stopped ringing. He grabbed it and flipped it over to look at the display. *Fuck.*

"Hey, Jax," he said, trying but failing to hide his disappointment.

"Leonidis, what the heck is going on?" Jax's voice was not the usual cool and calm it always was.

"Why? What is it?" Day asked worriedly.

"I'm at God's place and it's empty. The door was unlocked as usual, but he's gone and so is most of his stuff," Jax said.

Day's stomach dropped and his heart began to beat at a hysterical pace.

"Jax, is there any sign that there may have been a struggle or is there something like a note or object lying around that might suggest where he went?"

"You mean he's not with you?" Jax asked.

"Yeah, Jaxson, he's right here beside me, sipping a damn rum and Coke. I just wanted to ask you a completely asinine question that I already know the fucking answer to," Day snapped.

"Leonidis," his brother yelled in his reprimanding voice, "don't you take that tone with me, and darn sure stop cursing at me! No, there doesn't look like there was any type of foul play, and no there is no note that I can see. Now take a breath and tell me what is going on."

"Long story short. I called Cash's schizo brother on a hideaway phone that I wasn't supposed to see or especially use. But I did. Bit-bam-boom. God's angry brother is there yelling, hitting, scratching and clawing at God trying to kill him… and the fucker is built like a semi, so I couldn't take him down. Then the thuggish neighbors burst in like the brute squad and all hell breaks loose. God points a fuckin' cannon at everyone in turn, severely pissing off his neighbors. Last but not least, God throws me across the room and tells me to get the fuck out. Now I'm here and you're telling me my partner is MIA again."

"He hit you and then threw you out after all you've done!" Jax yelled.

"It was bad, Jaxson. I've never seen God look that defeated."

"It couldn't have been that bad that he had to hurt you, Leo."

"Oh no, it was bad. It was the fucking first twenty minutes of *Saving Private Ryan* bad, Jax." Day paced as he listened to his brother go on about God accepting responsibility for his own actions.

"Jax, don't get me wrong, I'm highly pissed off with my partner. I'm pissed off to the highest of pisstivity. But I still have to know that he's okay. That crazy brother of his really landed some hard blows on him and God didn't fight back at all."

"Because it's his brother. That I do get," Jax said softly. "But I can't check on him, Leo, because believe me, there is nothing here to clue me in on where he went." Jax paused before speaking again. "I must say I'm curious how he got all that heavy furniture out of here if he was in as bad a shape as you say."

"Well, that wouldn't be too hard to do. A lot of people owe God favors—both of us actually. If God called someone for help, they'd drop everything and come to help." Day took a deep breath. "The same as I would if he had called me." Day's voice was strained from the ache in his chest and he had no doubt that Jax was picking up on it.

"That asshole," Jax snapped.

"Whoa, big brother. Don't go cursing away your do-gooder image. You know you're not a vulgar-language type person... leave that for us heathens." Day laughed humorlessly.

Day heard his brother's irritated chuckle at him for trying to lighten the situation.

"Fine. But, after he apologizes numerous times, I'm going to give him a piece of my mind," Jax said.

Day did smile that time. He had no doubt his brother would do just that.

"Oh shit!" Day snapped his fingers at his recollection of something very critical. *Why do I always forget about this?* "I know exactly where he is... or at least I will in a second." Day hung up without another word.

He pulled up his track-your-lover app on his phone. He never did tell God how he'd found him in that alley in Buckhead. It took a few seconds for the app to open fully before he saw the red dot beeping on the map of their city. *You call yourself a detective, God. Pfft.* He immediately called his brother back.

"Jax, he's at the Fairfield Lodge in East Point. Please go check on him." Day didn't want to sound so pathetic. God had thrown him around and tossed him out like old leftovers, but Day loved him and would never want to see God hurt or in need of help but too proud to ask for it.

God was at the counter of the shady Fairfield Lodge hotel. It wasn't the worst but it damn sure wasn't the best. God pulled on his leather coat to try to conceal his weapons, not wanting to scare the clerk. It was almost ten at night, and all he had was one suitcase of clothing and one of his video games.

The clerk came from the back of the office and walked up to the counter, still not making eye contact with him.

"How much for a week?" God asked.

Maybe it was his deep voice or his drawl that caught the woman off guard because she jerked her head up from typing on the outdated computer to put a face with the rough-hewn voice. After taking in God's appearance she quickly turned her nonchalant demeanor into one that suggested God could have some company in his room tonight if he preferred.

God had to work hard not to frown at the small lady. He was sure she was a nice enough woman and could probably provide him some decent entertainment, but his mind was somewhere else… on someone else.

She batted large brown eyes that were enhanced with a little too much makeup, her lips painted a deep shade of red. Her hair was in a classic bob cut and framed her blushed cheeks.

"That will be two hundred dollars for a week," the clerk said around a wide smile.

God winced a little internally at the price. His payday was next week, but he had to make the three hundred and seventy-two dollars in his bank account last until then.

The clerk continued, "We have cable and Wi-Fi, there's a small workout room on the first floor, there's ice and vending machines on each floor, and a free continental breakfast on the weekends from six to eight in the morning."

"I'll take one with a king-size bed if you have it," God responded drily.

"No problem. Are you checking in anyone? Are you sharing the room?" she questioned.

"Single, please, and first floor if you have one." God didn't want to lead this woman on, but he didn't want to pay an extra charge either for checking in two people.

The clerk did a terrible job at concealing her excitement. She asked for his license and pecked away at the computer.

"You'll be in room 165 on the bottom, around the back."

"Anything on the front?" God asked. He liked to see who was coming and going.

"Anything for you." She winked, and he had to restrain from sucking his teeth and rolling his eyes. *Whatever happened to professionalism?*

"Okay. How about room 114, it's right there." She pointed out the window. He didn't turn around to look. He signed the papers that said he'd be a good guest or else pay the consequences, and went for the key card in her outstretched hand. When he tried to extract it from her claws, she jerked it back toward her and asked in what she thought was a sexy voice, "How about I come turn down the bed for you? We offer that to our special guests."

"Good thing I'm nothing special," God grumbled and pulled the key card from her.

He heard her mumble on his way out the door. *"Some motherfuckers are so blind; they can't see a good thing when it's staring them right in the face."*

God actually thought that was hilarious, but the irony was not lost on him. Day had been there in his face all along, and he'd missed it. Now he may have pushed Day out of his life for good... literally. God was still beating himself up for putting his hands on Day like that. But even worse was that Day had gotten up and still tried to help him.

He fit the card into the slot. When the light went from red to green he opened the door, entering the dark, damp room. He flicked the light on the wall and let the door slam shut and lock automatically behind him. Dropping the bag at the foot of the bed, he dug in his pocket for the pain pills Jax had left him and popped two in his mouth, swallowing them dry. He peeled off his coat and placed his holster and weapons in the one drawer in the bedside table right next to the Gideon Bible.

A hot shower and a little food might help how he felt. But he doubted anything could take away the vision he kept having of Day flying over the bed and slamming into his dresser. God squeezed his eyes shut. *Fuck. I'm so sorry, sweetheart.*

Too much happened in that room at once. God wasn't seeing straight. Genesis was beating the hell out of him. Day had violated his trust. His hood-rat neighbors had barged into his home and choked his brother. God had so much medication coursing through him he'd reacted without thinking.

Now he wanted to call Day so badly, but he needed to let things cool off between them. Then he'd have to figure out how he was going to make it up to him.

God opened up the brown shopping bag and emptied the contents onto the small dining table. He'd stopped and picked up some orange juice, a few cans of soup since his throat was still a little sore, some paper utensils, and some snacks. He poured some soup in a bowl and popped it in a microwave that was small enough to pass as an Easy Bake Oven.

God dumped his toiletries bag on the bathroom sink and looked at himself in the mirror. He looked like day-old shit. His deep wavy hair was all over the place, his beard had no contour to it, and his eyes looked like he'd just smoked crack. He rubbed his hands over his face and blew an exasperated breath.

Please have somewhat decent water pressure.

God twisted the faucet handles on the stall shower and turned the water up as hot as he could stand it. He washed quickly and then stood still, letting the water beat on the back of his neck. It wasn't as hard as he liked but it would do. He stood there until the water started to turn cool. He shaved his beard, leaving his goatee and a little bit of length under his chin. He combed his hair until there were no more tangles and left it down to dry. He felt better... physically.

With a small, scratchy towel wrapped around his waist, God went to retrieve his soup and sat in one of the small chairs at the two-person table. At least they were cushioned. His bed didn't look as inviting, with the typical hotel comforter that always slid off the bed and onto the floor in the middle of the night. God hoped the sheets were changed regularly, but his gut told him they probably weren't. *Thank the Lord I'm still on antibiotics. Could probably catch instant herpes in that bed.* He snorted and downed his bowl of soup in three quick gulps. He hadn't even realized how hungry he was until the bowl was dry and he immediately wanted more. So he popped open another can. *Day's soup was better.*

God wiped off the table and just as he was about to peel the covers back on the bed there was a light tapping on the door. He quietly opened the nightstand drawer and pulled out his 9mm. He pulled the curtain back just enough to peak and saw the night clerk from the front desk at his door.

Shoot me.

God cracked open the door. "Yeah. What's up?"

She smiled at the sliver of his chest she could see through the crack.

"Sorry to disturb you, but there's a man at the front desk asking for you and we have a firm policy of not giving out our residents' information."

God's stomach began to flutter. It had to be Day. Maybe he'd followed him there, God wasn't sure. "Did he tell you his name?"

"Yes. He said his name is Day," she replied, still craning her neck to get a better glimpse of his flesh.

"Give him the room number please, and thank you for checking first." God shut the door, not needing a response.

God had just enough time to throw on some jeans when a loud bang sounded on the door. He frowned and yanked the door open.

140

God looked into the angry eyes of the wrong Day. He wanted to see Detective Day, not Dr. Day. God huffed and stepped to the side to let Jax in.

"How did you find me, Jax?" God asked as his greeting.

"I didn't, your partner did. He seems to be able to track his lover anywhere in the United States," Jax said with zero humor.

His brow scrunched for a couple seconds before he realized what Jax was talking about. *Track your lover.* "He's actually using that goddamn app on our phones. Sonofabitch."

"If you weren't still sick and so freakishly huge, I'd punch you in the jaw for hurting my brother," Jax fumed.

God plopped down on the bed and hissed at the pain in his ribs.

"Jax, I don't make excuses. I fucked up and I admit it. I will fix this and soon. Leo means everything to me, and really, he's all I've got."

Jax dropped his large medical bag to the floor and looked God in his eyes. "But do you love him?"

God didn't speak.

"You already know how he feels about you. I've never seen him care for anyone else the way he cared for you while you were sick. He was scared and worried. He's still worried. He sent me here, wouldn't take no for an answer. You may care about him, but if you can't love him the way he wants you to, then let him know now... not after he's too far in," Jax said.

God knew Jax was telling the truth. He knew Day was important to him, but love? He'd never been in love before. It'd been even longer since he'd felt loved by another. What Day had done for him over these past few days must be what people in love did. He didn't need to reveal his feeling to Jax—like he'd noted when he opened the door—it was the wrong Day.

"I'll fix this, Jax. You know I'm a man of my word. It's all I have. I won't spill my feelings to you. But I promise you, I'll never hurt him again," God said seriously.

Jax stared him down for a few seconds and God never looked away. Not until Jax believed he was sincere.

"Fine. I'll accept that for now. Now lie back and let me take a look."

"I'm fine, Jax," God groaned.

"Shut up and lie back. I'm not going back to Leonidis without an accurate report that you're fine," Jax said while pulling out his stethoscope.

God mumbled some curse words as he positioned himself on the bed. He answered all of Jax's questions and let the man wrap his bruised ribs. Jax told him he was fine and his lungs sounded clear. He gave him some more pain pills and cough suppressant just in case. He also told God to rest over the weekend and he should be good to go to work on Monday.

He held the door for the short man. Jax and Leo were about the same height. His hair was in a simple buzz cut with neatly trimmed sideburns that stopped at the bottoms of his earlobes. God had a hard time looking into Jax's beautiful hazel eyes, so similar to his partner's. Jax shook his hand in a firm grip, surely firmer than needed, and God got the message. He quirked his lip up at Jax's protectiveness over his little brother, he knew what that feeling was like.

As soon as Jax was gone, God grabbed his cell phone and texted his partner. He thought for a second on what to send, but only two words came to mind. He typed, *I'm sorry,* and pressed Send. God only had to wait a few seconds before his phone buzzed with a return message. God opened it, and Leo had two words, too. God read Leo's response, *Fuck you.*

God laughed heartily as he stared at the two words with an angry-faced emoji symbol after it. Day was the only one that could make God laugh like that. *Oh, you're gonna make me work for this one, aren't you, sweetheart?* God climbed under the sheets, naked, and forced his mind to relax. He'd go get his man tomorrow.

142

Screw Your Apology

Day looked at God's weak-assed apology text. Day didn't care about a fucking text. He wanted God here on his knees begging for forgiveness. After Jax told him that God was fine and he looked very sorry for what he'd done, Day could think about nothing else.

Tomorrow was Saturday. Usually he and God would go work out, sometimes go to the shooting range, they'd do whatever they felt like doing. Then in the evening Day would cook and God would do or fix whatever Day needed him to around the house.

Damn, when I think about it, we sound so damn domesticated already.

Day tried to do things to keep him from going crazy with thoughts. He was an insomniac. It was only midnight now, what the hell could he do—short of taking sleeping pills—to calm himself enough to sleep.

"Fuck it. I'm not going to sit around here waiting like some lovesick girl who got dismissed by her guy. There's plenty of dick in the sea." Day lifted one brow at what he'd just said. "That made no sense."

Day showered and shaved as quickly as possible. He put a little product in his hair and ran his hands through it to make it look perfectly messy. He wore his well-worn, tight jeans and a button-down, tan collared shirt. He applied a small amount of cologne—Day never liked men that over did it with fragrances. He put his cell phone in his back pocket, his 9mm in the small of his back, and tucked his badge on the inside of his coat.

Day opened up his garage and straddled his Harley, revving the engine a few times to relish the vibration between his legs before he took off into the night in search of some fun. Day got on the interstate and opened her up, doing ninety miles per hour toward midtown. There was a cool sports bar on Piedmont that catered to men with specific sexual preferences. There wasn't a night Day went that he didn't get lucky.

Day parked his bike with all the other crotch rockets and strolled toward the entrance. He could hear the loud cheering on the inside before he even got to the door. He quickly shook hands with the familiar bouncer at the front and opened the large wood door. The crowd was rowdy and the party was in full swing.

Some people were dancing to the soft rock that blasted from the large speakers in the corner. Others were playing pool while watching various sports on the multitude of flat screens positioned around the bar. Day ignored those activities. Duff's was only open until two so that meant he had one hour to secure his date for the evening. There was a hotel by the hour just up the street, Day didn't even have to move his bike if he didn't want to.

He perched next to a man that from the back had a very small frame, tight waist, and bubble ass. When Day ordered his Coors Light draft, the man turned fully and looked in his direction. He gave the man a slight wink and watched those glossy lips curve up into a seductive smile. Lip-gloss didn't really turn Day on but it usually got wiped off while he was receiving head, so no big deal. The guy was cute though. Sweet, doe-like brown eyes, his hair was spiky with dark roots and blonde tips.

"What you drinking, cutie?" Day asked the petite fake-blond.

"A hard banger," he responded while licking his lips.

Day resisted the urge to laugh in his face, because if he did that might ruin his chance at a hard banger.

144

"Want another?" Day asked with plenty of pun intended.

"Wouldn't mind at all," he replied.

Day ordered another fruit concoction for… "What's your name, beautiful?" Day asked.

He watched those brown eyes roll to the right before his mouth finally responded. "Mick. Most people call me Mick."

"Sure, we'll go with Mick. It's fine if you don't want to tell me your real name." Day watched the man closely for more signs. When Mick responded to Day's question, his eyes went up and to the right, and since Mick was right-handed, Day concluded that he was lying. Day always looked for unconscious movements people made. It was why he was such a good detective. He didn't miss a thing… usually.

Mick giggled like a girl before answering, "It's not that, I just don't like to be called Michelangelo, so I tell everyone my name is Mick. But to be honest you can call me whatever the hell you want. You can also call me ready to get out of here."

Damn. I'd probably tell people to call me Mick too. Who the hell names their kid Michelangelo?

"I might take you up on that, Mick, but do you mind if I have a couple of drinks first?"

"Not at all." He watched Mick slide off his stool with the grace of a cheetah and attach himself to Day's right side. "And you are?"

Mick smelled like lavender and vanilla. Day wasn't an aftershave kind of guy, but he'd take what was offered tonight. Anything to stop him thinking about the big guy that had thrown him around like a ragdoll this morning. *Stop thinking about him.*

Day ordered three shots of vodka and another beer. The bartender lined up his shots and he downed each one in quick succession.

"Hey, slow down, cowboy." Mick laughed.

Day wanted to tell the man to shut up. He didn't know his plight. He was in love with his best friend and partner, but he wasn't loved back. Mick should be glad that he wasn't shitfaced already.

145

"My name is Leo," he finally answered Mick's question.

Day snaked his arm around the tiny waist and let the man nuzzle the side of his neck. He could hear him taking long whiffs of his cologne.

"You like the way I smell, honey?" Day asked, already feeling the liquor.

In answer, Mick wiggled a little closer and Day let his hand slide down to that tight ass. He gave it a firm squeeze, and Mick released a quick exhale against his neck.

"You smell delicious. I want to know if you smell like that everywhere. How long you gonna make me wait, big daddy?" Mick whispered with a slight slur.

Oh for fuck's sake.

Suddenly, Day wasn't in the mood. Just that damn quick, Mick had turned him off. Day didn't want lip-gloss and silly innuendos. He wanted his alpha stud. He wanted to be thrown down on the bed and handled. Day ignored the insistent whining from Mick and ordered another beer. After a couple gulps he was more than feeling a buzz. Day looked at his sports watch. *1:25 a.m. It's now or never.* He gave Mick another once-over before responding with an indifferent shrug. "Let's go, Mick."

Mick clapped his hands together and squealed like a pig, and it almost made Day decide he wasn't worth it. He hoped the man's moans were a tad more masculine.

Day held Mick by the hand as they made their way through the crowd and out the front door. He gave a quick nod in the direction of the hotel, letting the bouncer know he'd be back in an hour to get his bike. This definitely wasn't Day's first rodeo.

He and Mick stumbled a little as they walked, and Day began to laugh to himself. He felt like an idiot. When was the last time he had to get drunk in order to fuck someone? Hell, Day didn't even know if he'd be able to perform, because his cock was as limp as a wet noodle right now. Day turned the corner and ran smack into a large, hulking chest, startling the hell out of both him and his date.

Mick grabbed his chest. "Jesus!"

"No. God," the gruff voice responded.

Goose bumps popped up all over Day. He didn't need to look up; he knew exactly who that voice belonged too.

Day still had his arm around Mick when he heard the small man giggle. "Goodness you are huge. Sorry, didn't see ya big fella." Mick went to move them around God, but Day didn't budge.

Day finally looked up into fierce green eyes. *Holy fuck.* God looked good enough to pull into the small alley and fuck him for hours. He had on black jeans and a dark gray V-neck T-shirt. His black, mid-thigh leather coat was open and Day could see the butt of his Desert Eagle at his side… and just like that… Day was rock hard.

Mick pulled on Day again. "You coming, handsome?"

"No, he's not. Leave," God told Mick. His voice was rough and his posture was intimidating.

Mick looked back and forth between Day and God before asking Day, "You know this guy?"

Day was seriously at a loss for words as he stared at his partner that was supposed to be in a hotel room across town.

"Yes, he most certainly does," God answered for him.

God was restless lying in bed, unconsciously massaging his balls and playing on his phone. He played a couple games, surfed the Net, and began opening various apps. He scrolled past the track-your-lover application and opened it up. Smiling he saw that Day was at home. He'd debated calling him and trying another apology. After an hour of internal arguing, he'd finally convinced himself to do it, until he noticed the red dot on his was moving. *Where the fuck are you going this time of night?*

God sat up and turned on the small lamp attached to the wall by the bed. As the dot, Day, traveled toward midtown, God began to growl. He knew exactly where Day was going. It was his go-to-spot to get a quick piece of ass. *You little bastard.*

"I know exactly what you're doing, Leo. Teaching me a lesson, huh," God mumbled to himself as he quickly pulled some clothes out of his suitcase.

In less than ten minutes he was fully dressed and squealing his tires out of the Fairfield Lodge parking lot. God barreled down the interstate and into midtown Atlanta like he was on a high-speed chase. He pulled into the alley behind Duff's bar. He activated the alarm on his truck and made quick steps down the alley. As soon as he got to the end and was about to turn the corner, Day and his boy ran right into him. Now he was shooting daggers at Day's piece of ass and scowling at his partner.

He took in the young man that Day had on his arm and God had to fight the urge to yank his arm off. Spiky, bleached hair, a fucking midriff net shirt, wet lips, perfectly arched eyebrows—which God really hated—and a tiny frame. He decided to enjoy Day's loss of words for a couple seconds and slowly raked his eyes down that sexy body to the now-prominent bulge below Day's belt. God moved in until he was practically standing on top of Day.

"God, what the hell are you doing here?" Day finally spoke.

"Oh my stars! You really are God?" Mick squealed.

God watched Day pinch the bridge of his nose and roll his eyes in obvious embarrassment.

"Seriously!" God snarled, pointing at Mick.

"What. Are. You. Doing. Here?" Day snapped each word this time.

"You're not the only one that can track your lover," God said smugly while holding up his phone with the application still open.

Day's mouth fell open and the shade of red he turned was priceless. He decided to get rid of their excess company and take Day

148

back with him. God looked at Day's date and put on his best run-for-your-life face and spat menacingly, "Leave. Now."

"No," Day spoke before his date could move. "You don't have to go anywhere, Mick."

God looked back to Day and spoke in a harsh growl without moving his eyes from his partner's. "Mick, I say leave now. He says to stay. Whatever will you do?"

Mick turned and ran so fast his image practically blurred.

"That takes care of that," God said.

Day pushed God out of his space and turned to walk away without another word.

"Oh no, you don't," God snarled before grabbing Day around his waist and pulling him back into the darkness of the alley. He pushed Day up against the brick wall and pressed his forehead hard against his. "You think I'm just going to let you walk off?"

"Yep. Just like you did this afternoon," Day replied without a second thought.

He'd be damned if that response didn't hurt like hell. He kept their foreheads touching but lost some of his anger. "I apologized for that."

"You sent me a goddamn text message, coward. Now get off me. I'm going home... alone now, thanks to you," Day hissed.

"You were really going to fuck that guy?" God asked incredulously.

"You're goddamn right I was," Day retorted.

"Even though you're in love with me?"

Why did God say that? He watched his partner's face go from mad to stark raving livid. Before he could process what was happing, Day had caught him with a right punch twice to his rib cage making him cry out in pain at his already tender ribs.

"Fuck!" God yelled as he was shoved backward hard enough to almost knock him off balance.

"Can't believe you just said that, asshole," Day said while moving in on him again. "Think I'm going to let you string me along?"

God held his ribs and put one hand up to stop Day's approach, but it was useless. Day dropped like a martial arts master and did a backward spin kick, effectively knocking both God's legs from under him and sending him crashing to the ground—and two-hundred and fifty plus pounds hitting the asphalt really hurt.

"The bigger they are, the harder they fucking fall," Day snarled, and began to move in again.

What the fuck?

God knew Day was quick, he'd seen him in action enough times. God's only defense was his muscle, but he had to get his hands on Day first, which wouldn't be easy. God rolled and came up off the ground, quicker than Day expected, and he caught Day's left punch in mid-throw and spun him around. He yanked Day into his chest but took a hard right elbow to his right cheek before he was able to secure it with the other one.

"Enough," God growled in his ear. Day's back was pressed hard against God's chest, while God held both hands tightly in front of him. "Stop fighting me."

"No," Day snapped.

"Stop fighting me, Leo. Because I love you too." God said, his lips pressed firmly against Day's ear. "You can't fuck that other guy because you're mine," he whispered.

God felt Day's body go limp and he took the opportunity to spin him around to face him. He looked into soft hazel eyes and lost himself. "I do, sweetheart. I think I may always have. I just didn't know it until after you walked out of my apartment." God took a deep breath and shook his head; his eyes squeezed shut at the vision that popped into his mind. "After I hurt you."

Day didn't pull away, but God could see the hurt was still there. Man, how he wished he could take it all back. He swore he would

150

have done it all differently. "Leo. Please forgive me. I'm so sorry, and I promise I'll never put my hands on you in anger again." God watched Day for any signs of forgiveness. Day's head was down, he was still as a rock, and he still hadn't spoken.

God released Day's arms, took one hand, and slowly lifted Day's chin so he could look into those beautiful eyes again. Day's eyes were moist but focused.

"Say something, sweetheart. Tell me you forgive me. Tell me you love me, or tell me to go to hell, just say something," God begged, the silence driving him mad.

God was beginning to think he'd really lost his best friend until Day finally spoke. "I usually don't like endearments, but I think I like you calling me sweetheart."

He had to blink a couple times before he fully understood what Day had said. He released a harsh breath he didn't realize he was holding, grabbed Day in a huge bear hug, and turned him around until his back was against the wall. God held him pinned there and attacked his mouth with an urgency unlike anything he'd ever felt. At first it was hard, needy, urgent, before turning soft and gentle.

Day's lips were so soft and full. God pulled the bottom one into his mouth and sucked it tenderly, making Day release a sexy moan. God's dick was aching, pressed against his zipper. It'd been a while since he'd had sex, even longer since he'd had sex with a man, but never in his life had he made love. Love was something he thought only existed in cheesy romance novels and chick flicks. He never thought it could be real in him, but it was. He loved Leonidis Day, and was serious when he said he probably always had. His heart had ached tremendously when Day walked out earlier, and it ached all the way until now. Now he had him in his arms, and he wasn't letting go… ever if he could help it.

God ground his pelvis into Day, seeking some much-needed friction. Day grabbed God's stubbled cheeks with both hands and thrust his tongue in as deeply as he could. God thought he could orgasm right there in the dirty alley from the way Day was tongue fucking his mouth. God took as much as he could before he yanked his face away and gasped for air. "Jesus, sweetheart."

Day groaned. "Need you so fucking bad right now. Come home with me." It was a demand not a request. Day grabbed God's cock and gave it a hard squeeze.

"Ugh. Fuck yes," God hissed.

"Want you out of this dirty alley and in my bed in one hour, and don't fucking keep me waiting," Day demanded and turned to walk away without a backward look.

Yeah, make me pay, sweetheart.

God practically ran to his truck, ignoring the aches and pains he felt throughout his body. He could just hear Day's motorcycle revving before he slammed his truck's door shut.

Oh. My. God.

Day was excited, nervous, scared, terrified even, that he was about to have Detective Cashel Godfrey laid out, stark naked in his bed and ready for the taking. He'd pictured it a million times in the last four years. He'd had a sneaking suspicion that God was bi-curious if nothing else. Day noticed things, and he'd noticed God occasionally looking at men with more than just a passing glance. He just hadn't known if God would want to start something with him, but obviously he did and had for a while. Because God said he loved him… *loved* him.

Day was terrified because if this didn't work, where would that leave them as partners? Granted they had never been overdramatic, emotional bitches always ending a friendship if a romantic relationship didn't work, but how could he work with God every day if the man broke his heart? *Well, if it doesn't work, we'll have to be sure to be mature and not split on bad terms.* Day wasn't fooling anyone. What were the chances of a breakup ending on good terms? Slim to none.

Day used the garage opener and coasted his bike inside. He'd done almost one hundred miles per hour on the mostly empty interstate. He didn't worry about getting pulled over… they'd never ticket him. He was sure God would be right behind him, so he deactivated the alarm, unlocked the front door, and shot upstairs to jump in the shower. He'd be damned if he was going to be with God for the first time with another man's scent all over him.

Day stripped quickly and let his clothes fall wherever. He left the bathroom door open and started the shower. He dumped a quick cap of mouthwash in his mouth, swishing it around before spitting it into toilet. He stepped into the steaming shower and lathered up quickly, not wanting to waste another second of the night, because every second was a second he could have God's hands on him. He had his head ducked under the high-pressure showerhead when he heard God's gruff voice.

"Hurry up."

Day smiled when his cock jumped at God's sexy demand. He hurriedly rinsed off and turned off the water. He stepped out of the stall and began to wrap the large towel around his waist.

"Leave it off," God ordered from the now very dark bedroom. There was only a sliver of light filtering in from the hall, and it cast God in an eerie glow as he leaned against the door watching Day's every move.

Day wasn't shy about nakedness, but the raw sound of God's tone made him shiver as he tossed the towel away. Day stepped onto the beige plush carpet in his bedroom and stood a few feet from God. He slowly brought his hand to his now straining cock. He began at the base and gave it a torturously slow pull until he reached the blushing head, liking the clear pearly bead that formed at the tip, before sliding back down again.

God stalked toward him, grabbed Day's hand from his dick, and yanked him against his chest. "Mine," he whispered against his temple.

"Fuck," Day moaned. His cock was hard and leaking. He needed to touch it or Cash to touch it, just fucking something, before he went insane.

Day looked up into God's eyes and gasped at the feral lust he saw in the green orbs. "Cash," he whispered.

God held Day's wrist clutched to his chest with one hand, and used the other hand to swipe some of the clear precome that was leaking between them. Day watched the movement with half-lidded eyes as God's calloused thumb grazed tenderly over his cock head, making Day hiss at that tiny jolt of pleasure.

"Look at me," God ordered.

Day raised his head slowly and let God paint his lips with his own fluid. His mouth parted with his ragged breaths while watching God stare at his shiny lips before dipping down and capturing his mouth. God moaned so damn deep it vibrated Day's entire body. God lapped at his mouth and didn't stop until every single trace of his essence was gone. The jeans God still wore were coarse against his tender, wet flesh and he wanted God naked and now.

"Please," Day whispered.

God gripped the back of his neck and bit a trail to his ear. "Get on the bed," he commanded.

Oh my fucking God. Day had to keep himself from sprinting to the bed and jumping on it like a kid. Instead he walked slowly to the four-poster, California king-size bed and pulled back the black and silver plush comforter.

Day topped the twinks he'd brought home or to some seedy hotel for a quick fuck, but Day loved being dominated. He wouldn't say he was a full on submissive, but he craved a big, hulking man that wasn't afraid to take control and overpower his body.

Day tracked God as he stalked around his bedroom. The room was large, taking up most of the upper floor after he'd had one of the walls removed to connect both bedrooms. One side was a sitting area with a large flat-screen television, a dual reclining micro suede sofa, and his record player. In front of a bay window there was a moderately sized desk with a spotlight lamp attached to it where he built his model cars. The finished ones were in a large china cabinet downstairs in his den.

Day lay back and watched God remove his holster that held a very large and manly weapon. Day was a slut for beautiful weapons and God definitely had one. It was a Desert Eagle .50 AE with an interchangeable .44 Magnum barrel and black Micarta grip, and it was a force to be reckoned with. Day had jerked off more than once to thoughts of God holding or firing his weapon. Not just any man could wield a weapon like that. Day didn't care if that made him a nut with a seriously kinky fetish… to each his own.

God pulled off his shirt, his large chest muscles now on full display, and at some point he must have removed the wrapping Jax put on his ribs. The sparse patch of hair in the middle of his pecs made a silky, narrow trail down his ripped abdomen and disappeared into his jeans. Day made a mental note to lick his way down that treasure trail as soon as possible. God slowly undid his jeans and slid them down his thighs, never taking his eyes off Day. *When did he become a fucking tease?* Removing his jeans and boots at once, God stood before him naked as the day he was born.

Day's mouth watered at the fully erect eight inches of cut cock pointing toward him, just begging to be licked, sucked, and fucked; Day was just the man for the job. Day couldn't stop his huff of annoyance when God turned to walk into the other side of his bedroom, the sound causing him to pause and turn to look at him.

"Are we getting a little impatient, sweetheart?" God lifted one side of his mouth as he spoke.

Day groaned, but shook his head no. He didn't know what kind of torture God would put him thorough if he didn't behave. God's ass was just as muscular as the rest of him. *Give me strength.*

"Good. Because I don't like being rushed," he said nonchalantly and continued to Day's prized record player. In memory of his father, Day probably had one of the greatest jazz collections known to man and they were all vinyl, many of which he acquired at auctions. He was missing only one very special album he'd yet to find for sale.

He watched God flip through a few records before pulling one. He slid the vinyl out as carefully as Day would before placing it on the turntable. Soon Day's room was filled with the soft sounds of

George Howard's *Midnight Moods*. It was a smooth, sexy jazz album; definitely one for making love to.

Day's heart clenched. God didn't want to just fuck him; he wanted to make love to him. Damn, it'd felt like ages since Day had done that. Not since college if he were being honest with himself. He'd loved his college sweetheart, but they'd never actually got to the lovemaking part, since his college sweetheart was straight. But now he'd have the chance. Day reclined, letting the soft soprano sounds of the saxophone add to his euphoria.

He opened his eyes when he felt the bed dip from God's weight. God positioned himself on top of him and pulled the covers up over them, stopping at their waist. *Jesus Christ… and under the covers too.* Day's breathing picked up quickly as he stared into his best friend's face. They stayed like that for several long seconds, communicating silently. This was it. This was where there relationship changed from friends and partners to lovers. Were they ready for this? Is this what they truly wanted it to be from now on?

Yes, they thought in unison.

"Kiss me, Cashel," Day whispered.

God lowered himself fully on top of him and damn if all that muscle didn't feel blissfully heavy. God's kisses were so tender and soft that Day was swooning after only a minute. He never would've imagined rough and tough, bad-assed God could be so gentle. Their lips grazed back and forth over each other's, nipping lightly.

"Open," God moaned.

Day opened his mouth and his legs nice and wide to accommodate his lover. They kissed and rocked together, neither one seeming to want to rush things. God grabbed one of Day's thighs and pulled it up to his waist, wrapping it around his back, then did the same with the other. God was so large Day could only just hook his ankles together. God's elbows were braced on either side of his head. When he pulled back from their long make out session, that heat was shining in God's eyes again.

"Top drawer," Day said. God was thrusting that hard cock against him over and over, and he wanted to be filled with it more than anything in the world. God reached over and pulled open the drawer, feeling blindly for the lube and condoms. God reared up and pulled out the almost-empty box of condoms.

God growled and lifted Day completely off the bed, his legs still hooked together around God's waist. Day's eyes flew open as he held on to God's shoulders. God stared into his eyes, his teeth bared, and the muscles in his neck bulging in anger.

"You know I'm not a virgin," Day answered God's fury. "If you want me, you have me. Now stop acting like a bastard and take me."

God slammed him back down to the mattress and snatched the lube off the bed. He slicked three fingers and Day clenched thinking God might try to shove them all in him at once.

God lay back on top of him and moved Day's left thigh out to the side. "I'd never do that," he told him before slowly circling one thick finger around his tight ring.

"I know," Day whispered. "I just haven't bottomed in so long."

At the admission God licked Day's lips again and moved slowly down his body, licking and sucking in all the right places. He pinched one of Day's nipples between his teeth, flicking the black barbell pierced through it before licking the stinging sensation away. He did it a couple more times and moved over to the other nipple, giving it that same painful and tender treatment. Day's body jerked and spasmed with every move.

"I love these fucking piercings… so damn sexy," God murmured against the perky bud.

"More," Day begged. "I need so much more."

"I got you, sweetheart," God mouthed against Day's flat stomach. God's hot tongue wound its way through the ridges and valleys of Day's abs. His legs trembled with need and his cock jerked angrily at the lack of attention. God's breath ghosted over his cock and Day fought not to grab God's hair and force his mouth where he

158

wanted it. When his control was about to snap, God engulfed his entire cock down to the base and Day's back bowed off the mattress.

"Fuck!" God's mouth was hot and his tongue was like silk. "Oh, Cash, oh, Cash."

God hummed and dragged his tongue back up his shaft with plenty of suction and just the right amount of teeth. He lingered on the head, flicking his tongue under the cap, making his body jolt with each flick. Day shook his head back and forth. It was too fucking much. His hole clenched with the need to be filled just as Day felt the pressure of God's finger. He probed a little before pushing past the first ring of muscles, causing his hips to thrust up into God's warm mouth.

"Fucking more. More, babe."

God pushed in deeper and sucked Day's cock all the way down again, pleasantly distracting him from the slight sting in his ass. Day knew the sting would fade; he was ready to get to the good part.

"Now. I want you right now, Cashel," Day urged, while pulling on God's large shoulders.

God's throaty chuckle vibrated around his cock.

"Mmmm. Fuck."

"Patience, sweetheart." God dipped lower and sucked on one of his balls while adding a second finger. Day clenched this time, causing God to stop and withdraw some.

"No, no, no… it's okay." Day didn't want God prolonging the prep any more than he already was. God was damn near treating him like a virgin. He ground his ass down onto God's two digits and heard him groan.

"Fuck, Leo. So goddamn tight."

"Want you," Day moaned.

"You have me, babe," God responded and engulfed his cock again.

Dammit. Day didn't want to come like this. He wanted God inside him. God had three fingers halfway in him now and his finger

159

was rubbing that special place that had Day cursing and begging to be filled.

"I swear I'm ready," Day snarled.

God pulled his three fingers out and came back up to face him. "You're a bossy bottom aren't you?" he spoke into Day's panting mouth. "Want my cock, Leo?"

Day nodded his head yes like a bobble-head doll.

"Say it." God scrubbed his coarse beard over Day's cheek until his lips were pressed against the base of his ear. Day felt the hot tongue lick around his lobe before pulling the sensitive flesh inside that sinful mouth.

Day thrust his dick up, rubbing against God's hard cock. "Fuck, Cash! Yes, I want your cock. All of it," Leo practically yelled.

God yanked the condom off the comforter and slid the thin latex over his bulging erection, never taking his eyes off him. Day gasped at the love he saw in God's eyes. He couldn't believe that this was actually going to happen; he'd fantasized so many times. It was always God slamming him up against the wall and taking him roughly, never this gentle caressing, and terms of endearment lovemaking they were doing now. Honestly, Day liked this way just as much if not more. He was sure God could bring the thunder when he wanted to, but this was their first time, so Day let his mind clear and his body feel what God would give him.

God lay back down and positioned his cock at Day's pulsing hole.

"Leo. You are mine and only mine, are you ready for that?" God asked, staring into his eyes.

Day didn't hesitate for one second. "Yes. I'll be yours for as long as you'll have me." Day stroked the back of his hand down God's cheek. God turned and pressed a kiss into his palm. "I love you, Cash."

Day watched God close his eyes and push with enough force to breach him with just his head.

"Ugh!" Day's mouth flew open. Dammit, God's cock head was bigger than he thought.

God pressed his body into his and tilted his hips forward. Day brought his legs up higher to open himself up more to quench the fierce burning in his ass. *Fuck, fuck, fuck. Breathe.*

God's face was buried in the crook of his neck and his body shook against him. "Jesus, Leo," God hissed.

"Cash," Day said, his moans like a cry.

"Almost there, sweetheart." God pushed in deeper and Day grabbed at his hips to stop him.

"Ugh. Fuck, you're fucking big," Day groaned.

God took Day's hand from his hip and the other that was digging into his side; grasping them both he pulled them high over his head and pressed them into the pillows, securing them there with one hand.

God was shocked by his own self-control, but he refused to hurt his lover. Half of his cock that was inside Day and God slowly rocked back and forth trying to open him up a little more. "Come on, sweetheart. You can do it. Open up, take all of me," God whispered. He concentrated on breathing and not shooting his load before he got all the way in.

Day's erection was gone, his cock lying against his left thigh. *Fuck.* He had to make this good for him. "Breathe, Leo, and push out against me," he instructed.

Beads of sweat were popping up on Day's forehead and his body shook with pain or nerves, God wasn't sure. God lifted his head from against Day's neck and rose slightly to look into those beautiful eyes. Day's eyes were tightly shut and his brow deeply creased.

"Look at me, Leo." God kissed both of Day's eyelids.

God watched moist lashes part and Day's eyes focus on him. "I love you. Show me how much you love me too. Take all of me." God leaned in and parted Day's lips with his tongue and moaned into that pretty mouth. Day tasted so fucking good, he could kiss him all night, buried only halfway in him. He tongued Days mouth, licking the roof while using the hand not holding Day's wrists to caress his nipples. He felt him relax and go pliant, and God used that small window to push all the way in.

Day practically came up off the bed. "Cash!"

"Shhh, it's all right." God didn't pause; he pulled back a couple inches and slid back in again. Keeping the movements measured and slow, he brushed over Day's prostate with each stroke. "That's it. Take all of it, it belongs to you now, take it." He licked Day's open mouth.

God felt Day tilt his hips upward; driving God in deeper and he knew his lover was crossing over that thin line between pain and indescribable pleasure. God's balls had practically crawled up inside of him. He tried to think about anything that might ward of his orgasm, but Day's ass was squeezing him so damn tight, it was impossible not to focus on the sensation.

God pulled out almost to the tip and eased back in again. His body was pressed against his man from head to toe; only his hips moved his cock in and out of that heavenly cavern. God heard Day release the sexiest moan he'd ever heard in his life, and he thrust in with more power.

"Yes! Fuck, right there! Right fucking there," Day urged while thrusting his hips up to meet him.

God reared back and slammed into Day again. He was about to come but he wanted them to come to together. "Jerk that pretty cock for me, sweetheart." God released Day's hands so he could do what he'd asked.

God kept their foreheads together as they watched their union. God pumping in and out of that tight hole, his dick glistening and pulsing. Day's hand working his cock back to full-on hardness. God was about to come. *Fuck.*

God sat up and reared back on his legs. He gripped Day behind his back and pulled him up onto his lap. Day's legs instinctually wrapped around him as he thrust into him, using Day's weight to keep his dick fully buried. He shifted Day slightly and aimed left, pumping up into him, hitting Day's spot every time.

"Yes. Give it to me. All of it!" Day spurred him on, his hands digging into God's shoulders as he held on for the ride.

God watched Day throw his head back and bare his throat to him. He felt an animalistic urge to bite and mark his man… so he did. God brought his arms up and around Day's back and gripped his shoulders, slamming him down on his cock. He leaned in and bit Day's neck just below his ear. Day yelled out as his come spurted between them, hot and slick, propelling God into his own orgasm.

God squeezed Day and held him close as he shot his first jet of come. God growled deep in his throat with his teeth still latched on to Day's throat. He stopped biting only to pull the tender flesh into his mouth and suck as hard as he could until he stopped coming inside Day's spasming hole.

God stilled and caught his breath, his cock still buried inside his lover. He felt Day lick at the sweat on his neck and unhook his legs from around his back. God slid his hands down Day's back and palmed both of his ass cheeks, lifting him off his cock. Day hissed, and God gently laid him back down on the damp sheets. God was exhausted. He removed the condom and dropped it in the wastebasket beside the bed before dropping down beside Day.

"You all right, sweetheart?" God said, inching up against his side.

"Holy shit. You have no fucking idea how I'm feeling right now." Day half-moaned and half-laughed.

"Is it good or bad?" God asked, rubbing Day's smooth chest.

Day turned to face him with a sexy wink.

"It's real good. I'm just pissed that we could've been doing this four years ago." Day smiled.

"We weren't ready for this four years ago," God replied.

"Maybe you're right. Are you ready now, Cash?" Day turned serious eyes on him.

God used his thumb to tenderly stroke Day's bottom lip. "If you're asking am I going to hurt you or flake out, the answer's no. You know me, Leo. You're the only one who knows me. You're the only one that's seen this man in front of you right now."

"Do I know you, Cash?" Day whispered into the darkness.

"You will know all of me, but you'll have to wait until morning." God smiled, lightening the mood.

Day snorted at him and rolled out of bed, groaning like an old man and God had to hold in his laugh at Day's wide-legged walk to the bathroom. He heard Day cleaning himself up and he thought to himself while he waited. *He has a right to know.*

Day got back into bed and fully climbed on top of him, laying his head down on his chest. God laughed. "Uhh, sweetheart. You going to sleep like this?"

"Yep. I've imagined sleeping like this for years," Day said settling in comfortably.

God kissed Day's forehead and wrapped his arms around him, trying to calm his mind. *Please don't have a nightmare. Not tonight. Just let this night be perfect.*

The Truth is Revealed

Day woke at seven in the morning still settled comfortably on top of God's huge chest. It was like sleeping on a damn mountain… or a volcano. Damn God could give off some body heat. Day was sweating and so was God. Day slid off him and settled against his side.

God looked peaceful right now; Day hoped it was because of him that he'd not had a nightmare. He watched for a few more minutes before his admiration of God's beautiful body turned into intense lust and need. His cock was hard and ready for attention. Day slid down beneath the covers and leaned over God's semi erect dick. He licked his lips before taking all of it into his mouth. *Finally.* Day released a moan of contentment and licked around the head of the delicious cock before sliding back down to the base. Day had no gag reflex and he loved giving head as much as he loved fucking. He felt a large palm on his cheek and now that God was awake, increased the suction.

God moaned and spread his legs, allowing Day room to climb between them.

"Good morning, sweetheart," God said, his groggy morning voice sending tingles of pleasure to Day's balls.

Day answered with a fondling of God's balls and a slow, sexy lick along the large vein running up the underside of God's cock. He wrapped his mouth back around the head and went all the way down to the base again. God raised his hips and pushed the bulging head further down his throat. He swallowed a few times and God's palm moved from his cheek to the back of his head. God gripped his hair and held his face buried in scratchy pubic hair while he thrust repeatedly into his mouth. *Uhhh, yeah, fuck my mouth.*

"Leo, fuck. I'm gonna come," God moaned. "Ohhhhh… right fuckin' now. Auuugghh. Fuuuck!"

Day opened his throat and took every drop of delicious, hot goodness God had to give him. He swallowed until he was sure there was none left. He let God's cock slide from his lips and laid a tender kiss on the head before emerging from beneath the covers with a shit-eating grin. "Yes, it's a good morning now."

God breathed heavily while Day licked each nipple then tongued his way to the beautiful tattoos along the large biceps. The designs of Chinese art and intricate patterns wove around his side to his back. Leo loved the skull and crossbones engulfed in flames on his left pectoral muscle.

"I'm thinking about getting some more ink done," Day said. He had a Canterbury Cross over his left pec and a couple armbands on each arm… nothing major. Not like the beautiful art on the man that was splayed under him now.

"You hungry?" Leo asked between licks.

"No, if you mean for me to go out and get something. Yes, if you're going out to get it," God said.

"I mean I'll fix you something to eat, lazy ass." Day grabbed a large piece of God's flesh in his teeth, satisfied with the grunt he got from the big man.

"That sounds even better."

Day watched God's eyes meet his own. Beautiful green eyes stared at him for several minutes before he saw God turn away and take a deep breath. Day rose and fell with the movement. "If you're ready to talk, I'm ready to listen," Day whispered and lightly kissed God over his heart.

"Yeah, I think I am ready. Can we talk after breakfast?"

"Okay. Do you have something to do today?" Day asked.

"No. I want to go back to the hotel and change," God responded.

Day wondered if he should ask God about staying with him until he found another place. He didn't want to freak God out, they'd just said they loved each other, but it didn't mean they were ready to pick out china. He felt God's thick fingers under his chin, pulling him back to face him.

"Just ask already." God snorted a laugh.

Day rolled his eyes. Sometimes he forgot how perceptive they were with each other. Day could pick up most of God's thoughts, just like the man could pick up his. "Fine." Day grumbled. "Do you want to stay here with me? I'm not trying to clamp a ball and chain around your ankle or anything; I just thought economically it'd make more sense you know, not having to pay all that money for weeks when I'm right here with all this extra room. Then it'd be beneficial that you didn't have to travel to pick me up for work. We could split the housework, too because I hate raking the leaves and you don't seem to mind. Also, I thought—"

"Leo, shut the hell up." God's eyes were wide as he stared at him.

Day registered that he had rambled on; letting his nerves get the best of him while basically asking God to move in with him. The man was his partner but he was also so damned guarded.

"I could stay here with you until I find my own place." God kissed him on the forehead and nudged him off him so he could sit up and swing his long legs over the side.

Day had to fight to contain his excitement. Now wasn't the time to show his super serious partner his happy dance. Day just watched God run his hands through his deep waves. Hell, Day even liked the way the covers pooled between his bare thighs, just covering his soft cock that still shone from his spit. Day climbed off the bed and stood

167

in front of him. God wrapped his hands around Day's naked waist and kissed the slick hair between his navel and groin.

"Go fix breakfast while I shower," he commanded and popped Day's ass.

Day barely held in the hiss since his ass was still deliciously sore. He grabbed a pair of sweats out of the dresser, slipping them on as he headed down to the kitchen.

Day was pulling ingredients out of his refrigerator to make eggs Benedict—knowing how much God loved it—when his phone rang.

Day saw it was one of the detectives at the precinct and groaned quietly. *There goes my lazy afternoon.* He picked up after the third ring.

"This is Day." He listened to one of the surveillance detectives inform him of some glitches they may have regarding plans for the raid. The man said there would be a mandatory strategy meeting at two at the station and hung up without allowing Day respond.

It was only eight. That gave him plenty enough time to have a good chat and still get God's stuff to his house.

Day was just whipping the hollandaise sauce to pour over a perfectly poached egg when God wrapped him in his large arms. Day would never figure out how the hell the man could be so fucking stealthy at six foot fucking four.

"Smells good," God said, while licking the side of Day's two-day-old beard stubble.

"So do you," Day responded. He kept at his task, trying to ignore the persistent wood now pushing against his ass. He scooped a generous amount of potatoes onto both their plates. God released him and went to sit at the breakfast bar.

"An ex-boyfriend taught you how to cook, right?" God said nonchalantly while opening the morning paper Day had snatched off the porch before coming into the kitchen.

Day rolled his eyes. "Why do you ask that every damn time I cook something?"

"I do not." God harrumphed.

168

"Yes, you do," Day argued. "Then you say, 'Ummm, what was his name again?' Then I say for the millionth time, 'His name was Prescott Vaughan.' And then you say, 'Oh yeah, the miracle-worker chef.' And I just shake my damn head." Day couldn't help but laugh at God trying to hide his gorgeous smile behind the metro section.

"He is a miracle worker. Wasn't he like a great chef and then went blind, but somehow he magically built a huge culinary empire? I forget." God peeked over the edge of the paper.

"It wasn't a miracle, smart ass. He's just talented." Day looked over at God who was acting like he was no longer listening. "You know what else he can magically do? Those sexy boyfriends of his. He's in a three-way committed relationship." Day saw God peek back at him and then shrug.

"Uh-huh. They even let me join in once. Whew! Talk about fucking hawt." Day hid his laugh by looking in the refrigerator for some ketchup. Next thing he knew he was being hoisted up by massive arms, spun around, and slammed into the refrigerator.

God's eyes were electric. He held Day firmly against the cool appliance with his bulk and drove his thigh against Day's cock. "You fucked three men at the same time?" God snarled and bit Day's chin.

Day let out a startled grunt at the quick stab of pain, but it was quickly followed by a moan at the pleasure God's thigh grinding into his erection gave him.

"You thought they were hot, huh?" God thrust harder and grabbed a handful of Day's sensitive balls and squeezed.

"Ugh! You motherfucker," Day hissed. "No, Cash, fuck! I never fucked them. Hell, I've never even fucked Prescott. Jesus. Now put me down," Day yelled.

God stepped back and Day dropped none-to-gently down to the checkered linoleum floor. Day saw God smirk at him before sitting back down. He picked up the paper like nothing had happened. *Fucking bastard.* Day couldn't believe how insane God drove him. All that fucking brawn and strength was a crazy turn on for him.

169

Day plopped the plate down in front of his man, throwing him another eye roll before pouring fresh coffee. God had a regular sized mug while Day had a mug that resembled a soup bowl.

With all the condiments on the breakfast bar and their plates overflowing, they both began to eat as if they hadn't eaten in days.

"I have a question, Leo."

"Shoot."

"You dropped everything and went to see Prescott Vaughan a few months back when you said he sounded depressed."

"Yeah, and?" Day said around a mouth full of potatoes.

"Yeah, and, did you fuck him?" God asked, starring straight at him now.

Day swallowed his food, took a large gulp of his sweet coffee, and wiped his mouth before answering. "Didn't I just say I've never fucked him? Never means never."

God nodded his head like he understood. Day picked up their practically clean plates and put them in the sink. He was running some fresh dishwater when he heard God's gravelly voice.

"I killed my stepfather, Leo."

Chapter TWENTY-TWO

Now, Can You Handle the Truth?

God watched Day, checking his reaction to his confession. Day was a master at hiding his responses; it was what made him such a great interrogator. He never let his first reaction show. But God didn't want that, he wanted the truth. He needed to know how his man would feel about him after he'd laid it all out there.

"I need the real you, Leo. Not the disciplined detective," God stated.

He watched Leo turn off the faucet and dry his hands, never saying a word. He poured them two more cups of coffee, carried them by the handles with one hand, and grasped God's hand with the other.

God let Day lead them to his beautiful back porch overlooking a manmade lake. The screened-in porch was moderately furnished and equipped with a TV and mini-fridge. Day's house was definitely a bachelor's dream pad.

God sat down while Day adjusted the thermostat to knock off the chill. When Day sat beside him—their knees slightly touching—he looked into God's eyes.

"What did he do to you?"

God didn't know how he was going to be able to check his emotions. If he didn't already know he was in love with Day, he sure as hell knew at that moment. Day didn't ask why he had done it. He already knew there had to be a good reason, despite assumptions by

171

many that God had a hostile temperament. Day knew the kind of man he really was… he was caring, warm, and able to love. If he took a life, it was in defense of himself or someone he loved.

God huffed and took a couple more breaths before he released his secret to his best friend. No one knew this story except him and the DA of Clayhatchee, Alabama.

"When I was young, my mom and I really didn't have very much money. She was a single mom after the sperm donor she'd dated for about a month dumped her after she'd gotten pregnant with me. She did her best though. She worked at a local grocery store part-time, which was barely enough to pay the rent, much less keep us clothed and fed.

I was only ten when my mom got fired from her job for trying to steal some bologna to feed me. Her employer called the cops and even tried to press charges. Well, the cop that responded was a man named Jake Whittmen." God rubbed his hand through his now mostly dry hair.

"One thing led to another after he took her home instead of taking her to jail. Next thing you know… I have a new father." God huffed. He took a breather and watched Day take a sip of his coffee. His eyes were focused on the floor, but God knew the man was taking in even the minutest details of his story.

"Things were actually okay. He moved us into his small house in Clayhatchee, and it was better than where we'd been. It was obvious he never liked me, but my mom showered me with enough love so it was cool." God shrugged. "After my mom got pregnant with Gen, he seemed happy to have his own son so he laid off me a bit, and I tried to be invisible when he was home. I hung around with friends, did my football thing, and worked little odds-and-ends jobs to give money to my mom. All hell broke loose one day when me and him were arguing about me turning eighteen soon and still living there. My mom stepped in when he started pushing me around; he pushed her and she slipped and fell, breaking her hip." He gritted his teeth at the memories.

"While she recovered in the hospital, things turned from worse to flat-out unbearable. It didn't matter what I did he was on me. Gen was seven and I was seventeen. I was crazy about my baby brother. Still am. He was always with me if my mom wasn't home. I never left him home with dad." God put his hands up in air quotes when saying the word dad. "I didn't trust him with Gen, especially after the man had a few beers.

"Anyway, fast-forward a few months to me turning eighteen. He wanted me out. Trust me, I wanted to leave, but I had to protect them from him. I was big and he liked fighting with me... called it our own fight club, but really it was him taking out his frustrations on his own personal punching bag. He'd start a fight, usually when no one was home, then he'd tell my mom I was a troublemaker fighting at school and shit, or I was in a gang.

"He told me he'd take it out on my mom if I ever told the truth about my bruises. I didn't know if he meant it or not, but I refused to risk it. I'd seen him push her and hurt her before. I was in my room sleeping after football practice when he came in from fishing with one of his buddies."

God saw Day tense but he kept talking.

"He started letting his buddies have a go at me. It was getting harder to explain the bruises, and my mom started really pressing me for answers. I wanted to tell her so bad, but I wasn't sure if she would leave him and he'd turn into an even bigger psycho, or if he'd follow through on his threats to punish her if I told the truth. So I told my mom I was in a gang." God shuddered a breath. "She hated it. She and I grew further apart. When I tried to stop fighting with him and his friends, he said he would have a go at Genesis. I definitely wouldn't risk that. Maybe he wouldn't have abused his own kid, but I wasn't going to chance it. He was so damn drunk all the time by then, and his buddies on the force covered for him so he never got in trouble. One time he brought a few friends to my room who wanted to do more than fight. They held me down while two of the guys raped me. My dad wasn't in the room. He thought they were getting the best of me in a fight. After they were done they told my dad that I was a homo and I'd forced myself on them."

Day's head snapped up.

"Yeah, I know, that physically makes no fuckin' sense, but he acted like he believed it… probably to ease his guilty conscience. He let me recover for a bit, but it wasn't long before we were fighting again." God took a long gulp of his coffee to wet his dry throat. He couldn't believe how it felt to get this out, but it didn't make the memories any less bitter.

"The day he brought back those guys that raped me I think I lost my mind. I screamed for him over and over as they had their way with me. They left me bloody and I felt half-dead. After a few hours I hauled myself up to get cleaned up and he was in the kitchen still in his uniform, fuckin' eating a snack like nothing had happened. He started in on me. Calling me a faggot and telling me he wanted me out of his house immediately. He tried to fight me but I could hardly defend myself. He was beating the shit out of me when he pulled his service weapon." God took another shaky breath.

"Leo, I don't know for sure if he would've shot me. But after all the other shit he'd let happen, I fought for my life, I fought for my mom, I fought for Gen. I figured if I died, there'd be no one to keep him from hurting them. We wrestled around with the gun between us, and fell to the floor. The gun went off and I knew I was dead. We were both still for a long time until I realized that my pain wasn't from a gunshot wound. I pushed him off me and realized that he was dead, bleeding out from the bullet in his stomach. I managed to get up and I picked up the weapon off the floor. Of course, just like a damn movie, my mom and Gen walked in while I was standing over a dead body holding a weapon. My mom started screaming, Gen started wailing. I tried to explain, but she was afraid of me, telling me to stay away from them. I dropped the gun and ran.

"I slept in the park that night, the pain so fucking intense I wished for death. I ended up turning myself in. The police officers were not so gentle with me after I killed one of their own, but one officer believed me. He brought the DA to me and they got me to a hospital. There was clear evidence of long-term violence and gang rape. They didn't prosecute me, I was never charged, it was deemed a justifiable homicide. All the medical records and legal documents were sealed for my protection.

"When I got out of the hospital... I didn't have a family anymore. My mom let me grab a few things, but said she never wanted to see me again, that the gang I was in that told me to kill my father could be my family. She wouldn't let me anywhere near Gen either. I went to a homeless shelter and a couple of nuns helped me to set up residence to finish school." God finally looked at Day, he wasn't crying but his eyes were glistening and God realized that his eyes burned with unshed tears too.

"I made it through school and did one tour in the military before I joined the police academy. Since then, I've taken care of her and Gen from a distance. They don't know it's me that got them their house and pays for everything they need." God saw Day put it together immediately.

"That's why you don't have any money. Because you give it all to them," Day stated.

God nodded his head.

"Things may be different now."

God nodded his head again. "I went over there to fix the sink the other week. They came home early and saw me there after not seeing me in years. Let's just say, Gen was nicer the day he came to my place than when he caught me in their house."

"Your house," Day amended.

"No, Leonidis. It's their house. I'll take care of them until I can't anymore." God looked seriously at his lover, telling him it wasn't up for debate.

"Fuck, babe. Why didn't you tell me this before?" Day was up and pacing, his mind going a mile a minute.

"It's not exactly something you want to talk about while eating burgers and playing pool, Leo." God sighed like the story had drained him of energy. He closed his eyes for a couple seconds but when he opened them again Leo was on his knees in front of him.

"I want you to know that I appreciate you trusting me with this, and understand that it doesn't change a goddamn thing between us. But it kills me that you would rather your mom hate you for the rest of her life than tell her the truth." Leo ran his strong hands up and down God's thighs.

God put his large palm on that gorgeous face and placed his forehead gently against Leo's. "Thank you, sweetheart, but I'm okay with this. This is the hand life dealt me. But now I have you, right." God said it more as a statement of fact.

"Yes. You have me for as long as you want me." Day held him back.

God inched forward on the couch and pulled his lover to him. He kissed Day with all the passion and love he could. They rubbed and nipped at each other for several minutes before God pulled back.

"I know you better than you think, Leonidis, and under no circumstances are you allowed to try to fix this. I think you may be right. I think it may be time to tell them the truth, but in my own time, okay?" God licked Day's parted lips.

"Okay," Day whispered.

"Also"— God hugged Leo to him, rubbing his palms over the strong muscles in his partner's back— "thank you for taking such good care of me when I was sick. I may have been pretty out of it, but I remember a lot of it too. I think I knew then that you were the

176

one, the only one that would be there for me and have been for the past four years. I love you, Leo."

Day kissed him back and God pulled Leo into his lap, letting those strong legs straddle him. They'd had enough true confession time. God was feeling raw, exposed, and he needed his man now.

God gripped Day's ass, the cheeks soft flesh over hard muscles. He ground Day down against his hard cock while sucking Day's tongue into his mouth. "I need you so fucking bad right now, sweetheart." He breathed harshly.

"Take what you need you, baby," Day answered with a hard thrust of his hips.

"Mmm. Fuck." God dug inside the back of Day's sweats and kneaded the flesh before he let a couple fingers graze that tight hole. He felt Day jump at the touch. "You sore?" God nuzzled Day's neck.

"Not too sore for you. Need you inside me, babe." Day licked God's neck. "Uhh. You smell so fuckin' good."

God pulled one hand from inside Day's pants and brought his fingers to his lover's swollen lips.

"Open," he growled. God pushed his fingers inside and watched Day suck his two fingers into his mouth and swirl his silky tongue around them. God leaked precome in his pants while his hips pumped reflexively.

He pulled his fingers out and reached back around to Day's ass. He tapped against the quivering bud a couple times before pushing in one finger. Day's body went rigid for a split second before he relaxed and whispered for God to keep going.

God made quick work of getting his man ready. Day was writhing on his three fingers, moaning and whispering God's name again and again.

"Need a condom," God said breathlessly.

Day leaned over and pulled condoms and lube out of the coffee table drawer. God stared at him for a couple seconds before taking the condom and slick. "We're going to talk about this later."

Did Day really have condoms and lube stashed all over his house?

Day tried unsuccessfully to hide his smirk. God rolled the condom onto his aching cock and applied a generous amount of lube. Day got up and turned around, putting his back to God's broad chest. God let Day position his cock at his entrance and ease down onto him at his own pace.

God gritted his teeth at the perfect view of his cock being swallowed by this sexy man.

"Oh my fucking god. Leo, fuck," God groaned through gritted teeth.

Leo's back muscles rippled as he sat fully on his lap and he felt him breathe deeply while leaning back to kiss God on his lips. God gripped Day's hips and moved him back and forth on his cock.

The back of Day's head rested on his shoulder and God buried his face in the soft blond hair. "You feel so fucking good."

God let his partner set the pace. Day rocked his hips back and forth, keeping God's cock buried fully inside him. God spread his legs wider and inched down further on the couch. He gripped Day's chin and turned his face, kissing him again. It was sloppy, wet, and erotic. They moaned into each other's mouths and Day began to move faster, his breath panting with each gyration of those talented hips.

"Mmmm. Fuck yeah. Ride my cock."

Day brought both his arms up and wrapped them behind God's head. God rubbed Day's lithe chest and twisted the shiny black barbells in the erect nipples, wrenching a sexy moan from his man. God began to thrust up into that tight, perfect heat. Day's tight ass brought on his orgasm faster than he wanted.

"So perfect." Day gasped. "Right there, Cash, right fuckin' there. Gonna make me come. Touch me."

God thrust harder and stroked Day's rigid length in time with his thrusts. Day's cock was like a steel rod wrapped with satin. Day grabbed God's hand off his cock and licked the calloused palm from wrist to fingertips before guiding it back to his dick.

Holy fuck that was hot. God jerked Day a few times with his slick hand before he went completely still on top of him and ground the back of his head into the juncture of God's neck.

"Fuck, I'm coming!" Day yelled.

God felt the hot come run down his hand. Day's ass rippled and seized around his hard dick. God's eyes were half-lidded, his orgasm rocketing to the surface so fast he felt light-headed.

"Make me come, gorgeous," he moaned.

Day brought both knees up and placed his feet flat on the couch and rose almost completely off God's length before slamming back down again.

"Oh fuck!" God yelled, slamming his head back against the couch.

Day continued that move until God barely understood what the hell he was saying. He was probably promising Day a kidney if he'd just continue doing that on his cock. God tried to hold off coming, but couldn't any longer. He grabbed Day's hip and yanked the man down onto him while he pumped his hot jizz into the condom, wishing that the thin latex barrier wasn't there and he was heating his lover's ass with his come.

"Leo, dammit. So hot."

God rested his sweaty forehead against Day's shoulder while he labored to catch his breath. They lay there a couple more minutes before Day moved to settle beside him. He turned and kissed Day on his mouth, gently sucking his supple bottom lip into his mouth.

"Love you," he moaned while still sucking.

"Mmm. Love you too." Day smiled.

"What's so funny?" God asked while pulling off the condom, tying it, and dropping it in the wastebasket. He pulled Day close to him and buried his nose in his soft hair again.

"Everyone thinks you're this hard, evil, tough, sonofabitch that no one can get close to. And I have you snuggled up next to me, whispering sweet nothings in my ear," Day teased.

"Oh yeah," God said in his gruff voice. "Well I don't give a fuck what others think." God kissed Day again. "Only you."

Day kissed God back and began to stroke his already rising dick when God turned up the heat. He put his hand over top of Day's and stroked with him.

"You better stop. We still have to run some errands today." God licked Day's shoulder, tasting his sweat.

"I know. Oh yeah, and we have to go in for a meeting," Day said matter-of-factly.

God stopped stroking. "Nice you tell me now. What time is the meeting? You better not be fucking me while we're missing a meeting." God pinched Day's ass.

Day yelped and got up off the couch. "No, of course not. While it may be worth it, I wouldn't do that. The meeting's not until two. So we got time to go get your stuff and bring it back here," Day said while pulling up his sweats.

"All right, then let's shower and get going." God smiled at Day.

"I love that smile of yours that's reserved only for me." Day paused and brought his hands up to God's large chest.

"You're the only one that cared enough to make me smile. Now stop trying to start something we don't have time to finish." God grasped both of Day's hands and kissed them before spinning Day around and directing him back up the stairs.

He's Mine Hands Off

God had sucked Leo off in the shower when his hard-on wouldn't go away. He couldn't take his eyes off the big man as water sluiced down his body, weaving over all those muscles. Day knew he had it bad, he was crazy about God.

As God drove them recklessly to the hotel, Day thought about work.

What the hell could be going wrong now?

When they pulled up in the mostly empty motel parking lot, Day surveyed the area. It wasn't in the slums of Atlanta but it wasn't in the ritzy part either.

God got out and Day followed behind him to a room located on the first floor. When God opened the door, Day immediately had to check his first reaction. The hotel room was musty and offered the bare minimum as far as amenities. There was a king-size bed in the middle of the room and Day wanted to cringe at the thought of lying on it. There was one night table with a telephone and a 2005 phone book. The covers on one side of the bed were pulled back and Day thought about God tracking him on that app and springing out of bed to chase after him.

The small, two-person wooden table had two uncomfortable-looking chairs underneath it. The television was an older model but it did have cable, so that was a small plus.

"Stop looking like that, princess. Just needed a place to crash... it was temporary," God admonished him.

Perhaps Day wasn't checking his face as well as he thought. "You should've come to me in the first place. Before we became lovers last night... we were still partners," Day said and sat at the table while God re-packed his toiletries. Day noticed the empty soup cans on the table. "How's your throat feeling?"

"Fine time for you to ask after you've had your tongue down it most of last night and this morning." God half laughed.

Day flipped him off.

"It's fine, babe. Thank you for sending Jax yesterday too." God looked sheepish while he changed into something more appropriate for work.

"What do you think is going on with the case?" Day changed the subject. He didn't want to think about the fight they'd had ever again.

"Honestly, it could be anything. We're talking about a kingpin. He could have gotten word that the heat is coming down and could've gone underground. Could've changed the shipping schedule to throw off the Coast Guard. Anything to fuck up our plans," God said, picking up his weapons.

Day watched God eject the clip of his Eagle, check it, and pop it back in with ease. He cocked the barrel once before putting on the safety and snapping it in his holster. Day had to get his rising hard-on under control. He pushed his palm into his groin and shifted in the hard chair.

"Having some problems over there, gorgeous?" God threw him a sexy wink.

"Why?" Leo slouched down farther in the chair showing his bulge. "You gonna fix my problem?"

God walked toward him with that long-legged, lazy gait and smiled down at him. God had his deep waves pulled back with a thin band. His goatee freshly shaved. A tight black T-shirt and dark jeans hugged him in the most delicious way. His black Desert Eagle was large and in charge and Day wanted to throw God on the mattress—bed bugs be damned—and fuck the hell out of him.

Day rose until their chests touched. God stroked the back of his hand down his cheek and leaned in to kiss his forehead. They stared at each other for a few silent seconds before God finally spoke. "We gotta go." He leaned in and flicked Day's hard cock; then licked his lips. "Later," he promised.

God opened the door with his one large suitcase in his hand and tossed it in the back of the truck.

Day climbed in first and asked. "Where's the rest of your big stuff?"

God smiled. "Joker brought his guys and put everything in a SWAT van and stored it in his garage. I only had like five pieces."

"So he was the one you called to come to your rescue, huh?" Day asked and slammed the door to the truck.

"Hey." God turned Day's chin to face him. "I swear on everything, I was miserable for those few hours and you know it."

Day pffted.

"I tracked your ass down, didn't I." God stated.

"Yeah, you did." Day laughed when he thought about God scaring off his boy toy. He laughed so hard that God started laughing too.

They strolled into the precinct ready to hear what the heck was going on with their case. God dropped into his chair and Day sat on top of God's desk. Immediately one of the second precinct lieutenants approached them.

"Detective Godfrey, I heard you were sick. You doing better, man?"

"Yeah, I'm good," God said.

"Good. We need everyone at one hundred percent and fully operational."

Day watched the tall man look him and God over as if they were under inspection. Day frowned and stood up. "I'm going to get some coffee." Day walked off, leaving God to answer the unnecessary questions.

As soon as Day turned into the kitchen he skidded to a halt. *Fuck, not right now.*

"Well hello, Day. I was hoping to see you today," Detective Johnson continued stirring his coffee.

"How's it going?" Day said dryly and went about setting up his coffee machine.

"It's going better now that I'm seeing you." Detective Johnson moved to stand over him. Day had to practically reach around the tall man to start the machine. "Dude, want to give me a little room here?"

"No. I like being close to you." Detective Johnson ran one long finger slowly down Day's chest.

"Well fuckin' unlike it." They both jumped at the sound of God's gruff voice.

God walked up to Day and grabbed him by the back of his neck. He spun Day around so hard that he dropped the small packs of sugar to the floor. All he could do was hold on to God's massive biceps as he ravaged his mouth. Day let God completely control him until he was done proving his point. God released him and Day practically fell back into the counter.

"Fuck, Cash," Day whispered, completely out of breath. After Day got his wits about him, he noticed that God and Johnson were in a serious stare off over his head.

Johnson broke first and looked down at Day.

"You're fucking God now?" Johnson asked disbelievingly.

"Okay, it just sounds wrong when you say it like that, so I'm not going to comment." Day inched away from the two giants and propped himself up on one of the break room tables. "I think I'll watch this one from the sidelines."

"You're goddamn right he's with me. So you have to find someone else to harass every day, Johnson." God huffed. "Or are you going to run and tell daddy?"

Johnson stepped closer to God and Day watched God's non-reaction to the detective's scowl.

"I didn't know you batted for my team, God."

"Johnson, even if you were on the all-star team I wouldn't bat for your team. I'm with Day and that's just it." God crossed his arms.

"Well a man like Day requires commitment, effort, someone to put in full-time work. You are more of a detached from society kind of guy aren't you, God? I mean are you up for the type of job required to keep him as yours?" Johnson smirked and took a sip of his coffee.

"Yeah, I know all about that job, Johnson, because I worked the hell out of it last night." God stepped in even closer and mock whispered. "But you know what the difference is between me and you and our jobs? I usually quit mine; you end up getting fired. But seriously. You can stop applying with Day, because the position's been fuckin' filled." God caught the muffin Day threw at him and walked out the door.

Day did very little to hide his grin as he drank his coffee.

A.E. VIA

The Gayest of Them All

The meeting went almost four hours. They had received inside knowledge from an informant posing as a dockworker that the schedule had been changed and the shipment was coming in tomorrow, not three weeks from now.

They had no choice but to go ahead with the raid tomorrow. Everyone had their assignments. God and Day would be on the grounds rounding up suspects, and their primary target was the kingpin. They stood outside the conference room talking with a few of the department heads. Day had a hard time concentrating with God looking at him like that. True he would always think of God sexually, but he also knew that this takedown was going to be dangerous. What if he lost God when he'd just officially gotten him?

They estimated about forty-to-fifty men on the dock, not including those coming in on the container ship. This was not their first raid by far and God and Day operated like a well-oiled machine, but somehow this one felt different.

This is why they don't like couples working in the same precinct. Fuck. I need more coffee.

Day left God talking with the captain while he went in search of another refill. Day was sipping on a fresh cup of Mocha coffee with French vanilla cream when Johnson approached him.

"Are you and God seriously together, or were you just fucking with me?" Johnson asked in lieu of greeting.

Day groaned and turned toward his current headache. "That's an awful lot to go through just to fuck with you, don't you think, Johnson?"

Johnson threw both hands up in a gesture that said he didn't give a shit. "Hey, whatever floats your boat, man."

Johnson dug in the fridge and popped open a Coke. He turned back and Day thought immediately Johnson was going to try to convince Day he was making a huge mistake.

"So do you have any recommendations?" Johnson asked, not looking Day directly in his eyes.

"W-what?" Day stuttered. "Are you asking me who you should boink?"

"Jesus, Day, no." Johnson waved his hand at him. "You know what… never mind."

Day felt a little bad for Johnson. Maybe the guy was kind of lonely… perhaps in need of a good, hard boinking. Day was actually deep in thought when God strolled in with a thin file folder.

Day put down his cup and pointed at the file. "What's that?"

"It's nun-ya," God said opening the refrigerator.

"What?" Day frowned.

"Nun-ya business." God smirked.

"Oh you're just full of corny-assed jokes today aren't you, darlin'?" Day threw a packet of sugar at him.

God came up and kissed Day on his forehead. When Day looked over at Johnson, who was still slowly sipping his soda, the guy did look lonely as hell. Before Day could say something kind, his other headache strolled in.

"Oh hell. What the fuck is going on in here? This must be the officer's gay alliance club meeting."

Day blew an exasperated breath. "And now that you're here, Ronowski, all members are present and we can begin."

Day smiled as God and Johnson practically spit their drinks out laughing.

Ronowski fumed. "Day, you're going to stop calling me gay! I have never been gay! I will never be gay, and I don't like anyone that is gay! So stop saying that before people start believing your bullshit!"

Day clapped his hands together once. "Okay everyone those are the notes from last week's meeting, now on to new business." Day leveled Ronowski with a stern glare. "Ronowski, you are gay, man. You're tightly closeted. But you are indeed gay, ultra-gay. You're fuckin' Marvin Gay. You crash landed on Earth when your gay planet exploded." Day moved away from God and stood in front of an openmouthed Ronowski. "Come out of the closet already. It's so bright and wonderful out here. Dude, I've seen *Brokeback Mountain* too, don't believe that bullshit. No one cares who you fuck… ya know… like you tell me every. Single. Day. Of. My. Life," Day said exaggeratedly.

He stepped in so close to Ronowski that he could smell the body wash he used.

"Let a man bang your back out one time." Day leaned in to the man's ear and felt Ronowski's body give a fierce shudder. "I mean pound your ass so hard that you can't walk straight for a week, and I guarantee you, you'll want to march in the next gay pride parade, wearing nothing but a glitter jockstrap and a fuckin' hot-pink feather boa." Day stepped back and saw the beads of sweat that had popped up on Ronowski's forehead. Satisfied he'd proven his point; he refilled his coffee and left the break room.

God raked the leaves in Day's front yard while Day cooked their dinner. Both of them were quiet, no doubt the seriousness of tomorrow's raid weighing heavily on their minds.

What if he gets hurt… or killed?

God could barely breathe when he thought about that. He figured the only way to ensure that didn't happen was to keep Day by him at all times. God bagged up the leaves and set them at the curb.

He kicked off his boots before walking through the living room. Day's house was very nice. It had been his grandmother's and she'd left it for him in her will. Day did a lot of renovations on the three-bedroom, two-story home, and God found himself wishing he had a family to share that type of home with. He could see himself sitting on the large leather sofa in the den with Day snuggled up next to him, his mom baking them raisin bread, and Genesis upstairs blasting his music too loud. God shook his head at the nonsense and went in the kitchen to find the one thing he had in his life that was real. Day loved him, and as far as he was concerned, that would be enough for him.

He washed his hands at the deep sink inside Day's kitchen. The appliances were plentiful and spread around on the vast counter space, all of them either chrome or black. Name-brand pots hung on a mahogany pot rack over the large island in the middle of the black-and-white checkered, high-gloss floor. God pulled a bottle of water from the stainless steel refrigerator and inched a few feet over to press his body against Day's while he stirred a red sauce on the six-burner gas stove.

God buried his face in Day's neck and whispered behind his ear. "That smells really good, sweetheart. What is it?"

God saw the corners of Day's mouth turn up into a satisfied smile.

"It's chicken cacciatore," Day answered while scooping a small amount of sauce on the spoon. He turned around in God's arms and put the steaming spoon to his mouth.

God sampled the rich sauce and moaned at the succulent flavors. It was absolutely delicious. "Mmm. That tastes really good."

God looked around. "Is there something you want me to do?"

"Yeah. Stop moaning like that before I throw myself on that island and let you lick this sauce off my ass." Day gave God a quick kiss and turned back around to his sauce.

"You're a slut." God laughed and jumped out of the way before Day could swat him with the messy spoon. God perched on one of the three breakfast stools looking over the kitchen and picked up a *Guns & Ammo* magazine that was lying there amidst the day's mail. He flipped through the magazine, not really paying attention to the articles before asking Day, "So did you learn to cook that from your chef friend... what's his name again?" God said nonchalantly. A potholder hit him in his forehead, making him look up from the magazine in mock horror.

"You know damn well what his name is, and I'll be damned if I'm going to talk about Prescott Vaughan every time I cook us dinner." Day glared at him around a sexy smile.

God winked and let his man get back to cooking.

"So how about a movie tonight?" God asked.

Day's smile was bright with his response. "Yeah, babe, that sounds good."

God wanted to take that beautiful smile and hide it somewhere where no one could ever take it away. Day loved him and God didn't know why he'd never paid attention to it. Probably the same reason he didn't realize he'd been falling for his best friend for so long. It's like they say. Sometimes it takes almost losing someone to realize how much you'd miss them if they were gone.

"Go upstairs and wash up, you smell like the outdoors. Dinner will be ready in five," Day said while pulling out fixings for a salad.

"Sure thing, dear." God chuckled hoarsely. He was just out the door when he peeked his head around the corner. "I love your apron, wifey." God laughed and ducked quickly to avoid the carrot flying at his head.

"What woman do you know that wears a NASCAR apron?" Day argued to God's retreating back. "Plenty of men wear aprons, thank you very much. It's all about keeping your clothes clean. It's practical!" Day yelled even though God was upstairs.

God was still smiling when he went into the guest room for his suitcase. He looked in the closet and under the perfectly made bed. He even pulled out the drawers of the armoire on the far side of the room, but couldn't find it. He was about to go back downstairs and ask Day when he turned down the long hall and walked into Day's master bedroom. His suitcase was tucked neatly in the corner. He pulled it out but it felt empty. He looked in the first dresser; it held Day's clothes. A second, identical dresser was on the other side and God did a double take at his few toiletries that were neatly aligned on top. God rubbed his hand on the smooth surface and felt his heart clench at how domestic this looked.

His and his dressers... really.

God yanked off his T-shirt and threw it in the hamper along with Day's items. He washed up quickly and went back to *his* dresser to put on a clean shirt. His mouth dropped when he pulled out the dresser drawer. His shirts were neatly folded and placed in an organized arrangement. God went through all five drawers. His underwear, socks, shirts, and sweats: each arranged neatly and in its own place.

He dropped down on the bed and thought for a minute. At first he was joking, but Day really was domesticating him. Was God ready for that? Sure he loved Day, he'd take a bullet for him, but was he ready to play house? He pinched the bridge of his nose with his thumb and middle finger at the tension forming behind his eyes. God had been completely on his own since he was eighteen. He'd never shared space with anyone—hell, no one had ever wanted to.

Fuck. Just last night Day was getting ready to fuck mini Justin Bieber, now he was cooking and cleaning for God and doing his damn laundry. He tried to shake off his anxiety. He never used the word love lightly. He meant what he'd said last night. God had only loved three people his entire life and for the past four years only one of them returned that love. Should he really tuck tail and run just because this was new territory? *Hell no. All he did was unpack my suitcase. No big deal. He was just being hospitable. Damn sure is better than that seedy hotel.* "My boyfriend's just trying to make me comfortable." He smirked and tried the term on his tongue again. "I have a boyfriend."

"Get your ass down here and stop overthinking shit! Dinner is getting cold!" Day yelled from the bottom of the stairs.

Why did he always forget how well his partner knew him? God threw on his clean T-shirt, pushed the drawer shut, and jogged down the stairs. Day was standing there looking embarrassed. A bright red flush was creeping up his neck and settling in his cheeks. God stepped down to the last step and tilted Day's chin up so he could look into beautiful hazel bedroom eyes.

Day shrugged. "I just thought you'd be more comfortable in my room. I have a better mattress than what's in the guest room, it's one of those memory foam ones… ya know… better on the back. Also the other room only has one dresser which I guess wouldn't be a problem because you don't have a ton of stuff but I have the better shower with the ultra-pressure showerhead, and my TV's better too, I even have the Hustler's porn channel. I'm not saying I watch it but if you want to, then—"

God put a thick finger over Day's motor mouth, silencing his nervous babbling. He rubbed his finger back and forth over Day's plump bottom lip. He leaned in and whispered, "Thank you," before he kissed his boyfriend with as much love as he could put into a kiss. When he finally released Day's mouth, he let his lips linger there and spoke against Day's panting breath.

"I'm hungry. Feed me, sexy."

Chapter TWENTY-FIVE

From Partner, To Lovers, to ... Oh No. Back to Partners

God sat on the couch with his feet propped up on the ottoman. Day was stretched out down the length of the sofa with his head on a pillow in God's lap. They had enjoyed a great dinner and both were beyond full. The action flick they'd decided on was now almost over.

Day turned and looked up into God's eyes. He couldn't stop the satisfied sigh that left his body when he felt a large calloused hand cover his cheek. He'd wanted this kind of attention from this man for so long and now that he had it, Day felt like he was a boy and it was Christmas morning. He smiled lazily at his partner. "You getting tired, babe?"

"Yeah. I know you're not though," God said continuing to stroke his cheek.

"You know I can't go to sleep this early," Day huffed.

"If you didn't drink twenty cups of coffee a day, then maybe you could sleep. I think I'm going to cut your coffee intake by half, and see if that cures your self-inflicted insomnia," God said, laughing at the horrific look on Day's face and put his hands up in surrender. "Okay, forget I said that. Goodness."

God dropped his smile and his usually vibrant green eyes shaded to a forest green, dark with lust. God let his hands trail down Day's bare chest.

"Maybe I can think of another way to make you sleepy."

195

Day's back arched at the coarse touch of God's hands.

"I'm game for suggestions," Day murmured.

God pushed the ottoman out of the way so he could bring his legs down. He bent over and licked Day's lips before letting his tongue dive in for a taste. Day moaned at the bitter taste of the two beers God had consumed while watching the movie. Day's cock was already at full mast. God was so damn addictive to him, almost like his coffee. God sucked on his tongue like it was his cock and Day arched up again. His dick leaked in his jeans and he scrambled to free it from confinement. When his weeping cock hit the cool air Day hissed and stroked it a couple times before God caught both his hands and placed them over his head to rest on the arm of the couch.

Day grunted at the restriction. "I need."

"I know what you need. Now leave them there," God commanded.

God skimmed over Day's erect nipples and twisted the barbell in one, then the other. He attacked Day's mouth again and let his hand move down his muscled torso to his shaved pubic hair.

"I like that you trim these." God scratched at the prickly stubble while he nibbled on Day's bottom lip.

Day didn't get a chance to respond because God wrapped his cock in his large palm. His hand fully closing over his girth, he began to slowly stroke him. God swiped at the precome on the third stroke and it made his rough hand glide easier on the hard steel.

"Oh fuck." Day practically cried. God wasn't trying to prolong this; he was pumping Day's cock hard and fast. The squeeze and twist he gave his cockhead on every upstroke was fucking perfect. "Make me come."

Day felt more so than heard the deep growl that God released into his gaping mouth, and Day's orgasm hit him so hard all he managed was a split second of a hoarse shout. His mouth wide open in a silent yell, God licked all around and inside while milking every last drop from his dick before he stopped jacking him. Day hadn't realized his back was bowed in a C-shape until he released his breath and dropped back down to the sofa's cushion.

"Jesus Christ." Day gasped. His chest rising and falling rapidly. His eyes fluttered when God began to lick his fingers clean of Day's come. "Shit, you're gonna make me fucking come again doing that."

Day pulled God's fingers from his mouth and licked some of his own come off the thick digits. He leaned up and captured God's mouth, groaning at the taste of himself. "Need to taste you now."

Day loved God's dick. He was sure God had very few, if any lovers that could swallow his full eight inches. Day would show off his talent for as long as the sexy man would let him.

He flipped over and tossed his pillow to the floor. He could see God's hard dick bulging in his jeans. Nimble fingers undid the button and lowered the zipper. Day buried his face into God's black briefs and took a long whiff of his man's heady scent. He let God lift up and pull his pants and briefs down to his knees.

Just like God didn't make him suffer, Day was happy to bestow the same courtesy. He swallowed all that hard goodness in one gulp and buried his face in the prickly hairs at the base of God's cock. He felt God grab both sides of his head and he smiled inside. He wanted this man to come completely undone. Day wanted to satisfy him in every possible way so that he never had the urge to want for another… male or female.

Day pulled up slow and applied just the right amount of suction and teeth. He placed tiny nibbles on the full mushroom-capped head before diving down again. He could feel God's strong thighs trembling with the need to thrust into his warm heat. Day pulled back again and licked God's throbbing cock like it was a coffee flavored lollypop. He looked into his lover's lust-filled eyes.

"Fuck my mouth, Cash. Do it hard too, don't hold back." Day didn't wait for God's answer. He opened his throat and dropped all the way back down on the hard shaft.

"Fuuuck," was the long drawn-out groan Day heard as he felt God slouch down lower and spread his legs wider. The grip on Day's head tightened to almost painful and God began to ram his cock down Day's throat. Day squeezed his eyes shut, braced both hands under him, and took each punishing thrust. God's hips were strong and unforgiving as he pushed Day's head down with each upward drive.

"Take it all, Leo. Every. Fucking. Inch," God growled between lunges.

Day was loving every second of this blowjob. God's nasty talk had Day's cock twitching and filling up again. A few seconds later, God's thrusting became erratic, right before Day was rewarded with hot, salty come spurting down his throat. God held him down, not letting him move until he was completely spent. Day concentrated on breathing through his nose until God released him.

So motherfucking hot.

God unclenched his hands and began to stroke Day's hair, letting him know it was all right to come up for more air. Day let God's cock slip from his mouth and felt the big man jerk when it released with a *pop*.

"Damn, sweetheart. I had no idea you could take it like that," God said, breathing heavily and pulling his pants back up.

Day pulled his jeans over his ass but left the button undone.

"I haven't been able to let anyone do that in a very long time. I have a hard time trusting people," Day admitted and wiped the moisture from around his mouth.

He stared into God's eyes for several seconds and could see that the man believed him. God pulled him close and placed feather-soft kisses on his swollen mouth before releasing him. God stared at him trying to communicate with his eyes, but Day was having a hard time understanding this time. It was definitely something heavy that had his partner stressed.

198

God placed their foreheads together and let out a shaky breath before speaking. "Leo, I want you to stay right next to me tomorrow during the raid."

Day frowned in confusion and felt God tighten the hold on his neck.

"I mean it, sweetheart. You stay right next to me the entire time." God finally looked up into Day's eyes.

Day gently pried God's hand of his neck and kissed his palm before responding.

"I've had some pretty crazy thoughts about tomorrow too, babe. Been feeling like I wouldn't survive if something happened to you out there. But I contemplated and decided that you are a damn good cop and an even better partner. We've watched each other's backs going on five years. But you can't start thinking I need you in the role of bodyguard instead of partner now that we've become lovers."

Day dropped to his knees and kissed God's hands again before trying a different approach, because God's scowl meant he wasn't liking Day's answer so far.

"You're going to have to trust that I'm the same man and cop that I've always been. You've never doubted my ability or skills before, so if you want us to succeed as lovers and work partners, please don't start now. As much as I'd love to ask you not to move from my side either, I'm not going to emasculate you like that. We are God and Day, and together we've taken down some of the baddest motherfuckers in this city, because we are lethal as a team." Day sighed and rubbed his forehead tiredly. "But you can't turn me into the bitch of our team and tell me to stay tucked under your arm. Because if Captain gets wind that we're a couple and he feels it's interfering with our work, either you or me will be reassigned to another precinct. Then I'd have to quit because I'm not trusting anyone else to do this job with me. Tomorrow we go out there together as God and Day and take this fucker down, then when it's all over, we come home together as sweetheart and baby, and we celebrate with a nice hard fuck." Day smiled broadly at God's sexy grin and rose up to hug him. They embraced for a long time, neither wanting to let go. They both knew that tomorrow was going to be as real as it gets and one of them might not come back home.

Chapter TWENTY-SIX

Super Cops

It was six in the morning and God was sitting on the small chest at the foot of Day's bed tying his boots. He kept glancing up at his lover and saying silent prayers for the Almighty to keep him safe today. God was in his usual black T-shirt but he had on black cargo pants instead of his Levi's. He took his silver chain with his badge off his dresser and draped it around his neck. He hooked his gun holster and secured both his weapons before turning around to see Day leaning against the doorjamb waiting on him.

Day had on a black APD T-shirt with black cargo pants too. His boots were black steel-toed and laced up tightly over his pants. His badge was hooked to his hip and today he chose to carry his two chrome 9mm handguns in his holster. He'd trimmed his beard and had a little product in his hair, making it spike and stick out in the artfully messy way the models wore it. He looked delicious and deadly at the same time.

God tucked his wallet in his back pocket, snatched his keys of the nightstand, and dropped them in the side pocket of his pants. He turned off all the lights and slowly walked over to his man. Day was resting against the door and God propped one arm on the wall and leaned in to come into full contact with him while they were still just lovers.

They both had their eyes closed while they let the moment of silence be all that they needed. Perhaps Day was praying for his safety too. God finally opened his eyes and Day followed a few seconds after.

"I love you. Be safe," God whispered.

Day placed a firm grip on the back of his neck and God felt a power surge through him like he'd never felt before. He placed one of his hands on Day's neck too, hoping he'd somehow feel the same strength.

He watched Day grit his teeth at his touch, obviously feeling something strong. God crushed their lips together in a brutal kiss. It was raw, fierce, and full of promises. Promised to be safe. Promised to have each other's back. Promised to come home tonight.

When it was imperative that they breathe, God released Day's mouth. Their breathing was ragged and labored as they tried to calm their racing hearts. God knew they had to go but neither one was moving. He couldn't move until he heard Day say it too. God looked into those light-colored eyes and he knew the minute Day recognized what he needed.

"I love you too, Cashel."

The huge lump in God's throat prohibited him from speaking, so he nodded his head okay and turned to lead them down the stairs and out of the house.

The ride to the precinct was gravely quiet, but this wasn't uncommon. While things had changed dramatically with their personal relationship, things hadn't changed when they were getting into fight mode.

When God pulled in to the station they saw the parking lot was full of cars they weren't used to seeing. They had SWAT, sharpshooting teams, State Troopers, divers, Coast Guard, and countless task-force detectives from surrounding precincts. This was a collective effort by the city's officials to rid it of a virus that was killing the heart of their state.

As soon as God and Day walked into the chaos of their unit they were immediately pulled apart by administrative officers that were assigned to get them fully geared up with radios, wires, and vests.

Once God was fully set and weighed down by the heavy armor, he made his way through the throng of people to his desk. He looked up and tracked Day through the station and saw him heading to the break room, no doubt for his morning fix. He thought of following him but decided against it.

He's not my sweetheart right now.

Day was trying to make his coffee with all the extra goddamn weight on him and it was frustrating the shit out of him. He knew it was for his safety but, fuck. He needed to hurry up and get some coffee in him and get his head right for the fight. It was seven a.m. and in fifteen minutes the department heads would be getting the teams set to roll. Everyone knew their role; no more meetings were required.

Ronowski and Seasel came into the break room; both of them noticing the seriousness on Day's face and decided to simply fix their coffee and leave. Day shook his head in wonder. He could only imagine the look he must have on his face if Ronowski didn't want to risk fucking with him.

A loud siren pierced through Day's thoughts and he recognized the call for them to load up. Day headed out to the yard and eased up beside God. He discreetly rubbed the backs of their hands together before crossing both his arms over his chest. God looked down at him and gave him a slight wink before turning his attention back to their captain.

Once they were loaded in their police van along with Ronowski, Seasel, the captain, and four other officers from their precinct, the driver got the signal and they took off toward Interstate 75 South for the three-and-a-half-hour drive to the Savannah Ports.

Day settled his head back against the headrest and closed his eyes, afraid if he kept them open he'd only stare at God. Somehow the time passed fast as hell; like it tends to when you're going someplace you didn't want to go. The teams were getting into their positions. They were assuming the ready positions after receiving a confirmation that the cargo ship was in port as of a half-hour ago, which meant it was still loaded.

Alpha team, assigned to board the ship and confiscate its cargo had already rammed through the security gate and was moving fast across the ground to the pier. The security guards that were watching the gate and grounds were detained quickly.

Day held onto the handles above their heads as their driver sped onto the dock, positioning them several feet from one of the five hangars on the port... the one containing their kingpin. The other vans got into their positions as well. Some teams were there to make arrests, while others were responsible for collecting evidence, tactical support, and many others for a multitude of other duties.

The back double doors to their van swung open, and they moved quickly to the outer perimeters with their weapons pointed to the ground, surrounding the building within seconds. Day watched the other teams get into position at the surrounding hangars.

During the last meeting it was decided that an explosive would be used for breeching. This method required less strategic planning, a necessary change since they had lost two weeks of valuable planning time. Their combat engineers needed twenty seconds to place the small explosive charges on the doors and clear. The SWAT team leader's deep voice came across their earplugs with a fast count and a go on three.

Day felt God's heat beside him but his eyes were trained on the hangar bay doors. Day heard "three" then a loud bang as the doors exploded. They stormed in within seconds of the debris settling.

There were multiple booming voices yelling out "Freeze!" "Don't move!" "On the ground!" "Hands high!" "Georgia police!" as most of the dockworkers dropped to the concrete and others began to scramble behind anything that would provide them with cover.

The entire force had orders to treat everyone on the scene as hostile until proven otherwise. With the limited surveillance they'd been able to amass, it was unknown which of the dock workers were dirty and which were legitimate. If they were actual working for the state of Georgia, then they would be expected to surrender.

Day kept both his weapons trained in front of him while he moved with their unit further into the building. So far so good, everyone was cooperating. Bravo team was coming in to make arrests and load everyone into the extra vans. Day felt an eerie feeling slither down his neck, meaning trouble was coming. Day estimated about fifteen men were being taken out quietly as more officers and SWAT scanned every square inch of the hangar. Day turned to signal their group to move upstairs when all chaos broke loose.

A hail of gunfire from what sounded like automatic weapons erupted on the south side of their hangar. They ducked for cover behind large crates quickly trying to locate the shooter. Day's radio crackled on his shoulder.

"Officer down! I repeat: officer down with a fatal gunshot wound to the neck!"

Day cursed when he noticed more men with automatic weapons moving up the far side of the hangar and he quickly pushed the talk button on his mic. "We got multiple bogies coming in on the south side. Look alive!"

Day and God both began firing in the direction of the large garage-like doors on the far side of the building. This had to be their kingpin's army. Day could hear gunfire from the surrounding buildings as more voices came across the radio reporting emergencies.

Fuck!

205

Day gave a hand signal for Ronowski, Seasel, and two other officers to move to the other side so they could provide gunfire from both angles. He, God, his captain, and another officer laid down cover fire for them as they ran quickly to their position. Day gritted his teeth as bullets flew in their direction.

Day and God were back to back as always, watching all around them when God's recognizable gruffness came across the radio.

"Got a positive visual of the package. I repeat a positive visual of Joe Hansen, our kingpin. Upper level, hangar four, moving north, wearing a black suit accompanied by five heavily armed men, approach with extreme caution."

Day turned quickly and saw their kingpin moving down the stairs at the north end surrounded by human shields. The man had on a black suit with a red tie and black dress shirt. His guards had Smith and Wesson handguns aimed and ready to fire. Day cursed as Hansen was ushered into a room that had an exit into a back corridor with limited visibility.

Other team leaders were strategically placing their officers to get into a flush-out position and Day did the same. They moved in closer to the rooms at the back and Day saw bullets fly in from over their heads, the sharpshooters effectively taking out three of the kingpin's five-man guard.

Semiautomatics rang out in the hangar, Day and God dove behind a couple of metal barrels. Day saw God check the label on the container, careful that they weren't hiding behind anything explosive. God gave him a thumbs-up. When there was a brief pause in the fire from the dockworkers, Day and God rose simultaneously and opened fire, both men almost emptying their clips before they had to duck back down. As soon as they did, Ronowski's team rose and opened fire.

A loud scream pierced the air, and Day looked over to see Ronowski dragging Seasel into one of the back rooms.

Day clicked his mic on. "Officer down! Gunshot wound to the right arm."

Vikki had been hit.

Sharpshooters fired at two men closing in on Ronowski as he tried to tend to his partner. Day heard the SWAT leader yell through his bullhorn.

"You are completely surrounded. Lay down your weapons and come out with your hands up!"

Day leaned against God's back and peered around their cover. Two ducked heads were moving fast along the back end, trying to stay low and effectively moving out of sight of the sharpshooters firing from the rooftops seventy yards away. Day turned and saw that the back corridor intersected with the room where Ronowski was tending to Seasel's wound.

There was still too much gunfire going on for Ronowski to safely move Seasel out the back exit. Ronowski didn't even have his weapon out as he stayed low and used both his hands to apply pressure to the wound that was bleeding profusely. From where Day stood, he could see that Vikki had gone very pale and she wasn't moving. Ronowski was shaking her and yelling her name.

"Ronowski!" Day yelled but the gunshots were too loud.

The last of the dockworkers were either out of the building being taken down by the outside team, or were lying dead inside. But Hansen and his last bodyguard were closing in on Ronowski fast, obviously planning to use the room as a means to get to the outside. Ordinarily they'd fire in a couple of flash grenades and temporarily blind their suspects, but they had two of their own in close range.

Day had a split second to think. If he didn't move now, as soon as Hansen and his man entered the room, they would fire on his teammates.

"Cover me," Day yelled and took off toward the room.

"Day!"

Day heard God yelling for him, but he had no time. He barreled through the door, startling Ronowski, and charged into Hansen's guard as he turned the corner into the back door of the room. The hallway behind the rooms was narrow and there were few windows. He grappled with the bodyguard in the confinement of the small room. Neither man could fire their weapon nor could Hansen get past them. The bodyguard had at least three inches and forty pounds minimum on him.

Day slammed the large man into the wall, grasping the lapels of his suit jacket, yanking him away and spinning him around to slam him into the other wall. Day dropped his weapon as the man elbowed him in the ribs. With both hands free, Day connected rapidly successive punches with both fists. He landed at least half the hard blows to the man's face and kneed him with all his might in his stomach.

He vaguely saw Hansen turn and try to run in the opposite direction but gunfire from the sharpshooters stopped him as soon as his head came into view through one of the windows.

Day took a hard left to his temple before he kneed the man in the groin, causing him to crumble to the floor. He stepped back and kicked the guard square in the chin with his steel-toed boot, propelling the man back into the corridor.

Day turned and yelled to Ronowski, "Get her out of here now!"

Ronowski needed to get Vikki out of there and to medical attention fast while he had the chance.

Ronowski had just barreled through the side door leading outside when Day spun around and came face to face with his own chrome 9mm handgun that he'd dropped during the fight. Hansen had an evil glare in his eyes as he waved it at Day to move over toward him.

"Keep your hands where I can see them," Hansen snarled quietly through clenched teeth.

Day heard the SWAT leader on his bullhorn again.

"Joe Hansen, you are completely surrounded. Come out with your hands up or you will be fired upon!"

"Day, what's your position goddammit?" God's voice was strained coming across the mic on his shoulder.

The look Hansen gave him clearly told Day he was not to answer his partner.

"Do you really want to be charged with murdering an officer of the law?" Day said calmly, trying not to reveal his fear while staring down the barrel of his own gun.

"Shut up," Hansen snarled.

"That's the death penalty," Day said.

"I said shut up," Hansen growled, grabbed Day by the shoulder straps of his bulletproof vest, and put the gun to his forehead.

Day closed his eyes and took a deep breath… this was it.

A.E. VIA

Chapter TWENTY-SEVEN

Have You Ever Met the Devil?

God watched Day run to Ronowski and burst through the door like Superman. From God's position he couldn't see what was going on inside, but he knew Seasel was shot and needed medical attention. Day had EMT training and his brother was a trauma surgeon, so God assumed that's why he ran in after them.

God stayed low and focused on the bullets still flying around in the hangar. It was probably only a couple minutes, but it seemed longer until all of Hansen's army were overpowered and taken down.

God rose slowly along with the other officers, but stayed alert.

"Day, what's your position goddammit?" God growled, angry that Day had run off. God waited a couple seconds but didn't receive an answer.

God removed the mic from his shoulder and yelled directly into the speaker. "Day, come back... what's your twenty?"

God looked at the now closed door Day had barged through and spun around to his captain.

God faintly heard the door across the hangar open before registering the look of complete horror on his captain's face as he stared past God.

God closed his eyes, turned around in slow motion, and opened them knowing what he was going to see. Before him stood the love of his life with a 9mm pressed against his right temple and a very angry drug lord peering carefully around him.

211

God watched Hansen take a quick look behind him before speaking.

"I will blow his goddamn brains all over this floor if you don't back up!" Hansen's thick Southern accent echoed in the large building.

God vibrated with rage as he stared into his partner's eyes. Day was telling him to stay calm. God felt his vest being pulled from behind and he took a few steps backward before stopping.

"Easy, Hansen. You don't want to do this." The SWAT leader's voice was clipped but calm. "Put the gun down and step away from the officer."

"Shut up," Hansen screamed. "I want a car at the side door driven by one of my guys within three minutes or I kill him."

"Hansen, stay calm. Don't do anything that's going to get you killed. If you shoot him, one of these many officers is going to fire on you." The leader reasoned. "So think about whether you want to live or die. You pull that trigger; your life ends now, but if you surrender you can have one of your high-powered attorneys make sure you get your day in court."

"Don't try to con a con man, officer. I know all your tricks, and you're talking this man's fucking time away!" Hansen yelled.

God saw Hansen tighten his chokehold on Day until his lover was fighting to breathe. Day's ears and neck were bright red. His lips were darkening as his body was deprived of oxygen. Hansen pressed the barrel in deeper.

"Two minutes and fifteen seconds before I provide the great state of Georgia the luxury of one less narc," Hansen yelled.

God's mind exploded at the thought of living in a world without Day. He looked into his partner's glistening eyes; seeing him turning blue and nearing the point where he would faint. Day was still looking into God's green eyes.

No, no, no! He's saying good-bye.

God closed his eyes and released a loud, gut-wrenching growl, cutting off the SWAT leader's negotiations.

"Godfrey, get yourself under control," his captain said, trying to hold onto him.

God jerked himself out of the hold and stepped forward, his angry eyes boring into Hansen's. Hansen stared at him as if God were crazy. Little did he know, at that moment God *was* a little crazed.

"Godfrey, get back here and stand down. That's an order, Detective!" his captain barked.

God's large hands clenched at his sides, fighting his instinct to pull out his weapons. He ground his teeth so hard his jaw ached.

"Do you have any idea of the shit storm you're about to bring down on your life?" God snarled menacingly while his large frame shook with fury. "In your arms you hold the only thing in this world that means anything to me. The man you are pointing a gun at is my sole purpose for living. You are threating to kill the one person in this world that gives a fuck about me."

God took two more steps toward Hansen and was vaguely aware of the silence surrounding him. Hansen's finger hovered shakily over the trigger as he took two large steps back, Day still tight against his chest.

God growled again and he saw a shadow of fear ghost over Hansen's sweaty face.

"If you kill that man, I swear on everything that is holy, I will track you to the ends of the earth, killing and destroying everything you hold dear. I will take everything from you and leave you alive to suffer through it. I will bestow upon you the same misery that you inflicted on me."

Hansen shook his head and inched closer to the door behind him.

"Stay back," he yelled again, but this time the demand lacked the bravado he'd exhibited before.

"You kill that man, and you have no idea the monster you will create. Have you ever met a man with no heart... no conscience... no soul... no purpose?" God rumbled, his voice octaves lower than his already deep baritone.

God yanked his Desert Eagle from his holster in a flash and cocked the hammer back, chambering the first round. Hansen stumbled back again, his eyes gone wide with fear.

God instinctively tensed every muscle in his body and it felt like the large vein in his neck might rupture. His body burned as it had at the height of his pneumonia and he knew his wrath had him turning a brilliant shade of red.

"I'm asking you a goddamn question, Hansen! No soul! No conscience! I'm asking you if you've ever met the devil!" God's thunderous voice practically rattled the glass in the hangar windows.

"If you kill the man I love, you better make your peace with God, because I'm gonna meet your soul in hell." His voice boomed.

God slowly raised his gun and aimed it at that bastard's forehead, but God knew he wasn't going to have to take the shot.

Hansen took one final step backward and as soon as his heel landed, a single loud *pop* rang out in the silence. A split second later Hansen's head jerked back from the impact of the bullet lodged in his skull.

God had talked him back far enough that he was within visibility of the sharp shooters.

God caught Day's falling body before he was able to hit the floor. He dropped to his knees with his lover in his arms and held him close.

"Breathe, Leo." God coaxed while rubbing Day's cheek. He felt Day take in a few quick breaths before he opened his eyes and stared up at him.

God closed his eyes and pressed their foreheads together, not wanting to see what Day was saying.

"If he had killed you, I would've swallowed my own gun. There's no life without you," God whispered just for Day to hear. He felt Day grab onto his neck, holding him close.

"Let the paramedics take a look at him, Detective Godfrey."

God raised his head at his captain's order and slowly lowered Day's head while he moved back to let them tend to his partner. God watched them closely while they took a few quick vitals before placing him on the stretcher. One of them turned to look at God and his captain. God stepped forward.

"His blood pressure's high and pulse is erratic, so we're going to take him to the hospital to be monitored. He'll be at St. Mary's."

"I'm riding with him," God demanded.

"I'm sorry sir, but regulations don't allow that." The thin guy answered him as the other paramedic wheeled his man away.

God bared his teeth right before he felt a hand come down hard on his shoulder.

"Let them do their jobs, because you still have one to do too, Detective. Is that going to be a problem?" His captain leveled a hard stare on him.

God paused for a second, then gave a quick jerk of his head and turned in the opposite direction that his love had gone. God walked through the hangar aware of the many eyes that were on him. He just wanted to finish his job so he could go home.

A.E. VIA

A Truths

God was staring blankly at the forms laid out on his desk. How the fuck was he supposed to do paperwork right now, when all he could think about was Day? The empty chair directly across from him didn't help.

He almost felt like a kid being scolded by his teacher. "You can go out to play as soon as you finish your classwork."

Several officers had stopped by to ask about Day, all of them avoided mentioning God's psychotic threats against the kingpin. Hell, if his coworkers weren't afraid of him before then, they sure as fuck were now.

Day had called him as soon as the doctor left his room and told him that Jaxson was already there and would take him home soon. He asked God to be home when he got there and God was not going to disappoint him. He drowned out the whispers and stares in his direction and focused on completing his paperwork.

He'd just closed the file and was putting it on his captain's secretary's desk when the captain yelled for him to come into his office.

Fuck. If he says Day and I have to split up, I'm going to flip his desk over on his head.

God walked in to the small corner office and dropped into the hard wooden chair. He dragged his hand tiredly through his hair before speaking with a sigh.

"Sir."

"That was some performance you put on today." His captain sat back in his squeaky chair and stared at him.

"If you say so, sir," God responded.

"But it wasn't a performance was it, Godfrey."

God figured it wasn't a question so he didn't answer. He simply stared the man in his eyes until he spoke again.

"I think I'd know your response if I told you that I don't let couples partner together in my precinct." The captain leaned forward. "After what I witnessed today; you'd probably tell me to kiss your ass and no doubt Day would follow suit, and then I'd lose the best damn narcotics detectives in Georgia."

The captain looked hard at him and pointed a thick finger in his direction.

"If I hear of any problems with you two that aren't the usual headaches you numb-nuts give me... I mean any relationship problems, and I will split you up so fast you won't know your ass from his."

God couldn't stop the sly smirk that appeared on his mouth.

"Oh get the fuck out," the captain huffed, and God chuckled and stood to leave.

As God turned the knob to open the door, he paused.

"Any word on Vikki, Cap?" he asked.

God looked at his captain's weathered face.

"She's going to make a full recovery. She had to have a transfusion but she'll regain full mobility of her arm after physical therapy."

God was shaking his head at the good news when his captain added.

"By the way. You guys are both on leave for two weeks."

God frowned.

"Day needs to talk with the department shrink and do the mandatory six sessions and so do you," he ordered.

God opened his mouth to argue, but was silenced by a thick palm raised and a hard glare.

"This isn't up for debate. It's departmental procedure and you will both damn well follow it."

God turned to leave again.

"Hey, God."

God watched the captain stand, walk from behind his desk; and extend his hand to him.

"Damn good work today, son."

God took his captain's hand and gave it a firm shake. The wise man held his hand an extra second before releasing it. His captain didn't need to say anything else. The man could've lost several detectives today, but they'd all come through… maybe with a few war wounds, but they'd survived. They'd survived to fight together another day.

God left the office. He stopped by his desk to grab his coat and walked through the bullpen and out the front doors. He stopped mid-step when he saw Ronowski leaning against the front of his truck looking dog-tired.

God approached the man and looked him in his eyes. He could see the battle fighting behinds those sparkling blue irises.

God decided to speak first. "Cap told me Vikki's going to pull through. That's good news, man. You saved her life." God clapped the man on his back and moved past him to the driver's door. He needed to get home.

"No."

God turned at Ronowski's lone response. "What?"

He finally let his eyes focus on God's. "I didn't save her." Ronowski wrung his hands together. "Day did. He saved both of us. I treat him like shit all the time because he knows the truth about me and he almost got himself killed to save me."

God slammed his truck door back and came back to stand in front of the young man. God called him young because he looked it.

219

The boyish good looks and smooth, even-toned skin gave the man an innocent appearance. In all honesty Ronowski was gay-porn-star beautiful and any gay man would be very happy to satisfy him nightly… if the man would just be true to himself.

"Day did what any of us would've done if we'd been in his position. He was the only one that could see Hansen and his guard, so he reacted," God tilted the man's chin up to face him, "just like you would've done for him."

God saw Ronowski's eyes flutter before focusing on God's lips as he kept a firm grip on his dimpled chin. God stepped in closer to the man and noticed the increased breathing and rosy flush that crept slowly up those tanned cheeks.

God's voice was gruff, and he let it wash over the confused man.

"That feeling you're having right now Ro? Stop fighting it. That'll be a good way to thank Day."

God was surprised when Ronowski nodded his head. God dropped his hand and looked up when he saw Detective Johnson exit the precinct, heading to his BMW. He called out to him and saw the tall man squint to see them in the dark parking lot and God waved him over.

Ronowski looked scared when he asked God what he was doing.

"You shouldn't be alone tonight." God's tone clearly indicated it was a command not a suggestion.

"Hey, God. I heard Day is doing good and headed home. That's fuckin' awesome, man." Johnson stuck his hand out to shake God's and God gave it a couple good pumps before he released it.

"You never have to worry about me overstepping my bounds again. I promise you that." Johnson looked God in his eyes, and he knew the big man was giving him his respect.

"I appreciate that, Johnson," God responded.

Johnson released a harsh breath. "Well. Guess I'll go on home and see if a ball game is on. See ya." Johnson turned to leave.

"The Braves are on tonight," Ronowski called out to Johnson's back.

God had to close his mouth, gaping open in surprise.

Johnson turned and wasted no time asking the blond beauty if he wanted to watch the game with him.

Ronowski flushed when all their attention was focused on him.

"Uhm. Sure. I just need to get my stuff. I'll be r-right back," he stammered and walked quickly toward the precinct.

God saw Johnson watch Ronowski's ass move as he walked; not taking his eyes off him until he was inside the building.

Johnson turned back toward him and waggled his eyebrows. "Well my night is looking brighter."

God just shook his head at the now extremely happy man. He looked in Johnson's eyes and put on his serious face.

"You know that man's story already. He's just starting to believe what Day's been saying to him for years, but he's scared as fuck. If you hurt him in any way, Day will hurt you."

Johnson stopped grinning and looked back at God. "I thought Day hated him?"

"Day is complex, Johnson. He's crazy about Ronowski, that's why he rides the man so hard."

"I get that," Johnson responded. "All right. I don't mind doing the slow thing. We'll start with wings and a game tonight." Johnson shrugged and started inching toward his car. "Next week, maybe dinner and a movie."

"Sounds good, bro." God waved and climbed in his truck. Now that he was done playing Chuck Woolery and there were no more love connections to be made. He was going home to his sweetheart.

A.E. VIA

Chapter TWENTY-NINE

I Can't Lose You

"Jaxson, I'm fine really, and I won't be home alone. God is living with me now... remember?"

Day tried to reason with his stubborn big brother. Jaxson maneuvered the small sedan into Day's driveway and Day's heart rate picked up at the sight of God's truck already there.

"Oh and when did Cashel get a medical degree?" Jaxson huffed. "You may require medical attention in the middle of the night, and I won't be there."

Day smirked. "The only attention I'll require in the middle of the night won't require you being there to give it to me." Day winked. "The right man for the job will be there."

"You're a perv." Jaxson laughed. "Okay, okay. Just take it easy for the next few days and call me tomorrow."

"All right." Day leaned over and gave Jaxson a wet, sloppy kiss on the cheek until the man was pushing at him to get away.

Day laughed and grabbed his hospital bag that held his personal items. He looked at his brother.

"Thanks again for coming, Jax. I'll call you tomorrow. Tell Lisa I said hi and I love her."

"Will do," Jax replied and put his car in reverse.

Jaxson backed out of the driveway and Day gave him one final wave before walking up his Ardesia Stone pathway to his front door. Day didn't tell his brother everything that happened during the raid.

Only that he'd got caught in a bad situation and the captain thought he should get checked out medically before going home. Jaxson didn't like the vague answer, but Day wasn't ready to discuss the details with anyone else... not until he spoke to God.

He used his key to enter and noticed that not one single light was on downstairs. He went into the kitchen—not bothering to turn on any lights—took a couple bottles of water out the fridge and dragged his tired body upstairs.

He could hear jazz playing quietly as he walked down the hallway, and despite his exhaustion a smile crept across his face.

Day opened the door slowly and squinted at the dark figure standing in front of his window. There were no lights on in the bedroom either, only the light filtering in from the streetlamps outside.

God hadn't turned around. His back muscles were taut. He had one long arm braced against the top of the windowsill. He was shirtless and his sweats were hanging low on his hips, and Day could just barely make out the fierce lion on God's back in the pale lighting. Day could smell the freshness of God's shower. He dropped his bag and placed the water on the dresser.

"Cashel," Day said softly, his throat still sore from being choked.

God turned around slowly and faced him. Day choked up at the pained expression on his man's face. He could see that God's eyes were moist and red-rimmed. Day inched toward him and didn't stop until he was pressed against that broad chest. God's strong arms came around him and squeezed him hard. The guttural moan the man released against his temple made Day's heart seize.

God pulled back and gripped a handful of Day's hair, pulling so that he was looking up at him. God bent down and gently grazed his soft lips across his. Day's body vibrated from the sensual feeling. God rubbed his face all over Day's as if he were a cat marking him with his scent. God's grip tightened in his hair and he moaned again. Day could feel God's body trembling and Day didn't know at that

224

moment if the shaking was from residual fear or need, so he didn't move as he let his lover do what he needed to do.

God released the punishing grip and his large palms shook as they ghosted over Day's face. His chin was tilted up by firm fingers and again was blessed with feathery-soft kisses. God leaned back in and draped his arms completely around him and Day embraced him back. The soft piano from the album serenaded them and God just barely rocked their bodies back and forth in a very slow dance. Every few seconds he'd stop to place kisses on his forehead before leaning back in.

When the album finished and the needle lifted, God looked down at him and finally spoke, his voice much more hoarse than usual.

"Shower, sweetheart. I'll be waiting for you in our bed."

Day didn't want to release God, but he did and went into the bathroom, leaving the door open. He undressed quickly and got under the powerful spray. He scrubbed away the sweat, blood, grime, tears, and fears he'd been dirtied with today. He felt so much better after his third wash and finally shut off the taps. Day made quick work of drying his body, brushed his teeth, and walked back into the bedroom. God was already in bed, his large form taking up the entire right side of the California king-size mattress. The stark white sheet was draped loosely over his lower half. Day walked over, grabbed the two bottles of water, and set them on his nightstand just in case he needed them. He climbed onto the tall bed and was grabbed by strong hands and settled on top of his naked lover.

"Cash," Day moaned.

"Shhh. Just need to hold you," God said quietly as he rested his chin on top of Day's wet hair and squeezed him hard against him, protecting him as if someone might come in the middle of the night and try to snatch him away.

225

Day rose and fell with God's steady breaths. It was only nine-thirty but it wasn't long before Day's exhaustion had him drifting off to sleep.

He was jerked awake only a few hours later by God's twisting and grunting. Day was being squeezed to death and he was barely able to lift his head to glance at the small digital clock beside the bed. The bright green lights said it was a little after three in the morning.

Day jumped at the loud shout God released into the dark room and struggled to free his confined arms so he could wake his lover.

"Cash, wake up!" Day tried to hold God's massive arms down as he fought the attacker in his dreams.

"Cash, stop! Wake up!" Day yelled.

"No! Don't!" God grunted, thrashing beneath Day's weight.

Fuck.

God was so much stronger than Day and he worried that God would think Day was someone else and start attacking him if he didn't snap out of it. He was completely on top of God and trying to keep from getting hit. He shook God fiercely and saw him open his eyes wide in terror.

It all happened in the blink of an eye. God locked Day's arms behind his back and rolled, pinning him down to the mattress and pressing his full weight down on him. Day's heart rate skyrocketed at the realization that God wasn't awake yet.

"Cash, it's me! It's Leo! Wake up dammit!" he shouted at God and bucked to try to free his hands trapped painfully behind him. His large biceps bulged and flexed with everything he had. He needed to be able to put up his guard. If God started to swing, he had to be able to block the blows.

God blinked again and Day saw the reality seeping in. God's head jerked back and forth looking all around the dark room.

"Cash, its Leo. Look at me. Look at me," Day said quickly.

Cash turned and looked down at him and it broke his heart when God squeezed his eyes shut and let go of Day's arms. Day

226

knew God felt horrible, not only from the nightmare but from potentially hurting him too. Day held in the groan of pain caused by bringing his hands from behind his back and wrapped them protectively around God. He pulled God down to his chest.

"I got you, Cash. It's all right, it's just a dream," Day whispered softly while stroking God everywhere that he could reach.

God's heart was beating so hard Day could feel it against his own bare chest. He dug his fingers in God's long hair and massaged his scalp. God squeezed him back.

"He shot you. I couldn't get to you in time and he shot you," God said through ragged breaths.

"Fuck," Day hissed and held God tight to him. "No. You did get to me in time. I'm right here with you. You saved me. You will always save me."

Day opened his legs and let God sink in between them.

"Damn, I love you so fucking much," Day whispered.

Day placed kisses on the side of God's face while God had his nose buried in his neck, breathing him in. They lay still while both of their heart rates returned to normal.

Day moaned softly when God began to grind his hard pelvis in to him. Day's cock hardened almost instantly and he felt dizzy from the fast rush of blood to his groin.

"Mmmm. Fuck, yeah. Do it, Cash. Take what you need from me," Day spoke with his lips pressed to God's ear. His man needed to be assured that he was fine and right here with him. That God had saved him.

God brought both his hands down to Day's thighs and pulled them up so his feet were flat on the mattress on either side of him. The nightmare had left him hungry with need and power. Although in the dream, God didn't get to Day in time and Hansen had shot his lover, God had torn the man apart with his bare hands. His coworkers were yelling and cheering him on like at an underground, to-the-death cage fight. He growled, beat, and clawed at Hansen until the man was nothing but a large mass of blood, his limbs thrown in various directions from God's rage.

He woke up and he was on top of Day and it'd scared him. He didn't want to ever hurt him while he was asleep, he'd never forgive himself if he did. But Day was strong and capable. Although he was smaller than God—most men were—Day was muscled and fit. His strong chest had defined pecs and flat, ripped abs. His shoulders were sculpted and his biceps had thick veins that protruded when he flexed the large muscles. Day would fight back if he had to and God would be damned if that thought didn't make him crazy with lust.

Day was underneath him, driving his own hard cock up into him, and demanding that he take him now. God grunted with each hard thrust and bit Day on his shoulder to keep from yelling when Day gripped his aching cock in a tight fist and stroked it roughly.

"Fuck me, goddammit," Day cursed.

Day fumbled in the nightstand for the lube while they continued to hump each other like wild teenagers. When Day pulled out the supplies, he threw the condom at God and barked at him to put it on.

God's hands shook profusely while trying to pull the tight latex over his dick as he watched Day lube his own fingers and push two of them forcefully into his ass. Day's teeth clenched and his eyes slammed shut while he fucked his fingers, quickly reading himself for him.

He's mine.

God pulled Day's fingers from his ass, gripped both his wrists, and slammed them against the padded headboard, pinning his hands to the soft leather. He held Day in a submissive position with one hand and used his other to line his cock with Day's tight hole. He looked into Day's eyes and saw that his man understood what he needed. He pressed his mouth to Day's pursed lips and at the same time rammed his cock inside him until his balls slammed against Day's ass.

They screamed in both agony and bliss. Day's ass clamped God's cock in a viselike hold and scorched his dick with a heat that burned him to his toes. God didn't wait for Day to adjust. He pulled out to his head and plunged back into him repeatedly.

This was not going to be gentle, it wasn't going to be pretty, it was going to be fast, brutal, and uncontrolled. God held tight to Day's wrists above his head with one hand and dug into Day's smooth ass cheek with the other, pulling him open wider.

God's head was buried in Day's neck and he lived in his man's screams as he pounded his ass. Day was his and only his and anyone that challenged him would feel his wrath. His orgasm exploded and he roared loud enough that if Day had close neighbors they'd be calling the cops. He pushed in to the hilt and pumped his come into the rubber, filling it to capacity, again wishing he didn't have that fucking barrier.

As soon as he could he was going to make sure they were disease free and he could shoot his come so deep inside his lover that he'd taste it.

God panted against Day's sweaty neck, his cock still semi hard and throbbing. He just barely inched his hips back and let his cock slip out of its silky confinement. He realized his stomach was not only drenched from sweat but also Day's come.

Motherfucker.

Despite his brutality, his lover had gotten off, and judging by the amount of squishy mess between their muscled torsos, it'd been a damn good one.

God's cock rested against Day's hole and he absently pushed against the quivering bud. Day hissed and it made God latch his mouth onto the tender spot on Day's neck and suck as hard as he could. He was still satisfying his craving to mark Day as his own. If

229

he could have he'd probably have branded him with his name too. Somewhere very visible—maybe his forehead—God's Property.

Going Stir Crazy

Day woke up to the sun shining in his eyes; he turned to his back, and had to bite his fist to keep from yelling from the pain radiating through his ass.

Fuck, shit, damn, hell!

There just wasn't a curse word invented yet to describe how Day's ass was feeling at that very moment. *You better hope you got it all out of your system, Cash, 'cause I'll be damned if you're getting a repeat tonight.*

Day admitted to himself that although the first few seconds after God entered him were damn near torture, it did turn into some powerfully good sex that had him coming so hard he'd seen stars, and he'd never even touched his dick. It was just after eight in the morning and he knew God wasn't in the bed with him because there was no body heat coming from his side of the bed.

Day propped his elbow up, positioned himself carefully on his side; and grabbed the remote off the nightstand. As soon as he turned on the fifty-inch flat screen mounted on the wall, it flashed a special report about yesterday's drug raid and Day quickly flicked to another station… same thing.

What channel is Food Network? Shit.

Day quickly scanned the guide and selected a channel he knew wouldn't be reporting news of a drug kingpin being killed. He'd been there… lived it. He didn't need to watch it on television.

Day groaned at the reality cooking show that was on, but left it on anyway. He was just dozing back off when God came through the door carrying a tray. He wore a sexy smile on his face and no shirt... just muscles and tattoos on full display. Day couldn't believe his hole was actually clenching.

Glutton for punishment.

Day could see the newspaper hanging off one side of the tray, and a tall glass of grapefruit juice.

"I thought you might be a little, umm... sore. So I made you breakfast," God said proudly.

When God lowered the tray to the bed Day immediately had to halt his first reaction—which was to burst out laughing. Accompanying the newspaper and glass of juice was a small mug of coffee that was too dark for Day's liking, two pieces of burned toast with too much un-melted butter on them so the toast must be cold, and a big bowl of Cap'n Crunch cereal with a spoon large enough to stir spaghetti sauce.

God handed Day the coffee first. "Here. I know this is what you want first." God chuckled.

Day winked at him and took the mug. Day took a decent sip and cringed internally at the bitter, cold coffee. When Day looked closer into the mug, he could see quite a few coffee grounds floating around.

He looked up, gave his lover a genuine smile, and said, "Thank you, babe. It's perfect."

God looked so pleased with himself that Day vowed he was going to eat and drink every single thing on the tray. He picked up the toast, took a bite, and quickly chased it with some grapefruit juice. God climbed in bed from the other side and spooned him from the back, kissing him across his neck and shoulders.

"Are you feeling okay? Did I hurt you?" God asked in a low voice.

Day swallowed the mouth full of half-soggy cereal, almost gagging at the texture before answering God in a relaxed tone.

"No. You didn't hurt me at all. I'm a little tender, but it will go away soon."

"You're lying." God kissed his cheek. "I'm going to run you a bath in that swimming pool you've got in your bathroom."

"Only if you join me."

God kissed him again and went into the bathroom.

Day ate his food faster than humanly possible and scarfed down the horrific coffee in an effort to taste it as little as possible. He said a silent prayer that he didn't get indigestion and placed the tray on the floor.

He got out of bed and winced with each step he took into the spacious bathroom. God had the lights off and a couple candles lit on the outer rim of the Jacuzzi tub. He was already soaking, waiting for Day. Day licked his lips at the beads of water running down God's chest.

God lifted one corner of his mouth at him and that was invitation enough.

Day was already naked so he climbed inside the tub and settled between God's firm thighs.

"Jets or no?" God asked.

"No. This is relaxing just like this." Day leaned back, dropped his head on God's shoulder, and let the hot water soothe his soreness away.

"Oh shit." Day could feel God's growing erection poking him in his back.

"Relax, sweetheart, I'm not trying to do anything, but my dick has a mind of its own. You're just so fucking sexy." God kissed and licked Day's ear.

They were quiet for a long time and Day felt like he could fall asleep again until God's rough voice broke through his haze.

"You want to talk about it?"

Day took a deep breath and thought carefully about his answer. God massaged his shoulders with his strong hands and Day almost said he didn't want to talk; he just wanted keep being massaged. But there was something really important he needed to say.

"Cash. Thank you for yesterday." Day spun around in God's arms and faced him. "I've never been that scared in my life. At first I felt that if I died it would be okay, because I died while I was in love and the last thing I saw was your eyes. But when you said what you said." Day placed his palm over God's heart, felt the rapid beat there, and closed his eyes. "You said you'd have no soul, no conscience, and you'd take your revenge. That's when I got scared."

God cast his eyes down.

"You have to promise me. If anything ever happens to me that you'd go on. That's the only way I'd die in peace. You'd live for me. That you'd mourn me and then go on and love again. You've come so far in your life. The things you've endured made you strong. Some men have gone through less and it drove them to do unthinkable things because they couldn't handle what life dealt them. But you lived through it and now you're a highly respected detective." Day gripped God's chin and lifted his head. He kissed him passionately. "And you're the man I love."

Day didn't need God to answer him in words, his eyes and his kiss said it all. He told Day that he'd live for him.

God cared for his body; washed, massaged, caressed, and kissed him until Day was completely pliant and ready to lie back down.

Nothing else would need to be said about what happened in that hangar. They were partners and now they had an understanding. God told him that the file he'd gotten from the captain the other day was his medical proxy. He'd made Day his official. Day would have the authority to make any and all decisions regarding his medical care if he was ever injured on the job... or in life. God trusted him with his life and Day trusted him too. Enough said.

After a long nap they woke midafternoon with no idea what to do with themselves. They had two mandatory weeks off. God wasn't pleased with that at all, especially since their five-year anniversary as partners was coming up soon. That was a big deal for cops. Partners came and went all the time, but God and Day had been rock solid from the beginning. Five years with the same partner was a huge milestone celebrated throughout the department.

Day rolled his eyes and asked God to relax when the big man kept getting up and pacing around the house. God said he didn't want to lose momentum at work. Although they'd got the kingpin there were always more. The war on drugs was never ending.

Day had grabbed him and thrown him down on the floor in the den and sucked him off after God threw the remote control across the room and screamed that reality television was the stupidest shit anyone ever thought of. After the blowjob, Day took the remote and found a good action flick.

When it was over God rose and stretched his long body. "I'll fix us some lunch," he said and headed toward the kitchen.

Day's eyes widened and he shot up from his relaxed position, chasing after God. He barreled past him.

"No. I'll fix us lunch!" he practically yelled.

God quirked one eyebrow and stepped slowly away from the refrigerator.

Day calmed himself and lowered his voice to sound more nonchalant.

"I mean you made breakfast, it's only fair." Day shrugged and went about pulling out the fixings for some subs.

God still gave him a strange look, but nodded his head as if he understood and sat at the breakfast bar.

Whew. I don't know if my stomach could handle another one of God's meals.

Over lunch, God told Day about the exchange he'd had with Johnson and Ronowski when he'd left the station last night and Day

235

almost fell of his stool. He pumped his fist in the air at the victory and grabbed God's face and laid a loud, wet kiss on his cheek. He was so glad his lover decided to push his two biggest headaches together. Johnson could definitely give Ronowski the pounding his stubborn, tight ass needed. Once that happened, Day's hours at work would go way more smoothly.

Two hours after lunch and God was back to driving Day fucking nuts.

God had just come back in from cutting the already very low grass and was now sitting on the recliner in Day's bedroom aggressively pushing the buttons on the remote control flipping through the channels.

"Get cleaned up and let's go to Henry's," Day said.

Henry's was a great sports bar that had awesome all-you-can-eat wings, pool tables, darts, pinball machines you name it. He and Day would go there for hours some days after work, enjoying the atmosphere and good company.

"I don't want to go there," God grumbled.

Day looked up from the model car he was building at his desk and glared at his pouting lover.

"I didn't ask you what you wanted to do." Day tilted his head in the direction of the bathroom. "Now get your ass in there and get ready."

God stared at him for a few seconds before yanking some clothes out of his dresser and tossing them on the bed. He cursed under his breath as he stomped into the bathroom, slamming the door behind him.

Day held in his laugh and went back to working on his car.

This is going to be the longest freakin' two weeks of my life.

Are We All Bonding Now?

Day and God were so happy their required two weeks were over that they were both dressed and getting in God's truck three hours before they were supposed to be at work. They'd done their meetings with the shrink and even had two sessions together and she deemed them fit to return to duty.

Day had gotten a little nervous during one session when the doctor asked God how he would handle someone hurting Day now and his lover responded by jerking one side of his leather coat open and pulling his long blade from its sheathe.

"Easy, I'd cut their fucking arm off and beat the shit out of them with it," he'd said.

But Day quickly started laughing and told the concerned doctor that his partner was just playing.

After popping God hard in his stomach, God agreed and said he was indeed joking. When the doctor went back to writing on her legal pad, God mouthed to him, "No I'm not."

God still thought they just barely passed her requirements.

"Stop by Starbucks," Day said without looking up from his cell phone messages.

"You drink way too much coffee, Day. I mean all day every—"

"And you fuck too much. I mean all day every day." Day cut God off. "Do I tell you to stop? No. Instead I feed your addiction. Can't you provide me the same courtesy?"

God laughed and swung his truck into the crowded Starbucks parking lot. He parked in the back since his truck was too big to fit in the spots in the front. While Day was in the busy shop, God pulled out Mr. Eudall's TracFone and saw there still were no messages. God was going crazy wondering how his brother and mother were doing. He was so deep in thought he hadn't seen Day leave the shop and get back in the truck.

Day stared at the phone, watched God tuck it back into his glove box, and speed out of the parking lot. God's mouth was set in a firm line as his mind drifted to his last two encounters with Genesis. When he pulled into the station's parking lot ten minutes later he shut off the engine and turned to face his man.

"I think it's time I tell them," God said more confidently than he felt.

Day looked him in his eyes telling him that he would support him completely. God grabbed the back of Day's neck and pulled him to kiss him before it was time to clock in as partners.

"Love you, coffee slut." God chuckled softly against Day's lips.

"Love you back, sex slut." Day licked him.

God and Day walked into the station together and their entire department started clapping, yelling, banging on their desks, and whistling loudly. They made their way through the maze of desks as many of the officers patted them on the back and shook God's hand. The women were pulling on them and kissing their cheeks.

If God was nervous about catching some flak for being out and gay, no one in their precinct was showing it. Probably because who God was fucking was inconsequential to what was happening on the streets every day, and he was glad that he worked with a group of people that were smart enough to realize it.

After what seemed like a very long time Day and God sat down at their desks, anxious to get back to work. After the captain had finally gotten everyone to calm down they all behaved like Day and God had never been gone.

About one in the afternoon the captain called Day and God into his office with two of the city's Assistant District Attorneys to ask them about joining in on the interrogations of some of the eighty-five dockworkers who were confirmed to have worked for Hansen. The mayor was encouraging all law-enforcement departments to keep putting the hammer down on drug dealers. Although they'd cut the head off a very large snake, it might not be long before another one took up habitation in its place. Day and God were eager to accept. Besides, Day loved keeping his interrogation skills sharp.

Once that quick meeting was over, they both headed to the break room for more coffee for Day.

Of course.

"I'm gone for only two weeks and look at this mess," Day grumbled while wiping off the counter around his coffee maker.

God gulped his apple juice and leaned over Day to look at the nonexistent mess.

"Babe, I don't see anything." God propped his arm against the cabinets and watched Day huffing while taking inventory of how much coffee was left.

Day's cup was just about done brewing and he and God were staring at each other when Ronowski and Johnson came into the break room together. Day turned and looked at them both with a ridiculous look on his face.

Johnson went to the fridge and pulled out a can of soda while Ronowski stood there fidgeting nervously. God put his hand on Day's shoulder telling him to put the poor guy out of his misery.

"How's Vikki doing?" Day asked Ronowski. "Have you seen her?"

When Ronowski snapped his head up Day and God both sucked in a sharp breath at the huge hickey next to his Adam's apple. Johnson stared at them from over Ronowski's head silently asking them not to rib him.

No doubt the guy was still working on understanding and accepting his attraction to men, not to mention acting on it.

"Uhh. Yeah, I... umm... we went and saw her yesterday. She starts her PT next month so she's doing well. She'll be on desk duty for a while, and she's definitely not happy about that." Ronowski grinned shyly. "She wants to see you both... ya know... to thank you."

Johnson stepped closer behind Ronowski and his nearness seemed to relax him, because he looked Day in his eyes.

"I wanted to say thank you too. You both were nothing short of awesome that day and everyone knows it... including me." Ronowski stuck his hand out to Day.

Day put his coffee down, gripped Ronowski's hand, and pulled him into his chest startling the hell out of all of them. Day slapped the young man a few times on his back before releasing him. Day smiled broadly when Ronowski turned and smiled lovingly at Johnson.

The captain walked into the room and all four of them looked at him with grins on their faces.

Captain shook his head and moved to grab a muffin.

"For fuck's sake. What the hell is this; the champagne room now?"

"Yeah, except there's no champagne... only shame," Day said drily and gulped his coffee.

Ronowski laughed loudly and all heads turned to look at him. He cleared his throat quickly and tried to shrink back behind Johnson's huge figure.

Captain came to stand in front of them. "What do you and God got planned for the fourth?"

"Nothing comes to mind," Day responded first. "Why, what's up?"

"Ronowski's going to do some surveillance that he and Seasel had set up a few weeks back on a small-time meth dealer in

Buckhead. Since the fourth is next week, Seasel won't be in the field by then. So I want you and God to do the surveillance with him."

Day snapped his fingers loudly as if a memory just hit him. "Oh shit. Did you say the fourth... uh... uh... I thought you said the fortieth," Day stammered jokingly. "Sorry, we're completely booked."

God popped Day in the back of the head and saw Ronowski grin from behind Johnson and raise his middle finger at Day. "And no fucking in the backseat, Day... this is going to be real surveillance going on." Ronowski joked back.

Day couldn't help but laugh too. God was so glad Day and Ronowski had called a truce... work was a much better place this way.

"The fourth it is, Captain," God spoke over Day.

Day elbowed God in his gut.

"Do me a favor, Ro," Day said calmly.

"What's that?" Ronowski peeked around Johnson again.

"Johnson won't be with you all the time. Remind me to kick your ass later," Day said.

Ronowski came to stand in front of Day, looked at his watch, and smirked. "Sure, what time works for you?"

Day looked at his watch too. "Uhhh, let's see. Is five thirty good?"

"I just remembered I'm busy at five thirty."

"So what time can you be there?"

"I can do five thirty-five."

"Damn, that's cutting it close. I might be a little late, but wait on my ass whippin'."

"Will you dumb asses shut up? Lord help us... they've bonded." The captain tried to suppress his laugh. "God, how the hell do you put up with Day's mouth?"

"I got something that'll make him shut him up," God said in his deep voice.

Everyone groaned and scrunched their faces up in disgust.

"We don't want to hear that shit, God. Ugh," the captain said while pouring his cup of coffee.

God looked at Day and saw he wasn't the slightest bit fazed and if he knew his lover—which he most certainly did—Day would not let him get the last word.

"It's all a mind game that I play with God. He thinks he's shutting me up... but when he's finished with my mouth... I start talking again." Day winked.

"I'm leaving. I should write your asses up for sexual harassment or something." The captain hauled ass out of the room.

Johnson and Ronowski were shaking their heads, too and telling Day he sure knew how to clear a room.

"I got to get back across town," Johnson said then bent down to whisper something in Ronowski's ear that made the man turn red.

God tried to pull Day away but he refused to budge. When Johnson said good-bye to them and left, Day mock whispered to Ronowski. "I told you. One good pounding is all you—"

"For fuck's sake, Leo," Ronowski groaned, grabbing his soda and hightailing it out of there before Day could finish his sentence.

God slapped Day's ass, making him yelp. "You are too fucking much."

"But you love me anyway." Day licked his lips seductively at him.

"Goddamn right I do."

Chapter THIRTY-TWO

A Surprise Visitor

"Surveillance went great last night. That bastard is going down. Ronowski should have the warrant by morning and we'll be kicking down that asshole's door by noon," God said around a mouthful of Day's lasagna.

"Yep. Looking forward to it," Day said back.

"So are you going to tell me why Ronowski pulled you into the break room when we got back today?" God asked watching Day closely.

Day shook his head at him, smiling wickedly. "It was about sex."

"No fucking way. He came to you about sex?" God said, not hiding his shock.

"Who else is he going to ask... his priest?" Day said and quickly dodged the piece of garlic bread God threw at his head.

"Do I want to know?" God said.

"It wasn't too bad. He wanted to know the best way to pleasure Johnson." Day laughed when God scrunched up his face and made a gagging sound.

"There intimacy has been pretty one-sided from what I could understand. Ro was still pretty shy about telling me stuff, so I was mostly guessing." Day wiped his mouth with his napkin before continuing. "Being the stud that I am... I gave the kid a few pointers."

"Stud, huh?" God smiled.

"Yeah. I don't mind taking the little tyke under my homosexual wing and showing him how to fly." Day grinned.

"You're twisted. And isn't Ro like the same age as you?" God said.

Day blew an exasperated breath. "Regardless of age, Cash. I have more experience. Way more. Way, way, way more experience with fucking men than anyone I—"

"I fucking got it, Leo." God scowled at him.

Day laughed hysterically. "I told him all about how I make you scream my name every night." Day chuckled and bolted up from his chair, and God took off after him. Day ran back into the kitchen, jumping and gliding across the kitchen island on his hip and racing into the den. God was hot on his heels.

"I'll catch you, you quick little bastard. And when I do, I'm going to show you just how loud I can make you scream," God said in his sexy rough-hewn voice.

"Oh fuck."

Day was laughing so hard he could just keep ahead of God's grip. He dodged him in the living room, leaping over the coffee table, heading fast toward the stairs when he was caught around his waist with a strong arm and dragged back down the two steps he'd cleared.

God tore at Day's basketball shorts, practically ripping them in the process of taking them off. Day didn't have time to do anything before God's mouth wrapped his cock in hot moist silk.

"Oh fuck," Day groaned.

God was just dipping down and licking Day's balls when someone rang the doorbell. Day dropped his head back making a hard *thunk* sound on the stairs when God released his sac and released the hold on his throat. Day loved when God overpowered him, it gave him such an awesome high.

"Are you expecting someone?" God stood up and buttoned his jeans.

"Fuck no." Day looked at his watch. There was no way Jaxson or anyone in his family would make an impromptu visit at almost eight at night.

Day tried unsuccessfully to push his cock down as he made his way to the front door.

"This better be Ed McMahon with a big fucking check or else someone is getting hurt," Day said by way of greeting as he jerked the door open. He heard his lover laughing behind him, but turned very serious when they saw who their pop-up visitor was.

God quickly stepped around Day.

"Genesis. What are you doing here? Are you okay?" God said hurriedly.

His brother was standing there with a medium-sized box in his hands staring back at him. God saw immediately that there was no hate in his brother's eyes as he looked at him… only…

Sadness. Oh no. "Is mom hurt?" God said quickly.

Genesis shook his head no. God was getting a little nervous about Genesis's arrival. He felt Day place a protective hand on his shoulder.

"I don't like this, Cash. He tried to hurt you before," Day said from beside him.

Before God could respond, Genesis finally spoke up.

"I'm not here to cause any problems."

"How'd you know where I lived?" God asked.

"I followed y'all home from your job," Genesis admitted.

"You did what?" Day barked.

God placed his hand on Day's chest and moved him back some. He turned to face his lover.

"Let me speak to him please. He said he's not here for trouble. Why don't you go for a ride and let me and him—"

"I'm not leaving you," Day argued back.

"Shhh. Okay. I'm sorry. This is your house, I shouldn't have sugges—"

"See! I'm not liking this already. This is your house too and you know it!" Day scowled at God.

"I can leave. I didn't mean to upset anyone." Genesis turned to walk away.

"No! Gen, wait!" God called out.

He blew a tiresome breath. "Day, please just give us a little privacy," God pleaded with his eyes.

"Okay. I'll be right in the kitchen," Day said and turned to Genesis, raising his voice. "Only a few feet away."

Genesis's head snapped back at Day's tone making God sigh and roll his eyes at his lover. Day turned and walked away as slowly as he could.

"Genesis, do you want to come in or do you want to talk standing out here on the porch?" God asked him.

"Umm. Yeah, I'll come in."

God stepped back and let Genesis come inside. He closed and locked the door behind him. God led the way into the den and Genesis sat in the chair opposite the long sofa with God on the extended ottoman facing him.

God took in Genesis from head to toe. Damn, his brother had grown to look just like him; tall, brawny, bright green eyes with long, light-colored eyelashes. His hair was in a buzz cut and his sideburns were connected to his goatee. He had on a plain green-and-white-striped collared shirt that stretched over his broad chest and faded blue jeans. His low-top Converse were green and looked like they had a lot of miles on them.

"Your boyfriend is pretty scary," Genesis said.

God snorted and looked toward the other room. "He's all bark and no bite." God snapped his head back around at his brother. "Wait. How do you know he's my boyfriend?"

Genesis gave him a look that said, "Really?" and God shook his head.

"It doesn't bother you?" God said quietly, his rough voice already laced with emotion from having his little brother in front of him and not trying to kill him.

Genesis shrugged. "Why would it bother me? I'm gay too... well, bisexual I guess. I had a boyfriend for a while, but now I'm dating a girl. She's a cheerleader at my school. She's pretty cool."

God nearly had to pick his lip up from the floor. *He's bisexual. How the hell did I miss that?* Where the hell was all this coming from and why the hell was Genesis having such an easy conversation with him like they were best friends?

"Genesis, I have to say." God shook his head to clear it before speaking again. "I have no clue what the hell is going on. Why are you telling me this stuff?"

"Because I know," Genesis replied.

They sat staring at each other for a few long minutes. Suddenly, his brother's eyes welled with tears and his body began to shake.

"Whoa. You know what, Gen?" God frowned still at a complete lost.

"I fucking know, Cashel!" Genesis yelled surging out of his seat to stand over God.

Day ran into the den and God stood quickly holding his hand out to stop his partner. God had a feeling he knew what Genesis was talking about now.

"Genesis," God said slowly.

"The sick fuck recorded it." Genesis bent and picked up the box and shoved it at God's chest. "Mom and I saw it all. She found this box buried in the attic. We must have just put it up there without opening it when we moved here. It shows it all!" Genesis's tears were falling freely as he yelled. "The fights, the beatings, the threats." Genesis dropped to his knees as if he was in agony. He cried so hard his body jerked with the sobs. "Oh my god, oh my god," he groaned.

Cash shoved the box of old VHS tapes to Day and dropped down to embrace his brother, and Genesis clung to him for dear life.

"The rapes... we saw the rapes, Cash. All those men. Police officers." Genesis cried.

Jesus. No.

"Shhh, it's okay, Gen."

"No it's not okay." He sobbed against God's chest like a child. "You let us push you away, you let us hate you. Why the hell didn't you tell us, Cashel? We could've been a family. I loved you, man. You were everything to me, more than my dad ever was. Then all of a sudden, mom was calling you a killer and then I did too. You should have told us. I hate you for that."

"I know, Gen. Goddammit, I'm sorry. I didn't know how to tell mom the man she'd loved was psycho. I didn't think she'd believe me. I had no proof. More than that, I did what I thought I had to do to protect you." God released his brother when he felt Gen pull back. He looked into eyes so much like his own. "But believe when I tell you that I never left y'all. I've been watching you the entire time. I moved you guys here shortly after I did and I made sure you were safe and taken care of. I would never have left you and mom, Gen. I just loved you from a distance."

God let his brother have his moment. He cried silently into his hands. He knew how Genesis felt, he'd shed so many tears that he'd thought he had no more.

God helped him back on the ottoman and then paced the room. Day was sitting on the sofa sifting through the contents of the box. Did God want to watch them?

Fuck no. He'd lived it.

He'd burn them. There was no need for them now. His family had the proof and now it could all be over.

God stopped walking the length of the room and faced his brother. "Where is mom? How is she?"

He saw Genesis wince at his question as a fresh wave of tears flowed. He knew his brother was thinking of the response he'd give God anytime he'd ask about *his* mother.

God put his hand on Genesis shoulder. "Hey. Stop beating yourself up for how you treated me. You didn't know. It's in the past and that's where I want to leave it."

Genesis looked into God's eyes and answered him. "Our mother is having a hard time just like me. She hates herself for not giving you a chance to explain all those years ago. We've gone over and over it in our heads thinking there should've been signs. We've been in agony these past four days."

"Y'all found these four days ago," Day voiced in shock.

"Yes and I've been looking for you ever since. It took me a while to figure out what precinct you worked at. I remember him"— Genesis pointed at Day—"saying he was your partner on the force. So I went to the ones closest to where you used to live after I saw you'd moved."

God came over and knelt in front of his brother. "I know we've lost a lot of time, but we can let the past rest and look forward. You're about to turn seventeen." God gave Genesis a slight smile. "This is going to be exciting times for you. I'd like to be there, if you'll let me. There will be no more blaming, no regrets, and no what ifs. What's done is done. I'm all about my future now. My future with the man I love… and now… my future with my brother and my mother. How does that sound to you?"

Genesis wiped his nose on the sleeve of his shirt and nodded his okay. God was startled when Genesis jumped up and threw his arms around God's middle and held him as tight as he could. God squeezed his eyes shut at the burning in them and hugged his brother back. He hadn't seen this day coming, at least not for a very, very long time. After all the turmoil and heartache he'd endured for so long God was finally receiving some goodness in his life.

God and Genesis talked until almost midnight. Not about the past, but about the present and future. Day had gone up a couple of hours before, but God knew he wasn't asleep. When Genesis had called his mom during their talk and told her he was all right and Cashel was talking with him, God could hear her sobs over the phone. It took a lot for him to contain his feelings. He wanted to hug his mom so bad. It'd been almost seven years. Soon he'd be able to. Genesis had told his mom that God would be over this weekend for a visit.

When it was time for Genesis to go home, God had refused to let him take the bus. God called him a cab and waited on the curb with him. He hugged his brother tightly one more time before paying the driver and settling him inside.

God watched until the cab turned the corner before he went inside and locked up. Day was in bed watching TV when God went to the bedroom.

His lover sat up quickly at the sight of him. "You okay?"

The concern on his lover's face touched him deeply. God leaned down and placed a soft kiss on Day's forehead.

"Yeah, sweetheart, I'm good. Just tired. I'm going to wash up real quick, okay."

Day nodded his head and God closed himself in the bathroom.

The Not-So-Little Brother

It was Friday evening and God and Day were on their way to watch one of Genesis's football practices. God was so excited to be able to actually watch from up close and even talk with his brother's coach. He looked over and smiled at his partner, currently downing a huge cup of coffee from a convenience store.

"I'm really excited, babe. You should see him play, he's crazy good," God boasted.

Day looked over and smiled at him. "I'm really glad this is working out so well. I've wanted this for you. You and Gen are already doing so good. You guys talk on the phone for like an hour every night."

"There's a lot for us to catch up on. He told me last night that there's a tight end on his team that's been flirting with him, and he asked me what he should do." God couldn't wipe the wide grin off his face if he tried. His brother was asking him for dating advice.

"Hell, he's a tight end... there's only one thing he needs to do. Pound that tight ass. Did you tell him that?" Day smirked and took another large gulp.

"You are incorrigible. Damn," God said and wacked him in his shoulder.

"You should see the look on your face right now. I was at Jenkins's desk going over some interrogation notes with him this morning and he said that half the department hardly recognizes you now." Day chuckled.

"What does that mean?" God frowned.

"In a good way, babe. For years you looked so unapproachable and angry all the time. But now they said you look like—" Day stopped and laughed loudly.

"What? Spit it out!" God yelled.

"You look like a big, tattooed teddy bear." Day doubled over laughing.

God smiled. He didn't mind being called that. He was never mean and unapproachable; he just didn't have a ton of things to smile about back then. God pulled into the school parking lot and he and Day went to the far end of the football field. As they walked along the track that surrounded the field, heads began to turn, especially the cheerleaders that were there practicing too.

"Uhh, I think they're looking at you," Cash mumbled.

"Why me?"

"Because you look sexy as fuck today, that's why." God scanned Day's fit body lustfully.

"They're looking at you, brute, or those big-ass guns sticking out from under your coat." Day laughed.

They both looked like they were coming to arrest someone. God's gold badge hung from his neck, and Day's was attached to his hip.

Day had his leather coat in his hand, so his chrome 9mm handguns holstered under his arms glinted in the setting sun. His tight black turtleneck hugged his firm pecs and molded against his trim waist. The black, studded leather belt Day wore wasn't to keep his jeans up since they were tight enough. His dirty blond hair was free of product today, so after running his hands through it all day, its wayward strands only made him look even hotter.

God smiled when Day caught him ogling him for the millionth time today.

"What?" Day laughed.

"I'm gonna fuck you against the wall in the shower when we get home… that's what," God said, his voice deep and sexy.

"Fuck," Day moaned. "God, stop. I don't want to spring wood while I'm standing in front of a bunch of high school cheerleaders, dude."

God cracked up laughing again. "Sorry," he said with little sincerity.

The cheerleaders were waving and giggling as they walked down the track. Most of the players had turned from their coach's lecture to stare at them.

"Yo, someone's about to get arrested," one of the players yelled, making the players start ribbing and horse playing.

God saw when Gen turned and noticed them. His eyes went wide and a huge smile appeared on his face. God swore he'd never get tired of that for the rest of his life. Gen took off his helmet and started to jog over to them.

When Genesis was in earshot he called out to them. "What are you guys doing here?" He gave God a one-armed hug and did the same to Day before stepping back.

"Came to see your practice and see if you wanted to grab a bite with us tonight," Day said.

"Cool. Heck yeah. Practice is only another hour. I'll meet you guys out front after I shower." Genesis beamed.

"Hey, Gen, you cool man?"

The three of them turned around at the deep voice. A tall kid a couple inches shorter than Genesis was standing a few feet away with more than a little concern on his face. He had his dark hair pulled back into a ponytail, and despite the sweat and grime on his ivory face, anyone could see the guy was beautiful in an almost androgynous way.

"Yeah, Terry. It's my big brother, man," Genesis yelled back to him.

The kid's brow creased but he nodded and ran back to the huddle.

When Genesis turned back, the almost sweet smile he wore said it all.

"Is that him?" God asked the question anyway.

"Yeah, that's him," he said shyly.

Day shrugged and shook his head. "Not bad, Gen. He's hot in a twink kind of way."

God and Gen both groaned.

"Jeez. You really have no filter do you, Leo?" Genesis asked around a grin.

"No," God and Day responded in unison.

"Whittmen, get your ass back over here. I didn't say this was stop and chat time," one of the assistant coaches yelled.

God slapped Genesis's shoulder pads and nudged him. "You better go before you're running laps the rest of the practice."

"Can't you guys just wave your guns around or something to scare them?" Genesis joked.

God laughed and shoved him harder. "Get your ass back over there. Let me see what you got."

"You got it." Genesis snapped his helmet back on and jogged to join his teammates.

Day and God went up a few rows on the cold metal bleachers and watched the rest of the practice. He already knew Genesis was phenomenal but seeing him up close like this was unbelievable. God and Day didn't embarrass him by cheering him on, but they were barely able to contain their shouts every time Genesis completed a pass. His brother's tight end crush was a beast too. He and Genesis were almost in sync as he blocked for him on certain plays to get Genesis into the end zone.

At the end of the practice Genesis waved to them as he followed the other players into the locker room. Day and God were almost to the bottom of the bleachers when a man carrying a clipboard, wearing a white polo shirt and khakis approached them.

"Excuse me, detectives."

God and Day both turned and the older gentleman stuck his hand out to them. They both shook his hand and God saw the black-and-red "G" emblem on his shirt.

"My name is Joseph Myers and I'm the assistant coach for the University of Georgia Bulldogs. Are you family of Genesis Whittmen?"

"I'm his brother Cashel Godfrey and this is my partner Leonidis Day."

"It's a pleasure to meet you both. If you're waiting for Genesis, maybe I can have a couple minutes to talk with you men about Genesis's future."

While they sat in Henry's eating wings and drinking sodas, Genesis explained to him that there were always scouts in the stands watching him.

"If you guys come to the homecoming game next week, you'll see a ton of them."

"And they're only there to see you?" Day asked.

"Me, Terry, and one of our full backs are the ones they keep approaching. Terry already decided that he's going to his dad's alma mater, which is Virginia Tech, but Gibbs and I are still undecided. Coach shields me pretty good, ever since a scout from Florida tried to get me to take some money in exchange for signing a contract." Genesis wiped sauce from his hands and mouth. "I just want to get into a good school that has a great engineering program, football would be second. Besides, I need to stay close to mom; I'm all she's got." Genesis froze when he realized what he'd said, looking apologetically at him.

God was so proud of him he could've burst. God smiled to let Genesis know that he understood… things were different now, and it was going to take some getting used to.

"Aren't you a junior?" Day asked.

"No, he's a senior. He graduates in June. He took summer school classes for three years so he could graduate early," God answered first.

Genesis mouth was wide open. He shook his head with an expression of wonder on his face. "How did you know that?" he said so low God almost didn't hear him.

He looked into Genesis's moist eyes.

"I told you I've never left. Each year I buy the yearbook from your school and I get your school's newsletter too, which you're featured in just about every month. Then of course there's Facebook."

Genesis gasped. "You're one of my friends on Facebook?"

God looked a little uncomfortable. "Yeah, I am. I never post anything though. I just read yours."

Genesis just shook his head in amazement. He pulled out his cell phone and God knew he was opening his Facebook app. Then God saw him snap his head up and hold his smart phone out.

"Are you... do you pay for this too?" Genesis whispered.

"Yeah, Gen, I do," God said.

Things were real quiet for a little while as God watched the emotions play across his brother's handsome face. Sorrow, hurt, regret and maybe even betrayal all flashed quickly and God didn't know what else to say. So leave it to Day to break the tension.

"Okay, girls, let's not get your panties in a bunch. Stop all this pouting, get your asses up, and let's play some pool."

God and Genesis laughed while they inched their large frames out of the booth. Genesis fell in behind Day.

"I like you, Leo," Genesis said.

"Everyone likes me." Day winked.

"When you're ready for a real man, dump Cash and come find me." Genesis laughed hysterically when he couldn't dodge God's grasp quick enough and was wrapped in a tight headlock.

A Good Fuck and Then…..Awwww. Our First Fight

God and Day fell into the front door kissing and grabbing at each other. Day just barely kicked the door shut before he was yanked out of his coat. They'd kept the PDAs to a minimum while with God's brother, but Day was serious when he said he really needed to fuck his man.

God pushed Day against the wooden door and captured his mouth in a ruthless kiss. Day pulled Cash's coat off his shoulders, letting it drop down to the floor. Day squeezed the handle of God's Desert Eagle and sighed at the erotic way his dick jumped from the touch. Day stroked the long black chamber down to the felt grip panel.

"You stroke a man's gun like that, you might as well be stroking his cock," God said gruffly and moved Day's palm to his already fully erect dick and pumped his hips.

Day felt God fumbling with his belt. He yanked his mouth away from God's and moaned when God gripped the back of his neck, chased his mouth and sucked his bottom lip into his mouth and bit it. Day placed both his hands flat against God's massive chest and pushed him hard. God growled, knocked Day's hands back down and crashed into him again.

God spun Day around and pushed him hard against the wall while grinding his pelvis into his ass. God made quick work of unzipping Day's jeans and shoving his hands inside to give his balls a rough massage.

Day bucked back against God. "Ugh. You motherfucker."

"You going to give it up willingly, or do I have to take it, Leo?" God's whisky-rough voice vibrated through Day's body.

Day moaned at the assault, reared back and caught God in his hard abs with an elbow, enjoying the loud grunt from the big man before running up the stairs.

Day was rounding the landing when he heard God call out to him.

"I only enjoy it more when you fight, Leo," God said taking the stairs two at a time.

Day had shed his clothes in record time and was climbing into the shower without even waiting for it to heat up. Day had just closed the clear door when he saw Cash drop his pants, his blushed cock jutting out angrily.

Day turned his back on God and began soaping his body, ignoring his horny lover; in turn driving him crazy.

The door to the shower opened, and God stepped in behind him. God reached his long arm in front of Day and put the lube on the shelf. Day tried to suppress his smile. God's huge forearm came around Day's throat and pulled him against him. God licked his ear lobe.

"You insist on doing things the hard way... don't you, sweetheart?"

Day didn't respond and hissed when God punished him for it by biting his jaw. God took the soap from Day and put it back on the shelf, gripping both of Day's biceps from behind and pushing him roughly against the cold tiles, holding him in position with his bulk.

"Open," God growled in his ear.

"Fuck you," Day snarled back.

"As you wish," God said calmly and slid down Day's body. He parted his ass with both hands and speared his tongue into Day's tight hole.

Day squeezed his eyes shut and yelled his curses into the thick steam now filling the bathroom. "Fuck, goddammit."

God wedged his large body against Day until he had to either climb the wall or open his legs further.

"There, now that's better," God said smoothly and licked long and slow up Day's seam until he got to the base of his spine. God alternated from fast tongue fucking to lovingly relaxing the tight muscle. "Mmm, taste so fucking delicious." God tongue bathed him until Day couldn't see straight.

"Cash," Day whined pathetically.

God answered him by tongue fucking him again, this time flexing his tongue every three or four pumps.

"Fuck me now," Day begged.

God bit Day's ass cheek so hard it made him grind his teeth together to keep from giving God the satisfaction screaming. Day flexed his ass muscles to take the edge off the pain and felt God slap him hard on both cheeks.

"Ughh, Cash. Come on dammit." Day stroked his aching cock.

"Tsk, tsk, tsk. Patience, sweetheart." God teased him.

Day hated when God got like this. As soon as Day made God chase him, he'd turn around and make Day beg for it once he got revved up to go.

God lubed his fingers and pushed two into Day's relaxed hole.

"Yeah, that's it. Fuck me hard," Day moaned.

God pressed his body against Day's, trapping his erection against the slick surface of the shower wall. Day felt God's fingers leave his hole and the empty feeling made Day groan in frustration.

"Cash, please," he begged again. He couldn't take God teasing him anymore. He needed his man. Needed to be overpowered. His body needed to submit to its dominant.

Day felt God rubbing his lubed cock up and down his ass. Stopping every few strokes to press at his hole.

"Want me right now, Leo?" God whispered in his ear.

"Yes, right now, baby. Right now."

God pressed past the first ring of muscle in his ass and kept going until his balls were snug against his now red cheeks. It felt so fucking good Day wanted to cry out in thanks. God's cock was ramrod straight. It was hard and unyielding. Day pushed back into God's shallow thrust, grunting each time as God glided over his prostate with each stroke.

"Oh, shit. Fuck me, fuck my ass," Day whimpered. He spread his legs wider, dropped his chin to his chest, and braced his hands on the wall. The grip on his hips tightened to the point that he'd have finger marks, and that thought almost had Day coming. He tried to think of something else to ward off his orgasm but it was useless. When God was inside him nothing else existed. It was just him and his lover, taking him to places that could only be reached when he fucked him.

God kept his thrusts quick and deep. So fucking deliciously deep, burying his thick cock farther than Day knew existed. Day had absently risen up on his tiptoes to try to catch his breath. "Get back here," God barked, pulling him back down, impaling him onto his cock.

"Fuck!" Day's eyes rolled to the back of his head as he cried out and shot his come all over the wall. His ass clenched around God's cock, his own dick pulsing without being touched. Day's balls were completely spent as they rocked rapidly against his body. Regardless of his powerful orgasm, God continued to piston-fuck his ass until Day yelled he couldn't take anymore.

"Yes you can. Take my dick. All of it," his lover encouraged breathlessly.

God's hot mouth mixing with the steam from the shower had Day sweating profusely. Day dropped his head back to God's shoulders and clenched his ass as tight as he could, snapping his hips back into God's merciless thrusts.

"Oh you bastard. Fucking tight ass squeezing my cock." God grunted, his vicious rhythm becoming erratic as Day forced the orgasm out of him.

God held Day's ass snug against his pulsing cock as he filled him with thick ropes of hot come, searing him inside and claiming him at the same time. This, by far, was Day's favorite part... not *his* orgasm... but God's. God held him so close and tight when he filled him that it gave Day the feeling of unconditional love and of being one hundred percent possessed.

God's huge six-foot-four height was draped across his back while he caught his breath. "Damn. You are so fucking hot, Leonidis." God licked Day's neck and carefully slid out of him.

Day stayed still and let the hot water pound against his tender ass. Day could feel his lover's come seeping out of his hole and it made him shiver despite the heat. God and Day had stopped using condoms after they got their test results back a week ago. They didn't waste any time exploring new sensations with no latex barriers between them. The thought that they were in a monogamous relationship for the first time in their lives was comforting.

After a couple minutes he felt God washing his body gently with a thick, soapy rag.

"Just stand still," God said soothingly against Day's cheek, kissing him tenderly before going back to his job.

Once they were both cleaned, God dried them and led Leo by his hand to their bed. Day wished that everyone could see God like this. So strong, muscled, and yet so damn gentle. He pulled back the covers for him and waited for him to climb in before going around to his side. Day watched God from heavy-lidded eyes, check the safety on his gun and place it in the nightstand drawer.

When God got in he pulled Day to him like always, tucking him under him and wrapping protective arms around him. Day didn't remember God saying anything else, but if he did, Day had fallen asleep before he heard it.

Day didn't stir or even move again until the sun was beaming in the window on their warm bodies. He and God were in the exact same positions, clinched together, facing each other. God's arm was under Day's body, the other palm on his neck. Day's hands were tucked against God's chest. Judging by the amount of light in the room, it had to be after seven, maybe almost eight. Day smiled warmly.

"What are you smiling about, sweetheart?" God's rough morning voice went right to Day's already hard cock poking his lover in his thigh.

God's eyes were still closed when he pulled away from him and stretched against the cool sheets before returning to him.

"Good morning, beautiful." God stroked one finger down his cheek. "I don't think I'll ever get tired of waking up like this."

"Mmm. Me neither," Day agreed while palming God's hard cock. "Want me to take care of this before breakfast?"

God turned over and picked up his cell phone from the nightstand. "No, babe, I'm actually exhausted. Fuck," God murmured sleepily. "I need another five hours of rest."

"No can do, lover. You're supposed to go to your mom's today," Day said to him.

God released an annoyed breath. He didn't want to think about that just yet. To say he was nervous about speaking with his mom again was the understatement of the century.

"No shit, Sherlock. You really think I need reminding of that? What the fuck would I do if I didn't have you to keep me on schedule, Leo," God said sarcastically.

Day didn't say anything else. He rolled out of bed and went into the bathroom, closing the door behind him. Day knew God was stressed about seeing his mom but being an asshole wasn't going to make it easier. Day did his morning usual and left the bathroom to see God sitting in the chair in the corner of their bedroom with his head buried in his hands. Instead of inadvertently pestering his partner even more, he decided to just walk past him, get dressed quickly, and leave the room.

Day had just finished tying his biking boots and hooking his chain to his belt when God broke their silence.

"Are you gonna act like a bitch for the rest of the day and ignore me, Leonidis? If I wanted to date a sensitive-ass broad, I wouldn't be here with you," God said angrily.

Day locked his jaw and counted to ten, silently trying to calm himself. He tried to stay mindful that God was under a lot of stress. There were some things Day was willing to let slide, and other things that would be dealt with aggressively, and calling him a bitch definitely fell under the extremely aggressive category.

Day yanked his keys off his dresser and turned to glare at God before walking out the door. "You ever call me a bitch again, and I'm gonna show you just how much of a man I am."

Day walked out of the bedroom, down the stairs and straight out the front door. He opened his garage, grabbed his helmet off the shelf, straddled his bike, and revved the engine before he sped out his driveway.

God heard Day's bike rumbling nosily through their bedroom window. Day was leaving. *You gotta be shittin' me.* "I guess that means you're not coming with me!" God yelled angrily at no one. *If you don't want to be called a bitch, then don't act like one.*

God knew what he'd said to Day may have been a little rude, but damn, Day should have a little understanding. This was big for him today and he was past nervous to flat-out nauseous. God blew his frustrated breath out loudly and went about getting ready.

How cute, our first fucking fight as a couple. Yay.

God's thoughts went to his lover when he came downstairs and noticed there wasn't even any coffee made. He had no clue how to work that high-tech monstrosity.

God sat at the breakfast bar drinking his juice and reading the Saturday morning paper. His thoughts kept replaying this morning. He'd seen the angry muscle in Day's jaw ticking after God had said what he had and he'd immediately wanted to take it back, but it didn't work that way. Day would've still been angry. He was kind of pissed that Day left when he was supposed to go with him, but when he thought about it some more, this was probably something he should do on his own anyway. Day would be there for him when he came home—he wanted Day to be there waiting on him with open arms when he got home.

Fuck me.

God looked at his watch and saw it was just coming up on nine a.m. He folded his paper, put his dish in the sink, and left the house.

Momma I'm Home

When God pulled into the driveway, Genesis ran out and met him as soon as he got out of the truck. He'd quickly told God that he'd explained to their mom how God felt and what his wishes were. God was immediately relieved that his mom wasn't going to ask him those dreaded questions. How did it start, why didn't you tell me, how did it make you feel, and all those other questions he really didn't know the answers to. He didn't even know exactly what they'd seen on the tapes. Genesis said they saw it all.

He and Day never looked at the tapes. His man had taken them at God's instruction and burned them. Those were his past and God was all about the future.

When God came into the small house, his mom was sitting on the well-worn sofa with her hands clasped in her lap, a crumpled tissue visible in one hand. Her hair was pulled back in a soft ponytail and she had on a pink blouse and a tan tweed skirt that just covered her knees. Her makeup was minimal, but it wasn't needed on her angelic face. She smiled a sweet smile at him and waved him to her.

God removed his coat and Genesis was there to take it for him. He walked over and sat awkwardly on the small couch. His mom brought her hand up to lightly touch his cheek. She looked him over as if inspecting him and a quiet sob escaped her lips. He slowly brought his own hand up to gently wipe at the tears that fell from her eyes, trying desperately to keep his own from falling. Those seconds

265

felt like very long minutes before either of them spoke. After his mom was satisfied that he looked okay, she parted her lips and whispered to him.

"Welcome home, Cashel."

God told her about the military, about his job on the force, and he had them cracking up with stories about his crazy lover, promising her that he'd bring him around real soon. She'd popped God in the back of the head with her potholder when he told her that he'd pissed his partner off before it was time for them to come over.

"He sounds like a good catch, Cashel. Don't be a jerk to him." She admonished him right before serving him his favorite thing to eat when he was younger.

It was just after 6 p.m. and God and Genesis were devouring the entire loaf of freshly baked cinnamon raisin bread.

His mom smiled warmly at him and said in soft voice. "I was hoping it was still your favorite, Cashel."

God patted his mother's soft hand. "It will always be my favorite. You're going to have to give Day this recipe."

"He can cook?" His mom's eyebrows shot up.

"Mom, he's freakin' awesome," Genesis answered before God could. "When I was over there last week, he made us some kind of meat and noodles concoction." Genesis snapped his fingers. "What was it again, Cash?"

"Beef stroganoff." God laughed around a huge piece of sugary bread.

"Wow. Did his mom teach him to cook?" she asked while cutting God another huge slice and refilling his glass of sweet tea.

"I wish," God groaned.

"Uh oh." His mom smiled wide.

"Uh oh is right. He dated a real fancy-shmancy chef in college and he taught him a lot of stuff." God rolled his eyes and waved his hand dismissively. "I can't even remember his name."

"He remembers it all right. It's the one you love mom, that's on TV. You know him, the hot one... Prescott Vaughan, miracle chef." Genesis grinned slyly at God, who punched his brother in the shoulder as soon as their mom turned to go to the sink.

"Oww. Shithead," Genesis yelled.

Their mom gasped. "Genny, watch your mouth, Cashel, stop abusing your brother." She scolded both of them before turning around and continuing with washing the dishes.

"We're going to play some Madden in the living room before Cash has to go home and eat crow Mom," Genesis said while ducking God's left jab.

She laughed at them. "That's fine. I think I'm going to go on up to bed, I plan on going to church in the morning because I have so much to thank the good Lord for. My big boy is home." She leaned in and let Genesis kiss her cheek before turning and doing the same for him. God kissed and hugged his mom before walking her to the bottom of the stairs and telling her goodnight.

They'd been playing for three hours, Cash beating his brother two out of three games. They were having so much fun that Cash kept laughing and shoving Genesis, telling him to shut his mouth, their mom was trying to rest. When it was time for him to leave Cash asked Genesis if he wanted to come over and watch football with him and Day tomorrow; his brother eagerly accepted. God teased him by throwing out the invitation to bring a friend if Gen wanted.

"Do you need me to pick you up?" God asked before he put his truck in reverse.

"If Terry says he wants to come, I'll ride with him." Genesis waggled his eyebrows.

God smiled and shook his head at his brother's typical teenage thoughts before sobering quickly. Genesis moved closer to his window.

"Gen, you are using protection aren't you? I'm sure you're not a virgin." God looked seriously at his brother.

"No, I'm not a virgin but I always wrap up, Cash," Genesis answered him with a nervous chuckle.

"Always," God said sternly.

"Always, bro. I swear, man."

"All right then. I don't want to have to rush you to the hospital when your dick falls off." God laughed before barreling out of the driveway.

He saw Genesis double over laughing and flick up his middle finger at him before he turned and walked back into the house.

Never Call Me a Bitch

Day chastised himself when he checked the time on his cell phone for the hundredth time in three hours. When he'd left home he'd gone and sat in Starbucks, reading the latest issue of *Guns & Ammo* for about an hour while trying to plan what he wanted to do today since his previous plans were abruptly canceled.

He figured he'd visit his mom for a little while before riding to his favorite gun range and firing off a few rounds. Day didn't mind riding an hour to Carl's range because the man would let Day shoot everything from M16s to .50 caliber assault rifles. Day had one time fired a gun so powerful it had almost dislocated his shoulder... he fucking loved it. That would keep his mind off his lover.

He'd been home since around seven and was shocked to see it was after ten and God still wasn't home. He could only assume the extended length of the meant it was going well. He'd broken down and checked the track-your-lover app an hour ago just to be sure things hadn't gone to shit and God wasn't off somewhere stewing in his own anger.

Day was trying to concentrate on painting the tiny yellow strip on the back fender of the Ford Rod he was almost finished building when he heard God's truck pull up. Day put the paintbrush in the cup of water and got up from his desk. He could hear God coming up the stairs as he pulled the sheets back to get in the bed. He made quick eye contact with him when he walked through the door and assumed the smile he wore from ear to ear meant his visit went very well.

"Looks like things are good," Day said casually. "I'm happy for you."

"Things were better than good, sweetheart. My mom was so happy to see me. She made me raisin bread, and she even popped me in the head a few times when I told her I'd pissed you off. She wants to meet you real soon, sweetheart," God said breathlessly around all his excitement.

"I'm looking forward to it," Day said climbing in bed.

"Oh come on, Leo, you can't still be mad at me." God huffed. When Day still didn't speak, God threw his hands up. "Okay, fine. I shouldn't have said what I said. I'm sorry, all right. There. Does that make you happy now, or do I have to go out and by you some fuckin' flowers and candy and shit? Stop acting like this. I had a good day, babe, and I want to fuck you." God dropped his voice low.

"I have a headache and don't feel like having sex… since you're dating a bitch. Good night, Cashel." Day flicked the switch on the lamp by his side of the bed; putting them in total darkness. Day pulled the covers up, turned his back to God, and willed himself to go to sleep.

Day woke up before five a.m. and was pissed when he couldn't go back to sleep. Although his back was to him, he could tell God was also awake by his breathing. Day finally got sick of lying there and got out of bed. He slid his leather slippers on and went downstairs. Day got the paper off the front step and went to the kitchen for coffee. He was in the den watching Food Network, sipping his second cup when he had an urge to go back upstairs and climb back in bed with God.

This was bullshit. This was a stupid fight they were having and he wanted it over. Day was sure there would be real shit for them to fight about in the future, they didn't need to waste time on crap like this. But still... Day didn't move. Around seven, Day was back in the kitchen and cutting himself a grapefruit when God stomped into the kitchen looking like a speared bull. He wore only his pajama pants that were riding so low that Day could see most of his pubic hair. God's soft curls were disheveled and tucked behind each ear. Damn, he looked fucking delicious.

"Leo, come here." God turned; heading into the den, the large, roaring, lion head on his muscular back a reminder of who was in charge. God turned back around slowly. "I swear, get your ass in this fucking den, Leo," God said through clenched teeth when Day still hadn't moved.

Day saw the vein on God's neck bulge and recede as he shot daggers at him. Day abandoned his fruit and followed God into the den. God picked up the remote and flicked off the TV, giving them complete silence, and settled his large frame on the ottoman before beckoning him over.

Day walked over to him and saw God point to his lap. Day gave him a fuck-you look right before he was pulled forward and forced to straddle God's lap.

His lover looked at him and wrapped his arms around him before speaking. "Leo, this shit were doing right now is over. I fucked up and said some shit that was unnecessary, but I'm not going to kiss your ass for days over it. I apologized last night and I meant it. I apologize now, sweetheart. I'm sorry. I get a little agitated when I feel out of control and I lash out sometimes, but I'll definitely try to check myself and not disrespect you. Now you're mine and I refuse to have another night like last night. You belong in my arms when I'm asleep, got it?" God finished by slapping Day's hip.

Day didn't have a chance to respond because God grabbed a handful of his hair and slammed his mouth over his, stealing away any rebuttal Day may have said.

Day's dick quickly betrayed him, filling painfully at God's tongue darting in and out of his mouth. The taste of minty toothpaste and a sexy manly flavor that was all God was smeared across his lips, and Day licked at it greedily.

"Good. Now fuck me and show me how much you missed my arms around you last night." God's baritone drawl had Day standing to drop his pajama pants and briefs to the floor. He grabbed the lube from the drawer in the coffee table and settled back on top of that large lap.

Day and God's tongues battled while he lubed two of his own fingers and pressed one into his hole. "Oh fuck." Day breathed into God's mouth.

"Feels good, huh?" God reached around and settled his hand on top of Day's, feeling him fuck his own fingers. "That's so damn sexy." God took his middle finger and pressed it to Day's lips.

Day sucked God's thick finger into his mouth and moaned deeper, knowing exactly where that blunt tip was getting ready to go. Day's hungry hole clenched with anticipation. God slowly withdrew his slick finger and mixed some of his own spit to it before he reached around to Day's ass. Day already had two of his fingers inside scissoring him. He felt God's finger adding pressure and pushing in beside his.

"Oh fuck," Day groaned at the added burn. God's fingers were thick and long.

Day pulled his fingers out and let God's finger slip in, his lover immediately going for that spot that would make his back arch.

"Fuck. Right there." Day rocked back and forth on God's finger.

"You're so damn sexy." God licked up Day's chest and alternated between sucking hard on each pierced nipple. God twirled the black barbells between his teeth and flicked the tiny pebbled buds, driving them both insane. God looked at the now red nubs and used his thumb to stimulate them more while he watched Day's face.

"Now," Day growled.

God lubed his cock slowly while watching Day.

"This what you want, babe?" God stroked from the base to the bulbous head that was dark red with heat that seemed to be calling for Day's hot channel.

"You wanted my dick last night too, didn't you?" God gave him a sexy smirk while he lined his cock up with Day's hole.

"I want you all the time. Now stop all this goddamn talking and give it to me," Day said, impatiently trying to impale himself on God's shaft, his hole pulsing to be filled. God had one hand at the base of his cock steadying it for him. Day sank down onto all that thickness, his aching ass opening and swallowing his lover's dick in one quick move.

Day sucked in a sharp breath and sank down completely until his ass cheeks were on God's thighs.

God released the sexiest groan from so deep within that huge chest that Day felt it vibrate his own body.

"Fuck, Leo. So fucking tight." God's chin was tucked into his chest watching the connection of their bodies. Both hands on the perfect "V" that shaped Day's pelvis.

Day locked his arms around the back of God's neck and held on while he rocked his hips back and forth, grinding their pelvises together.

"Oh. My. Fucking. God. You're so damn deep." Day breathed. He kept himself fully seated while he gyrated like a striper doing a lap dance, and he could tell that it was driving his big lover crazy.

God's head lolled back on his shoulders, his mouth set in a hard grimace, his brows scrunched together with concentration. "You sexy bastard." God held his hands loosely on Day's hips, letting him wind and grind freely until Day began to pick up the pace. God dropped his forehead to Day's shoulder and murmured a bunch of nonsense while biting and grunting his cries into the muscle. Day wanted to pump his fist at the victory.

"Yeah. Say I'm your man," Day ordered, snapping his hips back and forth in fast, vicious motions.

"Ohhhh, fuuuuck." God panted as his hips were rocked back and forth by Day's powerful thrust.

Day brought both feet up to place flat on the ottoman for leverage and began to rise and fall on God's rigid cock. He rose until God's cock head was all the way out before slamming back down, his ass slapping God's thighs... and then again... and again.

"Shit," God yelled. "You're my man, yes, fuck. This is your cock, baby. Fuck it, fuck it!"

Day bounced up and down until God was yelling he was about to come. Day dropped his legs back to the floor and ground his hot ass against God's pelvis again. God's dick went concrete hard and pulsed inside him, waves of hot come searing his channel.

God's head was thrown back in ecstasy and Day squeezed and released his walls repeatedly.

God groaned long and deep. "Fuck yeah. Milk my dick. Mmm, fuck," God said, trying to hold Day's hips in place.

Day knocked God's hands off his waist, making God laugh a deep throaty chuckle. "You got something to prove to me, sweetheart, huh?" God mocked him.

Day leaned in and bit God's neck, sucking up a deep welt. God's strong hand was on his cock, starting to pump him with fast, determined strokes. Day slapped God's palm off his cock. He stood up, his legs still straddling God's wide body. He walked forward, forcing God to lie back, and prop himself on his elbows.

Day looked down at him with a possessive snarl and began to pump his cock with lightning-fast strokes, his wrist twisting when he got to the head. Day grunted and snapped his hips with his movements. God's eyes narrowed as he watched him closely. Day looked into God's bright green eyes and slowed his thrust just enough to reach back and scoop his man's come to lubricate his calloused palm. God sucked in a sharp breath and leaned in to lick Day's stomach.

"So fucking hot," God confessed.

"Mine," Day moaned and lowered his body so he was almost sitting on God's chest. He pumped furiously. Day fumbled for one of God's hands and placed it between his legs on his drawn-up sack. "Squeeze my balls," Day commanded.

"Oh you motherfucker," God watched his man in fascination.

God had Day's balls in a viselike grip, tugging them downward, the pain erotically sweet. Day threw his head back as his orgasm tingled at the base of his spine. His shaft throbbed in his palm; his thighs trembled with the intensity of his need to come. "Pull my balls… uuugh… fuck! Pull'em! Uuuugh, harder. I'm coming! Fuuuuck!" Day's body jerked violently.

"Can a bitch do this?" he hissed.

He grabbed a handful of God's silky curls and pulled, making him tilt his head back and show his throat. Day's senses snapped, turning feral. Day growled with the animalistic urge to leave a large bite mark on his man. Day bowed forward as his cock's first eruption of a thick, white rope of come hit God's Adam's apple, followed by much more painting his lover's neck and cheek. Day pulled slow, firm strokes up to his head before dragging back down until he was completely emptied.

"Mmmhmm. I'm yours, sweetheart," God said, giving him a sexy grin.

"Fucking right you are," Day said while he kissed and licked God's face clean.

Too Good To Be True

God and Day were on their way to pick up Genesis to watch the game over at their house. Day had also invited his brother, along with Ronowski and Johnson. The game wasn't starting until five, but God wanted to throw the ball around with Genesis, maybe even play a few games of *Madden* with him before the guys came over.

God swerved into the driveway and as soon as he dropped down from the driver's seat and slammed the door, Genesis rushed him, almost knocking him over. They wrestled with each other until their mom appeared in the front doorframe.

"Let them get in the house, Genny, my goodness." She laughed at their horse playing.

"Yeah, Genny." God teased his brother's nickname and was thanked with a hard pop to the back of his head. He chased Genesis around the yard until his mom yelled at him to get over there and give her a kiss.

"Hi, Mom, you look pretty today." God smiled and jogged up to her, picking her up in a bear hug and spinning her around on the porch. She giggled while swatting at his shoulders, urging him to put her down.

"Oh my Lord. Now I got two of you big oafs picking me up and spinning me," she said while turning to face Day. "You're not as big as them but you still look like a spinner to me."

"Oh I most certainly am; my mother still walks lopsided to this day. Com'ere, beautiful." Before God's mom could say no way, Day had swooped her up like a little girl and spun her around at least five times, making her squeal like she was on a roller coaster. He set her back down gently and kissed her cheek. She grabbed at her heart and panted, out of breath.

"My word. You may be smaller but you are just as strong." She laughed. "Leo, I'm so glad Cashel brought you by today. He had such wonderful things to say about you. Come on in, I'm sure you boys have a few minutes before you have to leave." She winked at Day. "Besides I made some homemade mac-n-cheese that I want Leo to taste since he was trained by the incomparable Prescott Vaughan."

"Oh no way," God groaned.

Day smiled proudly at God and walked into the house after his mom.

Genesis and God sat at the small kitchenette table eating the last of the raisin bread while Day explained to her that evaporated milk was a better substitute for cream in savory dishes. God grumbled more than a few times when Day told his mom what it was like to cook with her favorite television chef.

"If I have to hear how wonderful Prescott is one more time, I'm going to shove sharp sticks in my ears." God pulled Day to him and nipped at his chin.

"Oh be quiet you. You have him now, and you reap the benefits of the great recipes that Prescott left with him." She tsked at him.

"Yeah, whatever." God rolled his eyes and sat back down. He looked at the stack of mail and idly fingered through it, since technically they were his bills. The mortgage and utilities were paid automatically, so God was interested if his family had incurred additional debts that he didn't know about.

"Hey, Mom, what's this?" God held up an assisted-living-facility brochure with an acceptance letter inside it.

"Oh, honey. Genesis and I were going to talk to you about that. It just came yesterday, so now that we know I'm in, I can tell you all the details." She wiped her hands on the worn pink apron that covered the pale gray pantsuit she'd worn to church. She sat on the fourth chair and gently took the brochure from God.

"Since this will be Genny's last year in school and he'll be going off to college soon, he doesn't think I should stay here alone." She wrung the small dishtowel in her hand. "And I don't want to live alone either. So we found this really nice assisted-living facility."

"Like an old folks home. What's wrong with this house?" God interrupted, frowning.

He'd be damned if he sent his still relatively young mom to waste away in some tiny room in an old-age home. Day reached over and placed his hand over God's and gave it a couple pats, holding his gaze for a few seconds. His man was telling him to stop jumping the gun and listen.

He flipped his hand over and laced their fingers together. God took a deep breath before speaking again. "I'm sorry, Mom. I didn't mean to interrupt. Go on."

God saw his mom throw an appreciative smile at his lover before continuing.

"This place is wonderful, Cashel. Gen and I will never be able to thank you for what you've done all these years. But I don't want to live alone, honey." She hurriedly opened the tri-fold brochure and held it out for all of them to look at. "See. These are fully furnished apartments, not rooms; in a complex that's for either the elderly or anyone that has a disability and can't work. After Gen and I did a tour, the admissions manager said that I qualify because I'm on full disability—it has nothing to do with being old." She smiled and patted God's stubbled cheek.

"I can still do volunteer work. The complex has a van for transporting residents. There're also game nights and a recreation center, cinema, church, a full cafeteria, all right there in the community." She beamed. "The best part is, it won't cost anything extra, it's based on how much disability I get a month and I'll still get Joe's social security check."

God dropped his head down, while squeezing Day's hand tighter.

"Oh, honey. You've done so much. It's time for you to live your life and be happy with Leo. You don't need to keep running yourself into the ground, paying all of our expenses and your own." His mom shook her head as if trying to understand. "I still can't see how the heck you managed all these years. But you've done more than any son would have."

"Mom, if they have a vacancy now, then you need to take it. If you go back on the waiting list, there's no telling how long it would be before another apartment is available. I'll ask a friend at school if I can stay with him until Coach's son leaves for boot camp next month," Genesis said.

"Whoa, whoa. I'm lost. What do you mean live with a friend?" God raised his hand up to slow his brother down.

"Well, Coach said I could live with him after his son leaves for boot camp next month if mom was accepted into her new place. She can't have anyone living with her. We've been talking about this my entire senior year, but this apartment just became available, and I don't want her to miss it. I saw the place already Cash… hell I wouldn't mind living there. The cafeteria serves three meals a day for people that aren't able to cook for themselves and the food's ridiculously good."

God was listening to his brother, but he was staring at his man. He wanted to ask Day something but he just wasn't sure how.

"Genesis, you are more than welcome to live with us until it's time for you to go to school—of course, if it's okay with your mom—I have more than enough room and I'm sure Cash would like to spend as much time with you as he can before you go," Day said.

God stared at his man, his partner, his lover… his best friend. He'd known what God wanted to offer but felt it wasn't his place.

"Are you serious, Leo? That would be freakin' awesome, dude!" Genesis shook Day by his shoulders, not even trying to hide his excitement.

Day turned to look at God who was still staring at him in amazement. He winked and kissed God on his cheek.

"Cash and I would love for you to live in our home. The guest room is huge and you could do whatever you want to make it your own for these next nine or so months. It's out of your bus route for school, but I have an SUV that I never drive. I only ride my bike, or I ride with Dale Earnhardt, over here, so you can use it for getting around, as soon as I put you on the insurance."

God thought Genesis was going to knock Day out of his chair, he was shaking and hugging him so hard.

"Genny, for God's sake, don't kill the nice man." His mom laughed. "Leo, that's more than generous… are you sure?"

"Of course. Gen is family," Leo said while swatting away Genesis's groping hands.

"Aww man… this is going to be sweet!" Genesis grinned.

God was so happy. He would have a whole ten months with his brother before he went off to school in the fall. There was no doubt that Genesis was going to college. At this point it was just a matter of narrowing down the tons of options. God never thought he'd be this happy in his life. He was in love, he had the love of his mom and brother again, and if rumors were true—he was up for a promotion.

"Okay, Mom. As long as it's something you want to do." God leaned over and kissed his mom's cheek.

She stood and placed her hands on her lean hips. "Now I want Genny to go to a great school and kick some butt in their football program, and you and Leo to build your life together." She looked at them sternly. "And when all is right… I want some grandbabies." She beamed.

All of the guys started coughing and groaning at the same time.

"Okay, okay." She grinned and put her hands up to calm them down. "Cash, I want you to come with me to my walk-through so you can see it's a great place and there's no reason to worry. After you give your approval, I'll sign my lease and my big strapping men can get me all moved in." She leaned down and kissed all three of them on their foreheads. "Now I'm going to put on something comfortable and stretch out on the couch. I'll finally be able to watch my Lifetime Movie Channel on the nice TV since Genesis won't be hogging it watching football all day."

Cash smiled and walked her to the bottom of the stairs, kissing her on her cheek. "I'll have Genesis home by ten, Mom."

She turned on the third step. "He can stay the night; you don't have to drive all the way back here that late. I am capable of locking my doors and staying home alone, Cashel."

"Absolutely not," God said easily and smiled as she walked upstairs shaking her head at him . "'Night, Momma."

"Good night, sweet boy."

By the time they finished with their visit, God was convinced that the retirement community seemed like a nice place to live and it was only twenty minutes from his and Leo's home. His mom wouldn't be alone so Genesis wouldn't have to worry about her, and he could focus on school. God was going with her and Genesis next week to sign the lease, and then he'd put the house up for sale. God had to admit to himself that not having an entire household to keep up with was a wonderful feeling.

A Meeting Amongst Friends

Genesis and Jaxson were up out of their seats yelling like maniacs when the Redskins threw an interception on fourth down and the Falcons defensive end ran it back for a touchdown, taking the game into overtime. Living in Atlanta, most of them were Falcons fans, but Johnson was a Redskins fan and it'd made this game so much more fun than Day had imagined. Ronowski was more of a baseball fan, just like Day, but he was rooting for the Redskins along with his man.

When Ronowski and Johnson arrived together Day had welcomed them into his home. There was no longer any tension between them and after several nights of pool and wings at Henry's they'd become good friends. Ronowski was now comfortable discussing pretty much anything with Day, including sex. When Day told Ronowski to pull on Johnson's balls while he sucked him off, he'd turned so red he thought the guy's face was going to explode.

Day was spooning some more homemade guacamole into a bowl when he heard footsteps approaching him. He turned just as Ronowski slid up beside him, dipped his finger in the dip, and shoved it in his mouth.

"Mmm. Slide that finger in your mouth again and pump it in and out this time," Day growled.

"Are you always so sexual?" Ronowski laughed at him.

"Yes," Day said with complete seriousness. "I mean... have you seen my boyfriend? Yes, Ro, I'm thinking about sex all. The. Time."

Ronowski caught Day's arm when he moved to take the dip back to the guys. Day stared at him for a few seconds but he wasn't saying anything. Day had come to know Ronowski pretty well over the weeks they'd been partnered together while Seasel healed. Day set the bowl down on the counter and pulled the confused man into his arms. Ronowski slowly brought his arms up and put them around Day's neck. Day leaned back against the island and let Ronowski rest against him.

"Why are you holding me like this?" Ronowski said, his eyes focused on the buttons on Day's pullover.

"Because you want me to," Day said back. "What's on your mind?"

"I'm not hitting on you, Day." Ronowski pulled back a little.

Day squeezed tighter. He tilted Ronowski's chin up so the man was looking at him. "First off... I know that. Second, you know who I belong to and I don't think you're suicidal. Third, I know you love Johnson. So, I figured you might need a hug." Day laughed.

Ronowski smiled shyly. "I don't know if I do. I mean he's really cool and we have so much fun together. He's always coming up with this off-the-wall shit to do on our dates... like fucking bungee jumping or rock climbing! He's really funny and chill, ya know."

Day linked his fingers at the small of Ronowski's back and rubbed his thumb soothingly against the firm muscles while he listened. "So what's the problem, babe?"

"We were in bed last night and I was kind of almost asleep but not fully, and I felt him kiss me on my temple and he whispered that he loved me. I think he thought I was asleep." Ronowski worried his bottom lip while fidgeting with the collar of Day's shirt.

"You do love him though?" Day said it like it was a question and waited on the beautiful man to answer. Day watched Ronowski's crystal-blue eyes look up at his ceiling before focusing back on him.

Long, dark eyelashes fluttered up and down while he appeared deep in thought. His lips were naturally rosy pink and supple, a gay man's dick-sucking-fantasy lips. Ronowski wore a little gel in his hair with the front flipped up in a messy, tousled way. Hell, no wonder Johnson was in love after only a month.

"I don't know, Leo. How do you know when you love a man?" Ronowski blew an annoyed breath.

"Love is all the same, baby boy." Day smirked. He'd been calling Ronowski baby boy ever since the first question he'd asked Day about sex. "It doesn't matter if it's a man, woman, or hermaphrodite. Love is love darlin'. Let me put it to you this way; if you get a crazy feeling in your gut just from hearing his voice, then you know, if you can't wait to see him even though you've been apart less than twenty-four hours… then you know, if you find yourself doing anything in your power to make him smile, then you know. But the ultimate test to know whether you're in love or not, is to imagine that person suddenly taken away from you forever. If that thought makes you damn near tear up and want to run and put your arms around them and hold 'em close to you, then you damn well know you're in love."

"Holy fuck," Ronowski whispered and blinked rapidly. "I'm in love. Jesus. For the first time in my whole damn life."

Day couldn't help the smile that formed on his lips. He didn't know if other people would be happy for them, but he sure was. He'd been trying to drag Ronowski out of the closet for four years. Now finally, here he was in love with a man. Day squinted and studied the pretty man carefully while Ronowski stared curiously at him.

"What?" Day smirked. "You just realized you're in love with me too?"

"You're an asshole." He laughed and plucked Day's ear. "No, I'm not in love with you, but I'm glad you're… my… friend," he said slowly while arching one dark blond brow.

"Yeah, Ro. I'm your friend." Day laid a chaste kiss on those colorful lips and Ronowski puckered up and kissed him back.

"Ummm, bro, and J. You guys might want to come in here, because your boyfriends are in here getting down and dirty with each other." Genesis's deep voice yelled from the entrance to the kitchen.

Day shook his head and threw the closest object he could reach at Genesis while the kid laughed, grabbed the dip off the counter, and ran past God and Johnson back into the living room.

"Damn. Is it me or do they look fuckin' hot together?" Johnson nodded toward them while leaning against the refrigerator after pulling out another beer.

"Don't get any ideas in that twisted, perverted head of yours, Johnson." God laughed but Day didn't miss the sly wink he threw the man before he kissed Day passionately while he still hung onto Ronowski.

Day moaned and kissed his lover back for several seconds before pulling back. There was no denying the hard cock he felt pressed against him while God ravaged his mouth, but the sight before him now was nothing short of exhilaratingly sexy.

Ronowski's body was still pressed against him, his pelvis thrusting gently, of its own accord while his head was thrown back and resting on Johnson's chest, the big man kissing and licking all over Ronowski's pink lips. Johnson's mouth worked its way down to Ronowski's ear and sucked on the fleshy earlobe, flicking the gold hoop that was pierced through it. Ronowski let out the sexiest moan and Day couldn't stop his body's reaction. He pulled Ronowski's cock firmly against his own and thrust back. Day looked into the eyes of his lover waiting for any sign of anger or refusal, but was surprised as hell to see lust and excitement in God's electric green irises. God leaned in and sucked on Day's neck just like Johnson was doing to Ronowski.

Their lust was rudely interrupted when they heard Jaxson boo one of the post-game announcer's comments. Day pulled back and looked into Johnson's eyes over Ronowski's shoulder. Ronowski's half-lidded eyes were fixed on God's chest. No one spoke. There were only heated gazes, panting breaths and painful erections. Johnson broke the silence first with a very direct question.

"What's the verdict, God?"

Everyone turned and looked at Day's huge lover. For some reason, they needed God to say okay to whatever the hell this was.

God gently massaged the back of Day's neck and lowered his head to whisper in his ear, something meant for him and him alone. When God pulled back, Day let a wide seductive smile play across his face before asking Ronowski and Johnson, "You guys got plans tonight?"

A.E. VIA

Let's Do This. Playtime.

Day was upstairs in the bathroom freshening up while Johnson and Ronowski nursed their drinks downstairs in the den. God wrapped his strong arms around Day while he washed his face.

"Hey, gorgeous." God's smooth voice was against the rim of his ear.

"Hey."

"So we're really going to do this with them?" God licked Day's neck while watching his reflection in the mirror.

"Fuck, yeah." Day grinned and swiped the washrag across his face. "Have you ever played with another couple before while with someone?"

"I've had threesomes with chicks before, but I wasn't in a committed relationship with someone else. I don't want shit to get weird," God said.

"Oh, babe, you don't have to worry about that. Johnson is gay so he may already know, but some gay couples do play with other couples. It doesn't have a damn thing to do with cheating and I can see the gears turning in your head. No, we don't have an open relationship. I'm committed to you. I'd never go fuck anyone else or pick up random dudes to bring to our bed. We like hanging out with Johnson and Ro, they're cool guys, and we trust them, so it's just like having friends with benefits." Day winked.

"Your mind is very interesting, sweetheart." God shook his head at him.

"Did your brother like the truck?" Day dabbed a little aftershave under his chin.

"Shit! Hell yes, he did. I told him he had to be responsible and not fuck up or else we'd take it back," God said stripping off his V-neck shirt.

Day told God to go ahead and let Genesis take the truck home instead of God driving him home and then having to come all the way back. Day's Explorer was nice and it was hardly used, there was no harm letting Genesis have reliable transportation. The kid was smart, well behaved, and focused so Day didn't see why he couldn't be trusted with a set of wheels.

"Jaxson finally left too." God rolled his eyes. "I thought he'd never stop ribbing Johnson about how bad his Redskins are."

"So our company is down there alone." Day wrapped his arms around his man.

"I told them we'd call them up in a second. I just wanted to talk to you first and I'm sure Johnson might want to clarify what this all means to Ronowski too." God pulled the covers down on the massive bed and then checked the bedside table for the required supplies.

"I'm going downstairs to get them, lover." Day kissed God on his lips. When he turned, God grabbed Day's arm and spun him back around. He looked down into his eyes for a few long seconds, neither of them saying a word.

"He's going to want to fuck you." God looked at him seriously.

"Babe, if you can't do this, it's okay. I'll send them home right now and tell them this won't fly." Day stroked God's cheek.

"The thing is I want to do this. I just don't want Johnson falling in love with you again. I mean the guy chased you for damn near three years," God admitted.

290

Day pffted at him "He was hardly in love, it was only lust and he chased me because I was convenient. But I'm not concerned now because he's in love with Ro, and Ro loves him too. Besides, who wouldn't fall for that gorgeous man? Ronowski is fucking hot like Channing Tatum, but sexy cute like Zac Efron. It's a damn good combination... he's got the whole bad-boy-twink thing going.

"Fuck, I know. I want to kiss him and watch those pink lips slide up and down my dick." God palmed Day's ass and ground hard against him while voicing his fantasy.

"Fuck. I've got to watch that." Day grinned.

God spun him back around toward the door and popped Day on his ass. "Go get them."

Day went to the top of the stairs and yelled. "Get your asses up here!"

Johnson led Ronowski up the stairs by his hand. When they reached the top Day gave them a wide grin before leading them to the master bedroom. As soon as they turned the corner Day heard a loud gasp from behind him and he didn't have to see Ronowski's face to know why.

God was looking out the window. His long, muscular arms braced on the wall. His back muscles were defined and rolling with each breath. The roaring lion on his back looked as if it was daring anyone to touch it. The four long canines were fully extended, ready to shred something. The coloring was the most breathtaking; the golden-brown hue of the beast's mane was mixed with streaks of black and gold. The head alone took up the entire right half of God's wide back.

"Beautiful, isn't he?" Day stepped aside and let their company enter.

"I never knew that was there," Ronowski whispered.

"You can touch him, baby boy." Day smiled.

Ronowski shook his head no. "Umm, no that's okay. I'll just look."

"Come here." God turned around facing them. His green eyes set on Ronowski. There were multiple other tattoos across God's chest and various proverbs written in script on his pecs.

Ronowski turned and looked at Johnson who gave his lover a small nod of approval before he walked slowly across the plush carpet. Right before he got to God, Ronowski stopped dead and blurted too loudly that he needed to go to the bathroom. Ronowski scurried across the carpet like someone was chasing him and slammed the door behind him. They all waited a few seconds to see if they would hear the nervous man puking, but after a moment of silence, Johnson headed toward the closed door.

"Let me get him, Johnson," Day said and went inside the bathroom before Johnson could.

Day locked the door behind him and turned to face Ronowski. His hands were shaking as he repeatedly splashed cold water on his face.

"Ro, you don't have to do this, honey. It's supposed to be fun, not put you into cardiac arrest." Day rubbed Ronowski's back through his soft, cotton T-shirt.

Ronowski shook off the water droplets and turned in Day's arms.

"He's just so fuckin' big, I mean bigger than Johnson and definitely scarier. If I touch you, how do I know he's not going to choke the shit out of me?"

Day gave him an incredulous look before saying, "That's never going to happen."

Ronowski stared back.

"Again," Day amended.

Ronowski hit Day in his shoulder and they both laughed hysterically at the almost five-year-old memory.

"Why don't you guys bring the fun out here?" Johnson yelled at them from outside the door.

292

Day grabbed Ronowski's arm before he could turn the doorknob.

"Ro, nothing will happen that you don't want to happen. Hell, even if you just want to sit in a corner and watch… that's fine too." Day slowly pulled Ronowski against his hard cock and rubbed it against him. Ronowski's eyes slid closed as he licked his pink lips. "Or you could get in that bed and fuck me like you've wanted to for four years."

Ronowski's eyes got as large as saucers. "Really? I could do you?"

Day gave him a sly smile and brought Ronowski's hand to his cock and pressed into it. "I like that idea very much."

Ronowski grabbed Day's hand and practically threw him out the bathroom door. "Well hell, that'll be worth an ass whippin' from God."

Both of them stumbled out the door and Day ran into the back of Ronowski when he stopped abruptly, his mouth hanging wide open at the sight in front of them.

"Holy shit." Day breathed. "I think I'm about to come."

God and Johnson were both on the large bed. God had Johnson pinned underneath him, his large body wedged between Johnson's raised knees. God had one large hand on his throat and the other hand held a hand full of light brown hair, controlling the kiss. Day watched the muscles in God's back ripple as he thrust hard against Johnson, making the big man release an angry growl.

"Ugh, dammit. Fuck you, God. Feel so fuckin' good," Johnson groaned with little venom. He turned from God's mouth and looked at both of them standing just a few feet from the bed. "Come here."

God slid off Johnson and let Ronowski climb onto the bed and settle on top of his lover. Johnson held him close to him. "You all right, Ro? You say the word and we'll go home right now and get in my bed—"

293

Ronowski silenced Johnson by leaning in and kissing him softly on his lips. "No. I want to stay. Besides, Day said I could fuck him." Ronowski grinned.

"Oh did he now?" God grumbled and pulled a smiling Day on top of him. Each of them lying with their lovers.

They kissed their men, passionate moans filling the air. Day and Ronowski were back to back while the couples kissed. Day reached his hand behind him and felt for Ronowski's bubble ass. He messaged it roughly while he continued to kiss God. Day soon turned around and tapped Ronowski on his shoulder, making the man slow Johnson's kiss and turn to face him.

Day and Ronowski were so close that Day could feel the rapid heartbeat beneath his T-shirt. Day grabbed at the hem of the shirt and pulled it up over Ronowski's head and tossed it to the floor. Day smiled when he saw Ronowski's perky pink nipples were pierced with tiny gold barbells.

"No fucking way. How long have you had these?" Day flicked one of the shiny balls, making Ronowski shutter.

The smile the man gave him was absolutely gorgeous. "A month after I saw yours."

Day frowned at trying to remember.

"You had just come out of the shower at work. You had a towel around your waist and I saw them. I watched the water run down your chest before you pulled off the towel and began to dry yourself off. My dick went rock hard, so fucking hard I could barely breathe. I was so mad at you that the next day, I threw your coffee machine in the trash." Ronowski buried his head in Day's shoulder.

Day reined in his laughter but God and Johnson kept cracking up.

"That was you, you little bastard. I wanted to kill someone that day. No one knew what the fuck happened to it." Day bit Ronowski on his chest making them both laugh again.

Ronowski had the decency to look embarrassed. When they all stopped laughing and Day rubbed the small nubs until they were nice and erect Ronowski looked at him seriously. "I've been attracted to you since day one. It pissed me off, too, because you saw right through all the homophobic bullshit. I never wanted you to be my boyfriend, though, you talk too much." Ronowski grinned when Day sucked his teeth at him. "But you've become a good friend over this last month. So I guess what I'm trying to say is, I'm crazy about you, Day… ya know, in a you're-cool-but-don't-want-to-date-you-just-fuck-you kind of way."

Day lightly griped Ronowski behind his neck and pulled those pretty lips to his mouth. "I'm crazy about you too," Day whispered into Ronowski's mouth before he slid his tongue in for his first taste. The moan Ronowski released against Day's mouth was sinful. Day was hard as hell, his dick could probably snap in half right now. Day brought Ronowski's thigh up over his hip and ground against him with a ferocity that had all of them moaning.

God hooked his arm around Day's waist and rocked into him from behind, Johnson doing the same thing to Ronowski.

Day leaned his head back and let God devour his mouth while Ronowski licked a path from his chest to his neck and nibbled on his chin. Ronowski leaned in and let his tongue play between his and God's. A timid tongue licked around Day's lips until Ronowski found God's lips and began to tease the big guy with quick, unsure strokes, silently asking God for permission.

God growled against both of their mouths and Day felt Ronowski's cock go from hard to stone.

"Oh he likes that, baby," Day said to God.

God grabbed Ronowski by his neck and pulled him closer, kissing him until they both had to take a much-needed breath.

"Want you too, God." Ronowski confessed.

"Come here," God told him.

Day let Ronowski slide seductively over his body and settle himself on top of God. Day had to admit they looked good. God wrapped his large arms around Ronowski's waist and began undoing his pants. Day turned from the erotic show when he felt Johnson pressing his bulge against Day's ass.

"Hey, sexy," Johnson said against his neck.

Day climbed on top of Johnson and thrust back into him. Day leaned down and whispered in Johnson's ear. "You're one sexy motherfucker, you know that?" Day felt Johnson smile against his cheek. "I'm gonna sit on this dick and ride you until you come screaming my name." Day reached down and grabbed a handful of Johnson's cock and balls.

"Oh fuck," Johnson moaned, squeezing Day's ass. Johnson unbuttoned Day's jeans and began inching them over his ass.

Day rose so he could free himself of his pants and briefs. God and Ronowski were still kissing and fondling while inching their way over closer to them. Day straddled Johnson and stroked his own dick, putting on a nasty show for him.

Day winked when he saw Ronowski watching his actions with half-lidded blue eyes. Day pulled hard on his cock from the base to the tip, making a large bead of clear precome form on his flared head.

"You want a taste, sexy boy?" Day said, eyes still focused on Ronowski. He rubbed his thumb in the slick fluid and leaned over to paint Ronowski's soft lips with it, making them shine bright red like he'd put on cherry lip gloss.

Day moaned when Ronowski's pink tongue darted out to lick his lips, his eyes rolling in their sockets.

"More. You taste so good," Ronowski moaned.

God griped Ronowski's neck and licked the rest of Day's essence of his lips before directing his head toward Day's cock. Ronowski opened wide and let the bulbous head slip past his lips. God petted Ronowski's pretty blond hair as he bobbed up and down, making obscene slurping noises.

Johnson tucked both his hands behind his head and watched his man suck Day off. Johnson appeared to be proud, obviously having taught Ronowski what he knew.

Day tried to refrain from throwing his head back in ecstasy as not to miss a second of Ronowski sucking his cock... Ronowski was sucking his fucking cock. *Oh, how I've waited for this day.* "Fuck, honey. Your mouth feels so damn good... mmm... so warm."

Ronowski couldn't go down very far; every time he tried he'd gag. Day stroked his cheek softly while coaching him. "Just suck on the head, honey." Day hissed when Ronowski licked underneath his shaft before sucking as hard as he could on the tip of his cock. "Yeah, just like that."

Johnson and God began to kiss while Day got sucked off. They all looked so hot and sexy together that Day had to concentrate on not coming. Johnson and God were so big and alpha; it was a real turn-on to see them fighting for dominance with their mouths, Johnson eventually submitting and letting God tongue fuck him.

Ronowski's mouth popped off him and he directed his attention toward his own man. Johnson tapped Ronowski's swollen lips with his cock. "You want to suck me, beautiful?"

Ronowski answered by placing soft kisses on Johnson's uncut cock. Day leaned over and joined him. Day licked at his balls while Ronowski sucked on the exposed head. Johnson oh so slowly pulled his foreskin up until it completely covered his head. Ronowski sucked on it before using his teeth to gently nibble at the excess skin.

"Fuck, beautiful. That feels so good. Bite it," Johnson told his man. "Ugh! Shit." He practically yelled when Ronowski complied. Ronowski continued to nibble, then delved his tongue inside, searching for the hidden slit.

Day's cock leaked like a faucet. "Damn that's sexy." Day loved foreskin, the way it glided back and forth.

Day reached over to the side table and grabbed a condom. He tore it open with his teeth and slid one on Johnson when Ronowski finished with him. God moved behind Day and straddled Johnson's lower legs, leaning his weight on Day's back. He licked and bit at Day's shoulder, down his spine, to his ass. God pushed on Day's back until he was lying on Johnson's chest, and then he swirled his tongue around Day's puckered hole. God licked his finger and spread Day's cheeks wide.

"Give me the lube, sweetheart," God said to Day.

God lathered his fingers good and Day felt a thick finger massage the tight skin around his pulsing hole before it pushed in halfway.

Day moaned against Johnson's mouth. God rotated his finger while licking and sucking around his hole. Day rocked back asking for more. God added another and Day clenched his ass, God's fingers were so goddamn thick. Ronowski was watching Day's face carefully while God got him ready. Johnson began pulling on Day's balls by the time God was on his third finger. Day was moaning louder than a bitch in heat when Ronowski slammed his mouth over his to swallow the erotic sounds.

Ronowski's sexy lips were sucking and licking at his mouth too, a three-way kiss. Johnson pulled on his balls in the most torturous and deliciously painful way, while God was pressed hard against that spot inside him. Three of the hottest fucking men Day knew where sexually assailing him from all angles and he couldn't take it anymore.

"Fuck, fuck, fuck. I'm gonna fuckin come," Day moaned.

Johnson pulled harder, and Day threw his head back and loudly groaned his release. Come splattered Johnson's chest, some of it even landing on his cheek.

Day's breathing was ragged when he felt Johnson's strong hands lifting him and positioning his cock at Day's stretched hole. Day eased down on Johnson's sheathed cock in one smooth motion. Johnson was big, but he wasn't any more endowed than God, and since his man had done such a good job preparing him, he felt little discomfort. Day dropped his chin to his chest and cursed at the feeling of being filled.

God came around from behind him and settled beside Johnson, watching Day fuck another man. God rubbed his hand across Johnson's broad chest, rubbing in Day's come like it was lotion.

Johnson thrust hard into him as Day bounced with him. The grip on Day's hip was strong. Day buried Johnson's cock deep and ground against him, winding his hips in small, slow circles. Johnson sat up with a jolt and buried his face in Day's neck and let Day ride him hard.

"Ugh, I'm not gonna fucking last." Johnson breathed and bit Day's neck hard enough to make him cry out.

God rose up and leaned against Johnson's back. He put his lips on Johnson's ear while his orgasm built.

"You mark him and I'll kill you," God growled in Johnson's ear and bit the side of neck at his shoulder.

Day felt Johnson smile against his neck before he went completely still as his cock erupted inside him. Johnson groaned deep in his throat, his cock pulsing and throbbing in Day's tight channel.

Johnson breathed hard against Day's shoulder, licking and sucking his damp skin. Day felt Johnson's cock soften and slide from him. Day took both hands and gripped Johnson's face. He kissed his still panting mouth and spoke against the man's hot breath. "Now I'm gonna ride your man."

Johnson flopped back down to the mattress.

Day winked at God first and stalked over to Ronowski. "You ready for me, sexy boy?" Day said climbing on top of him and straddling Ronowski's narrow waist.

Ronowski stroked Day's rising cock while staring into his eyes. Day caressed the smooth cheek and couldn't resist leaning in to kiss those delectable lips again. They kissed until Day was hard again. Day pulled back and licked all around Ronowski's mouth.

"Hey, look at them." Day grinned and turned Ronowski's head to look at their partners.

God was lying on his side with one arm propping his head up while Johnson inched down the bed. He licked around God's wide cockhead before taking it in his mouth almost to the dark patch of hair at the base and pulled up slowly, flicking his tongue on the rim of the cap. God moaned and held the back of Johnson's head, guiding him back down. When Johnson had gone as far as he could go, God thrust his hips pushing his cock deeper, making Johnson gag and pull back. Johnson looked up and flicked his middle finger up at God. God gave him a sexy wink and propped his knee up to give Johnson more access. Johnson nuzzled the bristly hairs around God's groin before sucking God's sac into his mouth.

Day and Ronowski turned from that scene and focused back on each other.

"Can I taste you again?" Ronowski whispered against Day's hair.

Day worked his way up Ronowski's lithely muscled frame and straddled his shoulders so that Ronowski was unable to use his arms. Day's cock was poised at Ronowski's lips and Day sucked in a sharp breath when Ronowski opened his mouth and stuck out his tongue. Day inched forward a little more, letting the head of his cock just barely inch past those pink lips.

"You have the prettiest fucking mouth I've ever seen. Your lips were made to fucking suck cock," Day said, his voice hungry. "Open up, Ro. Let me feed it to you."

Ronowski whimpered and opened his plump lips. Day pushed in until only his head was buried completely inside. Day desperately wanted to shove his dick down this man's throat but he'd never do that knowing he couldn't take all of him. Day watched Ronowski's eyes slide closed while Day fucked his mouth with shallow pumps. Ronowski's moaning was sending pleasant vibrations up his shaft and Day felt his orgasm tingle in his balls, but he wanted to come while Ronowski was inside of him.

Day pulled his cock free and reached for another condom. He moved down until he was bent over Ronowski's cock. It was long but not a lot of girth. Day smiled because Ronowski's dick was darker than he expected and his pubes were trimmed.

Maybe I'll show him what it feels like to have your cock swallowed.

Day knelt down and licked the weeping head before putting both his hands behind his back. He opened his throat and swallowed Ronowski's cock to the root.

Ronowski slammed his eyes shut and arched his back, his pink lips forming a perfect "O" as Day swallowed repeatedly around his head.

"Fuck, fuck! Stop! I don't wanna come yet!" Ronowski yelled.

Day pulled back and grinned mischievously. "Fuck my mouth hard."

"Do it. You'll love it," God told him with a deep groan. Johnson was swallowing God's come down his throat.

Day took both of Ronowski's hands and placed them on the back of his head. He scooped his hands underneath Ronowski's ass and pushed him up into his mouth encouraging him to thrust.

Ronowski was a damn quick study because he held Day's head in a demanding grip and thrust his cock in as far as he could. He rapidly bucked hard off the bed while slamming Day's head down into his pelvis.

Damn this fucker's gonna chip my tooth.

Day grabbed Ronowski's hands from tangled in his hair and pulled his mouth off his cock, quickly snapping the tight rubber on him. Day positioned the long hard dick at his hole and sank down on him.

"Open your eyes," Day demanded.

Lively blue eyes stared back at him while Day rocked back and forth. Day reared back and fondled Ronowski's tight balls, knowing he was already at the edge, about to come any minute.

"You like that tight ass don't you?" Day teased Ronowski while winding his hips around in circles, working the man's cock like it was a lubed stripper pole.

It looked like Ronowski was about to blow, so Day was not expecting the strength from the man beneath him as Day was aggressively flipped onto his stomach and slammed face down into the mattress. Ronowski took both of Day's arms and pinned them behind his back as if he was arresting him.

Day's back bowed when Ronowski slammed his cock back into him and fucked him with an intensity that shocked the hell out of everyone in that bedroom. Ronowski held both of Day's wrists with one hand and wrapped his forearm around Day's throat with the other. Ronowski covered him from head to toe and thrust repeatedly into him barely pulling out before plowing back in.

"Yeah, I'm loving this tight ass you sexy fucker," Ronowski snarled against Day's ear.

Day just barely heard God and Johnson's curses as they no doubt watched Ronowski handle Day like he was a rag doll and ride his ass like a rodeo cowboy. Ronowski breathed harsh, sharp breaths against Day's cheek with each thrust.

"Come, you bastard." Day's words were barely audible since most of his face was mushed into a pillow.

Ronowski dug in deep and held there. He growled Day's name while his cock pulsed inside of his warm tunnel.

"Fuck," Day groaned. His ass was beyond sore but in the best way.

Ronowski pulled out slowly and flopped beside Day. The little shit propped himself up and stared down at Day—who still hadn't budged—as he gathered his wits.

When Day finally stirred he saw that all eyes were on him. "Oh fuck all of you. Okay, I'll admit I wasn't expecting that."

"Ya think?" Johnson chuckled. "Maybe I should've told you Ro hasn't topped yet… but he's really been wanting to."

God smirked while Day grumbled obscenities all the way to the bathroom leaving the assholes to have a good laugh at his expense. Day couldn't help but smile to himself while he adjusted the knobs on his large tub and let it begin to fill with steaming hot water. He let if fill half way and stepped in. God came in shortly after and bent down, kissing him tenderly.

"You okay, sweetheart?"

Day smiled up at him. He was better than okay. Ronowski had come out of his shell because of him; he couldn't help but feel some pride about that. The serenity he saw reflected in Ronowski's eyes when he entered him was a beautiful gift to Day.

"I'm wonderful, babe." Day's eyes widened. "Did you see his fucking power? Jesus."

"Yeah. You guys looked wicked together. I almost came again just watching," God said. He walked over to the toilet and relieved himself before coming back to the sink and washing his hands and face. "I'm tired, babe. I'll be in bed."

"All right, I'm going to relax here for a bit. Tell them to stay the night, okay," Day said before God could leave.

"Sure." God shrugged.

Why not? There's no reason for them to leave in the middle of the night. Obviously we all fit in the bed.

The tub was full so Day turned off the faucet and leaned his head back. He was just thinking of turning on the jets when Ronowski walked in.

"Damn that's a huge tub."

Day cracked one eye open. "Come on in then."

"Don't have to ask me twice. My fucking apartment's tub is too small to bathe a toddler. Your house is pretty awesome, man."

"My grandmother left me this place. Over time I made renovations. I like to build things and take on projects," Day told him.

Ronowski smiled and stared at him.

"Com'ere," Day said quietly.

Ronowski slid over and settled between Day's legs, leaning back against him and letting his head rest on his shoulder. Ronowski turned and nuzzled against Day's neck.

"I want us to be good friends," Day said rubbing a plush sponge over Ronowski's chest in soothing circles as he spoke. "I want you to forget about all the fights and arguments we've had, because I already have. I was simply waiting on you to come around, honey. I wouldn't fault any man for his indiscretions while he was denying his true self… the sexual frustration alone is enough to drive any man crazy."

"I'd like that a lot." Ronowski relaxed.

Day hit the buttons for the jest and let the pulsing water beat on his sore muscles. Ronowski turned his mouth to Day, obviously seeking another kiss. Day pressed a few simple kisses against his lips before licking him seductively. As if that was satisfying enough, Ronowski sighed and let his body go limp against Day, both of them content with the whirring sounds of the powerful jets while they unwound.

Day and Ronowski lay there with their eyes closed until Johnson came in the bathroom to relieve himself. "Okay you two gorgeous boys, time for bed."

Johnson helped them both out the tub.

When they made their way back into the bedroom God was all the way to the left side of the bed and Day could hear his soft snores. Day settled in close putting his back against God's chest and his man's arms instinctually came around him. Day held the cover open for Ronowski and waited for him to slide in next to him. Johnson got in behind Ronowski and wrapped his arm around his lover just like God did to him. Day and Ronowski faced each other. He linked their hands together and brought them up to their chests, letting their other hands rest on each other's waist.

Day's last thoughts were completely peaceful while he drifted off to sleep with the man he loved and his very good friends.

Special Kind of Friendship

Day woke up and immediately felt like he was in a sauna. *Holy hell.* The body heat radiating off these men was unbelievable. Somehow in the middle of the night—or early in the morning, however you think of it—they'd all squished in close together.

"Fuck me," Day groaned in a sleepy voice.

"Okay," Ronowski answered with his eyes still closed. His voice rough and sexy. He pulled Day's leg up on his hip and jabbed his morning wood at his navel.

"Seriously. Am I the only one that feels like this bed is the goddamn portal to Satan's lair? It's hot as fuck." Day bitched and wiped at the sweat on his forehead. He pushed Ronowski off him and climbed awkwardly out the bed, kneeing God in his hip in the process.

"Leo, shut the fuck up. It's too early for your whining," God grumbled and turned over.

"He's definitely not a morning person, huh?" Johnson's voice was deep and groggy.

Ronowski turned in Johnson's arms and began pushing his hard-on against him. Day spread out in the recliner in the corner of his room, picked up a flat album cover, and began fanning himself with it. He saw Ronowski reach back for God. God took the hint and settled in behind Ronowski while the horny man rocked back and forth between the two large men. God's hand was on Ronowski's hip, the muscle flexing under his palm with each move. Johnson's hand was already working its way down to Ronowski's cock, stroking him with purpose.

Ronowski came with a strangled cry before Day could really enjoy the show. Then Ronowski was going down south on his man, and Day was sure he'd flip over and give God the same good morning treatment after Johnson received his... so Day sat back and waited for it all to play out.

When everyone had gotten off, including Day since he'd jerked off while watching his live porno; Day told them he was going downstairs to make breakfast, since it was Monday morning and they all still had to go to work. No doubt they'd all walk into the station looking fucked-out and depleted.

Day made eggs Benedict for himself, God, and Johnson, while he made bananas-foster French toast for Ronowski, since he was informed the man was allergic to mustard seeds.

It was a little after seven when they finished breakfast. God and Johnson went in the den, drank their coffee, and watched ESPN while Day and Ronowski went back upstairs. Day loved showing off his model-car kits and his jazz collection. The men bonded with each other for another hour or so before Johnson and Ronowski had to go home and get ready for work, with a promise of hooking up for pool and beers after.

It was amazing that men could do this type of thing with each other and not make it awkward and complicated. Day and God were walking into the station and before they could even get comfortable at their desks the captain was calling them in to his office.

Day passed Ronowski at his desk on his way to the captain's office and was surprised when the man looked up and winked at them. The man sure had come a long way.

Day and God closed the door behind them and sat in the two chairs in front of their captain's cluttered desk.

The captain sat down and leveled a hard stare at them. "Well I'm not one to beat around the bush, so with that said; you guys are both being promoted to lieutenant."

Day and God's head snapped to each and back to their captain in complete shock.

The captain put his hand up to halt their questions and continued, "This has come directly from the Mayor to the police chief. The higher ups are real proud of the jobs you've done out on the streets, and with Hansen being taking down during an election year, it couldn't have come at a better time."

"Wait, are you saying this is a political-gain promotion," God grumbled sitting up straighter.

Day rolled his eyes at God's quick-to-bark mouth.

"Did I say that wise ass? No. If you think for a damn minute, you'd get it. Yes, it's a re-election year and the Mayor is recognizing the best we've got and showing that he's not taking this city's prime assets for granted. Damn, Godfrey. When I told them I needed two good lieutenants, your names were the first they came up with." The captain huffed. He yanked open his desk drawer and withdrew two brand-new, shiny-gold badges and slid them across the desk. God and Day took them and immediately replaced their second-grade detective badges.

"You guys might catch a little hate from some other seasoned officers. Some of these men have been here twenty years and are still third-grade. But that's their own fault. No one can doubt how hard you guys fight out there. I'm proud to call you my lieutenants. The promotion comes with a shitload of new responsibilities while still doing what you guys do best." The captain finally gave them a slight smile. He narrowed his eyes at them and shook his head in wonder. "In all my thirty-five years on the force, I've never run across two characters like you guys. I'm damn proud of you both. You're coming up on five years in a couple weeks, that's unheard of. Believe it or not you guys are making history in the APD. Long after you guys are gone everyone will remember you and tell stories of the dynamic duo that was God and Day."

Day and God stood and hugged each other right there in front of their captain. Day knew what God had overcome in his life and he was beyond happy for his lover. He had his family back. His brother was looking up to him as a confidant and friend, letting God help guide his future. His mom couldn't get enough of him and was moving closer. They even had an awesome set of friends that Day was sure would soon become invaluable to them. Everything had finally fallen into place.

"I love you, sweetheart. You saved me," God whispered just for him.

Day hugged him tightly. "I love you too. We saved each other." Day softly kissed his cheek.

"All right, all right. You guys can thank each other when you're not in my office," their captain teased them.

Day and God shook the man's hand again.

"Let's introduce you guys." The captain opened his door without another word and yelled in a voice only a captain can possess, causing everyone to stop what they were doing and face him.

God and Day stood beside each other, all eyes on them, while the captain spoke.

"I'd like you all to congratulate Godfrey and Day on five years as a highly successful and respected team on the APD and welcome them as your new lieutenants!" the captain yelled.

The whole department erupted in cheers and whistles. Cops were banging on the file cabinets and rattling handcuffs, trying to make as much noise as possible. Day saw Ronowski out of the corner of his eye running up to him, he had a huge smile on his face and when he was only a couple feet from him he held his arms out and collided with Day, wrapping him in a tight hug. Day lifted the man off his feet and held him close.

Day didn't know if Ronowski had forgotten where the hell he was but he placed a huge kiss on Day's lips before wrapping him up tight again.

"Congratulations, gorgeous," Ronowski said in his ear.

Ronowski pulled back and beamed at him again before moving over and hugging God. Ronowski gently fingered the word Lieutenant engraved in black lettering on God's badge that hung from his neck when his shoulders suddenly went rigid at the silence that had enveloped the entire bullpen.

"They're all looking at me aren't they?" Ronowski said quietly.

God just nodded his head and cracked up.

Ronowski spun around and threw his hands up in the air like he'd been busted. "Yes, I'm gay, get over it!" he yelled and turned back to them.

"Give us some credit; we're all detectives here, Ronowski. We figured that out years ago," one of the forensics detectives yelled back, and everyone start cheering again.

Day was proud that Ronowski took it all in stride even though his neck and ears were beet red. Most of the faces Day saw were friendly and looked genuinely happy for them. But Day was a people watcher, and he'd definitely noticed the few that slipped out of the station with displeased glares. Day shrugged it off. He'd learned very young that you can't please them all.

The women were coming up to them and hugging them while the men gave them strong handshakes and told them that it was a promotion well deserved. It was no secret that God and Day doubled everyone else's record in the amount of arrests they made and had taken over one-hundred million dollars' worth of drugs off the streets in their five years as partners.

Day and God were at their desk still feeling high from all the recognition when Seasel came over to them. She'd been on desk duty since returning two weeks ago. She still had six long months of physical therapy ahead of her before she'd be out in the field again.

"Ya know God; now that you're my lieutenant you have the authority to select my assignments." She winked.

"Of course I will, babe," God told her.

Seasel's brown eyes lit up.

"As soon as your doctor says you're finished with therapy," God amended.

He didn't try to dodge the hard slaps she landed on his shoulder.

"Asshole." She huffed and picked up God's gold badge, inspecting it carefully when a wide smile spread across her face. "So can I call you Leu?"

"Not if you expect me to answer," God retorted drily.

She rolled her eyes at God's sarcasm. "You're lucky your partner saved my life or else I wouldn't be throwing you guys a five-year celebration party next month."

"What party?" God asked.

"I'm not telling," she sing-songed on her way back to her desk.

Day and God's promotion really hadn't hit them until they came back from lunch and there were four detectives milling around their desk.

"Hey can you guys try not to take such long lunches. I've been waiting for like forty-five minutes," Detective Ross snapped at them before they could even sit back down. "I'm going to be taking my vacation in June this year instead of August like I usually do, so I put my request in your box for approval, Day. Thanks, buddy." The chubby detective slapped him on his back and returned to his desk.

Day blinked and looked at their in-boxes, which were overflowing onto their desks, and almost spit out his coffee. "What the fucking fuck?" Day yelled.

"You've got to be shittin' me." God looked around the office but no one was paying any attention to them.

Ronowski came up to them and plopped down in God's chair. "Hey, if you guys want the power and the big bucks... looks like you're going to earn it." He grinned wickedly at them.

"Ro, get the hell out of here before I do something to wipe that grin off your face." God yanked him out of his seat.

"Promises, promises, big boy." Ronowski laughed and took a couple steps toward his desk before turning and adding, "Oh, and lieutenants, I'm going to need one of you to question a suspect with me this afternoon. Does three work for you? Good," he said hurriedly, not letting either one of them get a word in as he laughed. He knew they were already swamped and was obviously delighted to add to their already chaotic workload.

God had only signed off on two requests for a different partner assignments and a complaint filed by a suspect against one of their officers when the captain yelled from his office for them to go with two other detectives to perform a search and seizure across town.

Day threw his hands up in the air. "I think we are being punked. How the hell are we supposed to do all of this shit *and* be out in the field?"

"Fuck if I know," God answered him, rubbing his eyes, throbbing from reading all those forms.

"Delegation, you fools."

God and Day both looked up at the thin man standing next to their desks with his own stack of paperwork. He lifted it high and let it drop down in God's in-box, making some of the other papers fall on the floor.

"What did you say? And pick those up, asswipe." God pointed to the fallen papers.

The IT geek squatted and picked up the couple sheets, sliding them back on the desk. Detective Halls wasn't a field officer; he was a computer crimes detective and an excellent hacker. The guy had like five different degrees in computer technology and a Masters in Forensic Science. He could take apart a computer blindfolded and put back together, or he could lift a usable fingerprint off a brick wall. He was a cocky sonofabitch who acted like he knew it all... which he actually did.

"I said delegation. You guys are lieutenants. That means you have sergeants, beat cops, and a whole office full of administrative officers at your disposal." Halls reached out and plucked the paper from Day's hand and flipped it over scanning its contents quickly before flicking it back at him. He sucked his teeth and shook his head at Day as if he was pathetic. "What type of three-star lieutenant spends hours approving vacation requests? The goddamn receptionist can input those, put a damn sticky note with a yes or no on it, and hand it off. Get it together, guys."

Day and God sat there with their mouths open as the tactless man walked through the station with his nose held high and closed himself back in his department, that consisted of ten laboratory stations, and what looked to be fifty or so computers.

"Damn that guy is a prick," Day muttered and started putting the papers in different stacks.

"What are you doing?" God asked.

"Delegating and then I'm getting my ass back on the streets where I belong." Day winked.

God quickly followed suit and after thirty minutes of sorting their paperwork they efficiently moved around the station issuing orders, behaving like real lieutenants.

By the end of the day God and Day were too exhausted to go out with Ronowski and Johnson for beers and instead picked up a pizza and went home to kick back and relax. They barely had time to digest their food before they were both in bed snoring loudly.

The Best Gift of Them All

A full month had passed and God and Day were just getting used to their new duties. Their true passion was being out on the streets, so the men had no problems with their newfound love for the art of delegation. They were good bosses, though, and eventually the coworkers who disagreed with their promotion at first were slowly coming around.

It was Friday night. Tomorrow all of the department, their family, and close friends would be at their house to help them celebrate their partnership anniversary. Day didn't think a time would come where his heart would be so filled, doubting he could handle another wonderful thing happening.

He was in bed watching the Food Network waiting on God to come out of the bathroom. He'd been in there for over an hour. The water to the shower had stopped twenty minutes ago.

"Hey! You didn't fall in did you?" Day called out.

No answer.

"Babe." Day pushed mute on the television. There was no sound at all. "Cash."

No answer.

Day pushed the covers back, got up and walked quickly over to the door. His nipples hardened in the coolness of the room, goose bumps popped up on his forearms. He tapped a couple times and before he tapped a third time God opened the door. Day exhaled a nervous breath. "Geez. Didn't you hear me call—"

God's hot mouth was on Day before he could finish his sentence. He was pushed back against the wall as God closed in on him, thrusting his strong pelvis into his. He grabbed both hands, interlocking their fingers and pulled them high above their heads. He pressed Day's hands against the cool surface, sliding his hands down his arms, landing on the front of his naked chest. God pulled his mouth away and kissed along Day's jaw to the base of his throat. He took a long inhale against Day's neck.

"Mmm. You smell good." God moaned in his ear.

Day lifted his chin, letting God do what he wanted. He could smell the fresh shower scent on his man. God's wet hair dripped down on his face, the smell of his masculine shampoo assaulted his senses. "You smell better."

God stopped his nibbling and licking long enough to stare into Day's eyes. "I love you so much." God whispered into his mouth.

"I know, babe." Day dropped his arms, so his fingers could tease at the opening of God's towel.

"I never thought I'd be someone special to anyone." God gently caressed the side of his face. Looking at him like he couldn't believe he was real. Day's heart clenched at the sincere look in God's striking green eyes. When he spoke again, his voice was strained and filled with emotion. "It's been five years, Leonidis, five years of me loving you."

"I don't know how I existed without you." Day whispered back.

God closed his eyes. His breathing was shallow and his jaw ticked with nervousness. Day could easily read him. "Cash. What's wrong?"

"I need to be with you," God replied gripping Day's shoulders, squeezing them tightly.

Day continued to watch his lover. Seeking out what was really going on inside of him. "I need you too."

"No. I mean I need you to have me. Make love to me." God bent slightly and placed his lips to Day's ear. "I want you to top me."

Day froze in place. His eyes lowered in contemplation, hands resting lightly on God's waist. *Top him.* Suddenly a ton of feelings washed over him. He simultaneously became excited, nervous, scared, and extremely turned-on. All those emotions swirling around inside his head and heart at once.

"Please. I trust you. I trust you to make it right. My only time bottoming was when—" God gripped Day tighter, pressing their bodies together, like he couldn't bear to say the word 'rape' right now. "I need you to make all that go away. Will you do that for me?"

God's deep voice vibrated Day's chest, and he knew what God was asking. All the demons of his past needed to be laid to rest. God had his family, his partner, his career. Love. He had it all. However, if he didn't come to terms with his past he'd never be able to fully enjoy his future.

"Yes," Day finally responded. "I will. I'll do anything for you. You know that."

God backed up a couple steps and reached out for him. Day put his sweaty palm in God's, and let him lead them to the bed. Day dropped his briefs to the floor while God tossed his towel and settled in the middle of the warm bed.

Day turned and went to his record player choosing Oscar Peterson's *Night Train*, a classy, elegant romantic jazz album. Only the best for his lover. Day turned off the television and all the lights in the bedroom, leaving only the moonlight to illuminate the room. God pulled back the covers, inviting him in. Day joined his man, immediately settling on top of his large body. He moaned deeply as soon as their hard cocks rubbed against each other.

"I'm gonna make this so good for you, Cash." Day moaned maneuvering himself so that his cock head was nestled underneath God's heavy balls. He relished the loud groan that erupted from the man beneath him. "Yes," Day hissed.

315

He was perfectly happy bottoming for God for the rest of their lives, but he did like to use his cock, he would love nothing more than to push into his partner's tight confinement. Making him scream out when he rubbed against that special place inside him. But he understood what God had gone through and he wouldn't dare ask him to do anything that would bring back those memories. Although it wasn't as frequent, God still suffered from nightmares about being repeatedly attacked.

Day stroked the wet strands of God's hair back, weaving it in between his fingers. His chest rose and fell rapidly as Day gyrated his hips. "It's okay." Day whispered, lightly moving his lips back and forth over God's parted mouth.

"Make it good, Leo. Please. I want my only memories to be of you. You taking me. The only one that has had me." God's pained voice made Day want to protect the man he'd called partner for the last five years, protect his lover from the nightmares, from those years of torture. He belonged to him now. When God thought of bottoming, he'd only think of him, not of those perverted assholes that had violated a scared teen.

"I got you, babe. Don't worry. I got you." Day settled deeply between God's thighs, while rubbing his hands over his face, his shoulders, his neck, his broad chest. Laying sweet, suckling kisses over every inch of him. Marking him in some places, teasing him in others. He inched down to God's weeping cock, rubbing his beard stubble up and down the length. God grunted his approval, pushing his hips up to feel more. Day opened his mouth wide and engulfed just the head. Stabbing his tongue at the slit, wanting more of the salty fluid easing from his man. "Taste so fuckin' good." Day moaned.

God's hands were clinched into fists, resting on the comforter as if he was unsure what to do with them. Day went down further, making sure to use just enough teeth to elicit a hiss but not enough to hurt. He didn't stop until his nose was buried in the scratchy hairs at the base of God's dick.

"Fuck!" God cursed, his shoulders coming up off the bed from the pleasure. Day knew God loved that he could take every inch of him and more. He pulled up slowly, dragging the flat of his tongue over that thick vein on the underside of God's dick. He moaned around the head and went back down again. Damn he'd never be able to get enough of this man. God was more potent than any drug, Day's own personal brand of heroin. His voice, his body, his attitude, his skills, and his intelligence all came together to make one helluva motherfucking man.

Day reached over to the nightstand for the Slick. God watched him, watched every move he made. Day came back and kissed him hungrily, pushing his tongue in deep so God could taste himself. God wove his fingers through his hair, holding him in place, taking control of the kiss. Day didn't mind. God needed to be in control of something, so he let him have this. He didn't stop until God released his head.

Day sucked in a few breaths, lifting up onto his hands. "Turn over, Cash."

A flash of worry appeared in those mesmerizing eyes right before God moved to do what he was told. Day didn't say anything about it. He didn't need to tell his man everything was going to be okay, he had to show him. Day closed his eyes while the smooth sounds of Peterson's piano calmed him, spoke to his spirit. He gently rubbed his palm up and down God's strong back. Stroking the large lion, taming the wild beast within his partner.

He maneuvered himself in between those solid thighs, spreading God open. *Fuck*. Damn, just a glimpse of God's dark hole had Day wanting to come. He had to compose himself. He couldn't get too excited, otherwise he'd lose his self-control and do something to mess up this special, very critical moment in God's life. He covered God with his body from head to toe, giving him security and protection, because that's how he felt when God was draped on top of him. He believed it worked both ways because his lover exhaled and sank down further into the mattress. He moved God's long hair out of the way and began kissing his neck while massaging his shoulders.

"Ahhh. Yes, Leo."

Day was doing it right. He wanted God to get vocal with him, let him know that he was enjoying this. Day ran his tongue down God's spine until he got to his hips. He rubbed his face against the soft hairs on God's ass. He gently opened one side of him and felt him tense under his palm. Day began to place soft kisses around his clenched hole before using his tongue to tease at it. God squirmed but he didn't shy away. Day placed a couple more teasing licks at the tight, furry bud, the dark hairs now slick from his spit, before finally pressing his tongue flat against it, feeling it pulsate. *Oh fuck.* God spread wider. *Fuck yes.* Day pushed down on his own aching cock while he swiped his tongue over God's hole again and again, licking, and blowing on the moist flesh.

"Again," God moaned, just slightly raising his hips up.

Day's chest was pounding with restrained energy. He rotated his tongue in figure eights in God's crease, pressing the tip in just a little. He pulled back and blew more cool air on God's puckered skin. "Ahh. That's good."

Day appreciated the approval so he did it a few more times. God was into it now. He kept up his tonguing while quietly flicking open the cap of the Slick and pouring some lube on two fingers, closing and tossing the bottle to the side. He pushed his tongue in farther, and goddamn his man was tight as hell. God was clenching his muscles at the intrusion of his tongue and Day could only imagine how that was going to feel on his bare cock. He was sure he'd lose it in less than a minute.

Day withdrew his tongue and God's body trembled beneath him when he rubbed one finger around his hole. He moved it in a circular motion for a few seconds before pushing in slightly. He pulled back, carefully watching God's reaction. His face was lying on the soft pillow, eyes closed, his brow creased with concentration.

"Relax. It's gonna feel so good." Day murmured, pushing his finger in deeper.

God nodded his head and raised his hips higher.

"Oh my fucking god. You are the sexiest thing in the world. Looking at you like this. Offering yourself to me. Jesus Christ. Thank for trusting me. I love you so much." Day panted out his gratitude while pushing his finger all the way in, simultaneously stroking his own cock. He couldn't help it. His cock was dark red and angry, needing release now.

God grunted again, but Day didn't stop. He pulled out to the first knuckle and pushed back in again, going deeper. His man jerked hard and yelled out his name.

"Fuck! Leo, it's good! That's so good!" God pushed back, seeking out more of that feeling.

Day reached between God's legs and pulled his dick back so he could lick at it while he finger fucked him. Day kept one finger deep inside pressing against that spongy gland and attached his mouth to God's balls, lapping at them, rolling them with his tongue. He heard his lover cursing but his own ears were ringing so loud he couldn't make out what he was saying. God's hot pulsing channel was squeezing the hell out of his finger.

Day dragged his tongue up behind God's balls and nibbled at his taint before moving back up to his hole. He swirled his tongue around his finger while he kept the pressure on God's prostate. His lover's bud had relaxed, taking his finger easily. "I'm going to give you more." Day said breathlessly.

God didn't answer, but his moan was enough encouragement for Day to keep going. He added a second finger, pushing in steadily. He felt God tense against the pressure. Day stopped and worked God's cock back into his mouth, sucking hard on the head until his man begin moaning again and slowly working his hips back and forth.

"Don't stop Leo."

"Never." Day pushed two fingers in, aiming for that sweet spot. "So fuckin' tight. Jesus."

He worked carefully to get God prepared for his first time. All the horrible violations that were done to him when he was young didn't count. This was what mattered. God willingly giving his body to his lover. He knew God was scared, he could feel it, taste it, he knew his partner better than he knew himself. But he could also feel the uninhibited trust God had for him, felt it stronger, deeper than the fear. Day was easily working three fingers in, and God's cries of passion were making his cock weep. *Holy fuck.* He'd never heard his lover like this, seen him spread open for him, so eager to be had.

"Now Leo. Right now." God said in his deep, sexy timbre.

Day reached for the lube and poured a generous amount on his dick and pushed some into God's relaxed hole. Day had to stop and just stare for a few seconds. In all his life, he'd never seen anything more beautiful than what was in front of him right now. *Please let me make this good for him.* Day sent up a silent prayer before pressing his blushed head to God's entrance. He wished he could see his face as he entered him but he knew this would be the easiest way for God to take him in.

"Relax Cash. It's going to be good, I promise." Day whispered in God's ear while he pushed past the ring of muscle.

God's body jerked beneath him, a startled grunt escaping his lips. Day halted, pressing his chest harder into God's back while massaging his shoulders. It took all of Day's strength not to push all the way inside and fuck God like it was his last act before death. But Day would do whatever it took, he'd be patient.

"I'm good," God said in a hushed voice.

Day rained kisses on the back of God's neck and over to his coarse jaw as he pushed in deeper. He licked around the rim of God's ear, speaking to him calmly, "Breathe baby. You know what to do. Show me how much you want me; show me that I'm the only one that has ever had you like this."

Day slightly rocked his hips, only moving in and out an inch or so, while God did what he needed to do so he could slide all the way in. Day kept rubbing, kissing, massaging, and whispering until God took a deep breath and pushed out against him. Day slid in with ease, until his balls rested against God's furry ass.

"Fuck."

"Fuck." They both hissed at the same time.

"Damnit, Leo. Feel... feels." God huffed.

"I know." Day released a throaty groan as he gently pulled out and slid back in. Making slow, shallow thrusts. The music was putting him in the lovemaking mood, the smooth jazz serenading them made Day want to keep it slow and sexy. When Day's balls were snug against God's ass he gently tilted his pelvis up, pegging that gland with his head. He knew he'd hit it when God's hands clenched into tight fists.

"Yes," God hissed.

Day kept that motion going for several seconds until he felt God moving with him. Finally, God was completely pliable beneath him, his chest pressed into the soft bedding, his legs spread wide, his ruggedly handsome face turned to the side, gusting shallow breaths into his mouth.

Day rose up and got a good grip on God's hips. He lifted him to his knees. He wanted to work God's thick cock while he fucked him. Day pulled out half way only to thrust back in with a little more force. God's hands scrambled for something to hold on to. Day grabbed them and linked their fingers together, anchoring them to each other. God's body shone in the darkness, the moonlight streaming in through the sheer curtains making the sheen of sweat on his back glisten. A sight Day would never forget.

He reached under and gripped God's cock. It was half-hard, but Day was about to change that. He stroked him in time with his movements.

"Mmm. Yeah, sweetheart. That's it." God encouraged. His body fully primed to take him.

Day snapped his hips and God cried out to him again. "Are you ready?" Day said, his control waning. He needed to go deeper, harder, or else he was going to fucking lose it. His man was so damn hot inside, squeezing him deliciously.

"Let me turn over," God answered.

Day pulled out very slowly. When God turned over Day didn't wait. He crushed his mouth to his and shoved his tongue in as deep as he wanted his cock to go. He kissed his man to within an inch of his life. Moaning and biting, licking and nipping, until God was begging him to fuck him. "Need you right fuckin' now, Leo."

Day ran his tongue along God's muscled pecs, sucking up moist red marks as he went. Dark nipples called to him, made his cock jump as he swirled his tongue around the tight nubs until they were hard. He tugged one of God's arms up, pressing his hand above his head. *Fuck.* God smelled so good. Manly and strong. Day buried his nose in God's underarm, rubbing his cheek along the fine hairs. Day licked him there. Another intimate and personal place, reserved only for him. He ran the flat of his tongue from the bottom of his pit to the top. God squirmed beneath him, held the back of his head in a firm grip, keeping him there. Day bit and laved at him vigorously, loving the rich, masculine smell of his lover. God growled, lifted his other arm and Day took the hint. He kissed and nipped at each nipple as he made his way over to the other arm. He gave the same treatment to that one. Damn. God's smell was an aphrodisiac.

When Day'd had his fill, he lined his aching cock up and pushed in to the hilt. They both gasped loudly and Day's eyes rolled in their sockets. God's legs fell easily to the side and Day started up a rapid, deep penetration. Keeping his body flush against God, only his hips moving up and down. "Shit Cash. Feels too damn good. Squeezing the fuck out of me." Day groaned into the crook of God's neck.

God nudged Day's face, seeking out his mouth. Day kissed him like it was their first time. He sighed as God embraced him. Hugging him tightly too him, his hips thrusting up to meet his. They were in that zone together. Where nothing else in the world existed, nothing mattered but them. There were no problems, no stress, no past, and no nightmares, only them in love. Making love. Sending all his lover's demons back to the depths of hell where they belonged.

Day could feel God's hard shaft rubbing against his abs. His balls tightened and his spine tingled with his pending orgasm. He reached for God's cock and jerked him in long tight strokes. He held God's shoulder, shoving him downward to meet him as he shoved deep inside. He was almost there, ready to come, ready to fill his man, make him whole again.

God gave a harsh grunt right before Day felt the first shot of warm come hit his chest. His lover's body jerked beneath him, while he pumped his dick for every drop God could give him. "That's it love. Come hard for me." God held Day's face while they looked down at their union, watched God's dick pulse in his fist while he released more pearly white fluid to coat his hand. When God was done he pulled Day in for another soul-searing kiss. God took Day's hand from his cock and brought up to their mouths. God stuck out his tongue, cleaning his come off of his hand.

"Oh my fuckin'—" Day's obscenities were cut off when God pushed his come-coated tongue into his mouth. Day shuddered as his cock jerked inside God's still pulsing channel. God moaned in his mouth while Day started to make love to him again. "Love you so damn much." God said on a sated sigh.

Day's eyes shone bright with his emotions. "I love you, too." He panted, his forehead resting against God's. Day didn't have much longer. His hips lost their rhythm when God's lust-filled green gaze bored into him. Their unbreakable bond. Talking to him without words. An amazing ability between soul mates. Silently he told Day to come deep inside him. Told him he was whole again. Told him that Day was perfect, he'd been perfect.

Day knew he'd do anything for this magnificent man, do anything he'd asked of him. Obey his every word.

Day held the back of God's neck, his other hand held God's thigh, keeping him splayed open for him. Day moaned low and deep. "I'm gonna come." God squeezed him tightly, held him to his hard chest. Day's back went stiff, his vision blurred as he slammed in deep and throbbed inside God's heat. He wanted his come inside this man, wanted him to keep it in him while they slept together. Day's body jolted from his first shot of come. He lurched and yelled like it was his first time. It was intense and powerful, it was mind-blowing to top a man like God. All of that barreled through Day's mind as he kept pumping his essence deep into him. He gave a couple more shallow thrust, before finally stilling. His cock completely drained.

His breathing was labored and harsh, panting while placing tender kisses on God's muscled chest. Day felt like a king. He sensed that God felt claimed, surprisingly, he did too.

Day lifted slightly, so his soft dick slid out of God. The moan God released was soft against his throat. When Day went to move off his lover, he was grabbed tightly. "Not ready for you to move yet."

"Want me to get a towel to clean you up?" Day said lazily.

"No. Leave it. Leave me just like this." God demanded and Day obeyed.

The 2nd Best Gift of Them All

Saturday afternoon Vikki was downstairs in Day's home putting the finishing touches on the decorations and getting the caterers in order for God and Day's promotion slash partnership celebration. A lot of people had pitched in to help with the costs of the event since Day refused to let them use the department's party funds. He looked out of Genesis's bedroom window and was really impressed with how they'd turned the back yard of his home into a beautifully decorated BBQ party. God and Day were simple men, so walking around in dressy clothes eating frilly finger foods wouldn't cut it.

God pulled Day into his arms, kissing his neck and shoulders before working his way up slowly to his chin. "I'm so in love with you. You were perfect last night."

"I love you back, babe." Day tilted his head back and thrust into him.

God slid down and grabbed both of Day's ass cheeks and massaged them while moaning in his ear.

"Hell! Come on guys, do y'all have to be sexing all the time?" Genesis covered his eyes as if he'd been blinded.

"Yes," Day snapped.

"Awww. Don't get mad Uncle Leo." Genesis teased Day... as usual. Genesis loved to get a rise out of his Uncle Leo. He started calling Day and his brother Jaxson "Uncle" since the guys rode his hide like they were related. Anytime Genesis got a speeding ticket or a "C" on a test, or made any kind of slip up… they were all over him.

After they'd moved God's mom into her new apartment, Genesis had moved in with them and Day loved how happy his man was to finally have peace within himself now that his family was whole again. Genesis was a great kid and Day could see more and more of God in him every day. Even when the big goofball went off to college he'd always have a room here in their home… especially since he'd only be an hour and half away at the University of Georgia playing in front of millions as a Georgia Bulldog this fall.

"Gen, how many times do I have to tell you to knock on our door?" God walked over to his brother and yanked him down into a headlock.

"I did knock but you guys were moaning and grunting so loud you didn't hear me." Genesis laughed and started elbowing God in his side so he'd release him. "I came up here to tell you that I invited my friend Terry to the party and I don't want you guys grilling him and asking him a million questions. We're not a couple or anything… we're just kicking it." Genesis shrugged.

"Okay, but you don't have to worry about us embarrassing you, because both our moms will be here, so I suggest you have this conversation with them." Day smiled at Genesis while lacing up his black-and-red Jordans. "You know my mom thinks you're this goody-two-shoes honor student who's saving himself until marriage. She doesn't see the actual pervert that we live with."

Day threw his head back and laughed when Genesis started shaking his head back and forth.

"Gen, go down and tell Vikki we'll be down soon. I have something to say to Day first." God shoved Genesis toward the door.

"Oh, I know exactly what you have to say to him and I think it goes like this… 'Ugh, yes! Just like that, sweetheart! Don't stop! '" Genesis shouted in mock ecstasy and ran from God as he chased him down the hall. Genesis's long legs took the stairs four at a time trying to escape his brother.

"I'll get you later, shithead. Don't fall asleep before I do," God yelled down the stairs.

Day laughed at his lover when he came back in the room. "I told you to be quieter when we fuck, babe." Day smirked.

God looked at Day like he wanted to devour him. "I can't help it if you make me scream, lover."

"He is good at that," the sexy voice said from the door.

God and Day turned knowing glares at their friends.

"What are you guys doing?" God smiled and walked over to kiss both men on their lips, Johnson lingering a little longer, like he always did.

Ronowski slunk into the room and settled in behind Day. He kissed his neck and Day turned and kissed him quickly. "You look good, baby boy."

"So do you." Ronowski smiled at him, nuzzling the side of his face.

Day had to admit that they looked pretty good for their party. God was in khaki cargo shorts and a simple white V-neck T-shirt. God's tan Timberland boots made him look like a roughneck. Day had on black shorts and a black-and-white collared shirt. They'd been sure to tell Vikki that everyone should dress casually, like they normally would for a BBQ. This was an informal party.

"Ro wants to know if you guys feel up to some company tonight," Johnson spoke up.

God grabbed Johnson's large biceps and jerked him forward, slamming him into his rock-hard chest. "Why? You ready for me to fuck you, Johnson?" God sucked hard on Johnson's neck but pulled back before he could leave a mark.

"Maybe I am," Johnson growled low in his throat and pushed God backward until their muscular bodies slammed into the wall so hard it shook the pictures. They both let grunted before Johnson finally pushed God's hulking frame off him.

"Holy fuck." Day panted squeezing his rising cock. "I definitely want to watch you two big motherfuckers go at it." They both knew where the boundaries lay when they played with Johnson and Ro. There was a silent understanding. No one would top God. That would always be something sacred and special for his one and only true partner.

"Well that sounds like a yes to me. We got our bags in the car. None of us have to work until Tuesday." Ronowski whooped. He was not shy about showing his excitement over being gay and in love anymore. All four of them had only been together a couple more times after their first time and each time it got better. They'd end with Ronowski and Day swooning in the tub and God and Johnson hugged up in bed watching *Sports Center*.

Ronowski jumped up into Day's arms and straddled his waist. He leaned in to lick Day's lips. "Until tonight, gorgeous."

Day let Ronowski kiss him with fervor before the beautiful man dropped his toned legs and went back into the arms of his man.

"Just let us get rid of Gen first. I'm sure he'll go over to Terry's tonight anyway," God said while hugging both of them. He told them to go on downstairs that he and Day would be down soon.

When they left God closed the door and locked it this time, making sure that there would be no more interruptions.

"I got a little gift for you, sweetheart, and I wanted to give it to you before the party," God said pulling a medium-sized wrapped box from underneath the bed.

Day smiled at him and turned and went into the closet and came out with a nice-sized elegantly wrapped box. "I got you something too." Day placed the box on the bed next to God. They both smiled at each other, still in awe of how much alike they thought. Somehow they both saw it fitting to get each other some type of gift to commemorate their five-year anniversary.

"Open mine first." Day beamed at him.

God turned toward the package and tore off the thin black-and-silver paper. He frowned when he saw it was a case surrounded with latches that needed to be unsnapped to open it. God looked up at Day with piqued curiosity before lifting the lid on the shiny wood-grain case.

"No way." God's eyes almost bugged out his head. "Those are freakin' beautiful... and so expensive. Sweetheart, what have you done?" God stroked Day's cheek tenderly. God carefully lifted one of the two identical custom-made .50 caliber Desert Eagles from the felt casing. God looked in amazement at the polished chrome ten-inch barreled weapon, accented with 24K gold appointments, the custom grips were black walnut wood with a lion's head etched into it.

God brought the piece closer and read the sexy cursive script along the long shiny barrel. *In God We Trust.*

God looked into Day's eyes and Day could clearly see, hear, and feel every bit of the appreciation his lover had for his gift. These weapons were worthy of the man in front of him. Day felt only slightly selfish for choosing this particular gift for his partner of five years, because he would reap most of the satisfaction every time his body reacted to God holstering those magnificent weapons close against his body.

"Come here, Leo." God's rough drawl interrupted his nasty thoughts.

God sat on the bed and pulled Day in between his legs. "I want to tell you before we go downstairs and celebrate our partnership with our friends and family that I love you more than I ever thought possible to love someone. Before I partnered with you I was a shell of a man going through life, simply existing. I felt like I was nothing special... but you believed I was someone worthy of your love. You've given me purpose, sweetheart; purpose to live. You saved me and I'll love you and only you forever for it." God leaned in and kissed Day softly. "This is for you." God held the box out to him.

Day quickly ripped open the shiny green paper and lifted the lid off the velvet box. "Oh my god." Day's hand went to his mouth as he stared inside the box. Day frowned and looked up at his man. "How the hell did you find this? Where did… How did you?" Day was at a complete loss of what to say. He picked up the album like it was a newborn fresh from the womb.

"An original first pressing of Coltrane's *Giant Steps*," Day whispered in awe, lifting the vinyl record while inspecting the condition of the cover. Tears formed in his eyes as he stared at the song titles on the back, remembering the smooth notes of every single cut. "I've looked all over for this. For so many years. I swear I don't even remember telling you about this. Jesus Christ." He looked into God's eyes, looked at the marvel that was his life partner. "My father used to play this for my mom and dance her around the living room." Day's voice caught on his feelings. He held the mint-condition record close to his chest and closed his eyes at the reminiscences. "All his albums got consumed in the fire. I was able to replace every single one he'd lost over time… except this one. I wanted this album so bad." Day smiled through the tears that fell from his eyes at the memory of his father. "She could never stay mad at him when he played this record. He loved her so much, until the day he died, baby."

God pulled Day into his arms and held him tight, letting Day release all the feelings he was having at that moment into him. "And I'll love you forever too, sweetheart." God released him and gently took the cover from Day's fingertips and withdrew the rare vinyl. He walked over to Day's player and placed it on the turntable, slowly dropping the needle on the outer edge.

At the first melodious crackling sound of the needle gliding over the grooves in the record Day clutched at his heart as memories of his father twirling his mother around invaded his soul. He could hear his father's deep voice singing off-key in his mom's ear while she flung her head back and laughed in his arms.

Day finally had his love for life. His partner in every possible way. He looked into God's soulful eyes and told him on a breathless whisper, "Dance with me."

Read Next: Embracing His Syn

Nothing Special Series

Everything's Not Always as it Seems

"Alright Syn, don't waste my fucking time. Let's see what you got."

Syn turned and looked at his hopefully future Lieutenant. God's gruff voice could really intimidate a man. Add in the guy's build and tattoos, and he intimidated most men ... but Syn wasn't most men.

He'd put in for an immediate transfer from his precinct in Philadelphia when he heard a vacancy opened up on the most notorious task force in the Eastern U.S. A task force headed up by Lieutenant Cashel Godfrey – known as God, and Lieutenant Leonidis Day. A quick-witted snarky bastard who wasn't afraid to cut you to the quick if you got in his face. The dynamic duo were both promoted to the rank of Lieutenant a couple years ago after having been Detectives for only five years. Being promoted so quickly had been unheard of – before they were recruited by the Mayor of Atlanta to head up their own task force made up of some of the toughest SOBs this side of the Mississippi. The new rules for God and Day were the same as before ... there were none.

Lieutenant Day was on one side of the bolt-locked door, a sarcastic smirk already on his face, his two chrome 9mm handguns pointed down at the rickety porch. God was on the opposite side of the door, his broad back against the house's red brick siding, his twin gold-toned Desert Eagles cocked and ready to fire. Syn took one final look behind him and saw Detective Ronowski at his six ready his shotgun. Syn gave him a quick nod. Everything was a go.

Syn steeled his spine, reared back, braced his weight on his back leg and raised his right boot in one swift motion and shattered the thin wood surrounding the doorknob. "Atlanta PD! Atlanta PD!" Syn yelled as he moved inside the small townhome, eyes forward but mindful of any movement in his periphery. God and Day were inside now and Syn watched them kick tables and chairs out of their path, making their way through the narrow hall that led to what looked like a couple of bedrooms and a small bath. After Syn shouted a couple of 'clears' for the living room and the kitchen, Ronowski quickly began rummaging through couch cushions, feeling underneath tables and knocking at areas on the wall, listening for hollow sounds. Drug dealers were known for concealing drugs, money, and guns behind drywall.

"Atlanta PD let me see your hands, now!" Day's command floated out to Syn as he made his way back to the front of the house. He saw Day leading out a man who looked to be in his early thirties. He was shirtless and his hair was matted to one side of his head like he'd been sleeping. His hands were secured behind his back with a zip-tie. Day threw him on the ratty plaid sofa and God's look dared him to try to get up.

"I guess you're not going to read me my rights. Fucking filthy cops. I heard you been asking around about me, God. I heard some other shit too."

"Maybe I should fix it so you don't hear anything else," God growled.

Syn watched God yank his twelve inch serrated blade from its sheath tucked underneath his left arm. He masterfully flipped the blade over his hand once like something you'd see in a Jet Li film and used his other hand to get a painful grip on the top of his suspect's ear.

The suspect became still and very quiet as the tip of the blade skated lightly across the side of his face and stopped at his earlobe.

"Chill the fuck out, God," the man hissed.

"What else did you hear, Goose?" God asked in a low voice.

"Nothing man! Nothing, alright!"

Syn saw God look him in the eye and he made sure his poker face was in place. Syn had read the entire file on this drug dealing trash over the last two days. Their suspect, Greg 'Goose' Jenkins, had taken over his uncle's illegal business after Day and God had gotten him locked up for twenty years. The men on their team had secured enough surveillance on Goose to conduct a legal search and get a solid conviction if they found drugs, cash or guns in the home.

After God tucked his knife away, Goose spat on the floor and leveled each of them with a hateful look. "Where's the warrant, God? Your boy is back there tearing up my goddamn house, let me see the fucking warrant."

Syn kept his eyes on the suspect, but the man's comments were raising Syn's hackles. Shouldn't they be calling this in by now? What were Ronowski and Day doing back there?

334

Syn was on the task force on a trial basis. He needed to prove he could follow orders, anticipate the need to act, and work efficiently as part of the team; but also show he was ruthless and dangerous ... just like all the other team members. He'd heard stories that these guys were badasses. So was Syn. He wanted to climb the departmental ranks, and being on God and Day's task force was a sure way to get his name recognized and get out from under his father's legacy to make his own.

God pulled one of the dining room chairs into the room, turned it around and straddled it. He stared at Syn, those green eyes drilling into him, but he didn't dare look away. God was intuitive as fuck. He knew Syn was thinking something was off about this bust.

"I heard you was crooked man," Goose snapped at God.

"You still hearing shit," Syn answered before God could. God briefly gazed at Syn.

"Where's your fucking warrant, God? I didn't hear you motherfuckers knock before you kicked in my door and just invited yourselves in."

"You don't invite the wind," Day said with a mischievous grin, coming back into the room with Ronowski trailing. "The wind just blows in."

"Fuck you," Goose snarled.

They hefted a medium-sized safe onto the wobbly dining table and Ronowski quickly pulled a small device from one of his pockets. He attached it to the front of the safe, next to the lock. Putting his ear to it, he listened intently as he turned the dial.

"I knew it. Dirty-assed cops!" the angry man yelled, bolting to his feet. God moved so fast Syn didn't have a chance to react. God's large hand gripped the suspect around his throat and lifted him several feet in the air before slamming him down onto the unforgiving floor.

"Ouch town, population you." Day chuckled.

Fuck. Syn's head was spinning. Something wasn't right. God didn't have a warrant, he hadn't read the man his rights, and no one was calling this in. *Oh fuck me ... this can't be happening.*

"You alright over there, Detective Sydney?"

Syn blinked and realized that beads of sweat were dripping down his face and his weapon was still out. Everyone else had returned their weapons to their holsters. Syn hoped he wasn't witnessing what he feared he was.

"Jackpot," Ronowski said.

Syn spun around and watched the smooth-faced Detective pull out stacks of rolled money. He didn't know exactly how much, but it had to be at least ten to twenty thousand since the rolls contained hundred dollar bills. Ronowski turned and winked at God, and Syn narrowed his eyes. *Please someone pull out an evidence bag. Please.* He watched Ronowski's bright blue eyes turn to Day and he'd be damned if the man he'd heard such wonderful stories about didn't reach into the safe and pull out several rolls of cash, putting it into the lining of his vest ... God and Ronowski following suit.

"Got a payday on your first seize. Looks like your lucky day Sydney." God's look was a warning when Syn refused to pocket any of the money.

336

Read Next: Here Comes Trouble

The Story of Detective Ruxsberg & Detective Green

Chapter One

"Ruxs watch out for the - Oh shit!" *Damn. Not another cyclist.* Green floored his huge RAM2500, barreling around the corner of Marrietta Street, keeping a close eye on his partner as he chased down one of their informants. He couldn't jump the curb, onto the sidewalk to cut off the chase there were too many pedestrians. Ruxs needed to get the bastard to turn off of the street into one of the many deserted alleys. Green divided his attention between maneuvering through the thick mid-afternoon traffic and not losing his partner. He roared the engine around a slow-assed Buick and flew through another red light, just lightly clipping the back end of a MARTA bus. *Opps. Thought I cleared that. Fuck.*

He saw Ruxs double his efforts, landing a hard slap to the informant's shoulder that sent him flying into an old lady, knocking her bags out of her hand. Green thought Ruxs had him but the fucker shimmied out of his coat, taking off again, cutting in between an office building and a parking garage. Green couldn't get over to cut down the small street with him. He gunned it, turning onto Cone Street. He'd cut him off at the other end. He blared his horn. Traffic was at a complete stop waiting on the light to turn. Fuck it. He cut the corner of the sidewalk, sending a metal trash can flying up into the air. At least there were no people on the sidewalk this time. He was almost to the exit of the alley when a he saw bright blue and red lights come up fast behind him and blast his siren. He ignored it, swerved over two lanes and put his front into the narrow opening of the alley. If their informant wouldn't have had his head turned to check Rux's closeness, he would've seen Green's truck and avoided slamming into the front of it. *That had to hurt.*

Green was out of the truck, coming around the front end just as Ruxs was picking up their man and throwing him back against the hood.

"Do you have to do that? I mean there's a dumpster right there." Green frowned at his partner. "Look at that dent, man."

"Shut up, Green." Ruxs huffed.

Green smiled teasingly, he knew how much Ruxs hated chasing. He stood there with his arms crossed over his broad chest watching their informant, doubled over from the pain of hitting his truck and for running the last ten minutes.

The police tires squealed to a stop right next to Green's back end. They both turned when the young cop jumped out, yelling at them to raise their hands above their heads. The cop finally got a good look at them and rolled his eyes, lowering his weapon. "Ruxs, Green, should've fuckin' known."

"What's up Michaels." Green shook the rookie's hand. He was one of the few uniforms that actually liked the guys on their task force.

"What'cha guys got there?" Michaels' eyebrows rose up in question when he looked at the disheveled junkie that was trying to ease around Green's truck until Ruxs pushed him back against the side of the building.

"You better go, Michaels." Green looked at him seriously. There was no way he was going to talk to their informant using their not so professional tactics around another officer.

Michaels blue eyes cast down as he fidgeted with his fingers. "Uhh. Yeah okay. Hey Green, did you get to talk to God about any openings he may have coming up on his task force soon.

Green suppressed his want to sigh. There was no way Micheals would make it on their task force. The guy was too nice and too easy going. He didn't have a harsh or cruel bone in him. You had to have pretty tough skin to take what their Lieutenants dished out... daily.

Green could see his partner gearing up to say exactly what he'd been thinking but spoke up before he could crush the kid. "Not yet. I'll talk to him real soon, okay."

Michaels beamed a megawatt smile and actually skipped back to his squad car. Green knew Michaels was gay, but damn. He chuckled to himself and shook his head sadly as Michaels gave him a friendly wave and drove off. He was just like so many others gay officers on the Atlanta police force. Wanted to work for God and Day.

"Why are you stringing him along? You know damn well he ain't getting in." Ruxs took off his black leather coat and tossed it inside the open passenger side window, after he'd handcuffed their informant to the dumpster. Neither of them were up for another chase.

"Yeah, yeah, I know. I'll tell him. But he's like a little puppy. I mean who can kick a puppy?" Green smiled at his partner who in turn gave him a look that said...

"What the fuck? Stop being an idiot. Tell the guy he ain't got it and move on. Besides he's always running errands for you and getting you coffee and shit. That's fucked up to do that, man."

Green opened his mouth in mock confusion. "I don't ask him to do those things."

"Can we talk about this later?"

Green shrugged. "Sure whatever," turning his attention back to their informant. As soon as Green leveled his hard brown eyes on him, he immediately got defensive.

"I swear I don't know nothing, Detective Green." The man whined sadly.

"Whoa, whoa. I didn't ask you a motherfuckin' thing." Green said back, calmly. "You lying to me already, Tommy?"

The man was shaking his head 'no' before Green could even finish. Ruxs stood by with a slight smile playing on his mouth as he watched him. Sometimes he felt like Ruxs loved this part a little too much, just sitting back and watching Green work. There only job was to secure suspects for their Lieutenants. Squeeze information out of people. Bring in whoever needed to be questioned. Arrest suspects. Basically they were God and Day's muscle, and they were damn good at it.

Green squatted in front of their informant, eyeing him carefully. His dingy clothes were hanging off his straggly frame and his hair looked like it hadn't been washed for days. His eyes were glassy and unfocused. The fucker was high. He wouldn't be good for shit right now. "Tommy. Tommy listen to me. Why'd you feed us that bullshit about the meth lab in East Point?"

"I didn't -"

"Shut the fuck up." Green cut him off, his voice at that low frightening timbre he used on suspects. A voice that sounded like he was so pissed off, he was too mad to yell. "Yes, you did. You gave us some straight bullshit. There were no real players in there. We got two lousy fuckin' bags. What the hell are we supposed to do with that?"

"I been in there myself. There be some highrollers in there, Detective Green. I swear it."

Green stood slowly. "You're still lying. Someone got to you. Who?"

"Nope. No one. I said I'd help you guys."

Green was done. This guy had been flipped. He was no use to them now. "Well it was nice doing business with you Tommy. But your services are no longer needed." Green stepped closer and draped his arm around Tommy's neck. He pulled out his wallet and held his badge up with one hand and gave a thumbs up with the one around Tommy. "Smile."

"What?"

As soon as Tommy turned his head back to Ruxs he snapped a picture of their pose with his cellphone. Green pushed Tommy away from him. "Now. We'll print out a few of these and post them around East Point, all the way up Church Street. Let a few of the fellas see who Tommy's been hanging with."

"You guys trying to get me fuckin' killed man?" Tommy yelled, pulling at the cuffs like they'd actually budge.

"I don't give a damn." Ruxs chimed in.

"Come on man. Don't do this. I gave ya'll good info. It ain't my fault you guys fucked it up." Tommy argued.

"Oh. So now we're the fuck-ups. I see." Green rubbed at his neatly trimmed goatee. "Let's go tell God how he fucked up that bust."

Ruxs quickly undid the cuffs and grabbed Tommy around his frail forearm. The man shook his head so hard, spittle landed on each of his cheeks. "No. No. No. Fuck no. I don't. I don't want to talk to God." Tommy looked like he was about to shit on himself.

"I sure as fuck, not gonna' give him your message. You said he fucked up, so let's go tell him." Green said casually. This was usually their trump card. No one wanted to talk to God or Day.

Ruxs was pulling Tommy to the truck, which took no effort at all.

"I didn't say God fucked up. You know I didn't. Okay, okay. Stop one second Detective Ruxsberg. I g-got a little s-something to tell you. I don't know a whole l-lot, but I know a little something about a l-little bit." He stuttered nervously, making very little sense.

Ruxs let go of Tommy's arm sending him falling back to the ground.

"Ouch. Damnit." Tommy rubbed at his wrist, glaring back up at Ruxs. He folded his legs Indian-style like he was on a damn Persian rug and not some filthy concrete. "There may be a pretty big shipment coming to the house on Cleveland Ave."

"How big?" Green asked, now slightly intrigued.

"Big, man. I don't know. Just f-fuckin' huge, okay. Got everyone uneasy, ya'know'".

"When?" Ruxs asked.

"Few weeks. Gonna be some foreigners coming with it. Chainz is up to some serious shit."

"You sure?" Green asked.

"My girl works in one of the houses Chainz keeps in the back. She heard one of his big boys talking about it. They setting stuff up for it already."

"In that shitty neighborhood. He's going to bring some foreign contacts and that much weight to a rundown piece of shit house on Cleveland Ave." Green said skeptically.

Ruxs shook his head. "That makes no damn sense."

"Exactly." The serious look Tommy gave them, said it all. He was telling the truth.

A.E. Via is still a fairly new author in the beautiful gay erotic genre. Her writing embodies everything from spicy to scandalous. Her stories often include intriguing edges and twists that take readers to new, thought-provoking depths.

When she's not clicking away at her laptop, she devotes herself to her family—a husband and four children, her two pets, a Maltese dog and her white Siamese cat, ELynn, named after the late, great gay romance author E. Lynn Harris.

While this is only her fifth novel, she has plenty more to come. So stalk her – she loves that - because the male on male action is just heating up!

Go to A.E. Via's official website http://authoraevia.com for more detailed information on how to contact her, follow her, or a sneak peak on upcoming work, free reads, and where she'll appear next.

Also By A.E. Via

Blue Moon: Too Good To Be True

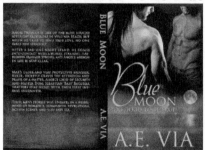

Blue Moon II: This Is Reality

You Can See Me

Nothing Special Series:
Embracing His Syn

Nothing Special Series:
Here Comes Trouble